Tiger in the Shadows is an inspired and eloquent account of the perils encountered by those who dare to exercise unfettered faith in China today. I pray this wonderful volume will spur believers worldwide to fall to their knees in desperate prayer . . . [but then to] go one step further and get up on their feet and find something to do that will make a difference in the lives of both believers and the lost in the Far East.

—TIM PETERS
Founder, Helping Hands Korea

A compelling read, *Tiger in the Shadows* draws readers into the Chinese underground church where intrigue, betrayal, and espionage affect the lives of people around the globe. Based on current events, this page-turning novel is well-researched, submerging readers into a covert foreign culture where accepting Christ as Lord and Savior is a crime.

—PEGGYSUE WELLS
Author of *What to Do When You Don't Know What to Say*

Tiger in the Shadows is a thought-provoking portrayal of the plight of Christians in contemporary China. Those who read *Tiger in the Shadows* will be challenged not only to pray for those currently facing persecution, but also to consider their own response to possible persecution in the future.

—SUSAN YOUNG
Communications Professor
Bob Jones University, Greenville, S.C.

Speaking as a Vietnam veteran and as a writer who has traveled extensively in the Far East, I can say that trying to understand the Oriental mind can be a challenge to westerners. Nevertheless, thanks to extensive research, Debra Wilson has created a work of fiction that rings true to portraying contemporary Chinese life. Her novel reveals the strong desire of the underground Christian church in China to know more about Christ and the lengths the communist government will go to suppress the spread of the gospel. The story has tension, drama, action, and a strong narrative drive, but it also has jubilation and celebration as it bears witness to the fact that the "Word of God will not return void."

—DENNIS E. HENSLEY
Associate Professor of English
Taylor University, Fort Wayne, Ind.
Author of *Man to Man: Becoming the Believer God Called You to Be*

Debbie Wilson took accurate research and combined it with her wonderful creative gift of writing to produce a novel that is both entertaining and enlightening. May God use this book to continue to keep this issue before the "free church" in America and to stir us to do all we can to "remember those in chains," as stated in Hebrews 13:3.

—DARCIE GILL
Mission Representative, The Voice of the Martyrs

Tiger IN THE Shadows

a novel

DEBBIE WILSON

Kregel
Publications

Tiger in the Shadows

© 2004 by Debbie Wilson

Published by Kregel Publications, a division of Kregel, Inc., P.O. Box 2607, Grand Rapids, MI 49501.

English translation of the lyrics for "To Be a Martyr for the Lord" are from The Persecuted Church Collection at persecutedchurch.com. Author and translator unknown. Used by permission.

Scripture quotations are from the *New American Standard Bible.* © The Lockman Foundation 1960, 1962, 1963, 1968, 1971, 1972, 1973, 1975, 1977, 1995.

The story of Christianity in the People's Republic of China is as vast and fluid as the heroic struggles of Chinese Christians and the political climate in which they live and worship. While careful re-search has gone into every aspect of this book to ensure an accu-rate portrayal of Chinese policies and life in the unregistered house churches, this novel is a work of fiction. Historical persons and events from China's history, as well as information on the churches today, are truthfully presented, and translations of actual govern-ment documents quoted, but the story's names, characters, and incidents are fictional, and places are used fictitiously. Any resem-blance to actual persons, living or dead, is entirely coincidental.

Cover design: John M. Lucas

ISBN 0-8254-4108-0

Printed in the United States of America

05 06 07 08 / 5 4 3 2

In loving memory of my beloved grandparents:

Marshall McLellan,
Lila McLellan,
and Marcella Wentworth

Grandchildren are the crown of old men,
And the glory of sons is their fathers.

Proverbs 17:6

There are fathers who do not love their sons;
there is no grandfather who does not adore his
grandson.

Victor Hugo

Prologue

"Do NOT BE AFRAID, my friends. It is only the wind."

The room itself seemed to release its pent-up breath. Faces relaxed. Wary eyes drifted away from the rattling unpainted shutters of the hut's single window. Attention shifted back to a slight peasant with a weather-creased face, who looked as if he had just come in from gathering the late-season crop of soybeans. He was known only as Lao, "the Brother."

Lao held up his book in the room's one bare light and smiled reassuringly. The matriarch, in a colorful, traditional Miao dress, smiled and nodded encouragement for him to continue. A girl puckered her lips against her fear. Other young people, little more than shadows in the dark, crouched or stood against the walls. Nearly thirty people huddled in the tiny room.

"So like us to fear the winds that rattle our lives," Lao said. "We fear spring drought or the summer monsoons that loosen mud and bury fields and houses. We fear the cadre. We fear that we won't be able to feed our children. But there was one who stilled the winds with a word of authority. As he did two thousand years ago, that same Jesus can calm the winds of life today and can carry us through each storm."

As if in response, a particularly heavy gust of rain-drenched cold moved the door against its leather hinges. A strong draft seeped in around the edges, bringing Lao a moment's relief from the stifling heat generated by the fire and the bodies packed into the room. With the fresh intake of air, the coals flared. A few elders and a young woman whose limbs already showed the deformity of untreated rheumatoid arthritis were pressed tightly together on the *kang*, the brick platform that doubled as a bed and fireplace. Others took turns sitting on makeshift benches around the room, which served as kitchen, dining room, and living area for a large farm family.

"We are all nervous, but I have only a few more words to say." He spoke slowly, reaching for words in the local dialect that differed from his native Mandarin. He had become expert in the varied dialects spoken around China through years of preaching, listening, fleeing, and hiding.

Brother Hu, in whose home they were gathered, had opened the meeting about two hours earlier. He stood next to the wooden crate on which Lao was perched.

"We have heard that Cadre Li knows that we are meeting tonight. So far he has given us no trouble. The Brother has come from Hunan Province to preach to us. If anyone wants to leave, we understand."

Apart from the Brother, none knew the cost of faith better than Hu. He had lived in a fine apartment while teaching mathematics at Beijing University of Aeronautics and Astronautics. That was before he was arrested in a raid on a meeting much like this one. When it became known that he was a Christian, the government banished him to this village in the western Guizhou highlands.

Hu cared for pigs during the day and taught in the evening, helping some of the village youths acquire the education needed to pass the qualifying exams to be able to go on to school and even college in the city. His own son, however, would be excluded from such an opportunity and might spend his life with the pigs or in the nearby coal mines. In a few years Hu Xiabo would become another work-worn peasant with deep lines scoured into his face from the sanding blast of the winds off Tibet's limestone mountains. Brother Hu's persecutors had not chosen to send him to the warmer climate of the sub-tropical rain forests in southern Guizhou Province but to Guizhou's foothills. Though the family enjoyed the delightfully cool summers and the above freezing winters, they struggled to stay warm when the cold, wet winds roared out of the mountains as they did tonight.

Tending pigs was the destiny chosen for the son because the father, a Communist Party member, had abandoned Mao for Jesus Christ. The Party made certain that every member of a family paid the price when someone showed a lack of loyalty.

None of the people left. Perhaps Cadre Li had noticed the coincidence that his wife visited her sister on evenings when the Christians were reported to be meeting. Now the cadre's wife hid her embarrassment by putting an arm around the poorest woman of the village, a widow with no family.

The Brother wiped a bead of sweat from his face. He edged farther from the fire, careful not to fall from his crate.

"The Lord tells us to carry one another's burdens. He has made us brothers and sisters through Jesus' blood. He tells us to love one another as He loved us, to care for one another, to feed the hungry, to clothe the naked, to comfort the grieving, and to lift the fallen as we would do with our earthly brothers and . . ."

At the door, Hu's nineteen-year-old son sprang to attention. "Footsteps. Running."

All that could be heard was the wind and the crackle of a coal that had settled in the fire.

Lao heard them now. *No more than one person. The cadre?* Not by himself.

Something landed against the door. Someone whispered, "Xiabo, let me in! Hurry!"

Xiabo threw the door open. A young woman, perhaps eighteen, squeezed past. "Get out. Hurry. A truck carrying police has entered the village. The captain is with Father now. Hurry. They will come soon."

Within seconds, the congregation had grabbed their coats and scarves and were passing into the night. Only their clothing whispered. In less than a minute, the makeshift church was a lonely hut once more.

Lao quickly wrapped his New Testament in oiled paper and stuffed it in his knitted hat. He ducked into his heavy quilted coat. Hu held his scarf for him.

"Xiabo will lead you out."

"Just set me on the path. I will find my way." Lao tossed the scarf around his neck.

"Xiabo knows the area."

"I have chased pigs through every *li* of it," the young man said with a confident grin. "I never thought that could be a blessing."

"Blessings come wrapped in strange colors," Lao said.

Outside, the Tibetan breeze flowing down Guizhou's mountains tickled his face with cold fingers, drying the sweat instantly. Lao silently thanked God for the clouds that had made him late earlier.

Again His protective hand.

Xiabo slipped past and led him at a quick but stealthy trot from the back of the hut. A twig cracked loudly under Xiabo's feet, and both men immediately froze and dropped to a crouch. There were no answering sounds. Hu Xiabo started again, and now the two slowed enough to brush feet lightly over the ground in front of them to avoid more dry limbs.

Xiabo passed downwind of the family's three ugly black sows. The younger man paused at a loud grunt as the animals shifted in their sleep. The breeze carried the rank odor of the tiny pig barn.

The sow settled down, but more disturbing sounds came from the central area of the village. Someone yelled. Heavy thuds of someone pounding on a door shattered the stillness.

"It has started," Lao whispered.

"They will be at our hut soon. They would be there now if Li had told where we were meeting," Xiabo replied. The two loped off, abandoning silence for speed. A gun was fired in the village. Xiabo glanced back but kept trotting.

They heard frightened murmurs from the peasants cowering behind the door of a hut as they passed.

The ground rose sharply.

"We follow the ravine here to the top."

"After that?"

"I will show you when we get there."

"No, it is safer for one than two. Go home before someone sees that you are missing."

The young man stopped and relaxed.

"Cross the road. About thirty meters west, there is another ditch. Follow that into the brush to the dilapidated hut."

"I know the way from there. God go with you."

The younger man pressed Lao's hand before disappearing in the direction from which they had come.

Sounds of turmoil increased in the village as Lao started up the ditch. He could make out wails, pounding on doors, yelling, screaming babies—the sounds of fear. He felt the tension in the pit of his stomach. It would be worse for them if he were caught near here. How bad it would be for him, he could only guess. He had always known that his preaching could cost him his liberty, if not his life. His long years on the road were quite unusual for an evangelist–teacher. A preacher's career was measured in months, even weeks. Then these servants were trucked off to suffer on China's western frontier, or they disappeared into the *laogai*, China's infamous reeducation-through-labor camps. Some preachers had been executed as examples.

Scenes of these martyrdoms were burned into his memory.

Lao paused to breathe and to knead a stitch of pain in his side. He despised the fear within him, but it pushed him on.

Resuming his climb up the ravine, he felt along the embankment with his hands. Stones rolled beneath his feet. A large stone clattered against another, bounced, and dislodged a hail of pebbles.

From above him and to his right, a gun fired. The bullet whistled past his head.

He threw himself to the ground.

"What do you think you are doing?" an authoritative voice yelled.

"I heard something, sir, from that area near the ditch."

A flashlight clicked on. The beam swept across the gully.

The Brother huddled against the mud with his face pressed into it, his eyes squeezed shut. His fingernails dug into the dirt. Silence, stillness, and prayer gave him the best chance. Cold pebbles embedded themselves in his cheek. The muted odors of soil, dead grass, and ancient pig manure washed from the fields seeped into his nostrils.

Help me to be faithful. Give me courage, Lord, and strength to finish my race.

Even with his eyes shut, he could tell that the flashlight had been shut off.

He waited with every nerve stretched toward his potential captors. At least his size made him a smaller target.

"No one fires without my orders. Is that understood? And no smoking," the officer said.

The Brother lay against the freezing dirt for ten minutes before pushing himself upright, his body stiff with cold. He shoved his glasses farther onto his nose, but he could hardly feel them. Rubbing his hands together offset the numbness enough that he could feel his way up the embankment.

He had to reach cover before dawn.

Part One

The turbulent wind precedes the mountain storm.
                                    —Chinese saying

There is a kind of man whose teeth are like swords
And his jaw teeth like knives,
To devour the afflicted from the earth
And the needy from among men.
                                    —Proverbs 30:14

Chapter 1

Stefanie Peng set down her briefcase and purse on the glistening gray tile of the entry hall. She kicked the door shut quickly to keep out the flakes of snow that drifted down on northern Illinois. Setting the brown paper sack on the stairs leading up to the main living area, she stopped and pensively lifted the top item from the bag to look at it more closely.

Small plastic figures of a handsome, blond Caucasian in black tuxedo and a black-haired, petite Chinese girl in a traditional white wedding gown faced each other in a garden of silk Chinese white lotus and red roses. This hint of East meets West had been intended to crown a large and very American tiered cake.

It occurred to her that the scale of this bride and groom wasn't quite right. The groom should tower even more over his diminutive bride. Not that it mattered. Through the plastic wrapper Stefanie brushed the groom's molded features and painted-on smile.

Roger, why? Why do you need to be high to be happy? Why do you need other women to feel like a man?

Resolutely, she dropped the topper back in the bag. Some Goodwill store shopper might be happy to top her wedding cake with a blond groom and a Chinese-Hispanic bride.

Stefanie hung her black leather three-quarter-length coat in the entry closet, wiped the melting snowflakes from it and stooped to remove her boots. Something seemed odd. The house was silent—no vacuum cleaner, washer, or dishwasher was running. Her grandmother's cheerful English or Mandarin chatter on the phone was missing.

Stefanie checked her watch. *Maybe Nanai went with Madre to pick up the kids.* Her eighteen-year-old sister, Amanda, and twelve-year-old brother, Jamie, would be out of school soon. And her mother had mentioned taking Nanai to a doctor's appointment.

Still, it felt wrong. No snicker of the cleaver cutting up onions, no sizzle and scent of vegetables cooking in the wok to the accompaniment of her grandmother's humming. Even the fuzzy little Chihuahua-Pekinese Amigo had not jingled his dog tags at the door in greeting. Amigo was both pet and family symbol, purchased as a joke by her father to represent the eclectic family over which he was head.

Nor had her grandmother opened the priscillas in the living room today. In her twenty-four years, Stefanie could not remember the house ever feeling so cold and lonely. It was the way her whole life felt these days. Putting her boots away, she wiggled her feet into slippers and padded up the steps, listening to a muffled sound she could not identify. She paused in the darkened living room to pick up a glass her father had left on the end table the night before.

That's odd. Nanai must have overlooked it.

Amigo whined as she entered the hall between the dining room and the two upstairs bedrooms. In the dimness she squinted to make out a very abandoned-looking dog, that was sprawled with his nose in the crack under Grace Peng's closed door.

Stefanie stopped with her hand on her grandmother's doorknob. The sound she had heard was sobbing. "Nanai? Are you all right?"

She must have startled the elderly woman, for her grandmother gulped audibly and sniffed but did not answer.

Stefanie pushed the door open.

"Nanai?"

The tiny woman pushed herself upright on the bed. She dabbed at the tears on her wrinkled cheeks with a wadded handkerchief. Her steel-gray bun was working itself loose. Her eyes were swollen and bloodshot.

Stefanie sat beside her grandmother, clasped one of her weathered hands in her own and stared into those dark, deep eyes.

"What's wrong? What happened? Are you all right?"

Her grandmother leaned against her. Stefanie stroked her hair until the woman could speak.

"It is not me. I do not mind for me. It is Chongde." She had lapsed into her native Shanghai dialect, as she always did when upset. Stefanie had never won more than a rudimentary understanding of her grandmother's native dialect, so she tried to lead her into Mandarin.

18

"You heard something about Grandfather? What happened to Grandfather?"

"I always thought we would be together again on this earth." She shook her head and leaned against her granddaughter's shoulder. The elderly woman's shoulders shook with the effort of controlling her tears.

Stefanie glanced around the room but saw no new letter. The picture that her grandmother had fled with from China during the Cultural Revolution lay on the bed. Thirty-year-old Peng Chongde and a smiling twenty-seven-year-old Grace held their only child, Andrew, a thin, somber child of six, between them. Friends who saw the picture would ask Stefanie where she'd had it taken, for her resemblance to her grandmother as a young woman was amazing.

Stefanie had grown up hearing the story of how her grandmother and father escaped Mao-crazed China during the Cultural Revolution with only the picture, her grandfather's violin, and a few other items wrapped in a quilt.

Her earliest childhood prayers had always remembered her grandfather. He was the family hero, who had insisted that his wife and teenage son rendezvous with a group of fleeing refugees, where he would try to join them. He was leading an aged university professor and his wife when they were captured by a band of ardent young Maoists.

The story that finally reached them was that Peng Chongde had thrown his body between the attacking students and a frail old woman they were beating. When the Maoists discovered that he was a Christian and a church leader, they had made him stand for hours in the "airplane position," bent slightly at the waist with his arms thrust back and out while they taunted him. For days they had ordered him to write confessions of his crimes as a rightist and a cow demon. They had beaten the half-starved man. Then they had imprisoned him.

Her grandmother and father escaped to Taiwan and later gained a resident visa to come to the United States. Not until the late 1980s, however, did the family hear rumors about Chongde's release from prison. He had soon been arrested again and reimprisoned. The family had written to him. One of Stefanie's earliest letters, written in laborious childish script, had been to Grandfather. They had written appeals to Vice-premier Deng Xiaoping, the "core" of the Chinese Communist Party. With every change of leadership, the family renewed their hopes and their letter campaign. The Chinese government had ignored all of their efforts. Over the years, only five letters had reached them from Peng Chongde. These now lay open and tearstained next to the picture on the bed.

Stefanie continued to hold her grandmother's hand and stroke the frail, brown-splotched skin.

"What did you hear about Grandfather?"

Her grandmother brushed her other hand across her chest, a common gesture lately.

"I miss him so. You could not understand."

Stefanie glanced at her left hand, at the finger that had so recently been encircled by a rather showy diamond. No, she couldn't understand completely, but she understood better now. Even knowing that Roger had deceived and betrayed her, she still missed him.

Nanai did not answer Stefanie's question. Instead, she returned to a story she had often told. Her words were filled with longing. "He had just been released from prison after Mao's campaign against rightists. He was so thin. I thought him plain, but the church elders asked him to play the violin for us. He played 'Amazing Grace,' and it sounded like the voices of angels. His face was transformed."

The lines on Nanai's face eased. Stefanie knew that inside her grandmother's mind a violin rendition of "Amazing Grace" was echoing. After some minutes she prompted, "And you fell in love with Grandfather at that moment."

Nanai nodded. "He had such a soul for God. How could I not?"

As if Nanai's love for God was one whit less than her husband's had been.

Nanai patted her hand. "You are such a comfort to this foolish, old woman." She rubbed her chest again. Her voice trembled. "Dr. Liu thinks I have breast cancer."

Stefanie stared at her grandmother. It was suddenly difficult to breathe.

"You must be strong, Stefanie. You must help me through this and be strong for the others."

"It must be a mistake. She is wrong."

"I have a lump, have had it for several weeks. Dr. Liu wants to do a . . . a . . ." She made a slashing motion.

"A biopsy. That will prove she is wrong. It will not be cancer. It will be benign."

Nanai shook her head. "She has seen much cancer."

In the silence, Stefanie realized that she was drumming her fingers on the spread. With some effort, she stilled her hand. "But they can treat cancer."

"With a knife. I cannot. I am too tired to fight cancer and knives and radiation and chemicals. I want to go home to be with Jesus and Chongde."

"Doctors do not always use knives now. Sometimes they use lasers. You might not have to go under a knife at all."

"Like your father worked on?" Andrew Peng was a research physicist who had been part of a team that researched military applications for lasers for the U.S. government.

"Yes. Remember how they used a laser on Mrs. Avery's mother's cataracts?"

Nanai shuddered. "So they burn a hole in me instead of cut me?" She shook her head.

Stefanie rose and paced the room. Though she loved her parents, she and Nanai had a special bond. When Roger had asked her to marry him, she had grappled with the idea that she would have to leave Nanai.

Not yet. Not now, she pleaded silently to God.

"I am ready."

Stefanie clutched her grandmother's shoulders. "You cannot give up. You cannot. Think of Grandfather."

She looked for something that could change her grandmother's mind. The room was simple—gray carpeting on the floor, the double bed Andrew Peng had bought years ago in expectation of his father's release from prison. Her grandmother had covered it with a wedding quilt that combined Christian and Chinese symbols in red. A dresser, a small desk and chair with a calendar above the desk completed the furnishings.

Stefanie stopped before her grandmother's dresser. Picking up her grandfather's violin case from the right side of the dresser, she opened it and removed the violin. After deftly tuning it, she poured her being into the music of "Amazing Grace," trying to reach out to snatch her grandmother from her precipice of sorrow and resignation. When she had finished, she quietly laid the violin back in its case and knelt beside Nanai—this woman who had been her life. Her grandmother's eyes were filled with fresh tears.

At that moment, Stefanie decided. She must renew the promise she had made as a child.

"Nanai, I promise that I will find Grandfather and bring him to you. But if I do that, what will it be for him if he comes to America, and you are not here? Think of all he's endured. Would you deprive him of that as well? What if it were the other way around? Would you want him to wait for you, to endure, to be strong—even if it meant having surgery?"

Nanai bit her lip. A tear slid down her cheek as she picked up the picture of her family. Nodding, she stroked Stefanie's long black hair.

"I will call Dr. Liu tomorrow."

Chapter 2

As Stefanie emerged from Wallace's Auto Repair the next morning, a red 1963 Ford Thunderbird pulled up. The driver leaned his head out the window.

"Hey, pretty lady, need a lift?"

For once, Troy Hardigan's short red hair was neat rather than tousled. His blue-gray eyes twinkled up at her. More amazing, he looked the part of a resplendent business executive in a pale blue shirt, a gray Zino suit, and a silk tie with intertwining streaks of blues, grays, and black.

"I don't know. My mother always told me not to accept rides from strange *hombres*—especially ones dressed like that. I don't think I know you."

Troy dropped his voice conspiratorially, "I won't tell your mother, if you don't."

"Deal."

Troy Hardigan had been a fixture around the Peng family home for eleven years, ever since her mother's youngest brother, Uncle Ramón, first brought him home on leave from the Marines. After he left the Corps, Troy had used his military background in electronics to gain a job in sales and marketing for a high-tech multinational based in Chicago. He had moved to a large, old frame house in Wheaton, about thirty miles west of the city and just a mile from the Pengs' upscale home in Glen Ellyn. Andrew and Delores had virtually adopted him, or vice versa. Stefanie wasn't sure which, but she'd had a spare brother around at most family gatherings.

Now Troy surprised Stefanie by jumping out of the car and opening the passenger door for her. She raised her eyebrows in question.

"When I pick up beautiful women, I fake them out by making them think I'm a gentleman."

"Good ploy." She slid in, and he closed the door behind her.

Stefanie glanced around the car. She had first seen it after its rescue from a car crusher two years before. She had thought Troy was crazy for wanting to rebuild it, but it was starting to take shape. The latest addition was a set of matching bucket seats that actually fit this make. The glove compartment still had no door, the visors were torn, but he had installed the radio.

As Troy slid in, Stefanie looked over the latest improvements.

"I never believed you'd get it running."

He beamed at her. "Like it?"

She looked around again for his benefit. "I'm impressed, but more impressed by you. You look," she shrugged, searching for the right word, "exquisite, handsome, elegant."

"You noticed?"

"Yeah, you even combed your hair," she said approvingly. She gave him the once over. The Zino suit clung to his big frame, emphasizing his wide shoulders and actually fitting the long arms that made buying anything off the racks for him impossible. She pulled his thick right hand from the steering wheel to examine it. "Not even grease under your nails."

"If you have shares in an industrial-strength hand cleaner company, sell. The value is sure to plummet when I am no longer buying their product by the drum."

They settled into the comfortable silence of long friendship. Stefanie glanced at him, wondering what to say about Nanai. He would take the news hard. Nanai had tucked the big, young Marine's heart under her protective wing when Troy had lost his grandmother to breast cancer.

Troy and Stefanie drew second glances when they walked down the street together. He stood a shade under six feet, and she stood, at most, a couple inches over five. Stefanie had the subtle upper-body tone of a gymnast, whereas there was nothing subtle about Troy's massive arms and chest, developed by years of weight training. In spite of his size, he had attained a leonine grace through the martial arts training he had begun as a Marine. When at home, he worked out with a practice group; on the road, he sparred with a few acquaintances who shared his enthusiasm for martial arts.

Those who studied Stefanie's features might see a hint of her mother's broad Mayan face and generous mouth. Mostly they could not see beyond her classic Oriental eyes and hair, and her china doll stature. Troy was imposingly large, but seldom had been accused of being handsome. His square jawline, faint dusting of freckles, and blue-gray eyes gave him an unkempt farmboy look.

23

His broad shoulders drew appreciative glances from women, but most thought him plain and disproportionately long of arms.

As she crossed into her teen years, Stefanie had thought Troy incredibly different and good looking. Since then, she had hardly given his appearance a thought. He was her "Uncle Troy," and if people didn't see the family resemblance, that was their problem. She could open her soul to Troy as to few other people, and it was years before she noticed that the openness was not reciprocated. Troy had the habit of hiding behind his size and generous gift of Irish blarney. He even used his empathetic ability to listen as a defense mechanism to control relationships. A great many people regarded Troy as a friend. Almost none could describe the inner man. The Pengs, especially Grace, knew more than most about Troy, but Stefanie had come to realize that even they had limited and provisional access.

"So what's the occasion?" she asked.

"Driving my favorite girl around."

She slapped his arm. "Really, what is going on?"

"We're releasing some new technology today. A bunch of hotshot international clients are in town so that yours truly can introduce them to the scientists who created it. All of Frontiers' head honchos will be on hand. Rumor has it that they're looking for a new sales manager."

A few moments later, Stefanie realized what he was saying.

"You mean . . . ? Why, Troy, that's great."

Troy stopped at a light. "You like the idea? I would be spending more time in a plush corner office, instead of wandering from time zone to time zone."

"It sounds wonderful, but you enjoy traveling."

"All hotel rooms start to look alike, Stef." The teasing tone dropped away. "I want something more lasting, maybe alongside someone who's glad to see me come home at night. In the past couple of years, I've started looking at life differently. I used to think that what I did mattered. I still do, it's just . . ."

Stefanie tilted her head, waiting for him to find the words. She knew the reason for his new perspective. For several months, Andrew Peng, with Bible in hand, had sat alone with Troy in the study far into the night. Troy had grown a lot more thoughtful and introspective as he enthusiastically listened to the older man explain the Scriptures and then began plunging into the Bible on his own. Eventually, he had confessed Christ in front of the Pengs and their church community.

"What I'm trying to say is that I want to have an eternal effect too. I need more stability so that I can grow spiritually, have a family."

He glanced at her and turned with the flow of traffic. No response came to Stefanie's mind as she looked through this new peephole into Troy Hardigan's life. She reached across the car to squeeze his hand.

"Then I hope you get that corner office and find that family."

Troy released the wheel with his right hand and intertwined his large fingers with her short delicate ones, lightly but firmly. Stefanie looked up at him with some surprise. He was big on jocular verbal gestures of familiarity, but he had always seemed overwhelmed by the unrestrained hugs and kisses dished out by Delores Peng whenever he visited the house. Troy had always shown a big-brotherly kind of affection, but this was different.

He let go of her hand to signal his turn into Frontiers Technology's drive.

"I'll be praying that today goes really well," Stefanie said.

Troy twisted in the seat and studied her for a long moment.

"Thanks. The meetings are supposed to end around 4:30. In case you get back early, I'll tell Nancy to let you into my office. If you're going to be late, leave a message so I'll know my baby's still in one piece."

"Thanks for letting me drive it." As Troy stepped out, Stefanie came around to the driver's side. "How do I adjust the seat?"

Troy pressed a lever on the side of the seat and slid the seat forward. It wasn't enough. When Stefanie seated herself, she could barely see over the steering wheel. Troy took the keys, went to the trunk, and returned with a folded blanket. He helped Stefanie out of the car and laid the blanket on the seat. "Your booster seat, milady."

A cab stopped beside them. A slender man around fifty stepped out from the back seat. He wore a turban with his conservative blue suit and dark gray overcoat.

"Troy."

Troy turned. "Devin, how are you?" The men exchanged hearty handshakes.

Devin stepped to the side. "Finally, I meet the lovely Stefanie. As you said, photographs do not do her justice."

Stefanie blushed and glanced at Troy.

"Stef, this is Devin Takheri, one of India's finest minds. He works for one of India's top communications firms."

"I'm pleased to meet you, Mr. Takheri." The man's erect carriage and cultured British accent gave him a refined presence.

"The pleasure is mine." The man's attention shifted to Troy. "Do you have good news to share with me, my friend?"

"It won't be long, Devin. Prince Saleem's retinue is here, and Mr. Kong and Mr. Tzu. Wait until you see the specs for the new satellite."

Stefanie noticed that a limousine had pulled up, with small flags for the kingdom of Saudi Arabia fluttering on each side of its impressive stern. A chauffeur stepped out to open the door for a stocky man sporting a fine tailored suit and an air of regal authority. He was attended by three aides.

With less pomp, two Chinese men exited a cab. The older of the two was of average height and solid build, but Stefanie's eye was drawn to the other, a tall, handsome man. He gave the impression of keen awareness and intelligence in his surveillance of his surroundings. Before she could get a clearer view of his face, he turned to speak to his companion.

A retinue of four men and one woman, all in fatigues, stepped from a car that was emblazoned with the name of the Venezuelan consulate.

"Who's who in human rights abuses," Stefanie muttered under her breath.

"Excuse me, Devin, I have to run. Stef. . . ." Troy helped her into the car and leaned toward her. "Have a good day, babe."

She didn't have a good day. Christmas shopping was approaching its climax and the checkout lines were unbearably long. All Stefanie could think about was Nanai's cancer and how she could keep her promise to bring her grandfather to the United States. It seemed impossible. She purchased her last few gifts quickly but with little pleasure, then turned onto 57th Street toward the sculpted concrete nest of cylinders known as the Regenstein Social Sciences Library at the University of Chicago. Three hours later, she left with a stack of printouts and a few books on contemporary life in the People's Republic of China. She was overwhelmed and somewhat discouraged by the Chinese enigma.

There was so much she did not know about the land where her father and grandparents had been born. Her first cursory look at the country revealed a vast territory of rich ethnic diversity and religious traditions that had drifted here and there with the political breezes of provincial and central governments. Officially, of course, the communist nation was atheist, and religion was expected to decline into oblivion as the generations left over from pre-Revolution China died off.

In practice, China's religions, from Tibetan Buddhism and Daoism to Christianity, resisted the enlightened dictatorship of the proletariat. The government's answer was to nationalize all religious expression under Party control. Christians, in particular, had proven uncooperative, more often avoiding the government-sponsored Protestant and Roman Catholic church structures rather than joining. That was at least partly the government's fault. Officials went out of their way to make registration of a Protestant Three-Self Patriotic Movement church, for example, nearly impossible. To join even the registered church invited harassment and lost privilege in some circles. In outlying provinces farther from Beijing, oppression had eased against these "unregistered" house churches, but local municipalities closer to Beijing were zealously and militantly fighting this avenue of dissent. Periodically, the governments cracked down on religion anywhere it might be found—especially when they heard reports of its explosive evangelistic growth.

Such information gave Stefanie a superficial look at what was happening. Peng Chongde had been sent to prison during the radical years of the Cultural Revolution during the 1960s. Why was this violin-playing preacher still regarded as an enemy of the people?

Maybe Troy could shed some light on the subject. He had international connections and had traveled to Beijing on a few occasions. He might have some ideas.

It occurred to Stefanie that she had developed a dependence on Troy for advice. Roger had plowed into her life like a wrecking ball and had left some gaping holes when he pulled out. But Troy was always just there. It would be nice to have Troy around more, but if he got married, he might not be so free to be part of the Peng family. It would complicate their friendship.

When she returned to Frontiers Technology, the lobby was teeming with men exuding machismo and women in power suits. Stefanie heard snatches of conversations about business, politics, investments, and economics. She felt the male eyes follow her to the front desk, where she waited in line to speak to Nancy, the secretary.

At her approach, the middle-aged blond woman leaned forward. "Hi there, honey. You're Stefanie, right? Troy said you'd be in. He's speaking in a few minutes. Would you like to go in?"

"I'd love to—if it wouldn't be a problem."

"Wait until some of this crowd clears, and I'll take you up."

Stefanie found a seat beside a tall potted plant that shielded her from some of the male attention. She always felt more comfortable watching without being watched. It was fun being the unnoticed observer, and one could learn a lot about people from behind a potted plant. Stefanie was proud of her unusual ethnic heritage, but it always made her feel the outsider. Chinese, but not quite. Hispanic to the core of her mother's nurture, but she didn't look the part. An American melted in the pot? To an extent, but she was too immersed in her parents' cultures to feel assimilated. To make matters worse, her petite size prompted others to lump her in with children who were years younger than she was.

A tall blond with an Australian accent and a small black-haired woman who might have been Filipino drifted by, discussing Indonesia's growing industrial base. The Saudi prince's entourage swept past, followed by Devin Takheri and two men who looked vaguely Nordic.

The lobby was clearing out, so Stefanie rose to examine a set of plaques. Troy's name appeared as Salesman of the Year. In fact, it appeared he had made that distinction twice in five years.

He never mentioned that!

He rarely discussed his work other than to tell the Pengs when he would be away. Then he would call to say he was home, or they would find him dozing in his car in the driveway some morning, waiting for them to awaken.

"I'm sorry for the delay, hon," Nancy said, bustling over. "You would not believe today! Troy may have already started, but . . ."

Stefanie grasped Nancy's elbow and pointed to the new plaque. "When was this announced?"

"December first, I think. Yes, the first was the Christmas banquet. He didn't tell you?"

"No, he never mentioned it."

"So that's why you didn't come to the banquet with him. I don't think Troy puts much stock in these things. . . . We'd better hurry."

Stefanie couldn't have gone to the Christmas banquet. On the night of December first, she had been angrily shoving pictures under Roger's nose, confronting him with the evidence of the three other women she knew about. Where Uncle Ramón had gotten the surveillance pictures was something of a mystery, but Ramón was a U.S. Drug Enforcement Administration agent, and he'd had devastating details about Roger's cocaine use. She'd waited for Roger to explain away the accusations, but he hadn't.

Now she dismissed that unpleasant thought and tried to keep up with Nancy, who was clearly devoted to Troy. Nancy was making it her personal business to bring Stefanie up to date on her boss's attributes and accomplishments. Obviously, Nancy thought this woman needed help in discerning Troy's virtues.

"He has a good chance of being the new sales manager. . . . He usually brings me a porcelain animal for my collection when he's been overseas. . . . He's always so courteous. . . ."

Putting a finger to her lips to end the conversation, Nancy ushered Stefanie through a doorway leading onto a balcony that overlooked a round conference room. The late afternoon glow from the skylights glinted on Troy's red hair as he spoke.

". . . new technologies that provide us with a better understanding of one another so that each nation here may progress in global communication, can better develop global trade, and work toward peace in the international community."

This authoritative speaker seemed so different from the merciless tease who made himself at home at the Pengs', stretching out on the sofa, giving Jamie martial arts lessons, lecturing Stefanie and Amanda on men, or wiping dishes with Nanai and Madre.

Troy finished his comments to polite applause and began a series of introductions that included a surprise for Stefanie.

"Several of you have requested greater facility in integrating our satellite technology with existing communication networks. Our new Comtalk.ts3 is what you have been asking for. Leading our research efforts is renowned physicist Dr. J. Derek Zinsser."

Dr. Jim!

A huge, bear-like man with an unruly mane of white hair rose and acknowledged the others. Dr. Jim was her father's mentor and her godfather. She described him to others as a cross between Colonel Sanders and Santa Claus. She had no idea that Dr. Jim worked with Troy's company. How odd that neither he nor Troy had said anything. The only thing that would have surprised her more would have been to find her own father there.

The senior Frontiers executives on the platform smiled benignly. Things seemed to be going well. The onlookers were attentive. A few seats were empty—one in the Venezuelan delegation, another at the table marked "Australia." The tall man was not at China's table, and two chairs were empty at the Saudi table.

As the next speaker took the podium, Stefanie returned to the lobby to ask Nancy to let her into Troy's office. On the phone, Nancy was saying, "Yes, Mr. Muranaka, I will schedule your appointment with Mr. Foo and Mr. Hardigan for January fifth. We're so sorry that you were unable to attend."

Nancy nodded toward Stefanie. She covered the phone and whispered, "I'll be up in a few minutes."

Stefanie took the elevator to the fourth floor and found the restroom. She took time brushing her hair before heading for Troy's office. Nancy must have gotten there ahead of her because the door opened easily when she turned the knob.

Troy's office always surprised her by its neatness. Other than papers he might be working on at the moment, nothing was ever out of place. She always thought it odd that he had done so little to personalize his workspace. His apartment abounded in models of classic cars, posters of James Bond movies, and *Star Trek* memorabilia from his younger sister, Patty, and her husband, Ian. But his office was all business.

Whoa! Nothing neat about this.

Patty's wedding photo lay broken on the floor. Books were pulled out from the shelves. Drawers hung out of his desk. A painting had swung out from the wall on a hinge, revealing a safe with something attached to the handle. She stepped closer. A bomb?

She heard a rustle, smelled a whiff of aftershave that reminded her of Roger, and then suddenly her face was rocked by a painful jolt. The world darkened.

"Don't move her. We've called an ambulance." The words drifted in from far away. Stefanie's jaw throbbed. She struggled to open her eyes and moaned. Forms of people bent over her, but her vision was too blurred to distinguish faces.

"It's all right, Miss Peng," said a woman's voice. "Just relax."

"Stef! Where is she?" That frantic voice from somewhere obviously belonged to Troy. Now if she could only remember why she was laid out on the floor.

A big hand seized one of hers, its size, roughness, and familiarity reassuring. "What happened? How bad is she hurt?"

She fingered her jaw to see if she dared speak.

"We don't know. We think she interrupted someone who was ransacking your office," the woman's voice said. "I came up to open the door for her and found her lying on the floor and your office torn apart. At first I thought she was dead." Sobs erupted.

Suddenly Stefanie's head cleared. That box attached to the safe. *Bomb!* Stefanie had to warn them. She forced her eyes open and squeezed Troy's hand. "Bomb! Get out." She tried to bring her body upright, but Troy pushed her firmly back down.

"Just lie still, babe. You're going to be all right."

"The ambulance is here," another woman said.

Stefanie grabbed Troy's lapel with her free hand. She licked her lips. "Bomb on safe."

Troy glanced at the safe. She could see his features now. "There's nothing there, Stef. You scared them off."

Paramedics barged into the room and began assessing the situation and asking questions. After an interminable time, Stefanie was lifted onto a gurney.

"I'll meet you at the hospital, Stef," Troy said.

"Go with her," his friend Alan Foo said. "Security's here. We'll check this out."

Considering the amount of pain Stefanie felt, it seemed impossible that no fractures showed up on the x-rays of her jaw. After pain medication was pre-scribed, she was ready to go home. But Alan Foo was waiting to talk with her, accompanied by two policemen and a man who said he was from Frontiers Technology's security department. They all crowded into a small examination room and closed the door. Troy seemed agitated by the questions and acted like he wanted to pace, if only he could find a few feet of floor space.

"Did you see your attacker?" Alan asked. He sat down opposite her.

She shook her head. The movement hurt her head, but talking hurt more.

"Any idea how tall he was? What color hair? Scars?"

"He was taller than me and had a hard fist." She had noticed something else. *What was it?*

"That narrows it down a lot," one of the officers quipped.

"Ms. Peng," the security man said, "have you had any contact with foreign-ers in the last few months?"

What a weird question.

"Yes. I tutored a student from Mexico, another from Ecuador, and three from China this semester." The security investigator demanded their names.

"When was the last time you spoke with them?"

"Look, Neale, Stef was in the wrong place at the wrong time. That's all," Troy said with a tinge of anger in his voice.

Alan Foo put a hand on Troy's arm. "He's doing his job. He's not trying to pin anything on Stefanie."

"Could we check your bag, Ms. Peng?"

Stefanie took Troy's hand to keep him from erupting.

"I understand. It's okay, Troy—Really."

The investigator turned her handbag upside down and rummaged through pens without caps, caps without pens, a wallet, loose change, combs, makeup, two small notebooks, a checkbook, an earring she thought was lost, two books on China, and a few sundry items. Inside a zippered compartment, he found her credit card.

"Why books on China?" He held up the two paperbacks she had planned to read in Troy's office while she waited. She didn't want to go into the story of her grandfather, her grandmother's cancer, and her promise. She had already embarrassed Troy enough.

"I'm doing research on the Chinese treatment of religious groups."

The investigator seemed skeptical of her answer. He spoke slowly. "All right, Ms. Peng, you can go now. We may want to talk with you again. If you think of anything that may help us find your attacker, please call."

Chapter 3

STEFANIE HELD THE HEATING PAD to her throbbing jaw. She had basked in her family's concern for her well-being, but she knew that the evening was about to turn serious. The dining table was packed, in classic Peng extended-family fashion.

Madre had not given Troy an option about staying for dinner when he helped Stefanie into the house. But if he thought he was being honored as Stefanie's protector, it was before Madre tore into him for not calling to tell her that Stefanie had been hurt. Troy seldom felt the lash of Delores Peng's tongue, and he wilted under what was, for her, a mild rebuke. Dr. Jim had gone to the Peng home as soon as he heard about the attack on his goddaughter. Unfortunately for Troy, that was how Delores heard the news.

As often as not, guests were at the Peng table at meal time, so English was the rule for all dining and most other family conversation. Otherwise, someone might forget and offend by saying something that a guest did not understand.

After dinner, the family gathered in the living room, where Andrew read Psalm 103. He removed his glasses, rubbed his nose, and donned the glasses again. Stefanie noticed how much gray had crept into his hair. He steepled his fingers with a thoughtful frown—certain indication that a serious family convocation was about to commence. Amanda and Jamie shot questioning glances at Stefanie.

"We have much for which to thank the Lord this night. He has protected our Stefanie from harm. However, before we pray, I have another matter that we need to lay before God.

"My mother went to see the doctor yesterday."

He paused and studied the Bible on his lap, struggling to preserve the stoic Chinese demeanor behind which he hid his problems. Clearing his throat, he continued, "Dr. Liu believes that my mother has cancer. We need to pray for her."

Dr. Zinsser recovered first. "Grace, I'm so sorry. My sister Dorothy has a list of specialists from when Helen had cancer. We'll do anything we can to help, and you'll certainly be in my prayers."

"Your suggestion is very kind, Doctor," Nanai answered softly, "but Dr. Liu good, very good."

Seated between Stefanie and Nanai, Troy leaned forward and studied the floor. Stefanie laid a hand on his shoulder, reading his thoughts of his grandmother's death. He ran a hand through his red hair and then engulfed Nanai's tiny hand in his big, hairy paw. She patted his hand as she would have one of her grandchildren. He could say nothing.

"What kind of cancer?" Amanda asked, her eyes watery.

"Are you going to lose all your hair, Nanai?" Jamie asked.

"Why didn't you tell us sooner?" Amanda demanded.

"That is not a respectful question," Andrew interjected.

"I did not know until now," Nanai said. "Not do well on doctor tests."

Amanda burst into tears, and Delores pulled her close, caressing her back until Amanda's sobs subsided. Delores's Incan heritage was more visible in Amanda's round face and impetuous personality. She felt things deeply and expressed herself on any subject, loudly and often. Andrew had loved such openness in the woman he married, but he did not appreciate it in his daughter.

Andrew was floundering, so Delores took over the discussion. She pushed back her shoulder-length black hair.

"We don't *know* that Nanai has cancer. She has a lump that the doctor believes *could be* cancer. We don't know what treatments Dr. Liu might want to do. If it is not cancer, then Nanai will not lose her hair, Jamie. If it is, we will deal with what comes."

"If the lump is large enough to feel, you need to know quickly. Has the doctor taken a biopsy?" Troy asked.

"She has not used the knife," Nanai said.

"But Nanai has promised to call Dr. Liu to set up an appointment." Stefanie leaned out so that she could look squarely at her grandmother around Troy. "Did you call?"

"January seventeen. Holidays. Many vacations. Dr. Liu gone two weeks."

"You really did call?" Andrew asked in shock. Cutting on the body was regarded with horror in traditional Chinese culture, and Andrew did not believe his mother would submit to such an invasion of her body.

"I promised. I called."

All eyes turned to Stefanie, who had accomplished this feat.

"Nanai and I have an agreement. She will stay alive for Grandfather, and I will find him and bring him home."

Nanai smiled contentedly. Everyone else stared at Stefanie.

Her father cleared his throat. "Perhaps we should pray now."

Each knelt to pray silently. When everyone was again seated, Father started singing "Abide with Me," and others joined in. Stefanie could not sing because of the pain in her jaw. Amanda and Jamie were not trying.

Madre and Nanai accompanied Jamie and Amanda downstairs. Stefanie remained, knowing that only the opening gun had been fired in this battle.

Drumming his fingers on the arm of his recliner, Andrew waited until the women were out of earshot.

"You have promised your grandmother something you cannot do."

"Father, I intend to do it. I don't know how it will happen yet, but I will go to China and look for Grandfather. I have already begun doing research."

"Unthinkable. You have no idea . . . and if by some miracle you could get there, what would you do?"

"I don't know yet. Remember, I was going to China for my honeymoon with Roger. I arranged some magazine writing assignments to help cover our travel costs."

"If I might suggest, sir, we can't know what steps could be taken until we learn where your father is today," Troy offered. "Stef, you can't go until you know whether your grandfather is even alive."

"It is useless to even try. We have tried to find information a dozen times," Andrew said bitterly. "Especially since Tiananmen Square, they ignore us. But if anyone goes to China, it must be me. I could take a leave of absence if there is any chance it might do any good."

Troy looked down. "I'm sorry I haven't helped in this, but you all say so little. I work with some Chinese businessmen who have connections in industry and government. You'll never find out anything with a direct approach. You work relationships. I know people who might know the people who can find this out."

"The former ambassador and I attended college together," Dr. Jim said. "I could ask for his assistance."

"Yes, that's how it's done," Troy said. "Andrew, think about your students. Do any of them have connections that would allow them access to the *Dang An Chu?*"

"What's that?" Dr. Jim asked.

"The Chinese government maintains files on all citizens," Stefanie said. "These are compiled in the *Dang An Chu.* They probably still have files on Father and Nanai. Birth records, work reports, school records, marriages, divorces, arrests, all of that."

As the others continued talking, Stefanie reviewed the names and backgrounds of Chinese students she had tutored. Her grandmother and mother came back upstairs and said good night. Dr. Jim rose and stretched. "I'm getting old, and this has been a difficult day. The thought of your guest bedroom appeals to me." Stefanie kissed him and her father on the cheek before they left the room. Much more would be said on this matter, but at least the issues were laid on the table.

Troy leaned back on the sofa, eyes closed, hands clasped behind his head. Stefanie dropped down beside him. They sat silently together for several minutes. Troy tipped her chin around to look at the bruise on her jaw. "You okay?"

"It doesn't hurt nearly as much as thinking about Nanai . . . and I've also been thinking of Roger. But Troy, I didn't intend for you to hear about Nanai like this. I meant to tell you earlier today."

Troy gestured to dismiss any thought that he had been mistreated. "Forget about Roger and concentrate on Nanai. He's not worth thinking about."

"I also wanted to apologize about Roger. You tried to tell me I was making a mistake, and I just got mad." She shook her head and ignored the twinge of pain it caused in her jaw. "I should have seen through him. I can't believe I was so stupid."

"It's easy to make mistakes around chameleons. He fooled Pastor Avery and your folks and—"

"But not you and Uncle Ramón. You never trusted him. Nanai didn't either."

Troy picked up her left hand. "Ramón and I are in the business of looking under the skin."

Uncle Ramón certainly had to read people as a DEA agent who sometimes worked under cover. Evaluating character kept him alive. She hadn't really thought about Troy needing the same skill. But he was a salesman who dealt with scientists and world-class power brokers. Yes, he did have to read people.

"I had to watch my own prejudice with Roger," Troy continued. "I knew that at least part of what I was feeling might be jealousy."

Jealousy? She waited for development of the thought, but Troy hurried past it.

"Don't you think Ramón and I have gotten taken in by some pretty faces? Chalk Roger up to experience and forget him. He doesn't deserve the pain you're inflicting on yourself." Troy glanced at Stefanie. "Easy for me to say?"

Stefanie glanced at him and decided to change the subject.

"I worried about telling you about Nanai. I mean, your grandmother and all."

"It does hurt to think of Nanai going through all of that." Troy squeezed her hand. "You know that whatever happens, I'm here for you."

She smiled up at him. His blue-gray eyes were gentle and wistful, his red hair mussed.

"Troy, you have been my best friend. Even when I didn't appreciate what you said about Roger, I knew you were looking out for me. To change the subject, do you really know of anyone who might be able to help find Grandfather? I'm sorry to say that my contacts within the halls of power in Beijing seem pretty weak."

"Oh, you might be surprised who you know. Yes, I can think of people. Problem is, I'm not certain they can be trusted. But one thing I'm going to do is talk to a Marine sergeant that Ramón and I had in the Gulf War. Chou, Ulysses Chou. 'The Big Chew,' we called him. Of course, we also called him other things that your tender ears shouldn't hear."

She nodded. Uncle Ramón and Troy had laughed about The Big Chew when they came home on leave. It was part of the foreign language of Marine-speak that had fascinated and mystified Stefanie as a young teenager.

"Chou's involved in security at the embassy in Beijing. He's made a lot of Chinese friends while chasing his roots down."

"Well, I'm glad to have the help of a Chinese-American Marine named *Ulysses*, but I—*Yuliang*! I forgot Yuliang. I was so focused on trying to remember all my tutoring students that I forgot the most obvious person." Stefanie trotted to the coat closet for her purse. On her way back to the sofa she flipped through the pictures in her wallet. "I don't know whether you remember her." She found the picture. "Here. We roomed together one semester at the Foyts', until Mr. Foyt got sick and we had to move out."

In the picture, Stefanie stood between two Chinese girls in front of a monkey habitat at the zoo. One of the girls was flirting with the camera, her lips pursed, eyes laughing, makeup perfect. The other girl had a restrained Madonna smile and thick glasses that hid her eyes.

"She's much prettier than the picture. She is the only 'true believer' Maoist I ever met. She kept trying to convert me."

Troy settled his arm around Stefanie as he studied the picture she held. "She always wear her hair so short?"

"Umm-hmm. She said the only reason women wear their hair long is to please men."

Troy tugged Stefanie's long hair. "Decadent bourgeois female. How scandalous to please a man."

"She might have used those exact words," Stefanie said as she pulled her hair free from his grasp. "It's a strange relationship. I think we're friends, but we always argued a lot when we talked. Come to think of it, Yuliang introduced me to Roger." Her mind drifted to the meeting in the library where Yuliang had been tutoring Roger. He had asked Stefanie on the spot to go out with him. She had turned him down . . . that time.

"So what does our pretty Mao fan do?"

"She works on China's literacy program. For a while, she traveled around the rural provinces, studying the schools. I call her every so often, and we chat. Sometimes she acts like it's a bother even talking to me, but other times she really seems to need someone to talk with. Last time we talked she was fretting over an important speech she was giving soon."

Troy was still leaning against her looking at the photograph. Stefanie shoved him back playfully and handed him the picture. "Yuliang comes from a rural village, and she has family there, so she really cares about improving the education. But she gets frustrated that the government takes so long to do anything about school needs."

"So did she risk her career to tell them what they need to hear instead of what they want to hear?"

"I haven't heard."

Troy checked his watch. "Tell you what. I told Nanai I would take her Christmas shopping tomorrow. I'll come over around seven in the morning and we'll call your friend. It will be night there, but not too late. Then let's go Christmas shopping and to lunch with Nanai."

Stefanie walked him to the door. He paused at the threshold and placed his hands on her shoulders. She had to crane her neck to look up into Troy's eyes, which were nine inches above her own. She decided that she kind of liked Troy's more relaxed openness around her, but it seemed odd.

"You know that fretting tonight won't make Nanai any better. You need to sleep," he said softly.

She nodded. "You're right."

"Good night, babe." He pressed his lips to her forehead and left.

That was the same Troy, a kiss-on-the-forehead thing to say good-bye.

It had irked her when she was thirteen and had a massive crush on this red-headed giant.

As she locked the door, she decided that it still irked her.

She turned off the inside light, then glanced out as Troy opened the door to his car. As the car's dome light came on, she saw that someone else was in the car, someone big who filled the passenger side. Minutes passed, and she remained glued to the window. Then the passenger door opened, and Dr. Jim got out and faded into the shadows of the walkway back toward the kitchen door. Troy pulled out.

She tiptoed to the living room doorway to peek as Dr. Jim let himself in to the kitchen, looked both ways before easing the door shut, and crept toward the guest bedroom. Stefanie waited until she heard his bedroom door close.

Why would these two family friends sneak outside to meet?

She was suddenly too tired to wonder about it. She would ask Troy tomorrow.

Chapter 4

THE DONKEYS WERE COMING.

For two millennia, the ancient city of Canton was the southern gateway to China. In its modern incarnation, Guangzhou, the city was eclipsed as a world trade port by its near neighbor, Hong Kong, but it remained a gathering point for businessmen, tourists, and smugglers, one of the nation's most open and profit-driven centers. Despite its relatively relaxed Western aura, Guangzhou's airport was watched carefully by the police, who tried to intercept all kinds of contraband. The knot in Lao's stomach tightened as he waited for the Bible couriers to arrive. Gao Wenzao, one of the younger donkey guides, waited by the drinking fountains to meet the Bible smugglers. Did Wenzao's eagerness make him appear suspicious? Lao scanned the faces of the security personnel. None showed interest in the college student, who was nearly dancing with excitement.

As Lao mixed unobtrusively with the large groups of people in the terminal, he enjoyed the gleam of the world-class airport, a symbol of progress that all Chinese could be proud of. He also prayed silently and tried to relax. *Please continue to blind their eyes to our donkeys and guides.* At this moment, more than a hundred people were praying for the arriving shipment.

Carefully keeping their distance from each other inside the terminal were the young guides who would meet the arriving smugglers at the Brother's signal. He hated these arrivals, because there was so much pressure and the danger of arrest was so high. But all the praying Christians were depending on him to bring Bibles, and they all looked to him for leadership. No, he corrected himself, they looked to him to be responsive to God's Spirit. If it were God's will, their church would receive a Bible.

No wonder my hair is gray. My faith is too small.

Four dozen Bibles were due on this trip, and each had already been assigned to one of the many churches scattered across China. *So few Bibles to meet so many needs.*

An elderly couple carrying large beach bags entered a customs line. The tall, white-haired woman wore off-white slacks, with a matching broad-brimmed hat, and a flowered blouse. The man, a few inches taller, wore white pants and a flowered shirt. He carried their jackets over one arm. As the Brother watched them, the man threw back his head and laughed at something the woman said. These people were experienced. If they were nervous, the Brother could not tell.

Slowing his stroll, he observed the various security personnel, his stomach quivering. The guards and customs agents were alert today, but not unusually so. That was a good sign. The plainclothes police were the more dangerous ones. They were less obvious than their uniformed counterparts, although the Brother had learned how to spot them. Today they seemed relaxed, even bored. Also a good sign.

The woman asked the customs officer about two Cantonese restaurants, her bracelets jangling as she gestured. The customs officer said something, probably in English, because the Brother could not understand anything but the restaurant name. The agent hardly checked their luggage before passing them through.

Lao nodded to Gao Wenzao. Without acknowledging the Brother, the younger man intercepted the elderly couple, making discreet eye contact before turning to lead them away. Only the sharpest of policemen would have realized that contact had been made.

Quelling a sigh of relief over the first safe arrival, the Brother watched for the next pair of donkeys. Trying to raise a church without Bibles was like growing a garden without hoes. False doctrine sprung up like weeds, and only the Word could pluck it out.

The Brother wandered past rows of customs officers until he spied two college-age girls stepping up to the customs counter. Their guide stood by a nearby newspaper stall.

Children. So young. Was I ever so young, so innocent?

The girls, laughing and chattering, dropped their bright red backpacks on the counter. Fishing a tube of lipstick from her purse, one of the girls spilled her purse. She flushed bright red at the feminine articles that scattered across the counter and tried to stuff them back. The female customs agent helped her, hardly perusing the back packs, and wished both girls a good day.

The guide, a Chinese girl whom the Brother had assigned to meet the smugglers, greeted them both with hugs and a welcome in broken English. Anyone would think they were old friends, rather than strangers forging a new bond of shared faith. The three young women soon disappeared amid the throng in the terminal.

The Brother knew that the next donkey was in trouble as soon as he saw him. The young American licked his lips constantly, his eyes darting around. The Brother shook his head at the waiting guide, who quickly turned toward the exit before the donkey could give them both away. Moments later, one of the customs agents was calling security. Soon they led the young man away, along with his six contraband Bibles. *A half dozen disappointed churches.*

The last donkey was a big, brown-haired young man in jeans and a red ball cap with a book in his hand. He practiced Chinese on the people ahead of him in the customs line. The middle-aged Chinese couple good-naturedly helped him with his pronunciations. When he reached the customs agent, he greeted her in Chinese. She questioned him in English and he searched the book for Chinese answers.

"Are you carrying anything you should not have?"

"I do not carry bad things," he managed in fractured Chinese. He grinned at her triumphantly, his enthusiasm infectious.

"Why do you come to China?"

"I play my Chinese." He winced and said in English, "I don't think that was right."

The customs agent laughed at him, scanned his luggage, and passed him through.

The Brother caught his eye and took a position several paces ahead. Glancing at the security officers, he led the young man to a bus stop and bought a ticket to a smaller village. The donkey did the same.

They sat in separate seats. Even now, the Brother did not relax his vigilance, though his stomach had stopped quivering.

The big American continually attempted to converse with the people around him. His friendliness broke down the cultural barriers. Most of the people, though chuckling at his attempts, answered his awkward questions about the crops, the city, and what parts of the bus were called.

When the bus stopped in a small village, the Brother got off. The young man followed. Both purchased tickets for the next bus and waited without acknowledging one another. They rode all day, deeper into the countryside, the young man continuing to make more friends along the way.

At the next bus stop, the Brother faded into the darkness. When the young man finally stood alone at the bus stop, the Brother stepped out of the shadows. "Come."

They shook hands. The donkey's hands were smooth, thick, and warm. The Brother winced at the strength in the enthusiastic handshake as his knuckles rubbed together.

Without another word, the Brother led the young man along the dark road. Night birds called from somewhere in the distance. The smoke from coal fires and the aroma of cooking meat and spices hung in the air as they passed a cluster of homes.

After a while, they turned onto a rough path through a field. The young man stumbled several times in the darkness. Finally, the Brother paused, placed his new friend's hand on his shoulder, and led him to a small single-story house.

When he knocked on the door, a teenage girl opened it and stepped aside for them to enter. Her parents and grandmother welcomed them and quickly seated them on the floor at a low table. A simple dinner of rice and vegetables was waiting. After the Brother offered thanks, they ate. With his appetite dulled, the young man patted himself on the chest and said in Mandarin, "My name is Jim."

Their hosts repeated, "Je-im."

Jim pointed at the man, who said, "I am Likun."

The young guest kept them entertained with his attempts to pronounce each name. At each failure, the others laughed and corrected his intonation. Jim exaggerated the changes, provoking new laughter. The Brother smiled at the quickly established friendship.

When Jim pointed to the Brother, Lao said, "My name . . ." He paused. *No, my name is no longer my name.* "Call me *Lao*—which is 'Brother,'" he said, following the Chinese with its English translation. This was his only identity since his family had disowned him, the only name people knew. Those who knew him by his old name were not friends, and if they knew who "Lao" really was, they could use that identity to track him more easily.

To change the subject, the Brother pointed to Jim's backpack.

The young man dragged it to the table, opened it, and removed a handful of tightly rolled clothes. Unrolling a pair of jeans, he pulled out a Bible and passed it to Lao, who offered it to the elderly woman.

She accepted it reverently, raising it toward heaven. As she kissed it and held it to her heart, she began to weep, the tears coursing down her face.

"They destroyed my husband's Bible in the Cultural Revolution. They took him to the *laogai*, and we never saw him again. Our only Bible has been the verses we copied down from memory."

She clutched the Bible to her heart, rocking back and forth and murmuring thanks to God. Tears filled the eyes of her son, daughter-in-law, and granddaughter.

Jim and Lao slept that night on straw in the shed. Before they lay down, Jim touched the Brother's arm. "I did not understand Grandmother. Why she cry?" he asked in awkward Chinese.

The Brother tried to distill the story into a few words that the Westerner could look up in his book. "Cultural Revolution. Husband *laogai* die. No Bible. Church seven hundred."

In the lamplight, Jim's hair glowed golden as he bent over the phrase book. The Brother was not sure what the expression on Jim's face meant as he straightened. "Seven hundred people? No Bible?"

The Brother repeated the words.

The next morning, following a small breakfast of rice, the Brother led Jim to the bus stop after giving him their next destination. Before the bus pulled out, the Brother bought a ticket and climbed on. They exited with several others in midafternoon.

Jim followed the Brother to a small factory. The foreman led them to an office where the Brother pointed to the backpack.

Jim dug out a Bible. The foreman took the Bible in both his hands. Grinning, he set the Bible carefully on his desk and hugged Jim and the Brother.

Moments later, he left the room, returning shortly with several men following him. Each one in turn picked up the Bible. Some opened it and ran their fingers along the characters. One carefully wiped his workstained hands on his handkerchief before he touched the book with the tips of his fingers and grinned. Each man shook the Brother's hand and Jim's.

When these men left, others came in groups of a half-dozen at a time, men and women, their hands callused, their faces deeply furrowed. They, too, touched the Bible, some caressing it, others kissing it. Then they shook hands with Jim and the Brother.

For the next few days, the Brother and the brown-haired American took bus rides north and west through the vast countryside. They met with individuals, families, and church groups crowded in apartments or small dwellings. On the road, the two did not sit with one another. Jim garnered too much attention just by his size and exotic looks. Rarely did a Western tourist wander so far into the provinces. During their stops, the two managed to converse enough for the Brother to learn that Jim was a college student in America, studying business management.

To deliver the last Bible, the Brother led Jim to a meeting in the back of a small barn in Sichuan province, where two dozen young evangelists had gathered. As they were sitting on the floor, a young woman entered. A smile lit her pleasant but pale face.

The Brother jumped up and rushed to clasp her two small hands. "Welcome, Ling. We had not heard they released you."

"Last week. I should not have come, but the cadre is away. I am so hungry for the Word."

"You honor us with your presence."

Surrounding her, the others shook her hands or embraced her, their voices excited. She was thin and frail, but her face glowed with joy. The Brother wondered if the young donkey could recognize the marks of her love for Christ.

He read the questions on Jim's face. "*Laogai.* Three years." He held up three fingers.

Jim repeated the phrase and nodded his understanding. "Why?" he asked in Mandarin.

The Brother picked up the Bible, mimed reading it, and held his hand at different levels to indicate children. Jim nodded.

Slowly the Brother read from 1 Corinthians 1 as the young evangelists worked feverishly to copy the words. The Brother read a brief section, then painstakingly explained what Paul was saying as the others took notes. As Lao taught, Jim stared at Ling, who fastened her whole attention on the words.

The teaching continued without a break for six hours, until the Brother could hardly speak. Then two women brought stew and he ate and rested. After a few hours, the men and women returned with their notebooks, and the Brother taught by the light of an oil lamp until the oil ran out.

The next morning, Jim and the Brother began their return trip to Guangzhou. On the night before their separation, they stayed at the home of a man who taught English in the high school. With the teacher translating, they visited late into the night.

"I had heard that Bibles are now available in China, so I was amazed when someone asked for volunteers to smuggle them in," Jim said.

"One printer is authorized to produce Bibles for the registered churches. There are shops that sell them in the large cities. But distribution is controlled and very limited. Some years ago an American book publisher came to the Beijing Book Fair with hundreds of Bibles and asked permission to give them as free samples. Police had to be called in, not to confiscate the Bibles but to manage the lines of people who wanted them. That was a great miracle. Even the police begged to receive copies. Especially in the western provinces, though, there are entire villages with people who have been Christians all of their lives who have never held God's teaching in their hands. You see how few we have even for the evangelists who teach the Word. It is sad and dangerous to our understanding of the truth."

The next morning, before he left, Jim hugged the Brother and the teacher. "You have changed my life. In America I can buy a Bible anywhere—a bookstore, a department store, on the Internet. I don't need permission. I can listen to preachers on the radio and television all the time. I didn't understand the importance of what I was being asked to do in coming here."

He lowered his head. When he raised it, Jim had tears in his eyes. "A few years ago, I was bored with church. We went three times a week, and it was just someone talking at us, lecturing us. My friends and I didn't want to hear what the preacher said. We would sit with our feet on our Bibles."

The Brother stared, dumbfounded. He could picture the faces of people who had died for those words.

"Why would you put your feet on God's Word?"

Jim hung his head. "I never met anyone like Ling, who would go to prison for those words."

Chapter 5

STEFANIE SILENTLY PRAYED that Yuliang's mother would not answer the telephone. Once, she had spent fifteen minutes and more dollars than she cared to remember talking to the garrulous woman. With Troy lounging on the family sofa across the room, Stefanie lay back in the beanbag chair, listening to the buzz that told her the connection was completed.

With relief, she heard Chen Yuliang's voice.

"*Ni hao*, Yuliang. This is Peng Stefanie," she began, shifting easily into Mandarin.

"Stefanie! Are you in Beijing with Roger now?"

Stefanie winced. "No, I am at home in Glen Ellyn. How are you?"

"Upset, but less so than last night. I told you about the report I was ordered to prepare?"

"The one on literacy?"

"I gave it yesterday at an annual educational conference. I made several suggestions for changes. People were agreeing with me, applauding my policy recommendations. During the break, several important people complimented me on my report."

Stefanie could hear the crackle of anger in Yuliang's inflections.

"But something went wrong?" Stefanie prompted. Across from her, Troy was stretched out on the ancient sofa, listening.

"Then the assistant to the minister of the Religious Affairs Bureau gave a speech about how we have failed the children in the countryside because we have not taught them enough against cults. He said this must change. Afterwards, everyone talked only of what he said, and they forgot what I said. He will probably be the next minister of the Religious Affairs Bureau, and I will stay where I am."

"Cults?"

"*Xie-jiao.* An evil religion. They try to fill the people's minds with superstition and turn them against the government."

"You mean like Christians?" Stefanie felt the dig of condescension in her friend's voice as they entered a zone of previous conflict.

"Some say they are Christians. But if they were really Christians, they would join the Christian church and obey the government. Besides, there are other groups, like the Falun Gong. Even you would say that they are false." Yuliang didn't seem to be in a mood to press her usual insistence that all true Chinese Christians were in Three-Self Patriotic Movement churches.

"The assistant director was especially concerned about one called Lao, an infamous cultist who does nothing but go around the country teaching people that his religion is better than communism and that they should obey his God rather than the government."

This conversation was not tracking as Stefanie had hoped. It was not the time for an atheism-versus-Christianity argument. She tried to think of what to say.

"I am sorry about your report. I know you worked hard on it."

"I thought if I worked hard, perhaps I would advance. Then I could have my own apartment instead of living with my aunt and cousins and mother. Can you imagine five people living in two rooms the size of your living room?"

"No."

"Do you know what's even worse? The only way I can think of getting out of this apartment is through my supervisor. Several times he has asked me to go to his apartment to watch videos with him. He has a three-room apartment to himself since his wife died, and he keeps telling me that he bought contact lenses for her." Stefanie could picture Yuliang shoving her hated horn-rim glasses back onto her nose with one finger.

"Is he a good man? Do you like him?"

"He is twenty years older than me. He looks like a beetle, with skinny legs and arms and a huge belly. But he thinks he looks handsome. Stefanie, you cannot imagine!" Stefanie would have laughed with Yuliang at this description, but her voice sounded so discouraged.

"Are you really considering him?"

"What else can I do? He may be my only chance to get ahead. He has connections, *guanxi.*"

"But would you be happy with such a man, even if life were better, Yuliang?"

Stefanie had to hold the receiver away to protect her ear from the explosion that followed.

"How do you know what would make me happy? You have everything—a nice home, good opportunities, good eyesight, a car, Roger. Your life is perfect. Love is a bourgeois Western tradition for those who can afford it. I have to make my own way, and I will do whatever it takes to get ahead."

Stefanie tried to place herself in Yuliang's position, but she didn't understand the bitterness. "I am sorry, Yuliang. I know you have disappointments, and now they are ignoring your ideas."

After a moment of strained silence, Yuliang cleared her throat and spoke softly, "I have been unfair, Stefanie. Please understand that this was just my disappointment speaking. You have been a good friend, and thank you for sending the laptop computer and tape recorder. What did you call about?"

"I wonder if you could give me advice on how to find someone." Stefanie quickly described her grandmother's cancer, Nanai's fear of surgery, and her own promise.

When she finished, there was silence on the line, and Stefanie wondered if they had been cut off.

"Yuliang?"

"I am thinking. I will be right back."

Troy propped his head up on his hand while Stefanie waited. "Well?"

"She said she'd be right back. Toss me the throw, please. I'm cold." He pulled a small blanket with a Navajo design from the back of the sofa, balled it up, and lobbed it at her. It spread out over her head. She yanked it to the side and tucked it around her with one hand.

"If you're still cold, let me know. I'll see what I can do."

She made a face at him. He laughed.

Stefanie heard an exaggerated sound of inhalation on the line. Yuliang claimed that tobacco helped her think, but her smoking in their apartment had been another source of arguments when she and Stefanie roomed together. "Now tell me about your grandfather. I remember that he was a cultist?"

"He was a Christian preacher."

"Umm, tell me everything you can think of about him."

Stefanie rattled off his birth date, his marriage date, what she knew of his arrests. When she finished, she waited while Yuliang inhaled and blew. The sound made Stefanie want to clear her throat.

"I know someone who might be able to find out."

"You do?" Stefanie waved to Troy who rolled from the sofa and squatted beside her, pressing his ear to the phone. She held it out so that they could both hear.

"He will want money."

"How much?" She had saved so little and wasted so much on her wedding preparations.

"I would guess a thousand U.S. dollars to begin with."

"A thousand dollars!"

"You are marrying a rich man. He will give you a thousand dollars to find your grandfather."

"I am not marrying Roger. I ended our relationship," Stefanie said.

"You did what? Why?"

"He has been cheating on me."

"So? He is rich and handsome. What do you expect?"

Faithfulness? Character? Loyalty? Stefanie didn't think Yuliang would appreciate her reasons, nor her ideal that money wasn't a reason to marry. She did have more options in life than her far-off friend.

"Will you still be coming to China?" Yuliang asked.

"No, I am looking for a job."

"What about the articles that you wanted to write about China?"

"The magazine was not offering to pay my travel expenses. They will have to find some other Chinese American to write about returning to the land of her ancestors. I will try to sell my car to raise the money for your contact. It will probably take a few days."

Beside her, Troy pulled his checkbook from the pocket of his jeans. "Find out where we send it."

"Hold on, Yuliang. What are you doing?"

He was already signing his name to a check for a thousand dollars. "We need an account number that we wire it to." He tore off the check and pressed it into her hand.

Stefanie covered the phone. "I can't take this from you."

"Fine. You just sold me your car."

"You know my car's not worth much."

"Get the account number. We'll argue when you're not running up the phone bill."

She uncovered the mouthpiece. "Where do I wire the money? A friend just bought my car."

"I would like such a friend. I suppose you can wire it to my account. Here is the number . . ."

When she had finished giving Stefanie instructions, Yuliang said, "You know I can promise nothing, and it will take a week, maybe two, to get back to you."

"I understand. Thanks, Yuliang. I will appreciate anything you can do. And maybe those people at the conference *were* listening. I know you don't like it when I say this, but I care about you, and I pray for you."

Yuliang hung up without saying good-bye. Stefanie laid the phone on the base and cast tired eyes toward Troy.

"I hope we didn't just waste your money and my car."

"Be patient, Stefanie. This is how these things are done."

That afternoon, Stefanie listened to the easy banter between Troy and Nanai in the front seat of Troy's "regular" car, a Ford Taurus. The two never had trouble communicating, and Troy had taken Mandarin lessons from Stefanie, to the delight of Nanai. He had picked up more from his time with the family.

"Nice lunch. Enough present," Nanai said happily.

"It was a nice lunch, but now we're shopping for your present," Troy said.

They went through the same discussion every year.

"Nanai, you are going to lose this argument. You always do," Stefanie said.

Nanai turned to look back at her. She patted Troy's arm. "Troy enough present."

"You think that, and I think that, but Troy doesn't think that." Stefanie raised her eyes and encountered Troy's in the rearview mirror.

"If you don't help me pick it out, I'll just have to go and spend extra to try to please you, Nanai," he said.

"And you know he will," Stefanie said. "Have you decided what you want?"

"What you want?" Nanai asked.

"I already have Stefanie's present this year," he answered.

Again Troy's blue-gray eyes met her gaze in the mirror. *Why is he looking at me that way?* She had seen that look in Roger's eyes—intense, as if he were looking into her soul. His eyes dropped back to the street. *I imagined it.*

"Spend too much," Nanai said.

"Naw, I bought her a seat cushion so that the police won't think she's a ten-year-old out joy riding. I got it at Goodwill."

Nanai nodded vigorously. "Good buy. Take me Goodwill."

Troy's cell phone rang. He pulled it from his coat pocket, passed it back to her, and said, "Answer it for me, will you, Stef?"

"Hello, Troy Hardigan's, Stefanie speaking."

The voice on the other end was so soft that Stefanie had a hard time hearing it. "Toy Hardgan? Speak Toy Hardgan."

"Whom should I say is calling?" Stefanie asked. She strained against the phone to hear the answer. On an impulse she repeated the question in Mandarin.

The woman hesitated, then answered in Mandarin. "I am Guangmei."

"Just a moment, Guangmei." Hearing the name, Troy swerved into the right lane and quickly turned into an alley. "He is finding a place to park the car so he can speak with you," Stefanie said into the telephone, clutching the arm rest to keep from falling over.

As soon as Troy pulled the car to the side of the alley, he reached for the phone. "Guangmei, this is Troy. Where are you?" He spoke in awkward Mandarin. He checked his watch. "When land?" He pulled a card from his wallet and a pen from his shirt and jotted her answer down. "Guangmei, do not cry. I am coming. Stay customs. Wait customs. Stay people. Do you understand?"

He handed the phone back. "Stef, repeat that to her. I can't remember the words. Tell her not to go anywhere once she passes customs."

As Stefanie put the phone to her ear, Troy backed the car into the street and swung into traffic, flinging Stefanie sideways in her seat. "Guangmei, Troy is coming. Go through customs and wait. Stay with lots of people."

"I am scared. A big man follows me. He knows what I have."

Troy was merging onto Interstate 90 West. "Get her flight number."

"Troy is coming, Guangmei. What is your flight number?"

"Wait. I do not know. Wait." Stefanie heard her ask someone. She returned and gave the information.

"Good. I have it. That is KLM Royal Dutch flight 8611 from Amsterdam, at the Northwest terminal."

"He will help me stay in America? I am helping him; he will help me?"

Stefanie braced herself for another quick change of lanes. Once Troy had safely inserted the car into a space between a Chevy and a semi, she asked, "She wants to know if you'll help her stay in America."

"Tell her yes. Alan and I will help her stay."

Stefanie repeated his message.

"They say I must turn off the phone. We will land soon. You will come for me?"

"We are on our way. Traffic is heavy, so it will take time, but we are coming."

"Tell her again to stay where there are plenty of people," Troy said.

"Stay with people, Guangmei. We are coming."

They had gone only two miles on Interstate 90 when the traffic slowed and then stopped. Troy pounded the steering wheel. "Not now. Please not now." He turned, met her eyes, and ignored its questions. "Where's the phone?"

He punched in a number. "Hardigan. Where are you? Guangmei is landing at O'Hare in about five minutes."

"I'm stuck on I-90. It looks like an accident. Can you get someone to meet her and protect her? . . . She says she's being followed. . . . I know. . . . This could be the break."

Troy glanced in the rearview mirror as he listened to Alan. "Listen, Alan, I can't discuss this right now. She caught me out Christmas shopping with friends."

Stefanie watched him. *What is going on? Who is Guangmei, and why was she so scared?* Stefanie pinched pleats into her skirt. The thought flashed across her mind that maybe Guangmei was someone special to Troy, but that didn't track. This had something to do with Alan Foo and work—and it sounded serious.

"Okay, Alan, it looks like we're moving a little. Do what you can." Troy folded up the phone and tossed it back to Stefanie. "If it rings, answer it. If it's Guangmei, explain that we've been slowed down."

Troy hunched over the wheel, as if his will alone could part the sea of cars before him. He darted into holes in traffic that Stefanie would never have tried. She clutched the armrest and prayed.

Nanai had not said a word since they started their crazy race. She, too, clung to the armrest and kept her head bowed.

Stefanie sighed relief when they turned into the Arrivals lane for the Northwest terminal. Then traffic stalled again. Troy unbuckled his seatbelt.

"Stef, I'm going to run for it. Park somewhere as close as you can and meet me at Northwest baggage claim."

Before she could respond, he had already swung out of the car, leaving the door open as he sprinted toward the terminal.

Behind Stefanie a car horn blared. She quickly took Troy's place behind the wheel, tried to move the seat enough to reach the accelerator and brake pedals. When the driver behind her laid on the horn again, she gave up trying to get the seat all the way forward and just stretched her leg. She grumbled in Mandarin, "He is certainly eager to see her."

"You know it is not like that," Nanai said. "Troy will help her. You do not need to be jealous."

"I have no reason to be jealous of Troy," she muttered back, then rolled down her window to answer security questions at the short-term parking lot guards' station. She got out to open the trunk for inspection.

Heading into the parking lot nearest the Northwest Airlines terminal, she tried to clarify her relationship with Troy for her grandmother.

"Troy's a good man, a good friend. I want him to be happy."

She spotted an empty lane and headed for it.

"Troy is a good man," Nanai agreed, "but happiness is not as important as his walk with God." Then she smiled. "I want you both to be happy."

Climbing from the car, Stefanie realized that Nanai had just offered a little grandmotherly interference. She also knew that Nanai had never said in any fashion that Roger was a good man.

Always one of the world's busiest airports, O'Hare bustled more than usual with the early wave of holiday travelers. Though her height didn't allow a good vantage point for spotting people in the crowd, Stefanie watched for Chinese travelers as she and Nanai reached the baggage claim area. According to the display on one active carousel, Guangmei's flight had landed. The last luggage from that flight was spilling out from the conveyor belt.

Stefanie spied a small woman who appeared to be looking for someone. "Guangmei?" she asked.

The woman glanced at her coolly. "I beg your pardon." Her accent carried a British stamp.

"You aren't Guangmei?"

"I beg your pardon?"

"Is your name Guangmei?"

"No, it is not."

"I apologize."

Another Chinese woman was standing near a water fountain. Stefanie approached, but the woman waved and ran off. Stefanie half expected to see her run into Troy's arms. Instead, she was hugging another Chinese woman about her age and two little girls. The four all talked at once.

Nanai had parked herself in a row of plastic seats and was chatting with a tall, rail-thin man in a cowboy hat and boots who was pointing beyond Stefanie. "Yes, ma'am, red hair and wide shoulders. I think I saw someone like that over near customs."

His eyes traveled over Stefanie as she joined them. "I'd be glad to see you ladies over to find the red-haired fella."

"Was he with a woman?" Stefanie asked.

"He was talking to customs officers, I think, and some policemen. If that's your man."

"Thank you very much. We'd better go, Nanai."

"Thank you. God bless you," Nanai said.

"I'd be glad to come along, just to help out," the man said hopefully.

"We'll be fine. Thank you anyway," Stefanie said. She took her grandmother's arm and steered her gently but firmly toward the customs area. When they were out of the man's earshot, she said, "Nanai, you don't know a stranger."

"If he is a stranger, I cannot know him. If I know him, he is not a stranger."

Stefanie rolled her eyes and peered through the crowd until she saw Troy. He turned toward them as a guard walked away.

As he approached, Stefanie could see that his brow was creased with worry. "I can't find her. I'm going to check in baggage claim."

He walked off in the direction from which they had just come, leaving them standing near customs.

"Where would she go after customs?" Nanai asked.

"Probably to retrieve her bags or possibly to get a bite to eat."

"Bathroom," Nanai said, and wandered toward the restroom signs.

At the end of a side hallway, an electric cart was parked. It was hitched to a small trailer dumpster for emptying trash bins. Something black lay on the floor beyond the tractor—a woman's black pump.

Nanai turned into the bathroom, leaving Stefanie in the hall, staring at the shoe. Digging through her handbag, she found her cell phone.

"Troy? Have you found her?"

"No, nothing. Why?"

Stefanie's hands were shaking. She walked toward the shoe, then stopped by the dumpster. A piece of black fabric hung out from the lid of the can. "I think you'd better come back to the restrooms near customs."

Gingerly Stefanie lifted the dumpster's lid. The black fabric was part of a woman's skirt, and under the skirt she could see part of a woman's leg.

"Stef? Stef? Are you still there? What is it?"

Stefanie dropped the lid.

"I think I found her."

Chapter 6

"YOU SURE YOU DON'T want to come?" Stefanie asked her younger sister, Amanda. Amanda was pushing radio buttons in the passenger seat of Stefanie's ancient Ford Escort.

"You'll comfort Troy better than I will. I'll wait here." A bubble gum bubble sprouted from Amanda's mouth and then deflated with a *puff*. Amanda settled back to listen to her favorite radio station.

"I just want to be sure he's all right. I shouldn't be long."

"It's okay, Stef. Madre won't have dinner ready for another hour."

Stefanie closed the car door. Troy had taken Guangmei's murder hard. After endless discussions with airport security and police in the customs office, both with Stefanie and Nanai and in private with the officers, he had said nothing on the way home. Once he had slammed his fist into the steering wheel. When he hadn't called and he hadn't shown up for church the next morning, Stefanie decided to check on him on the way home.

Troy rented an apartment in an old two-story brick home owned by an elderly widow. His landlady, Mrs. McClellan was quite taken with her handsome, red-haired boarder and had tried to match him up with a succession of single young women connected to her large circle of family and friends.

Irregular thudding sounds brought Stefanie to a stop outside the two-car garage near the covered stairway leading to Troy's apartment. Remembering the attack in Troy's office, she crunched through the snow on the walkway to the garage.

What if someone's beating Troy?

Silently opening the side door to the garage, she peered in, her eyes still dazzled by the brightness of sun on the outside snow. She squinted to see Troy pivot on one foot and kick high into a bull's eye on a boxing bag. As his kicking

56

foot dropped, he slammed one fist and the other into the swinging bag. In almost the same catlike movement he whirled his body toward her, his hands raised in an offensive stance.

As if a switch clicked in his mind, he dropped his hands. Sweat stood out on the red stubble of his unshaven face and on the curly hair of his upper arms and chest under a sagging athletic T-shirt. He approached her but said nothing as he picked up a towel from the hood of his T-Bird.

"Are you okay?" she asked.

"Yeah. Fine. What do you want?" he asked brusquely

"I wanted to check on you. I was worried."

He reached around her and pulled the door shut. "If you're too warm, I'll turn off the heater."

Standing so close, she realized how strong he looked with the muscles bulging on his chest and arms. She stepped away. "I'm sorry. I didn't mean to let your heat out."

She leaned against the T-Bird to put a little more distance between them. Half turning toward the car, she ran her hand over the shiny finish of the door.

"Afraid I was being a bad boy? You had to come check on me?"

Surprised at the harsh tone, Stefanie turned toward him. "That's unfair. I said I was worried about you."

No response.

Why is it so hard to find the words? "I wanted you to know how sorry I am and that I'm here for you. We all are."

He stood with the towel over his shoulder, watching her.

"She seemed. . . . You were so. . . ." She shrugged. "I don't understand all that happened yesterday, but I'm just so sorry."

He nodded. "Thanks."

Thanks? What does thanks *mean? Go away? Give me a hug? Drop dead?* She waited, but he said no more.

She sidled around him. "I'd better be going, I guess. If you need to talk. . . ."

"Yeah."

She paused at the door to look back. He stood in the same spot as if frozen there. He looked so alone. Ever since his father had kicked him out at seventeen, he'd pretty much been a loner. He had kept a relationship with his grandmother until she died and with a sister. Otherwise, the Pengs and Uncle Ramón were his only family.

She opened the door, then stopped, without looking around.

"You need to let somebody in. If not me then . . . somebody."

"Stef?"

"Yes?" Troy still hadn't moved.

"Uh, thanks for coming by. Later, huh?"

"Sure, Troy."

She waited another moment before leaving quietly.

By that evening, Troy still had not called. Again he did not come to church, and her mind drifted constantly from the children's Christmas program. *What if he doesn't call? Does he still want me to drive him to O'Hare for his flight on Tuesday morning? Is he okay?*

Only her position as secretary of the College and Careers Class made her stay for their Christmas fellowship. *Okay, he is grieving. He needs space. But he isn't going to get by with pushing us all away and shutting himself in a closet.*

She'd call him on Monday if he did not call first.

Her most ardent admirer, Reb Carver, cornered her in the kitchen as she placed cookies on plates.

"Stef, seems we've been playing answering machine tag."

Stefanie didn't look up. She had deliberately returned his calls when she knew he would be working. It wasn't that she didn't like Reb as a friend, but he seemed to want more of a relationship. Laura had tried to get his notice from the first day he walked through the church doors, but he had eyes only for Stefanie. He actually looked striking tonight in his state police uniform.

"I've got some tickets—"

"Reb, please don't." She held a hand up between him. "I'm not interested in a relationship now. It's too soon. Why don't you ask Laura."

"Would you be interested if Troy had the tickets?"

"This has nothing to do with Troy."

"Except that during the past two weeks, every time I call I find out you're with him."

Lani Avery stuck her head in the doorway behind Reb, heard the conversation, rolled her eyes, and slipped away.

Reb stepped closer. "I can respect that it's too soon after Roger, but I want to know whether I have any hope with you."

"Reb, I'm . . . Troy!"

Troy stood in the doorway, cleaned up and casual. She was so relieved to see him that her conversation with Reb dropped from her mind.

"I didn't mean to interrupt. I didn't see your car, Stef. Do you need a ride home?"

"Yes, I mean Lije and Lani were going to . . ."

"That's okay. I can take you. Come out when you're ready. Sorry to interrupt, Reb." Troy held out his hand.

Reb shook his hand. "That's okay, Troy." He glanced at Stefanie and smiled. "I think we're done."

Stefanie hurried through setting out the refreshments so that she could leave. When Troy saw her coming, he got out of the car and opened the passenger door.

While they were leaving the parking lot, she searched her mind for what to say. "Thanks for the lift home."

"Mind if we drive some first?"

"That's okay, but I ought to call my family."

"I already called and told them."

They drove without speaking for nearly ten minutes until they ended up at a park. "Mind if we stop a while?" Troy asked.

She was about to joke about her rule of never parking with a date, but Troy didn't look like he was ready for humor just now. Besides, he wasn't a date, just a friend who needed to talk. She almost changed her mind when he reached out to take her hand.

"I acted like a jerk today. I just didn't want to be around people. Not even you. I couldn't talk about the weather and how cute the kids are and how good the sermon was. Ever feel that way?"

"Most of us feel that way sometimes, especially when we lose someone we care about."

"Care about?" He dropped her hand, turned to face her more directly, and put a hand on the back of her seat. "Do you have the idea that I had some sort of attachment to Guangmei?"

"Well, you are thinking about settling down, and you were so eager to reach the airport. Then it was all such a nightmare. I thought you took her death extra personally—really hard."

Troy looked pensively out the window. "I am taking her death personally. It's a tragedy in more ways than I can say just now. But I hardly knew Guangmei." Then he looked at Stefanie and chuckled. "When I decide to get married, you'll be the first to know." He tugged her hair, then wrapped the strand around his finger.

"Stop teasing." She pulled his hand loose and held it to keep him from pulling her hair again. "You can see why I thought you were interested in her."

"No, not really. I can tell you a little. You know that we market satellite and communications technology across the world. The U.S. government determines what we can sell and to whom. All sales contracts are reviewed by the State Department and some even by the CIA. Some technology in a satellite, for example, has to stay secret even from the people who buy the satellite. Some of it has military applications or could give a lot of economic power if it was abused. That makes software and technology companies targets for industrial and military espionage. Guangmei works for a company in China that may be a cover for espionage. They seem to have access to our processes."

"And she was carrying proof?"

"Probably. Alan and I thought we might be able to get something certain. Alan met her several times. I offered to help her get permanent resident status in this country. It was strictly business."

"She said she had information."

"She had my card in her pocket. That's all we could find. I'm going over the situation tomorrow morning with some hush-hush government spooks. They are taking this very seriously."

"So whoever killed her knew that she was bringing information to you. Are you in danger?"

Troy ran a finger over her hand. "Probably no more than usual. I'm sure they got back whatever she had. But I let her down, babe. I told her I'd protect her, and I didn't."

"You didn't know she was coming. You did your best under bad circumstances."

"My best isn't over. She had no family, so it's up to Alan and me."

"Troy, was that what the attack in your office was about?"

Someone knocked on the window. Troy rolled the window down and stared into the glare of a large flashlight. Next the light flashed over Stefanie. "You folks having a problem?"

"No, we were just talking, officer," Troy said.

"I see." He stretched the "see" out while he kept his light on Stefanie. "I'd like to see some identification, please, from both of you. Would you get out of the car slowly, please, sir?"

Troy turned on the interior lights. With exaggerated slowness he exited the car and removed his wallet from his back pocket. Another police car drove in behind them with lights flashing.

While Stefanie rummaged through her wallet for her license, a woman in uniform came to her door. She opened the door for her. "Would you get out please, miss?"

"Have we done something wrong?"

"Could I see some identification, please?"

She passed her license. A flashlight played on her license and then on her again. "Your birth date?"

Stefanie told her.

"That would make you—"

"Twenty-four last September."

"You don't look twenty-four. How well do you know the man you're with?"

"Troy's been a family friend for eleven years. We stopped on the way home from church to talk over some problems."

"Wait here, please."

Stefanie pulled her coat more tightly around her. Snow drifted into her hair.

The female officer returned. "Would you open your coat, please, miss?"

"My coat?" She unbuttoned it and opened it. The policeman ran a light over her.

"Here's your license, miss. For your own protection, come back during daylight hours. The park is closed after dark." The woman held the door for her.

Stefanie pulled her coat tightly around her. Troy didn't say anything until they were on the road. He took her hand. "Don't be upset."

"Do you know what they thought?"

"They thought I was an adult male who was seducing a juvenile." He patted her hand. "Calm down. You can't blame them."

They said nothing until Troy pulled into her driveway. "You okay, babe?"

"I'm mortified."

He squeezed her hand. As she put her hand on the door handle, he leaned across and grabbed it. "I'll get your door."

He walked her to the door. "I have a meeting at eight on Tuesday. It would be better for me to pick you up before the meeting. Then we can have breakfast, and you can drop me off at O'Hare?"

"Fine, but I'd prefer to drive my car—or your car that was mine. I will pick you up." She rummaged through her purse for her keys. He took them from her and reached past her to unlock the door.

"All of this gentlemanly attention is going to spoil me for all my other guys."

Troy didn't smile. He paused with his face a few inches from hers.

"Thanks, Stef. Thanks for being here." His lips brushed hers before she had time to react. Then he pushed her through the door and closed it behind her.

Stunned, she stood in the foyer for several seconds without moving. She locked the door and turned on the lights that would take her to her basement bedroom.

He was just saying thanks.

As she made her way downstairs, the more honest part of her emotions knew that this man was asking to be more than her best friend. When the dust settled from the Roger wrecking ball and the dilemma of finding Grandfather, she might have to review Troy's status as adopted big brother.

Chapter 7

KONG QILI STUBBED OUT his third cigarette in the restaurant's ashtray. He leaned back in his chair and blew a stream of smoke toward the ceiling.

"So we still do not know her contact," he said in Mandarin.

"We were fortunate to find an opportunity to get Du Guangmei alone," his associate, Tzu Chuin Man, replied. "We had a matter of seconds. I disabled the surveillance camera, and Qian did the rest. He was most efficient. I have been through her briefcase and luggage, but there is nothing to indicate who she was meeting."

"If you had been seen, your action could have had serious consequences. I still worry that there was a camera you did not notice. It would have been better to take her from the terminal. We could have intercepted her contact."

"You saw the papers she carried. There should have been an armed escort waiting for her. If we had not acted, there also could have been serious consequences."

Kong nodded. "I was only reflecting on the dangers. You acted with daring and courage. I assume Qian could not search her."

"There was no time. Even with a good hiding place, I am told that a child stumbled onto her within a few minutes. People were searching."

"I believe you said a *Chinese* child with an old woman found her. That is curious."

Tzu slid an envelope across the table and Kong slipped it into his brief case without comment.

"I understand the police also spoke with a man, but I never saw him," Tzu said. "These pictures show the old woman's face. I did not get a clear shot of the girl, but that did not seem important. Perhaps they are distant relatives not in the files. The girl is perhaps fourteen. The grandmother is not likely to be an agent either."

Shoving the ashtray away, Kong tapped his fingers on the table. "We are missing something. Why Chicago?"

"She had contact with companies here."

"And one of her contacts was CIA, but which one?" Kong raised a warning finger as the waitress approached. Her smile lingered on Kong, who returned it. Tall for a Chinese, ruggedly handsome, and accustomed to feminine admiration, he rubbed the scar on his chin, a reminder that he shouldn't be cocky in this business.

"He is coming," Tzu said quietly. Both men rose to greet Troy Hardigan.

"Mr. Hardigan. Thank you for moving our meeting forward," Kong said in fluent English. He prided himself that some English speakers with whom he did business assumed that he had been raised in Hong Kong because of his ease with the language.

"I'm sorry that it had to be under such sad conditions," Hardigan said. Kong noted that the hand he grasped was rough, a peasant's. Only in America could there be such a ridiculous corporate sales representative. Kong glanced into the American's guileless blue-gray eyes.

"I read of the murder in the paper," Troy said, shaking his head. "Please accept Frontiers Technology's condolences on the death of your associate and apologies on behalf of our country. We trust that the killer will soon be brought to justice."

Kong folded his hands in front of him and acknowledged the courtesy by bowing his head. "Thank you." Extending a hand toward a chair for Hardigan, he resumed his seat and signaled the waitress. "Will you have something to drink?"

"Coffee. Black, please," Hardigan said as he brought a sheaf of files from his briefcase to the table top. "I hope you don't mind that we get right down to business. I have a lovely lady and an unpleasant plane trip waiting."

"I too have a plane trip ahead, to take home a lovely lady who sadly is deceased," Kong said somberly. Du Guangmei had not been lovely, but Hardigan did not show any response to the statement.

"You'll be accompanying her body home?" Hardigan asked.

"Yes, I must personally comfort her widowed mother and her only brother."

Hardigan nodded slowly. "I don't envy you your task." He leaned his folded arms on his files. "Telling family that a loved one has died must be the hardest thing anyone has to do."

"Did you know her, Mr. Hardigan?" Kong stirred his coffee.

"I've been trying to remember. I met several staff at your office, but I don't recall the name. Was she a friend?"

The question surprised Kong. "No, I scarcely knew her." He had known her cousin, who had died during a botched abortion. He also had learned that Du Guangmei held him responsible for her cousin's death and her aunt's subsequent suicide. He tapped his fingers on the table, then reached for a cigarette. *Was that Du's motivation? All that matters is, who was she delivering the information to?*

Kong measured Hardigan once more. No, this was not the CIA contact. His reputation offered no inkling of undercover involvement, nor did he show the intellect or sophistication to be an agent.

Hardigan opened a file and offered copies. "These are the estimates we discussed." He handed one copy of the report to Kong, another to Tzu, and opened the third copy. "You'll find the cost summary with total estimate on page two and some of the variations we discussed following. Description of each item begins on page thirteen."

Kong focused his attention on the pages before him. "These estimates are lower than you first quoted. Lucrative government contracts help."

Hardigan leaned back, affable, natural. "Government contracts help when we can get them, but we have focused our work on serving business needs."

"I was impressed by the caliber of scientists working with you. Dr. Po and Dr. Zinsser, in particular."

"We are very proud to have such powerhouse physicists, I assure you."

The men were silent as Kong and Tzu examined the documents. Finally Kong set the report down. He checked his watch. "Everything looks in order, Mr. Hardigan. I'll take these to my superiors and hope to give you a final answer in March in Hong Kong."

Hardigan replaced his report in the briefcase and extracted business cards for the two men. "If you have any questions, please contact my office. I'll be out of the country for a few weeks, but I can be reached by e-mail, and my office will forward calls. I will return your call at the first opportunity."

Kong glanced at the nondescript business card and shook hands with Hardigan with the appropriate banalities.

As Hardigan walked away, Tzu leaned closer. "What do you think?"

Kong drew in the cigarette smoke and blew it through his nose. "If we had manpower to spare, I'd set someone to watch him, but he is not CIA. A simple peasant."

Stefanie was having trouble concentrating on her book as she waited in her car for Troy's meeting to end. She had awakened with the troubling half-memory that Troy's kiss had found its way into a dream. Then an argument with Amanda had started the day badly. When Stefanie had returned from the shower to dress, Amanda had rolled over and looked down mischievously from the top bunk. "Ooo, good choice. Troy likes you in that."

That remark almost sent the red skirt and sweater back into the closet, but she ignored the little-sister impertinence and pulled them on.

"You two were late enough last night. Where were you?"

"We were talking."

"Just talking?"

"What else would we be doing?" Stefanie's patience was wearing thin as she tugged the comb through her hair.

"Well, with Troy being in love with you. . . ."

That did it.

Stefanie spun from the mirror. "Don't be ridiculous. Troy's not in love with me. He still thinks I'm a little kid."

Amanda leaned out over the bunk and rolled her eyes. "No wonder he and Uncle Ramón say you're a babe in the woods. You are so-o-o-o naïve!"

"And you read too many romance novels." Stefanie returned to her combing.

"You should read a few. You'd learn what a man in love acts like, instead of falling for Ro-o-o-ger." Amanda ducked out of the way of the flying comb.

As if that hadn't been enough, she had stopped at her computer to check e-mails on her way out the door. An e-mail with an attachment was there from Dr. Jim. He asked if she would do him a favor and put the attachment on a disk for Troy, since she would be seeing him this morning. The attachment looked like gibberish, and she fumed as she copied it to the disk. Why didn't Dr. Jim just send the file to Troy, and how did he know she would be seeing him? People were showing altogether too much interest in her personal life.

Troy, however, had shown a corresponding lack of interest as he got in the car with a perfunctory greeting and immediately immersed himself in paperwork. Work had already taken him. That hadn't lifted her spirits either.

Now she jumped at Troy's knock on the passenger window.

"You don't have to look so gloomy, babe," he teased. "I haven't left yet." He climbed in and pulled on his seatbelt. "So where are you taking me for breakfast? Your choice since you're paying."

"If I'm paying, we'd better go home. My father still extends me credit." She started the car.

Troy put his hand on the gear shift lever to halt her putting the car in gear. "Hey, don't worry about finding work. It's just slow now, especially with the holidays." He turned her chin toward him. "You're a good writer, Stef, and some editor's going to snatch you up. You've got experience, credentials, ability."

"Too bad you aren't hiring."

His blue-gray eyes, reassuring and warm, looked deeply into hers. Suddenly aware that she would miss him, Stefanie nodded her thanks and forced a smile.

He settled back into his seat. "I need to make a call, then how about Pancake House?" He punched a speed-dial number.

"Yeah. Hardigan. I just had an interesting meeting. He was probing about Guangmei. . . . Naw, you know I'm just a good ol' country boy. . . . Yeah. Watch your back."

Stefanie pulled the disk from her purse. "Dr. Jim sent this for you this morning."

Troy took it without question, slipped it into his briefcase, snapped it shut, and gave the locking mechanism a spin.

"I opened the file to make sure it came through. It just looks like gibberish. What's going on with you and Dr. Jim? And why did he sneak out to your car last week when he was visiting?"

Troy opened his mouth, then shut it.

"I saw him in your car. I watched him sneak back into the house."

Troy ran a hand through his hair, leaving it standing on end. He slouched back into his seat. Tapping on his briefcase, he finally spoke. "Some of it you're just going to have to trust me on. It's related to my job, and I can't talk about it. I can say that Dr. Zinsser is worried that your father may take it upon himself to return to China to look for his father. Your promise to Nanai is making him think about doing it. He can't. It would be too dangerous."

"Lots of people who fled during the Cultural Revolution go back to visit now."

"Not top-flight physicists, Stef. Not people doing your father's cutting-edge work."

"His work is all for medical application. At least, that's all he's ever talked about."

"That is mostly, but not entirely, accurate. In any case, some medical technology can have more sinister applications, and your father's knowledge could be vastly useful in weapons research if they could use your grandfather as leverage to force him to cooperate. If he refused, it could make things a lot worse for your grandfather. So Andrew can't go. We can't allow it."

"I understand the concerns, but I'm not sure how you two have a say in Father's travel plans."

"Let's go eat. I'm hungry."

Stefanie put the car in gear. "Okay, but I still don't understand why Dr. Jim talked to you about my father."

"He hoped that the two of us could prevent his going."

"How?"

"He was looking for ideas. Now let's talk about something more pleasant."

During breakfast and the drive to O'Hare, Stefanie's mood lifted. They laughed through much of breakfast. But she was feeling down once more as they took the Departures exit ramp.

She found a place in the short-term lot and turned off the car.

"Anything else you want to discuss before a cop shows up at the window again?" Troy said.

"Now that you mention it, I have a couple of questions about the way you've been acting around me lately. I know you hate to talk about personal stuff, so I'm just giving fair warning that some personal things will be on the table when you return. Also," she added, wagging a finger at him, "whatever the police may think, I am not a child, and I am sick of condescending little girl kisses on the forehead. We can shake hands, or you can give me a hug."

Troy thought it over. "I think I've got it: Serious talk later; no more forehead kisses; and no longer a little girl. Really, though, I already had that last one figured out. Can I still call you 'Babe'?"

"You call half the women in Chicago 'Babe.' Why should I be any different? Come on, I'll help you take your bags to check-in."

While Troy carried his suitcase, suit bag, and laptop into the terminal, Stefanie brought his briefcase. He checked his luggage.

"Are you in a hurry?" he asked.

She shook her head.

"Good. Whatever they say about security check-ins, at this time of day it doesn't take an hour to get through. I'd rather spend a little more time with you than sitting in there missing you."

His comment touched her. "I'll miss you too."

He led her to a couple of seats.

Stefanie began, "You've been such a comfort to me with Nanai's cancer and with Roger." She looked up at him. "Three months seems an awfully long time for you to be gone. How long will you be in Washington?"

"Just until the end of the week."

All too soon Troy decided that he had to go through security. Stefanie held her hand out to him.

"It won't seem like Christmas without you and Dr. Jim here."

"Yeah, not for me either."

"I'll be praying for you and e-mailing you."

"Good. I'll need both." Troy took her hand, then put his other arm around her. She walked into the hug willingly, but she was not prepared when his lips closed on hers in a firm kiss.

Troy lifted his head, his eyes twinkling. He caressed her blushing cheek.

"Grown up enough for you, babe?" He winked at her and joined the line to go through security.

She stared after him.

Maybe I should *borrow a few of Amanda's novels.*

Chapter 8

THE BROTHER SHUFFLED into one of Guangzhou's more modern apartment buildings through the back door. With a rag from his pocket, he started dusting the stair railing. He smiled as he worked past a cleaning woman mopping the floor, but she ignored him.

No one pays attention to cleaning people, not even other cleaning people.

Dusting his way to the fourth floor, he glanced around to be sure that no one was around before knocking on one of the doors.

Donkey guide Gao Wenzao grinned when he opened his door. The apartment was a wonder, the largest Lao had been in. He removed his scuffed shoes before crossing the white carpet through two large rooms and a hall leading to Wenzao's bedroom. He shook his head.

A whole bedroom for one boy. Some of today's youth have life so easy.

Five elders waited for them in the lavish room. Wenzao had a thick, soft mattress on a wooden bed frame with colorful sheets and blankets. Bright posters of the basketball hero Yao Ming and pictures of Wenzao's family and friends adorned the clean, bright walls. An entire bookcase was devoted to books, small boxes, and electronic devices that the Brother could not identify. A television sat on a videocassette player, and a computer occupied a desk in the corner. Clothes poked out of a dresser piled with papers and gadgets. The Brother marveled at all of Wenzao's possessions.

The young man sat on the corner of his bed and invited the Brother to join him. The others were seated in chairs.

One of the elders, small and thin from several years in the *laogai*, prayed. When he had finished, another elder in a nicer suit turned to the Brother. "What can you tell us about the Bibles?"

"One of our donkeys did not get through. We lost six Bibles, but we can thank the Lord for the others. We have delivered nearly two dozen already." He pointed to the college student. "Wenzao is the only donkey guide that I have not talked to yet."

Wenzao beamed. "Two dozen Bibles, two commentaries, and a concordance."

The Brother closed his eyes in thankful praise as tears burned his eyes. How had the two elderly donkeys carried so much?

Around him, the other elders murmured their praise to God. After a time, their eyes settled on the young man again. Instead of looking excited, he seemed a little nervous.

"Before we go on, I want you to see something," he said.

As the elders nodded, Wenzao licked his lips. "I asked you to meet me here today because I have several things to show you, and my parents are both working. I told you we had all of these Bibles, and it is the truth, but they did not all come in the form we expected."

Sweat was forming on the young man's forehead.

"What do you mean, Wenzao?" Lao asked.

"Three of them came in this form." Wenzao flicked on the television with his remote control. The men watched a dark-haired man in a long robe as he walked among a group of poor people teaching them the Beatitudes—in Mandarin.

"What is this?" the thin elder asked.

"It is a film about the life of the Savior," the well-dressed elder told him. "I have seen some of it before."

Wenzao fast forwarded. He stopped at the resurrection of Lazarus. The men watched, spellbound, as the dead man came from the tomb. Wenzao sped the film forward again until they watched the Savior being led to Golgotha.

As the spikes were pounded into Jesus' wrists, the Brother closed his eyes and covered his ears with his hands. Still, in his mind he heard the nails being driven in, the shrieks of pain. *Oh, God, forgive me. Forgive me my sins. I know you have, but I cannot forget.*

"Brother, Brother." A younger elder shook him gently. "Are you all right?"

Looking around the room, he recalled where he was. For a moment he had forgotten. The scenes had disappeared from the television, and with them the scenes in his own head. Wenzao and the young elder questioned him with their eyes, but the two older were looking at the Brother with understanding and compassion.

"Are you all right?" the younger preacher asked again.

The Brother rubbed his hands along the coarse fabric of his trousers. He nodded. "It was so powerful. I could not watch it. To see again the suffering that my sins caused!" He blinked back tears.

"I am sorry, Brother," Wenzao said. "I thought you would be pleased that we have these tools for evangelism."

"The Brother has not said that he is not pleased at having the film," the thin elder explained. "The film shows how evil our sins are that they could cost our Jesus so much."

"So they are a powerful tool?" Wenzao asked uncertainly.

"I would rather have Bibles," said the Brother. "Our most needy areas are rural. Seldom do we have access to such things as your television. Many still lack electricity."

"I thought of that. Look at this." From the bed Wenzao picked up a flyer from his father's store. "Battery operated televisions. They are small enough that we can carry one with us."

The Brother read the advertisement and passed it to the next man. He remembered torture, but would the film be powerful to those who suffered from poverty and despair every day of their lives?

"We will find uses for them," he said without enthusiasm.

A solidly built elder cleared his throat. "We have another matter to consider."

The others turned to him.

"We need to make sure that this film does not teach false doctrine or downplay doctrines that might be less popular in the West, such as the miracles of Jesus."

The well-dressed elder nodded. "Before we distribute these, we must make sure they are accurate. We do not need to import more doctrinal problems from the West than we already have."

A cell phone on the dresser rang, and the elders jumped. Wenzao picked it up.

"Ni hao."

While the young man talked on the telephone and the other elders talked among themselves, the Brother looked around the room again. *So many things. So much wealth.*

Wenzao had become a zealous young Christian in the past year. He had bought and read the entire Bible. He had started a Bible study among his college friends. He had been a donkey guide and distributed Bibles in the countryside twice. With such a love for Christ and yet so much to make life easy, the Brother wondered whether the young man would continue to love Christ first, would remain faithful under hardship, threats, and deprivation. When the Brother added in Wenzao's family position, he worried for the young man.

Oh, my son, my son, have you counted the cost? So many love the world more than they love Christ.

Wenzao opened a dresser drawer and pulled three Bibles from it. He laid them on the bed.

The elders looked from the Bibles to the young man. The frail elder asked, "Where are the others?"

The young man winced. "That is what we must talk about. They are here." From the desk next to the computer he picked up a stack of small plastic boxes, each with a picture of singers and dancers visible through the plastic. Each of the elders lifted one from the stack and turned it over. The Brother held a box with the picture of a Hong Kong singer whose picture he had seen in a train station.

Wenzao opened one box and lifted a shiny silver disk from the box. It reminded the Brother of the large black disks of Western music that he and other students had destroyed during the Cultural Revolution.

"Each disk contains the entire Bible," Wenzao explained nervously. He turned on his computer, inserted the CD, and showed the elders how the Bible software worked.

"Is this all they brought?" the thin elder asked sadly. "This will not be much help. It is very nice, perhaps, but we need Bibles at churches that don't have computers."

"That is true." Wenzao turned away from the computer. "Those churches also do not have printing presses. It would be nice if they could have a printing press they could go to for copies of Bible texts they were studying."

He opened the desk drawer and removed a stack of papers stapled together. "Computers are increasingly used throughout China. With these," he held up a disk case, "you can print just the chapter or book you need." He passed them each a bundle of papers. "Here is 1 Corinthians. Is that what you have been teaching, Brother?"

The Brother nodded blankly as he flipped through the stapled pages.

Wenzao leaned toward him. "How much more time could you teach if you did not have to wait for everyone to write the passage?"

"That is true," the stocky preacher said, "but writing down God's Word also helps our young evangelists learn it."

The Brother thought of the amount of time it took to write out the passages, especially for some of the less educated. "You both make good points," he said slowly. "The brothers and sisters could copy the words accurately later and give the copies to others. Sometimes they write down the incorrect characters and mistakes are taken back to the people. We could avoid mistakes this way."

Wenzao looked relieved that the Brother was not dismissing his idea.

"And the time that you have to train the evangelists is so limited. You could double the teaching time," he added.

Several elders nodded, but two looked skeptical.

Wenzao had one other argument. He picked up another CD case.

"If the Public Security Bureau goes through the belongings of younger evangelists and finds a few compact disks of popular singers, will they be suspicious? Young people carry music disks everywhere. But if they find this," he held up the Bible, "they will know at once what they have."

The Brother had to agree. In the few areas where communications towers were available, cell phones had increased the safety of the church. Lookouts could instantly warn if police units seemed to be gathering for a raid. The church could not afford to ignore technology that would help them carry out the Great Commission.

"We do have one more problem, or at least a challenge," Wenzao said. He placed a different disk in the computer. "The commentaries they brought us are on disk and in English. I thought I could give a few pages at a time to some of my friends who are studying English to translate."

"I do not think that is a good idea," the stocky elder said. "We need someone who knows English and also is grounded in the Word."

Wenzao opened his mouth, glanced at the Brother, then closed his mouth.

"I know someone I could speak to at the seminary, but I am not sure he will agree," the Brother said.

"Talk to him," the thin elder said. "This is not a job for children who are learning both English and theology."

"When I speak to our contact, I will explain the difficulties with the English commentaries. Perhaps Chinese commentaries can be found like this in Hong Kong," the well-dressed preacher said.

The elders discussed which churches should receive the few actual Bibles that had been brought in. After further consideration, the elders identified a number of rural churches where members had access to computers. Each took several of the disks with them. The stocky elder had access to a video player, so he took one of the videos to study. The Brother placed the three Bibles into pockets inside his coat and stuffed several computer disk boxes around them. He hoped he would not appear suspiciously bulky as he left the building.

Singly and in twos the elders left the apartment several minutes apart until only the Brother remained.

"You have done well in thinking all of this through," the Brother said. "Without your knowledge, we would have thought that this shipment was of little worth to us."

"I am glad," Wenzao said. "Brother, could I talk to you?" He led the Brother into the kitchen, with its gleaming appliances, and sat down at the table. The Brother seated himself across the table so that he could study his young friend's face.

Wenzao rubbed a finger along the shiny table top before speaking. "It is my father. He does not understand my commitment to God. I do not know what to do."

"This is not an easy matter." The Brother scratched his chin, then leaned his elbows on the table. "What does the Scripture say?"

"It says that I should honor my parents."

The Brother nodded.

"But how can I do that and love God with my whole being when my father wants me to follow him in business? What I want, what I believe God wants, is for me to preach."

"You must do what God wants, but that need not conflict with your father's wishes. You have an opportunity that so few young people have to go to college. You need time to learn the Bible. You can learn to speak well, to teach well, and to use technology to spread the gospel in ways I cannot understand. You can learn to translate English materials that we cannot get in Chinese.

"Also, your father is probably watching your faith to see whether it turns you from an obedient son into a spoiled Westerner. By obeying the command of Scripture, you show him that you can be both a Christian and a dutiful son. And you can pray for your father that God will use your proper submission to open his eyes."

"I had not thought of that."

"If we are to confront cults like Budding Rod and show the people that this false female savior is anti-Christ, we must have effective leaders who are grounded in the Word."

Wenzao nodded. He sighed. "Sometimes I feel as if I am wasting so much time."

The key turned in the lock of the apartment's door and Gao Mingfu strode in. Closing the door behind him, he said, "Wenzao, is your mother home yet?" He turned and scowled as he saw the Brother in his rough clothes. "Ah, you are working on our apartment?"

"Father, this is my friend who prayed for me, the one whose prayers saved my life," Wenzao said.

"Oh. I apologize that I did not recognize you. Please do not think I am ungrateful for what you tried to do, but Wenzao refuses to recognize the potency of the drugs that cured his leukemia." Gao Mingfu laid his coat and briefcase on the table.

"I was dying, even with the drugs, father. They did not start working until Lao prayed for me."

"Sometimes God uses drugs alone to heal, sometimes prayers alone, sometimes the two together," the Brother said. "We can both be happy for Wenzao's healing."

"That may be, but Wenzao does not need to listen to superstition and throw his future away. You should not be teaching him to disobey his father and his government!" Gao Mingfu stood glowering at the Brother.

"He did not teach such a thing, father." Wenzao rose, his face as stern as his father's. "He told me I should honor your wishes to get my education. He told me that in obeying you I can obey and honor God who gave me back my life for a purpose. And I will honor God by giving Him back the life He spared me."

Gao Mingfu's face reddened. He strode from the room and slammed the bedroom door.

"Gently, Wenzao. Your tone dishonors your father, especially in front of a guest," the Brother said. "You must understand that he only wants good to come to you. Remember that it is more difficult to rebuild a wall after part of it has been knocked down. I know this is true."

Chapter 9

KONG QILI SAW "THE DRAGON," the special assistant to the Minister of Public Security, before she saw him. The woman guarded the minister's door against unwanted intruders, breathing fire on any who might consider wasting his precious time. She ruled over his underlings with a clawed hand. In the years Kong had known her, she had never varied her appearance. Her steel gray hair was always arranged in a short, squared-off cut with straight bangs. Gone was the unisex Mao suit that had once accompanied her Mao-approved hairstyle. But the dark blue, square-cut jacket she had assumed at the minister's insistence was not a significant improvement.

The pool of secretaries quailed every time the Dragon's eyes swept over them. Her ever-present frown deepened at the sight of Kong. Without speaking, she nodded toward a chair.

Kong pulled the notebook he had bought in Chicago from his inner jacket pocket. A page of the notebook listed several high technology companies in the Chicago area. Another listed people working for those companies who might be U.S. government intelligence agents. Some names were circled as deserving further scrutiny. Others had been pared off as improbable candidates to be CIA. For example, the thought that Hardigan with his transparent demeanor, freckles, gorilla-like build, and Midwestern "aw-shucks" honesty could be an agent was laughable.

He flipped another page. Here he had listed twenty names of American physicists, with J. Derek Zinsser's name at the top. Zinsser was indisputably the head of the satellite project, but he would not be easily corrupted. Indeed, back in the latter days of the Cold War, a Soviet agent had been kicked back to Moscow for trying.

Kong's agents had found nothing with which to blackmail Zinsser, but they had been able to work one of his assistants. Then Zinsser's attention had been drawn to a change in his assistant's spending patterns. Zinsser had asked the Americans' Federal Bureau of Investigation to investigate. Knowing he was under suspicion, the assistant had threatened to identify his Chinese contacts unless he was paid more handsomely. The next day, he'd had the misfortune of stepping in front of a speeding car. The threat was ended, but unfortunately so was the access.

Four names under Zinsser's on the list had been crossed out. James Bartlett, May Chin, Harold Dedelmeyer, and Heinrich Gaust assisted Zinsser, but they were hand-picked by Zinsser and evidently shared his values system.

Kong lighted a cigarette and studied his notebook again. If he appeared unperturbed by the wait, the Dragon would relent sooner. She continued reading from a folder.

About ten minutes later, the Dragon's imperious glare summoned a nervous young secretary. From the look on the girl's face, Kong expected her to bolt.

"Tell the assistant to the director of the Religious Affairs Bureau that the minister will see him in twenty minutes." The Dragon turned to Kong. "He will see you now."

She led the way into the office, walking through the cloud of smoke that was enveloping the minister, and seated herself beside his desk. "Mr. Kong has arrived, sir."

The minister peered at Kong through the haze. A man of medium height with short-cropped silver hair, his mild manner had deceived many into thinking he was easy to please. After a warm greeting, he congratulated Kong on the progress made in upgrading the United States technology intelligence network, then got to the point. "What can you report on the contact of the traitor Du?"

"We found no contact information in her belongings, but the fact that she went to Chicago indicates it is someone in one of the companies that have done business with us. Placing an agent in those circles would seem in keeping with American intelligence practice. We have eliminated two salespeople from consideration. One is out of the country, and the other obviously knows nothing."

The minister leaned forward. "Tzu will continue searching?"

"Those are my orders."

"Good. I want you to place Tzu in charge of the network for now."

Am I being blamed for the security breach with Du Guangmei? Kong felt the shock of the minister's statement in his stomach. He clamped his jaw shut.

The minister rolled a pen between his hands.

"You have completed the initial reorganization in the United States, and I need you to oversee a rather unusual special project. I personally do not see the need to assign an operative of your caliber to this assignment, but several bureaus with rather weighty influence do. I chose you because you are our best hunter and can probably take care of it in less time than others might require." A twitch of his lips hinted of a smile. "I also want to keep you close at hand for awhile. A vice-ministry position will be available shortly, and I would like to see you fill it."

A vice-ministry! Kong enjoyed the travel and financial opportunities of his position, but the influence of a vice-ministry was a plum well worth plucking. The perqs alone were worth it: Opportunities to make more money, a better apartment for his mother, a car, and serious influence.

The Dragon checked her watch, went to the door and opened it. The assistant director of the Religious Affairs Bureau stood there with his hand raised to knock. Behind him stood a slender girl with thick glasses.

A smirk flashed across Kong's features for an instant as he stood. The old devil had opened the door on him like that once, leaving him with the same awkward embarrassment now worn by the assistant director. The minister introduced Assistant Director Chang Rongwen and Chen Yuliang. Then he asked Chang to explain the project.

Chang was passionate about his work and roused himself to a fury as he explained the unique difficulties he faced with the cults.

As if he had heard this sort of thing many times before, the Minister of Public Security leaned back in his chair, turned away from the speaker, and closed his eyes. Kong also found his mind drifting in the warm room as the assistant director strutted around the room expounding, "A danger to the people . . . a cause of instability . . . revival of superstition . . . an assault on the principles of the glorious Revolution . . . an estimated five thousand converts a day."

Stifling a yawn, he noticed that even the Dragon's eyelids had drooped. Then Assistant Director Chang renewed Kong's attention as he whirled on him.

"They must be stopped, Kong!" He pounded his fist into his hand. "They endanger the People's Republic. These religionists destroyed the Soviets. Now their forces expand daily, undermining socialist principles and political stability."

Kong stared at Chang. Speaking slowly to cover his anger, he said, "Do I understand you correctly? You want me to hunt down uneducated religionists?"

"These Christians endanger the national stability. Their teaching promotes divisiveness. They convince people that this god of theirs they call Jesus is coming to take over all governments. They refuse to follow the people in family planning initiatives and education."

"On the other hand, my comrade, you have to see our perspective on the issue of religionists," the minister remarked. "These Christians have hardly been a public safety issue for my department. By all accounts, they are good workers who do not cause trouble beyond sneaking off behind the backs of their cadres to talk about their god. They do not beat their wives. They do not even drink. I appreciate that you must deal with complaints about family planning and proselytizing. But I have more immediate and more dangerous threats."

"So they said in Moscow, and look what happened to the Revolution there. These are dangerous subversives who cloak their opposition to the Party and socialism with their religious platitudes. They are a knife at the throat of the people's will, as they undermine authority with their misbegotten loyalties." Chang lowered his voice at the cool look on the minister's face. "You are accustomed to looking at threats from world governments who would strangle us into submission to their will. We deal with a cancer that is destroying our own society by rotting away the socialist will. It was not an invading army that destroyed the Soviets. It was the failure of their own socialist ideals and revolutionary will. This baby must be destroyed in its cradle."

"That was tried once before, I recall," Kong quipped. He prided himself on being well-read, able to pick up on the allusion to the Christian's belief in a god who became a human child. "It looks as if he's already up and toddling about the countryside."

As the assistant director's face reddened, the minister intervened. "The project for which our help has been requested has to do with finding only one or two leaders of the Christian cult who have been particularly good at evading the police and are identified as a serious national threat. I have asked you to sit in on this meeting because I think you can quickly and efficiently take care of this problem for Assistant Director Chang, and we think there could be a connection here to another of your assignments."

Kong's head snapped up at this last bit of information. He waited for elaboration, but Chang had gotten a new burst of energy:

"Yes, our specific concern is one agent who sneaks about the country, living off the labor of the people without working. He organizes teams of one or two who stir up the people. We know him only as the 'Brother.'"

Chang Rongwen leaned forward and hushed his voice as if sharing a national secret. "I believe this Lao is behind the whole thing. If we catch him, we can destroy these Christian cults. That is why you are here, Mr. Kong. The minister said that you are the 'Beijing Tiger,' who always brings down his prey."

Chang straightened his body, seated himself with a flourish, and gestured to the silent young woman who had faded into the room's furniture.

"Miss Chen has a way to make Lao into dinner for the Tiger," the minister said.

The girl with the glasses rose, placed her briefcase on her chair, and opened it. She passed a file folder to each person seated around the desk.

"This gives a brief background history of the teams of cultists who spread corruption and superstition through the people. Their work is well established. It actually began in 1934, before the Japanese invasion, with a religionist named Yang Shaotang. At that time, Westerners were still spreading this poison throughout Asia as a means of subjugating and colonizing our ancestors. Yang became their puppet so successfully that he was known throughout the West as David Yang. Yang worked his agents, called Spiritual Work Teams, until the Japanese disrupted his operation.

"Yang's strategy still is followed. Evangelists spend weeks learning at one of their hidden bases of operations. Then they spread across the countryside disseminating their anti-socialist rhetoric to villages and cities on their circuits.

"We believe that Lao oversees much of the operation. Though we do not know who he is, wherever he goes the illegal churches fester."

Although the subject bored him, Kong was impressed by the woman's efficient presentation. And he would certainly take out this "enemy of the people" if it meant a promotion. The possibility of a vice-ministry could arouse his interest in anything, even another of Mao's anti-sparrow campaigns. Who was he to argue with what the fools in power regarded as important?

"We believe we have found a way to infiltrate this network through a man who is now in prison, whose name is Peng Chongde. You are holding a summary on his life and considerable influence among the cultists. As a young man, he followed Wang Mingdao in opposing the Three-Self Patriotic Movement.

"Men and women such as Peng and Wang acted as traitors to the people in fighting the government's approved, legitimate expressions for traditional

Chinese religions, Christianity, Islam, and other cults. You know that through the approved TSPM movement we avoid the confusion, sectarian violence, and instability inherent in religious imperialism by foreigners and sects."

"Of course, of course. But it says here that Peng has been in various penal institutions for over forty years. He is very old news. Is he now willing to work with us if we let him die in a warm bed?"

"Peng Chongde has resisted rehabilitation. Numerous attempts have been made to physically rehabilitate him."

"In other words, torture did not break him. That sometimes is the case with such prisoners."

"Yes, it is. But instead of abrogating their relationship with him, the house churches have continued to honor and look to him. For a time in the late 1980s, he was allowed freedom in Shanghai, though under supervision. Religious leaders from all over China visited him."

"So you think he has the identity of the Brother."

Chen smiled. A hard glint formed behind the thick glasses. "When a tiger is about to jump and kill, he always looks back to make sure the cub is all right."

"Peng has a family. Then why . . . ?"

"The Pengs fled to the province of Taiwan in 1967, abandoning him here. From there they went to the United States."

The Minister raised his hand.

"We are coming to a reason I want you on this case, Kong. I believe you will find a connection here to other matters on which you have worked. Peng's wife and child ended up in the United States. The son was given the Western name Andrew. He took a doctorate in physics at a top American university called Harvard."

Andrew Peng? That name is familiar.

"He now teaches and is a research consultant—*in the Chicago area,*" the minister added. "He is involved with at least two companies of your acquaintance."

Kong's heart quickened as he made the connection. *Associate of Zinsser. Yes, close friend of Zinsser. It must be the same man.*

"I have not met Andrew Peng, but you are correct, Minister, that we have some interest in him. His specialty is lasers—medical applications, mostly, but he has worked in satellite development. To have leverage through a member of his family could be most useful."

"All that is fine," the assistant minister threw in. "Just remember that our primary concern is the Brother."

"We stalk other game besides your rabbits."

Chen had lost control, and this presentation was in danger of developing into a brawl between Kong and the assistant director.

"Sirs, there is no reason why the Tiger cannot pursue the rabbits while keeping an eye out for his other prey. Andrew Peng is . . . uh . . . Mr. Kong has accurately described his work. He married and has three children. The oldest, Stefanie, is twenty-four. She has an advanced degree in journalism and a second undergraduate degree in Asian studies."

Chen Yuliang caught her breath and directed the men to a picture in the dossier of three young women: Chen Yuliang and two others.

"Stefanie Peng is the short one in the middle, Mr. Kong."

"I assume you know this woman."

With a practiced eye in evaluating attractive women, Kong noted that Stefanie Peng stood several inches shorter than Chen Yuliang. Long wavy black hair framed a petite oval face with large dewdrop eyes and a large expressive mouth. He shifted his attention to a photo of a man who must be Andrew Peng, standing beside an elderly woman.

"Yes, I know her quite well. The old woman in the other photograph is Chu Dehong, Peng Chongde's wife. She took the name Grace Peng in the United States. The man with her is Andrew."

Except for the longer hair and larger mouth, the granddaughter looked like a younger version of her grandmother.

"Chu Dehong has breast cancer. She is eager to see her husband before she dies, and Stefanie Peng wishes to find her grandfather so that she can take him to America."

Kong smiled. "Ahhhh! Lure the girl here. Put her in a cage to dangle before the old man. Perhaps the old fool will dance for us."

Chen's eyes looked huge behind her thick lenses. "And the same would go for your other interest, Mr. Kong. Andrew Peng would do much to save his daughter."

"I am sure he would."

"Once she is in China, Stefanie will be easily snared. She is an ardent religionist herself and an aggressive researcher and journalist. She probably will break criminal laws without any help from us, though we can always give her a hand. If you were a lonely old man, Mr. Kong, would you not relinquish a mere acquaintance to save your granddaughter, who is the living picture of a beloved wife you have not seen in forty years?"

"My compliments, Miss Chen. Not many intelligence agents could have put together those threads into such a plan. And yes, Minister, this could do much good with the father. How unfortunate that Andrew Peng does not desire to return to the land of his ancestors himself." Kong frowned as he mentally reviewed the basics of the scenario.

"But you see problems, Kong?" The minister asked.

"Details that need refinement. There are multiple steps involved, so more chance for complications. An assistant would be most helpful. Is Miss Chen available for such work?"

The girl behind the glasses blushed with pleasure. The minister nodded toward the Dragon, who wrote on a file.

"A most subtle plan." Kong said, rubbing his chin.

"And you will remember its goal, Kong?" Assistant Director Chang asked with a remaining tinge of distrust.

"Oh, certainly, certainly."

Kong tried not to gloat. He was the master at playing these games.

I have been handed the key to Zinsser, with a vice-ministry thrown in.

Chapter 10

THE SLAP OF HER HANDGUARDS against the lower parallel bar claimed Stefanie's attention. With her arms straight, she went into a fast backward hip circle, letting her body swing under the bar. When her body topped the bar, she released the lower bar, snapped her back into an arch and grabbed the upper bar in an eagle catch.

The clock on the wall across from her sailed by in a blur. She caught a whiff of the kerosene heater in the corner. The sports room that her father had added to the back of the garage years ago was a refuge from life's problems. Sometimes, the floor routines knocked the tension out of her; but on days like today, nothing but rigors of the uneven parallel bars could vanquish her turmoil.

The three routines she had already performed had eased her into a more complicated one. She did not look down as the door to the garage opened. Rising to a handstand on the top bar, she swung down, tucked herself, and turned a double forward somersault to dismount. She staggered a little on her landing as her right leg reminded her of a past injury.

Watching from the doorway, Grace Peng gasped, her hand pressed to her chest. When she recovered herself, she brought Stefanie the towel that lay on a pile of rolled-up mats.

"When you do that, I hear your leg snap again." She shuddered. "Why must you do that somersault?"

Stefanie picked up the sweat pants she had left on the mats.

She had broken her leg at age thirteen while performing the double somersault dismount in competition. Coming down too soon on her right leg had snapped her femur.

Stefanie wiped her face. "Uncle Ramón told me, 'If a horse throws you once, you get right back on to show both of you who the boss is.'"

Nanai shook her head and lapsed into Mandarin. "I am also afraid of horses."

Amigo scampered over with a scarlet plastic flying disk that was almost as large as he was. Stefanie tossed it for the dog to catch. He panted after two tosses and settled down on the mat between the two women.

As Stefanie pulled her sweatshirt over her head, she saw the wall clock. "I guess I'll be late for my honeymoon flight." She turned her back to the clock and squatted down to roll up the mat she had spread beneath the uneven parallel bars.

"It has been a hard day for you."

Stefanie did not answer.

"We worry for you, but you shut yourself away."

"I had not yet written to explain to a couple of editors why they would not be receiving my series of articles on China." Stefanie's jaw ached with the building tension. The pleasure she had felt from her exercise dissipated as she thought of this aborted wedding day and all its complications to her life.

"Did you finish your letters?"

"First drafts. I just did not feel like being around people."

"Stefanie, remember that this is a hard day for all of us who love you." Her grandmother's face furrowed in concern and she rubbed her chest.

Ashamed, Stefanie hugged her. "I am sorry."

"This is your way. I understand this. When someone hurts, you are first to comfort them. But when you hurt, you shove others away. It is not good for you. It is not good for your family. We need to share this grief, for it is like a death in your heart."

Nanai tucked a loose black strand of hair into Stefanie's ponytail. "Remember your gray kitten. It jumped out the window and was killed in the street. We searched everywhere for you. We were getting very frightened. Finally I heard a tiny sob coming from under my bed. You were hiding there crying."

"This is not a kitten." Stefanie dropped to the rolled mats. "It is not even just Roger's betrayal and the wedding that is not happening today. My whole world is getting run over—you, Grandfather, Roger, my career that is not happening. . . ."

"And someone else you avoid mentioning."

Stefanie nodded. "I suppose he is part of it."

"You do not open his card. So I bring it to you."

Her grandmother held the small envelope that had come with a dozen roses that morning. She had already received a mixed bouquet and a book of Chinese poetry for Christmas. Now these flowers and an envelope addressed in Troy's bold scrawl. He must have ordered the roses before he had left for Washington and India.

Stefanie ruffled Amigo's fur and switched into English. "I have enough on my mind without Troy." She winced at her tone of voice. "I'm sorry, Nanai. I didn't mean to sound that way. I couldn't ask for a more supportive friend than Troy. But he seems to want our relationship to be more . . . complicated."

"Not complicated. You are not ready to give your heart. Troy knows that. But these flowers say that when you are ready to pick up your life once more, he is there. That may be uncomfortable, but it is not complicated."

Amigo rolled onto his back for a belly rub. Stefanie scratched him half-heartedly. She switched back to speaking in Mandarin to try to explain.

"I have failed to help you. I have failed to find Grandfather. Roger disrespected me and faked his relationship with the Lord and with me. I counted on my articles on China to help my career. Now I am not going to China. Troy was a constant that I thought I understood, and now I do not think I have understood him at all. Maybe what he feels is becoming clear, but he is a complication—and one I cannot accept right now."

Nanai slowly lowered herself to the mat beside Stefanie and put an arm around her. Stefanie returned the gesture. Her grandmother's bones felt less substantial than the candy canes they handed out to the children after the Christmas program. A wave of helplessness washed over her.

"I too have struggled with feelings of complication about a man," Nanai said. "For many years I could not understand why Chongde sent me away. I could not understand that he thought I could not stay with him and serve Christ as he did. I could not understand why he took the chance that led to his arrest.

"Finally I decided that I must trust the love and wisdom in Chongde's actions—and in the Lord's. I think Chongde suspected that he would be captured by the Red Guards. He made me promise to take Andrew and escape, even if he was not at the meeting place. He trusted that we would never be alone, even if he could not be there. Such a man I will trust and love, even if I do not see him until heaven."

Stefanie hunched her shoulders.

"You do understand what I am feeling? I do not think I can trust a man again."

"I know your heart well, little one. I also know this man's heart—better than you do, I think. He is not Roger."

Stefanie shook her head. "How do I know he won't become another Roger?"

"You have seen the changes in him since he became a Christian."

"I saw changes in Roger too, Nanai, or I wanted to. How do I know that Troy is being honest about his faith?"

Nanai leaned forward to look her in the eye. "Because his relationship with the Lord does not depend on whether you love him."

The door burst open and Amanda came in. "Phone, Stef. It's Yuliang."

Stefanie jumped to her feet and ran from the room, calling back over her shoulder, "Amanda, help Nanai get off the floor."

Rushing into the family room, she pushed through a quickly gathering group of family members to reach the telephone. Her pent-up breath exploded as she grabbed the receiver. "Yuliang? Hi. This is Stefanie. Sorry to keep you waiting."

"I hope you will pay me for this call. It is expensive," Yuliang said.

Not a thousand dollars worth of expensive. Her family, huddled in the bedroom doorway, did not know of Troy's loan. "Of course. What did you find out?"

"I think I have found your grandfather, Peng Chongde." Yuliang reviewed the facts that Stefanie had given her and added new ones.

Stefanie rolled her eyes at the recitation. "That sounds right," she interrupted. "Where is he? How is he?"

"He is in a reeducation-through-labor camp in Xining."

"Xining?"

Amanda and Nanai were coming into the room, and Jamie ran to the map of China on Stefanie's bedroom wall, nearly knocking over Amanda's easel, to search for Xining. He pointed to a spot in eastern Qinghai province.

"He works on a loading crew and helps the *laogai* medic."

"Is he all right? Is he healthy?"

"Of course! Do you think we mistreat him?" Yuliang's voice seemed sharp, even for her. Then she added in a softer tone, "He is to be considered for release sometime this winter."

"Release?" Stefanie gasped.

"Release?" voices around the room echoed. "When?"

Her father's eyes, normally so calm, danced like Jamie's. Stefanie waved them silent.

"I am sorry, Yuliang. Could you say that again, please?"

"I said I talked to some corrections officials who said that a family member's presence could expedite the release and secure an exit visa."

Stefanie repeated the conversation to her family. Tears streamed down her grandmother's cheeks as she pressed her fingers against her lips. The family was rapidly boiling into a mass of hugs.

"When is the hearing?" Stefanie covered an ear to keep out the excited chatter around her.

"Sometime between the end of January and the end of April. There is a backlog."

"Oh." She tried to hide her disappointment. She could not spend four months in China. She needed a job.

"When? When can he come?" her family begged.

"Yuliang, wait a minute, please. We are all so excited." She covered the receiver. "She says between January and April, and it would help to have a family member there."

Her father looked anguished. "My passport has been recalled for some problem. I'm not sure how soon I can go."

"I will go," Nanai said.

"You don't have an up-to-date passport," her mother reminded Nanai.

Stefanie turned back to the phone. "Sorry. I'm back, Yuliang."

"I looked into another possibility for you."

Yuliang's voice oozed with uncharacteristic sweetness, making Stefanie uneasy.

"What is it?"

"A friend in my department hires foreign English teachers for colleges. He told me that Beijing University needs an English teacher for next term. Someone became ill. I told him about you."

"Me?"

"Your qualifications fascinated him."

"I do not have a teaching certificate. I am a writer."

"You are bilingual and you have tutored. There are two classes in speaking English and one in writing English."

"Well . . ."

"He will call you tomorrow to see if you are interested. You would have no trouble with the work. Remember that it would put you here for your grandfather's hearing."

Stefanie paused. She glanced at the yearning expressions on her father's and grandmother's faces. Concerns pricked at her, but she mustered a look of excitement. "That is wonderful, Yuliang. Thank you. Have him call me."

When Yuliang set the phone down she raised her eyebrows in Kong Qili's direction. "Well?"

He removed the earphones he was using while he taped the call. "Well done, Miss Chen." He opened a bottle of bai jiu, and poured a measure of the sorghum liquor in two glasses, passing one to Yuliang. Lifting his glass, he said, "To the tigers. May the lambs always yield so easily."

Part Two

If you are ugly, do not blame the mirror.
> —Chinese saying

For now we see in a mirror dimly, but then face to face; now I know in part, but then I will know fully just as I also have been fully known.
> —1 Corinthians 13:12

Chapter 11

THE BROTHER PUSHED HIS BICYCLE into the gorse and rhododendron bushes, wincing at the scratches, and bent over. His eyes watered from the cold wind sweeping down the hills. Nothing unusual seemed to be going on. Most people were enjoying the warmth of their snug cave homes. These were dug in the loess deposits, near a settlement of more conventionally constructed apartment buildings and houses that rose from the plain.

Burrowing his head deeper inside his collar, he slipped his hands inside his sleeves and squatted even lower to lessen his exposure to the wind-whipped dirt as he watched. If government agents were watching for him, he wanted to take no danger to his Christian brothers and sisters. He would finish his journey after dark.

Even after darkness had descended, he unerringly found the door of Baoti and Sufen's cave. As soon as he knocked, the door opened and Baoti pulled him into the cave in which he and his wife lived. The scent from one of Sufen's pork and noodle creations filled the air, its ginger teasing his nose. The warmth stung his cheeks.

Smelling of coal smoke and fish, Baoti engulfed him in a hug. "You have come at last. Now I think you expect a share of my noodles and pork." He turned back into the room. "Come out. It is safe."

Sufen appeared as if from out of the walls and smiled shyly at him as she rolled his bicycle away. She leaned it against the wall beneath a picture cut from a magazine of the Three Gorges, one of China's most spectacular tourist spots. The tiny woman with veins of silver that ran through her hair had brightened the cave walls with numerous posters and pictures. A picture of their ten-year-old son, taken a year before he drowned, sat in a frame on a shelf in the wall with their clock.

The door to the second room, the couple's bedroom, stood open. The bottom panel of a bookcase that leaned against the back wall of the cave slid aside and a slender, young man poked his head through with his bowl and chopsticks in his hand. Wen Dengfu grinned up at the Brother before crawling out the rest of the way.

The Brother helped him to his feet and hugged him. "I have something for you."

The young man's grin widened. "A letter from San? Have you seen her? What about Mary? Are they both all right?"

"What is the hurry? It is a piece of paper," Baoti teased. "Let us consider a more important matter—food."

"You eat. I am hungry for news from home." Dengfu hunched forward with extended hands as the Brother searched his pocket.

"I bet he left it with Chou, thinking you would get it there," Baoti said.

Disappointment flashed across the younger man's face.

Sufen touched her husband's arm. "Do not tease."

"No, I planned to leave it here. Here it is." The Brother tugged a folded sheet from among several other letters.

Dengfu grabbed the letter, retired to the corner, and unfolded the rice paper page. Baoti and the Brother smiled at each other. Dengfu had not seen his wife and three-year-old daughter for almost a year. He had been running from the Public Security Bureau and preaching where he hid.

What if Jizhong . . . ? The Brother canceled that line of thinking as the younger man sniffed and brushed at his eyes.

I am not strong enough to make their sacrifice.

"Come, Brother," Sufen said. "I have your favorite meal ready. The others will be here soon."

The small woman bustled about to close the panel of the bookcase and set the table. She held out her hands for his coat.

By the time the Brother struggled from his coat, Dengfu was ready to join them. The younger man dashed tears from his eyes and grinned widely. He waited until they had finished giving thanks to spread a paper in front of the others. Circles with lines running off in various directions made up the picture.

"Mary drew me a picture of her and San and me with Jesus in heaven. Did you see them?" Dengfu asked the Brother.

The Brother swallowed two bites of the pork and noodles. "No one makes pork and noodles like you, Sufen."

She blushed and lowered her head, the silver in her hair reflecting the light from the lamp on the table.

"I stayed with your parents while I was there," he said to the younger man. "They all miss you."

Dengfu nodded.

"The little one is a miniature version of San, except that she has your grin."

Dengfu grinned.

"She chatters like her mother."

"Has San found work?" Sufen asked.

The Brother shook his head. "Work is hard to come by, but the money you sent helped."

"Sometimes I think I should go back," Dengfu said. He lowered his head.

Sufen patted his arm. "You would be arrested. How would that help the gospel or San and Mary?"

"It is hard for them, of course," the Brother said. "But Mary's prayers for her father must bring joy to the heart of God. That little one loves the Lord."

Dengfu's eyes watered and he nodded.

Behind them the door opened and the first church members entered. They crept in a few at a time to avoid drawing attention to the gathering. Sufen put out the fire in the small coal stove while the men finished eating.

When everyone arrived, nearly seventy people packed the two rooms of the cave. Laughing, talking, and hugging, they helped one another out of their coats, then wedged themselves together on the floor, knee to knee, toes brushing the seat of the pants of the person in front of them. Small children perched on a parent's lap.

When Baoti rose, everyone quieted. He opened in prayer, then others prayed. The Brother felt that if he opened his eyes, he would see the smile of God upon them.

How can heaven be any better, Lord?

In a space empty of prayer, someone began singing "To Be a Martyr for the Lord."

> From the time the early church appeared
> on the day of Pentecost,
> The followers of the Lord all willingly sacrificed themselves.
> Tens of thousands have sacrificed their lives
> that the Gospel might prosper.
> As such they have obtained the crown of life.

At the first chorus, the Brother could not make himself sing.

> To be a martyr for the Lord,
> To be a martyr for the Lord,
> I am willing to die gloriously for the Lord.

He pictured again fingers being broken, one by one, heard the anguished screams as the bones snapped, the thuds and moans of beatings. He dabbed at his tears.

While the others sang the Mandarin gospel song about being willing to leave everything and to die for the Lord, the Brother stifled a sob. He had left everything, his family, his sweetheart, his position, but to die, to suffer pain, or to be beaten and killed was more than he thought he could bear. He was so tired, and the fear swept over him.

> Those apostles who loved the Lord to the end,
> Willingly followed the Lord down the path of suffering:
> John was exiled to the lonely isle of Patmos.
> Stephen was crushed to death with stones by the crowd.
> Matthew was cut to death in Persia by the people.
> Mark died as his two legs were pulled apart by horses.
> Doctor Luke was cruelly hanged.
> Peter, Philip, and Simon were crucified on the cross.

Baoti, pressed up against the Brother by the tightly packed crowd, threw a brawny but tender arm around him. The big fisherman squeezed.

The Brother prayed silently, *Lord, I am not worthy. I am so weak, so scared. How can you use me?*

> I am willing to take up the cross and go forward,
> To follow the apostles down the road of sacrifice.
> That tens of thousands of precious souls can be saved,
> I am willing to leave all
> And be a martyr for the Lord.[1]

After the song, a woman praised God for her supervisor's conversion. She introduced him to the group. Tears streamed down the face of a new believer who thanked God for delivery from opium addiction. A middle-age man repented for visiting a prostitute. Someone asked prayer for an aging mother's illness, a cadre's salvation, a brother's spiritual growth.

The group did not have to speak in whispers, as in apartment meetings. They could even sing loudly, as they could not in a house, for the thick dirt walls absorbed the sound. Amid the others' joy, the Brother prayed for wisdom, for the words to say that would strengthen and minister to these precious brothers and sisters. His fear seemed to block all his thoughts on the Word.

Over the passing of hours, the singing, prayer, and praise subsided. Faces turned in hungry anticipation toward the Brother.

Lord, give me fishes and loaves for them. My basket is empty.

Beside him, Wen Dengfu touched his arm. The young man's eyes sparkled and pleaded. Thankfulness flowing through the Brother, he nodded to the younger man, who stood.

Dengfu described the misery and hopelessness of the world without Jesus. Then he described the sufferings of Jesus so powerfully that the Brother could not help crying. Others nodded, wept, or bowed their heads with teary eyes.

"He asks us to be willing to suffer for Him, to take up our cross. What was the cross? It was the instrument of His torture and death. For us we may need to face the rifle, the electric baton. We must be willing to give up everything—job, home, security, and . . . and family."

Dengfu's voice caught. In the warmth of the packed cave, he paused to steady himself.

"After His sacrifice for us, nothing is too great for Him to ask." Dengfu looked toward the ceiling with his arms spread. "The troubles here are hard. Being faithful is hard, but when we see Him, what will the suffering and the sacrifices matter? We will rejoice that we were counted worthy to suffer for Jesus."

The young preacher's face glowed with zeal.

The Brother nodded as the fear inside shrank.

Yes, Lord, glorify Your name in us, in me. Your grace will be enough for the hour.

The Brother awakened in total darkness. He listened as he struggled to remember where he was. Rolling over, his hand brushed cold metal, and he remembered that he was lying beside the printing press. Then he heard the sniffling that had awakened him.

"Dengfu, are you all right?"

"No. I am a hypocrite."

"A hypocrite?" The Brother pushed himself up on his elbow, careful not to bump his head on the press.

Dengfu must have moved, for the subtle whisper of his blanket reached the older man. "I preach to others that no sacrifice is too great for our Lord—and I believe it."

"I know you do."

"Then I dream of San, of holding her in my arms, of bouncing Mary on my knee. We are all laughing. San's laugh is like spring after winter, rain after drought, the song of a lark. Then I wake up."

The Brother waited.

Dengfu's words choked on a sob. "I tell the Lord I cannot go on. I am not strong enough. It is too much." The younger man's sobs filled the silent darkness.

Searching for the wisdom to comfort his friend, he laid a hand on Dengfu's shoulder. "When Jesus called the rich, young ruler, He asked for him to sell everything and follow Him. When the possessed man freed of Legion asked to go with Him, He sent him back to his own people. He took away the pride of being a Pharisee from Paul and the nets from the fishermen, the sword from the zealot, and the tax books from the tax collector. He requires of each of us the sacrifice of what matters most to us."

"It hurts so much."

"Yes, I know the hurt. But you do it. If it did not hurt, how would it be a sacrifice? How would it be worthy of *His* sacrifice?"

The smoke from the coal-oil lamp and the sharp tang of the ink drove the two men from the hidden room behind the bookcase in the afternoon. They had printed fifty copies of their small hymnal to pass out to believers on their journeys. The house churches never had enough Bibles, teaching materials, or hymnals. Baoti and Sufen had finished the fifty New Testaments, but a broken piece on the old printing press had prevented them from finishing the hymnals. Dengfu had brought the replacement piece with him.

Baoti arrived home. He sat down on the benches with them, told them of his day with the nets and asked about the press. His stomach rumbled. "I hope Sufen will not have to work too late. I am hungry."

He prowled around the cave's two rooms for several minutes before opening the door to peer down the street. "She will be here any time. I should start the fire."

The Brother and Dengfu helped. After a few minutes, Baoti drifted to the door again. The Brother, done with kindling the fire, followed. Dusk was settling across the plains.

"Here she comes. Why is she so late?" Baoti stepped outside and waved.

Peeking around him, the Brother saw Sufen glance over her shoulder. She plodded toward them.

"Get into the back room. Something is wrong." Baoti closed the door. He propelled the Brother toward the back room. "It is our signal. The police must have stopped her again after school. It happened once before when a brother was staying with us. Hurry."

They glanced around the room but saw nothing that would give away their presence.

"Do you think there is a spy in the assembly?" Dengfu asked.

"That is a common problem."

The two men crawled through the opening, closed the sliding door, and wrestled a block of clay through the tunnel from the other side to block the hole. Baoti sprinkled pepper in front of the bookcase in case the police brought dogs. Dengfu started to wedge the block tight.

"Not yet," the Brother whispered. "We should have time."

"You are home late tonight," Baoti said in a falsely hearty voice. "Did the police stop you again?"

"No, they did not talk to me, but they talked to the principal." The evangelists pushed their ears to the block's edge to hear Sufen's soft, frightened voice.

"It will be all right," Baoti said. The pair was silent for several minutes before Baoti said, "You had better fix supper."

Because Baoti did not give them an all-clear signal, the Brother and Dengfu remained in the hidden room. As Dengfu pasted more hymnals together from the freshly printed pages, the Brother lay near the tunnel entry in case Baoti called.

About a half hour after the men had retired to the hidden room, someone knocked on the cave's door. Sufen answered. "Principal Lai, please honor our home."

The Brother cracked open the sliding door in the bookcase. If he positioned his eyes carefully, he could see a stout, dignified woman standing near the door.

"Niu Sufen. Zhang Baoti." Principal Lai nodded to the fisherman.

"Principal Lai." Baoti bowed slightly. "Join us. We were just preparing to eat."

The woman glanced at the table. "Thank you, but I came to return Niu Sufen's grade book."

Baoti exchanged a glance with Sufen, then he put on his coat and left the cave, leaving the women alone.

"Is something wrong, Principal Lai?" Sufen asked.

"You were very kind when my son was ill, Niu Sufen, and I would show you a kindness."

Her head tipped, Sufen waited.

"Men from the Public Security Bureau came this afternoon to ask questions about you. They asked if I had heard anything about your brother."

"My brother?"

"I told them he was a fisherman, but they said your brother is an agitator who seeks to overthrow the government and the Communist Party." The woman stared at Sufen.

"My brother is a shy man who scarcely opens his mouth."

"That was my memory as well, and that is what I told them. They asked about another man named Wen. I told them I had never heard of him."

Principal Lai touched the doorknob. "You may hear somewhere, Niu Sufen, though it would not be from me, that the policemen's supervisor comes tomorrow morning. Early tomorrow morning."

The woman opened the door.

"Thank you, Principal Lai, for returning my grade book," Sufen said loudly.

"What if it is a trick?" Dengfu asked when he and the Brother had come out from the hiding place.

"I do not think it is," Sufen said. "The Lord has been dealing with Principal Lai since her son's illness."

"I trust her," Baoti said, "but the decision is yours. If the police supervisor comes, he may order them to watch us. He is a stubborn one and could watch us for weeks."

The four huddled around the table, trying to decide what their safest move would be.

"They may already be watching," Dengfu said.

"What do you think, Lao?" Sufen asked.

"We endanger you while we are here. I will take some of the hymnals we have ready and leave tonight. I have to get to Hebei Province." He turned to Dengfu. "You must make your own decision."

The young man bowed his head, then nodded. "I will go with you."

Chapter 12

Kong Qili tapped the end of an unlit cigarette on the pile of papers in front of him. He glanced at the three Public Security Bureau agents assisting him who stood near the door of the dingy room of police headquarters in the third poverty-stricken rural village they had visited today. Scowling at the peasant seated before him, he said, "You were in the room with this man for hours, but this is all the description you can give us?"

The peasant sitting across from him rolled his hat in his hands and eyed the tape recorder in front of him distrustfully. "He was just so ordinary. I do not know if I would recognize him." The man licked his lips and hunched forward. "When he starts speaking, you forget to watch him."

"You mean he is boring."

"No, I mean you see his words. He talks about this Jesus and you see Jesus healing people. I cannot explain it. The story comes to life and you feel this Jesus in the room with you."

Kong shoved himself back in the chair. "So he is small, graying, middle-aged, has a loud voice, and is a good storyteller. You cannot think of anything else about this Brother?"

The peasant slid forward on his chair. "I asked about him, who he is, where he comes from, but nobody seems to know. They just say God sends him."

"Do you mean as if he were an angel, a spirit, or some supernatural being?" Chen Yuliang asked from where she stood behind Kong.

"Not exactly." The peasant squinted and wrung his hat. "I do not know." He shrugged. "That is all they said."

"You can go," Kong said.

The peasant hurried to the door.

"If you find out more about this one called Lao, helping us capture him would be worth a year's wages to you," Kong said.

The peasant turned. "A year's wages?" He bobbed several times to Kong. "Yes, thank you, sir. Thank you."

Qian, the man who had followed Du Guangmei to Chicago and ended the problem she had presented, closed the door. "Do you want us to follow them, pressure them?"

They had talked with three other peasants in this shabby little town and been told the same information.

Kong threw a pencil down on the pile of papers. "No, they are telling all they know. They cannot describe him. He is ordinary. Nothing unusual. This man is successful because he is drab, and he knows how to use his drabness to be invisible." Kong leaned his fist on his thigh. "We will go with your plan, Chen Yuliang, but we still need a backup plan."

Qian leaned his massive hands on the table. "I could romance the girl."

Kong fought back a smile at the idea of the massive middle-aged man with a receding hairline romancing the Peng girl. "Thank you, Qian, but you are too valuable to tie that closely to the girl. I will require your expertise elsewhere."

If Qian felt any disappointment, he hid it well. "Thank you, Mr. Kong."

"Miss Chen and I will wait for you outside while you pack our equipment."

Kong held the door for Chen Yuliang, then followed her outside into the fresh air. Glad to wash away the scents of human waste, sweat, and cooking cabbage, he inhaled the cold air, coal smoke, and diesel fumes. He offered a cigarette to Chen Yuliang and lit both his and hers with a lighter.

"What are your thoughts, Chen?"

"We do not need spies if we have Stefanie. The old man may not know the Brother, but he knows the people who know him. We can roll them all up and this master deceiver with them."

"But one should always have a backup." He watched a boy riding a bike and thought of how much he had wanted one when he was young, especially after Shaoqi received one.

Shaoqi. Hmm, Shaoqi. Yes.

"Repeat that, please, Chen."

"I said we should also insert Stefanie into the house church movement. She is the sort who would learn much. Then when we spring the trap we could predicate her release and her grandfather's on finding the Brother."

Kong paused with his cigarette halfway to his mouth. "Not bad, Chen. How pliable is your friend under such pressure?"

Chen blew a long puff of smoke. "I do not know. Stefanie holds strange principles. She is very stubborn."

"I have another question, which I hope will not offend you." He watched her from the corner of his eye. "I have had problems working with women before."

"What kind of problems, Mr. Kong?" Her question sounded emotionless, giving him no feedback.

"Emotional bonds with an enemy can get in the way. The Peng girl has been your friend. In a moment of casual laughter, you might decide that you were wrong to bring her into this."

Yuliang's eyes narrowed into dark steel behind her thick glasses.

"I assure you that my emotions will not be a problem, Mr. Kong. No friendships come before China." Again Kong could not interpret the bland detachment.

Kong turned to face her directly so that he could study her openly. "I am asking you to smile into her face every day and sell her out, Chen. Can you lie to her, invite her deepest secrets, and hand them over without thinking about your betrayal?"

"Of course, Mr. Kong." Chen Yuliang smiled coldly. "I already have."

Stefanie could not keep her mind on her father's voice as he read a lengthy Bible text for the night. The room seemed unusually warm, her father's reading dry, and the room stacked with tension. She prayed silently for her family to agree to her going to China, especially her mother, the key to the debate.

"Do we have additional prayer requests?" her father asked. No one said anything, so Stefanie surged ahead.

"Mr. Kong will be calling tomorrow, Father. I need to give him an answer," Stefanie said.

"Stefanie, the money—"

"—has been provided, Father."

"How?"

Stefanie licked her lips. "The College and Careers Class gave $500. Dr. Jim sent $4000."

"You asked for this money?" His dark eyes sparked angrily.

"Of course not, father. I asked for prayer." Stefanie tried to stifle her irritation. Sometimes her father treated her as if she were still a small child, as though her petiteness reflected her maturity.

Delores stepped into the conversation. "My mother has sent the breeding fees from two stallions. And I didn't ask either. Nor did we ask for the $2500 that the church mission board gave toward the ticket to bring your father home."

Andrew Peng bowed his head as he fought for composure. Clearing his throat, he said, "I will call tomorrow to ask when my passport will be returned."

"This has nothing to do with your passport, father. Mine is in order. It's the one good thing from my engagement. I'm ready to go to China," Stefanie said.

"I am head of this family, and I must go for my father."

"It's too dangerous for you. You fled China. They won't forget that."

"And Communist China is not dangerous for you?"

"You're an influential physicist. I'm nobody."

"My position offers me protection. My prominence makes me visible."

"Prominence doesn't help Chinese who return to China and get on the government's bad side. They arrested a scientist and her entire family even though she was doing research that they'd given her permission to do."

"No argue," Nanai burst out. "I will go. It is my place."

"Nanai, you can't. All they'd have to do is put you in prison for a few months to kill you," Stefanie said.

"Stefanie, you simply cannot go to China. I forbid it," her father said.

Words were threatening to explode from Stefanie, but her mother rescued her.

"Andrew, *mi amor*. You told Stefanie that she could not go because of money. We prayed. God provided the money. And now you say that our prayers and God's provision meant nothing."

"That's not what I'm saying, Delores. Don't put words in my mouth."

"Then what are you saying?"

"It's too dangerous."

"*Mi amor*, I once agreed to accompany a sweet Chinese man to a movie because I was impressed by his mind, and I had noticed an inner integrity and courage. I was more impressed on that first evening when that man wanted to pray with me. That night as we prayed I learned that he had a father who was in prison for his love for the Lord, and we prayed for his release. I decided to find out if tamales and sweet and sour pork might make a dish. Never before have I doubted that man's trust in God and courage. But now that it seems possible, he is telling God that he doesn't like God's way of answering prayer because it is *too dangerous*. After all of these years of praying, you are telling God He can't use whatever means He wishes to answer our prayers?"

"We are not talking means; we are talking about Stefanie. Are you telling me you want Stefanie, our little girl, to go to the hands of the very government that has kept her grandfather locked away all these years?"

Stefanie opened her mouth to respond, but a sharp glance from her mother closed it once more.

"I would rather cut off my right arm than see her go to China."

"Delores, for once be logical! If you don't want her to go, why are we disagreeing?"

"Because what you and I want is not the issue. It seems that God has opened the doors for Stefanie, not for you, nor for your mother, nor for me. And I understand why Stefanie might be the tool that He would use. I, for one, won't tell the Lord, 'No, thank You, Lord, I don't like the way You do things. Answer our prayers some other way.'"

Her father ticked off his reasoning on his fingers. "Stefanie has no experience dealing with communists. China is dangerous. It is my responsibility to take care of my children."

"She's also God's child, *mi amor*, just as your father is. You have always taken care of your children, but they are His more than they are yours. Your place as a father is not being challenged."

Delores looked again at Stefanie, who knew that this was the cue for the daughter to speak—wisely.

"Father, I love and respect you, and I have always submitted to your wisdom, even after I became an adult, and it was no longer required. I am twenty-four years old. In the American way of thinking, I could make this trip without your blessing, but I know that would not honor God or you. I will follow the Chinese way and the Christian way. I believe this is God's will, but I leave the decision to you."

Delores drove in the last nail. "Andrew, I for one cannot pray for your father's release if we turn down the only means He has given us to accomplish that." Her mother shook her head.

Andrew Peng looked at his wife, eyes misting but his mouth hinting at a bemused smile. He surveyed the others and watched his mother for some seconds. She remained silent, her face inscrutably set toward the floor. Then he looked at Stefanie.

"You have always looked and even acted as my China doll. But, whoever you look like, Stefanie, you *are* your mother's daughter. That gives me some comfort. I almost feel sorry for the government if they take you on."

Chapter 13

WHILE OTHER PRISONERS on the third shift at the Xiyu Coal Mine, also known as Provincial Number 3 Labor Reform Detachment, finished eating their watery rice porridge and hard roll, Ren Shaoqi hunched over and closed his eyes. He was not asleep, but rather conjuring up the face of the man he intended to kill. Yes, he still could form in his mind the long, lean, saturnine good looks of his childhood friend, Qili. Here was the man whose future death kept Shaoqi alive.

Someone elbowed him in the ribs. He grunted from the sharp poke.

"Ren Shaoqi," an army officer in the front of the room announced.

Several prisoners glanced back at him. He stumbled to his feet, supporting himself on the table.

"The rest of you are dismissed," the head guard snapped.

Two soldiers stepped behind Shaoqi. A few prisoners, the closest things he had to friends since No Taolin's release, glanced at him sympathetically. The guards' presence prevented their speaking to him, but he knew what they were thinking—firing squad. Somebody wanted his retinas or kidneys.

His meal turned to a heavy stone in his stomach. He could not die until he killed Qili.

The captain led him to a shower. His hands still shaking from eight hours of swinging a pick and hauling coal cars through the tunnels, Shaoqi lathered the soap on, sniffing it and scrubbing at the coal dust pressed deep into his pores. He wiped on the luxury of a thin gray towel and dressed in clean prison clothes. Although the shower did not kill the lice, he felt better.

His mouth went dry as he approached the infirmary. The guards whisked him past the disconsolate prisoners lined up in front of the door.

A woman doctor studied papers and ordered him to undress.

Though not as pretty as women he had known, to Shaoqi she appeared exquisite after a half-dozen years of not seeing a woman. He held his hands together to keep from stroking her soft, clean skin.

Her temperament did not match her skin. She poked, probed, and drained him of blood without mercy, ignoring the crude comments of the guards. Without a word or glance that suggested he meant any more than a microbe under her microscope, she ordered him to dress. He took his time, his hands stiff.

He was still tying his rope belt as guards shoved him toward the door. The captain, pacing in front of the door, led him down a hall to the right, through another hall, up two flights of stairs, down another hall, and into a conference room.

The sunlight coming through the windows blinded him. He threw his hands in front of his face to block the pain of the glare.

"Leave us," a man ordered.

"Are you sure, sir?" the army captain asked.

"Yes, wait outside."

Shaoqi knew that voice. He had not forgotten. He started to sweat. His hands trembling, he forced them to his side and straightened.

"What do you want?" he rasped, blinking into the light.

"*Ni hao*, Shaoqi. It has been a long time."

Eyes burning, he squinted until he located Kong Qili leaning his elbows on the table. Someone else, maybe a woman, stood behind Qili. He quickly judged the distance across the table to the throat he wanted to tear out.

"What are you doing here?"

Qili lit a Panda cigarette and offered one to the person behind him. *Yes, it is a young woman.* Then the pack and lighter were tossed across the table toward Shaoqi. The thought of a Panda cigarette and the smoke of the other two set his mouth watering.

"Sit down," Qili said.

Shaoqi glared at him. After a moment he sat from exhaustion.

He could see the woman now. Though she wore thick glasses and her hair was short, she was much prettier than the doctor. If it had not been Qili who sat opposite him, he would have had a hard time keeping his eyes from her slender figure.

He stared at Kong Qili. Only the small silver scar on his chin marred the sophisticated handsomeness.

"At least you still carry a token of our relationship," Shaoqi said.

Qili rubbed the scar. A large ring on his right hand flashed in the sun.

Shaoqi glanced at the coal dust and grime under his nails and ground into his skin. He plunged his hands beneath the table.

"How would you feel about being released?"

"How do you think I would feel?"

"What would you do if you were released? Visit your mother? Watch your sister's performance? Find a woman?"

"I would kill you."

Qili laughed and leaned back in his chair. "How would you do that? Just because you left your mark on me, does not mean you can take me, any more than you ever could."

"I would drown you like a misborn cur." Qili's eyes lost a bit of their sparkle. *He must still fear the water.* Qili might outfight him but he never could swim. Qili recovered himself so quickly that the girl probably had not noticed his discomfort.

"You could earn your chance to do me in."

"How?"

Qili's hands showed no trace of dirt as he smoked. Shaoqi could not remember what it felt like to be so clean. "A general is looking for a kidney donor whose profile matches you and one other prisoner. I give you an opportunity to live, Shaoqi."

He is telling the truth. Shaoqi began to sweat. *I must kill him before I die.* He lit a cigarette from the package, rose, and paced.

"Go on."

"You will be transferred to Provincial Number 3 Labor Reform Detachment in Xining. There you will become friends with an old man who works part of the time in the infirmary. His name is Peng Chongde. He is a cultist, a Christian. You will express an interest in his religion and befriend him. When you have earned his trust, you will find out anything you can about a man called 'the Brother' and his base of operation."

"That is all? You must have offended someone. Your masters have you chasing cultists?"

Qili's cigarette went to his mouth. Shaoqi tossed his own cigarette to the floor and clenched his fists. Though Qili's hands were well manicured, they were stained with blood—including the blood of Shaoqi's father, Ren Muhang.

"Why do you want me to do this?"

"Shall we say for the sake of my childhood friend. All you need to do is discover the identity of this man called the Brother and his home."

Qili stretched out his long slender hand to knock ashes from his cigarette into the ashtray. Not only was no coal dust ground into his finger, but he had no calluses. His hands looked as smooth as the woman's. Shaoqi knew that those hands were as deadly as a knife blade.

Shaoqi closed his eyes. He pictured the thick calluses on his scarred hands next to Qili's smooth hands. A drop of sweat rolled down his forehead. *Concentrate on what he says. You have to live.* He forced his eyes open. "What assurance do I have that I would go free?"

Qili's insolent grin filled Shaoqi's vision. "You have my word."

His word!

Shaoqi launched himself across the table with agility that surprised even himself. He reached for Qili's throat, wanting to remove that cruel grin forever. As he struck, Qili deftly stood with a sideward movement and grabbed Shaoqi by the shirt. The chair fell backward, and Shaoqi came down on top of it, the breath knocked out of his chest and belly. The wall stopped his forward motion as his head crashed into it. The blackness cleared from his eyes just in time to see Qili's shoe aiming for his jawline.

"So much for old times, Shaoqi. I gave you a chance."

Rough hands grabbed his arms and dragged him. His head lolled. With his jaw throbbing, he had no strength to protest. As his legs bounced down the step, he passed out.

Ren Shaoqi was drowning. Coughing and spitting, he fought his way to consciousness. He blinked at the captain standing over him in his green People's Liberation Army uniform with the dripping bucket.

"Name," the captain said.

Shaoqi answered between gasps.

The captain demanded his work unit, his age, and his crimes.

"Crimes against the people, fomenting insurrection." His head hurt too much for him to remember the other legal terms they had used for his being a leader of the Flying Tigers. Taking their name from Claire Chennault's squadron of American pilots who fought the Japanese in China in World War II, the motorcycle band had warned students in Tiananmen Square of the government's movements before the massacre in 1989.

Qili had been at his side then. But soon he learned that his friend was a government agent who had infiltrated in order to betray. He tracked down leaders to gain *guanxi* in the government. Shaoqi had nearly reached Tibet's border with India when Qili found him.

"Look up," a guard said. He snapped Shaoqi's picture.

The female doctor gave him a shot.

"What is that for? What are you doing to me?" he asked.

"An anticoagulant," the doctor said.

"Silence," the captain said.

Two guards approached him with ropes, handcuffs, and leg irons.

Shaoqi stared at them, trying to sort the situation out in his aching head. They planned to kill him. He rolled to his hands and knees, but the larger guard knocked him to the floor. The guard's knee drilled into his backbone.

He kicked, but the smaller guard threw himself onto his legs.

Shaoqi screamed as his arm was yanked backward. The cold steel of the handcuff clicked tight on his wrist. Then the guard wrenched his other arm back.

The leg chains dragged his legs down. Still, the guard at his feet worked.

The guard with the knee in his back wrapped a rope around his throat.

Shaoqi wanted to scream and curse. *Do not kill me. Qili is still alive.* Not until Qili had tracked him down near the Indian border did he learn that Qili had arranged for thugs to attack his father the night before the exams that determined college entrance. His father had died; Shaoqi had been forced to work in the factories because he had not gone to take the test. Qili had entered the university.

If there are any gods out there, let me live long enough to see Kong Qili dead, he prayed.

The guard with the rope rose. He pulled Shaoqi up with him, the rope cutting off Shaoqi's breathing momentarily.

When Shaoqi gasped for breath, the big guard stuck a cigarette in Shaoqi's mouth and lit it for him.

Twisting his neck to ease the rope's irritation, he saw that his pant legs had been tied shut and his shoes tied on. He studied the rope to make sense of it. The ropes tying his shoes on bunched under his feet, unbalancing him.

The big guard said, "When a man gets shot, he cannot control himself. A lot less mess this way."

Shaoqi stared at him. *They really mean to kill me.*

The guard showed no animosity. "It is not so bad. We are good shots."

"Take him out," the captain said.

Because of the short leg chains, Shaoqi stumbled with his first step.

The big guard caught him. "It is easier to hop."

Refusing to hop to his death, he shuffled past the captain.

Blinking against the brightness of the sun—*a sun I will never see again*—he saw the canopied army truck backed against a loading dock. Soldiers and prisoners occupied the back of the truck.

When Shaoqi's guards shoved him onto the truck bed, he stumbled against two soldiers guarding another prisoner. Silent tears trailed down the face of their prisoner, huddled at his chin, and dripped off his jaw. Another prisoner glared around the truck defiantly. With a start, Shaoqi recognized him as a student leader during the Tiananmen uprising.

He squinted into the shadows of the truck, counting himself as the sixth prisoner. Two soldiers guarded each of them.

Shaoqi turned to face the sunlight. *I die, but Qili will live to see the sunshine.*

The truck jolted forward with the soldiers steadying the prisoners.

Shaoqi stared out the open back of the truck. It clattered through the sunlight and shadows, past apartment buildings, restaurants, and factories. He clenched his top teeth to his lower lip to hold in his screams of anger. The truck's gears ground down as it slowed to turn.

Behind him, the man who was weeping said, "I did not mean to hurt him. I only wanted some money to feed my son. He is so little and he cries."

No one answered.

The truck bounced across a field or perhaps a rutted road, Shaoqi could not tell which. As it slowed and stopped, the soldiers again steadied their prisoners.

Two black cars pulled up behind the truck. After six guards climbed from the vehicles, they went to the trunks of the cars.

A soldier let down the tailgate. Shaoqi's soldiers pushed him to the tailgate between them, steadied him, and jumped down with him between them. Without waiting for him to regain his balance, they pulled him, bouncing awkwardly, into a field.

When they turned him around, he gasped as he saw what the soldiers from the two vehicles were doing. Chatting among themselves, they loaded rifles. *They really mean to kill me.*

"Do not take it too bad," the big guard said. "It will be over quick."

Shaoqi whipped his head around. A half-dozen ambulances were lined up ahead of the truck with the medics chatting and smoking in a relaxed huddle. He had heard that as soon as the prisoners were dead, the medics would load them onto the ambulances to harvest their kidneys or retinas. They would take his kidney for some fat, old general who had lived his life but whose influence let him steal Shaoqi's life too.

He hated them, all of them except the two prisoners calmly shuffling to their deaths—the student leader and a calm-faced middle-aged man. Most of all he hated the fat, old, bai jiu-drinking general who wanted his kidney. He hated that unknown general almost as much as he hated Qili. Qili would see the sunshine, drink bai jiu, love a woman, perhaps sire a son to carry on his evil line.

As the soldiers with the guns approached, his two guards tripped him to his knees, jolting him so that he bit his tongue. The other prisoners likewise were forced to their knees. He had not realized how cold he was. Now he had to clench his teeth to stop their chattering. The cold pebbles drilled into his knees, but the guards refused him any relief. The wind drilled through his thin, wet prison clothes into his bones. Unable to spit the blood from his tongue, he swallowed it.

One of the soldiers carrying a gun approached Shaoqi, passed him. Shaoqi felt the armed man hovering behind him like some evil spirit, waiting to whisk him into whatever lay beyond.

He tipped his eyes toward the sun and the blue sky. Alive and free, a crow winged across his view. He stifled a sob.

Carrying a red flag, the captain who had been doing the paperwork walked into his view and turned. The safety on the guard's gun clicked loudly with its release.

The captain called the guards to attention. While stamping his feet, he made a brief speech about purifying the socialist society from incorrigible criminal elements. He might as well have been reading his wife's grocery list for all the emotion he showed.

Shaoqi's mind drifted to his family, then focused on Qili once more—Qili in the sunshine, living, breathing, loving, killing.

The captain's call for the soldiers to prepare snatched his mind back to his plight. The soldier behind Shaoqi racked the bolt, the clack of the metal against metal sweeping down the line. Shaoqi felt the cold barrel of his gun as it was shoved against the base of his skull.

Shivering and sweating, Shaoqi wanted to close his eyes, but he could not break his gaze free from the captain with the raised flag.

The captain swept the flag down. The red blurred against the blue sky.

He heard shots.

He felt the blow.

Then nothing.

Ren Shaoqi opened his eyes. His head hurt so much that he snapped his eyes shut. He had seen nothing but darkness. He heard nothing but silence. He faded in and out of consciousness. The blackness never lightened. No one came near. He shivered, naked, against the coarse cold stone on which he lay.

Gradually the throbbing in his head decreased so that he could recall what had caused it. He had been executed.

"Am I dead?" he asked. The words echoed, but no one answered.

His grandmother had secretly burned incense to her ancestors in the spirit world. Was he now in the spirit world and punished? Would he remain here in the darkness, hungry and cold forever?

He felt his way around the walls and stumbled on the grate covering the hole that served as a toilet.

He licked his lips, but his fat, dry, and swollen tongue held no moisture. He huddled against the cold stone wall on his bunk. He grew weaker. He shouted. He wept. Always he hated Kong Qili.

The hunger worsened, faded, and worsened after he slept again.

Something in the darkness awakened him. Something was happening—a sound. A foreign sound, a series of clicks, and the creak of hinges as the darkness behind him split apart.

Prepared for a demon, he cowered on his bunk. He tried to cry out, but his mouth was too dry.

Light spilled into the room from the hallway. Shaoqi flung his arm up against its brightness. A man's shadow, tall and lean, blocked the light.

"You are still alive, Shaoqi, for now," Kong Qili said. "But the only way you stay alive is to work for me. Do you understand?"

Shaoqi opened his mouth but could not force it to work.

"The soldiers are waiting, Shaoqi, to take you back to the execution grounds. This time they will shoot you. You will get no third chance to live."

Shaoqi's head wobbled on his neck.

"Will you work for me?"

The terror of not knowing whether he was dead or alive in the darkness filled him. What lay beyond the bullet in the brain? He squeezed his eyes shut against tears he could not cry. He croaked, "Yes."

Chapter 14

TROY HARDIGAN'S GAZE SLID from the notes on which he was working to the picture on the desk of Stefanie and him, taken a year before. On the day before the photograph was taken, Roger Eddington had become angry with Stefanie and to spite her had backed out of cohosting the Valentine's banquet for the high schoolers at the church and Christian school. Instead of giving in to him, Stefanie had asked Hardigan to take Eddington's place.

That was the evening he had realized that he loved her.

Troy picked up the picture and gazed at Stefanie. A red comb with a large heart pulled her hair back on one side, giving her an exotic flair. She wore a simple, long-sleeved red dress with darker red hearts in a raised pattern on it. He didn't know what the fabric was called, but he could still remember the gratitude in Stefanie's eyes when she looked up at him as Steve Avery took their picture. Lani's younger brother had said, "Come on, Mr. Hardigan, make Roger eat his heart out."

Troy's work among foreign government officials, businessmen, and scientists required a stable persona. Even when he looked on Stefanie only as his tiny Chinese "little sister," he had a picture of Stefanie on his desk as a prop. He seemed more respectable as a businessman if he could show a picture of the girl back home. He had pictures of her in his laptop, his wallet, and his business card holder. It all gave the impression of a man in love. Originally he had woven his cover story of waiting for his fiancée to finish her education before they married. Somewhere along the line, the photographs had ceased being props. He had found himself thinking of Stefanie while on dates with beautiful women.

I miss her. Lord, be close to her today.

At a knock on the door, he set the picture back on the desk. After a glance at the clock, he peeked through the peephole and unlocked the door.

"Devin, come in."

"I apologize for arriving so early," Devin Takheri said in his precise India and Oxford accent. His dark hair was combed back immaculately, his conservative suit impeccable. "I am interrupting your work."

"My daydreaming. I'm finding it harder to work all the time." This trip he was missing Stefanie to an intense degree, more since he was wondering whether he really had a chance of winning her love.

The tension in Takheri's brown face eased into a smile. The furrow bisecting his forehead softened. He picked up the photograph. "You are a fortunate man. She is truly lovely."

"It remains to be seen how fortunate, depending on whether I can convince her to set a date." Hardigan closed the folder he had been working on and returned it to his briefcase. "She's finally finished her masters."

They discussed Stefanie's major and Takheri's daughter's education. Takheri's smile broadened when Hardigan asked about Kailasa's pre-med studies. Troy noticed that Takheri described his daughter with the same pride that Andrew Peng showed toward his children.

"Thank you so much for asking, but please excuse my digression."

"I enjoyed it. No problem."

Takheri's smile faded. "I fear there is—a problem, I mean. We have experienced a problem with the new communications satellite."

A problem that couldn't wait an hour?

"What kind of problem?"

The furrow deepened. "You should see the data yourself."

"Mr. Dalal is my supervisor at BSNL," Devin Takheri said as he introduced Troy to a squat man with one eyebrow lifted in a permanent air of cynicism. Hardigan folded his hands at his chest and bowed slightly in the traditional *namaste* greeting. Sur Dalal did not return it, but nodded, his eyebrow inching higher.

Had Dalal discovered that the communications satellite purchased from Frontiers Technology was sending out an extra carrier signal toward an American satellite? Likely. Troy had warned executives that the Indians were no fools. They would figure it out. A superior had deep-sixed his warning. Americans forever underestimated the Indian specialists. Troy doubted that they would have tried this stunt with the Japanese.

Devin Takheri led them to a clean, cool screening room. One of the off-white walls contained a white board, another a large-screen TV, and a third a series of maps with a map of Asia rolled down. A long table in the center of the room held a carafe of iced tea and several glasses.

"Refresh yourself whenever you like, Mr. Hardigan," Takheri said.

So I'm Mr. Hardigan now.

Takheri inserted a video into the VCR. Hardigan seated himself, opened his laptop, and prepared to take notes. Dalal was watching him.

Surprised at the contents of the video, he frowned. This was not what he had expected; someone else had been detected trying to communicate with the satellite. He began taking notes. When the presentation on the video ended, Sur Dalal folded his hands together on the table and leaned forward, his black eyes piercing. "Do not do us the disservice, Mr. Hardigan, of telling us that you are merely a salesman instead of a technician. We require an explanation of what is going on."

"Truly I am not a technician, Mr. Dalal, but it doesn't take a technician to see that another party is communicating with your satellite."

"Who?" Takheri demanded.

"I don't know. Would you allow me to contact my company?"

He spoke for several minutes with two technicians before turning to Dalal and Takheri. "They need permission to communicate with your satellite, and I need permission to release your passwords to them."

The two men took him to the control room and Takheri provided the technicians with the required information. He remained on the phone with them.

Wondering if the person who had broken into his office had cracked his safe to acquire lists of partial passwords, Hardigan paced. *What if Stef had seen him?* He shuddered at the thought. She might have ended up like Guangmei with a broken neck.

His face pale, Takheri leaned forward. "Are you certain? Thank you."

Takheri strode back to the conference room and whirled on Hardigan and Dalal. "This could hardly be worse. The Chinese are trying to communicate with our satellite. The Chinese!"

"We realized that China has not tripled its trade with us inconsequentially. Now we know their price," Dalal said.

Icy relations between India and China had begun in 1962 with China's invasion and seizure of a strip of the Himalayas claimed by India. To further freeze the relationship, China had supported Pakistan's and Kashmir's movements toward independence. When Indian intelligence discovered Chinese weapons sales to Pakistan, India had pushed fast-forward on its nuclear weapons program. India had also done its best to antagonize the Chinese leaders, including an offer of refuge to Buddhists escaping Chinese brutality in Tibet.

During the 1990s, Sino-Indian tensions had eased for economic reasons. It was to their mutual benefit to increase trade. The two nations even pledged to find a diplomatic solution to their Himalayan border dispute. There were limits to good will, however. One still could not fly directly between India and mainland China. Troy had tried.

Before Troy could respond, Takheri, his forehead deeply furrowed, said, "You must realize our predicament. With the exception of Japan, India is the most stable democracy in Asia. Unlike the Japanese, we are surrounded by hostility, as well as by people who sell us technology that comes complete with a back door, so that they can enter when they wish."

Hardigan winced inwardly. *Here it comes.*

"You will notice that I have not raised the issue of what your company did. Of course, we expected nothing less and we have financial leverage to get Frontiers to pull the plug on its industrial espionage if it becomes a problem. But if the Chinese have a way in, it could be disastrous.

"Let me clarify the record. Frontiers Technology has committed no industrial espionage." Troy leaned on his fists atop the table. "Anything that we may have done to your satellite has been done with regional security, including yours, in mind. You must know that your nuclear weapons are a concern to the U.S. I think my government may feel better with a finger on the pulse of India and your neighbors."

"You care about our weapons program, but not China's or Pakistan's?" Takheri slammed his hand on the table in frustration. "Your President Clinton destabilized Asia when he allowed China to proliferate nuclear weapons. He even opened the door to North Korea! It seems to me that the United States has more important things to worry about than India's nuclear program. Your government's errors encourage the very nations that menace us."

"Many of us realize that, sir. We have grave concerns about India and Pakistan as long as your nations stand on the brink of mutual annihilation. The U.S. is very concerned about China's military buildup and the spread of her weapons capabilities and technologies to the most dangerous countries in Asia. However, Pakistan, North Korea, and Burma cannot afford to purchase our satellites. So we do not have the option to sell technology to them with any back door such as you have most tactfully mentioned. Any improprieties on our part have been motivated by the desire for a stable and financially healthy society in India."

Takheri paused. "Troy, I think you know that we are not angry with you personally. I know you have been as candid with us as you are able. But we are frustrated with American policy."

"I understood perfectly what you meant, my friend."

"The question of the moment is how to stop the Chinese from infiltrating our satellites," Dalal said.

"What did the technicians tell you, Devin?" Hardigan asked.

"The diagnostic they ran indicates that the Chinese have obtained password access to some systems. The software allows a process for locking them off of these systems. It will take a little time, but not long. They have not gained password access to the entire system. We will change the uncompromised passwords anyway, in case they have a source for those as well. We ask that you initiate a security study at Frontiers to determine whether security was breached at your end. We certainly will do the same."

"I'm sure as soon as the technician pulled up your data, an alert shot up the channels, but I will make a call as soon as this meeting ends to make sure that we initiate a full investigation."

Takheri nodded.

Hardigan seated himself. "Have you had any suggestions of Chinese spying? We have always known that a network of operatives works in the United States. Companies such as Frontiers are, of course, key targets. We have extensive safeguards. Meanwhile, it's the old story of tracking down their agents."

"So your company may have been compromised?" Dalal asked, leaning back, his arms crossed, waiting.

"Any organization can be compromised at any level, whatever their safeguards. One of our researchers on the satellite project was killed in a hit-and-run accident. He had an unusually high bank account that his wife could not explain. This researcher, though, did not have access to the type of information that would allow infiltration of your satellite. That would narrow it down to a limited number of people who are considered highly trustworthy."

"Who would have access to our satellite data, Mr. Takheri?" Dalal demanded.

"Also a handful of people. I can get you a list."

"Good."

"I know you have intelligence specialists, but you should especially be looking for people with money problems, romantic problems, and those with even a remote Chinese background. Increasingly, romantic ties and ethnicity are incentives for spying, more than fidelity to a cause," Hardigan said.

"Perhaps someone with a Chinese girlfriend," Devin added coolly.

Troy smiled. "Exactly. I'm just the kind of person that you should put under the microscope. I'm sure my company will look into my personal life. That is just part of the cost of doing this kind of work. Oh, and for the record, my girlfriend is a Chinese-Hispanic American."

Takheri's fists unclenched. He forced a grin. "I will remember that in case we learn that Mexico also is accessing our satellite."

Troy edged back toward serious matters. "I'd be interested to know if you've been doing business with Black Cat Industries, Eastern Sea Communications, or Guangdong Communications Specialties."

The glance between Dalal and Takheri told Troy they had done business with all three. That didn't help Hardigan identify which of these Chinese companies was spearheading the espionage network. Hardigan's money was on Kong Qili at Black Cat Industries.

"What will the United States do about Chinese spying?" Dalal said.

"Proceed cautiously," Hardigan said candidly. "Americans are of three minds about China. Businessmen and politicians are eager to open China's markets and make lots of money; the human rights activists, some people in religious circles, and a small number of military people and politicians are concerned about abuses and expansionism. The rest neither know nor care what China is doing."

"Indians have to care, because of what China has done in our neighborhood over the past thirty years." Takheri ticked off the series of encounters on his fingers, his voice rising with each one. "They annexed some of the Paracel Islands from South Vietnam during the last crisis of the Vietnamese civil war in 1974, attacked Vietnam in 1979, have been gradually taking over the Spratleys, seized Mischief Reef from the Philippines in 1995, and fired on Taiwan in 1996. They provide weapons, advisers, and intelligence help to Afghanistan, Pakistan, and North Korea. Bases monitor our every move from Burma, and a major railway is being built across Burma. When they annex San Francisco, then maybe Americans will care?"

"Takheri, calm yourself," Dalal said. "The Americans are happy children, playing with the toys they buy from China. Don't expect spoiled children to be farseeing."

Hardigan poured tea from the carafe for Devin Takheri and himself.

"Mr. Dalal's assessment gives one of the more unflattering insights into the problem, Devin. There are other factors. A century ago, Americans became accustomed to seeing Asia, and to an extent Africa, as stabilized colonies that we didn't understand and didn't really have to. Our focus of interest has been Europe. China and India and the other Asian and Arab societies were complex, exotic netherworlds that could never really affect us. We've been forced to look hard at Asia only when they knocked us in the head to get our attention. We paid a small price for our ignorance in the Boxer Rebellion and a much larger price in World War II, Korea, the Japanese industrial revolution, and Vietnam."

Troy sipped his tea as he thought a moment more. "We were pretty thoroughly knocked out of our Eurocentrism by our dependence on Arab oil, the Middle East wars, and attacks on U.S. soil by Islamic radicals. What is happening in many parts of the world could keep us all awake at night. I guess the bottom line is that the politicians don't want to frighten people needlessly or give them too many places to worry about at any one time."

He raised his hand at Takheri's attempt to interrupt. "In our defense, I would add that the U.S. is quite aware that China has more than fifty subs and five thousand military planes. We know that they are supplying some very dangerous things to nations that are very unfriendly toward us and toward you. Internal Chinese propaganda targets *us* as their major enemy, not India."

"In other words, we won't get a place on your news programs until five thousand lie dead in a bombed town. The extent of your concern is that India and Pakistan behave toward one another as obedient subordinates of the great American superpower. So where does that leave us? The Chinese are sitting in Burma, monitoring everything we do," Takheri said. "They are challenging our eastern borders again. We lost forty thousand soldiers, my uncle included, in 1962 when China seized our land in the Himalayas. Many of us have not forgotten that incursion."

Dalal leaned forward. "Hardigan, I see this as the bottom line: We require that the security of the satellite that we bought from you be protected. Until it is, we expect you to stay here and head the investigation or get someone here who can."

"I will stay if you feel that is necessary, Mr. Dalal, but I don't really understand what my presence will accomplish. I really am a salesman, not a technician or an investigator."

Dalal stood with his fists on the table. "I am sick of games. You are not just a salesman, but if you are interested in sales, I pledge to you that you will see a marked drop in sales throughout Asia unless our interests are protected."

Dalal stalked out, followed by Takheri.

Hardigan sank back into his chair to finish his tea. His superiors had wanted an excuse to install a second phase of satellite surveillance technology onto the Indian communications satellite. This wasn't what they had in mind, especially since the first phase was hardly a secret to the Indian government. They might as well send a memo to Dalal about their plan. In fact, Dalal would respect them more if they did.

Troy hoped that a technology team could resolve this situation shortly; otherwise, Stefanie might forget who he was by the time he got home.

Chapter 15

"Feeling amped to be coming home, eh?" Pete Weston, Stefanie's seat companion since Hong Kong, stretched his lanky legs into the aisle of the China Air jet. Her nose was glued to the window where the first scenes of China, the land of her grandfather's persecution, were stretched out below in hues of brown, gray, and green, sprinkled with white and blue.

"Umm, no. I'm American. This is my first trip to China."

"I thought it might seem like coming home. The racial thing you know."

"No, home is where the people I love are." She pictured her grandmother's instructions in etiquette as she packed Stefanie's clothes for the trip, her mother's precautions, her father's tearful prayer for her in his office, her siblings' excitement. She touched her waist and the money belt her mother had insisted that she wear. She missed everyone already.

The engine's whine changed pitch. The ailerons extended, and the plane tipped toward the mainland.

Stefanie sighed. The past four days had been exhausting. Besides packing, she had cashed in the U.S. Savings Bonds she had inherited from Grandfather Martinez, to complement the gifts of friends and family. Her contact with the Chinese Department of Education, Mr. Kong, had called twice to reassure her that the articles she had agreed to write would cause no problems. She looked forward to meeting the pleasant-voiced man.

The seat belt sign flicked on. Pete Weston fished inside his pocket and drew out a business card. "Do you have a pen?" His thick Australian accent reminded Stefanie of Eliza Doolittle before her transformation in *My Fair Lady*.

He wrote a number on the card. Passing the card and her pen back, he leaned closer, bringing the reek of Chinese beer with him. "In case you need a mate or a few pictures shot."

"Thanks, Pete." Friendly without being pushy, he had told her of his Chinese girlfriend and of his life as a photographer—"a camera boffin," he had called himself—in China.

The plane landed with a bounce. Weston slouched more comfortably into his seat. "You don't need to beetle off?"

She shook her head.

"Good. I hate fighting crowds. The worst thing about China is that everything's done in flocks. The only thing you do as an individual is get thrown in prison."

His words startled her. Weston had worked in China since the mid-1980s, before Tiananmen Square. She leaned closer so that he might hear her without shouting. "Do you know much about their prisons?"

"I'm awake up to know I don't fancy a stay in one. Why?"

By the time she finished telling about her grandfather, the plane had found its parking place, and the queue of passengers was inching past.

Weston's mouth tightened. "How about going on a grand tour-a-rama with me? I'll show you some sites the tour guides overlook."

Stefanie finished hanging skirts next to sweaters in her half of a small closet. She tugged the three dresses and the suit clear of the garment bag and laid them on her bed. The bedroom, smaller than the one she shared with Amanda at home, contained her roommate's meticulously made bed near the closet, a dresser, and Edda's cello, music stand, and folding chair. Edda had hung three Nordic photographs of fjords so vivid they made Stefanie cold as she looked at them. When Mr. Kong had introduced them, he had said that Edda had come from Germany three years ago to teach German, but Edda said little of herself.

Wishing she did not have to go to the reception for foreign teachers, Stefanie separated the hangers and shook the dresses to settle the wrinkles. As she tugged her red wool coat from the suit bag, the front parted to reveal another dress.

"Now who . . . ?"

It was the semi-formal dress she had worn to host the Valentines' banquet with Troy. She pulled it free from the hanger. The fabric slid between her fingers. After Roger had refused to come, Troy had worked hard to show the kids a good time. He had even rented a limousine to pick up Amanda and two of Amanda's friends, as well as Stefanie. He had thrilled the girls with flowers and had turned the romantic dreamer Amanda into his eternally devoted follower.

She lowered herself onto the bed, realizing for the first time that Troy's attitude had changed toward her after that night. He'd stopped being "Uncle Troy" and had adopted a more thoughtful and less playful demeanor. Her mind had been so full of Roger Eddington that she hadn't given a thought to the indications that Troy wanted more from their friendship.

"Hmm."

Stefanie glanced around at the sound.

Tall, angular Edda Ansgar pointed at her watch.

Still clutching the dress to her heart, Stefanie pulled her sleeve up to read her own watch. She had ten minutes to reach the van. "Oh, thank you, Edda."

Edda nodded. During the two hours they had shared the apartment, the middle-aged blonde had spoken exactly two words—her name, by way of introduction—and she had not yet even smiled. Stefanie wondered whether Edda put all her roommates on this kind of probation.

"By the way, did you take those pictures?" Stefanie pointed at the fjords in the photographs.

"Yes. On my honeymoon." Edda strode past her to the closet, removed a nononsense green woolen coat, and left.

Stefanie stared after her. *I can't say I'd recommend her for a "Norway-is-for-lovers" tourism ad.*

Arousing herself, Stefanie thrust the red dress into the closet and ran to the bathroom, slamming the bathroom door behind her. She carefully pinned a gold alpha fish pin to her blouse. She tore the brush through her hair, forced her feet into her heels, and grabbed the doorknob. The door did not open. She turned the knob and pulled harder. Still, it didn't move. She leaned backward with all her weight, but the door did not budge.

She checked her watch. She was due in the van in five minutes. "I can't believe this." *Wouldn't Lani and Laura be rolling about the room in laughter about now? I can't be late.*

She bent a hook from her curlers to wedge between the latch and the casing. She yelled, but no one came. She searched through her overnight bag for something that might help her get out but could find nothing helpful—bath aids, perfume, a few cosmetics, facial lotion, her slippers, hair dryer, the pink footed pajamas with Bugs Bunny on them that her sister and brother had given as a Christmas joke.

She turned the door knob gently. It turned freely, too freely in fact, but the latch did not release from the striker. In frustration, she kicked the door.

The only way out seemed to be through the bathroom window. A tree stood a few yards away, but the night obscured it. With her gymnastics training, reaching the closest limb would not be a problem in the daylight—assuming she could get her window open—but who wanted to jump out of a window in the dark to try to catch a limb she could barely see? She might fall the three stories and break her neck or be otherwise injured and freeze to death.

She kicked off her heels and climbed into the bathtub. The window slid open easily. She peered at the tree but could see it only as a black mass in the darkness. Propped on the window sill, she glanced at her plaid wool skirt and jade silk blouse. She was not dressed for gymnastics.

She thought she saw a movement in the light of the next building.

"*Ni hao?* Is anyone down there?" she called in Mandarin. After a few moments a shadowy figure moved from the building to the tree and looked up at her.

"Did you speak to me?" She could not see him, but it was a man's voice.

"Yes, thank you. I wonder if you would ask someone in building maintenance to help me." She explained the situation.

"I will get help for you."

"Thank you so much."

She closed the window and waited. Finally she heard a knock on the door of her apartment. The door to the apartment was only a few feet from her bathroom door. Leaning against the bathroom door, she called, "I cannot come to the door. I cannot open my bathroom door."

She heard a key turn in the keyhole of the apartment door.

"Ms. Peng, are you all right?" She recognized the warm voice of Kong Qili from the telephone.

"I am fine except for my embarrassment, Mr. Kong. The latch is stuck, and I cannot open the door."

The knob turned, but the door did not open. The door rattled as though Kong had shoved it. The knob jiggled.

"Ms. Peng, I will get someone to take the knob off."

"That's fine. I'm sorry to delay you from the reception."

"I'd rather help you, Stefanie, than go to a reception." She frowned at the Western sort of familiarity. She did not think that most Chinese would speak this way to a woman they had only met by telephone.

"We will have you out shortly. Then we can go to the reception together."

She opened her mouth to object, but he was being so nice that she thought it would be rude. He was doing his job of looking after the foreign teachers.

Between his search for a maintenance man and the removal of the doorknob, Stefanie's stay in the bathroom stretched another half hour. After she thanked Mr. Kong and the maintenance man for getting her out, Kong ordered the maintenance man to reinstall the knob assembly while Stefanie got her coat. Kong helped her with it.

"You are a lovely woman, Stefanie—certainly worth the wait. We'll make the best looking couple there."

She took a first look at her supervisor and unsuccessfully avoided staring. Surely Kong would be one of the most attractive men at the reception. His conservative black suit accented dark good looks. Unusually tall for a Chinese, he would draw women's eyes. But what riveted her attention was the immediate impression that she had seen this man before. Perhaps it was just his cologne, one of the same expensive American brands that Roger wore. Something about the cologne made her uneasy, but she pushed the thought aside. She didn't want to get to the point where anything that reminded of Roger would unnerve her. She would have thought little of this in the United States. But here?

As they reached the sidewalk, he offered his arm, which she accepted. "The sidewalk is uneven here and there. We would not want you to fall now. I hope you do not mind the walk."

As they strode toward the reception hall, he told her of his education at Beijing University, his family life, and his work at the Education Department. Such openness also surprised her. Her father and her grandmother were not so open with details about themselves. What was it about this man that disturbed her? Perhaps his personality was a bit too much like Roger's—the way he invaded her space, the suave good looks, the stylish dress, even the aftershave. She would have to be careful not to bias her relationship with her boss because he reminded her of a bad experience.

When they reached the auditorium, she thanked Kong for his kindness. He took the hint graciously.

Stefanie found her favorite sort of place for people watching, a chair in a quiet corner near an enormous potted palm. She seated herself in its shadow to wiggle her toes in her heels. She had missed the program. She picked out the few people she had met. Many of those in attendance would ship out to other schools in a few days.

Kong Qili left the room. Seconds later a tall, slender Chinese woman seemed to follow him. *That almost looked like Yuliang.* The woman glanced in Stefanie's direction, and light reflected off her glasses.

Stefanie's head ached, and she longed to go back to the apartment, clear off one side of the bed, and fall into it. No, she had to force herself to mingle.

Mr. Kong returned to the auditorium after ten minutes without the woman who looked like Yuliang. Where had she gone? Stefanie waited until Kong was distracted by someone, then slipped through the door where she had last seen the young woman. She found herself in a dark hallway with a slate floor and a number of office doors closed on either side. But light seeped from under one of them. At worst she would disturb someone who was working late, so she knocked tentatively. The door opened, framing Chen Yuliang.

"Yuliang, I have been looking for you." She reached for her friend, but Yuliang stared at her. Her back was straight, and red blotched her cheeks as if she were angry. Stefanie backed off and touched her friend's arm. "Are you all right?"

Yuliang relaxed. She hugged Stefanie. "I am sorry, Stefanie. You startled me."

"I had hoped to see you, maybe set up a time for us to go to lunch together or dinner. One of the articles I am writing is a comparison of restaurants that appeal to different publics. I thought maybe we could sample a little food together."

Yuliang answered slowly and without enthusiasm. "That sounds like fun."

"Is something wrong?"

Looking over Stefanie's shoulder, Yuliang wet her lips. "I have been busy at work. Let me check my calendar. Maybe later this week."

Stefanie stepped to the side and turned to see a shadowy Kong Qili behind her, his face lit by light from the doorway. He switched the conversation to English.

"Yuliang works too hard. I think it's a great idea for the two of you to spend time together."

Yuliang looked away. "Mr. Kong's right. I'll call you, but right now I need to get back to my work."

"I'm sorry to distract you. Call when you can."

Stefanie still felt ill at ease alone with Kong Qili in the dark hallway, but he stepped to her side and drew her arm through his with practiced ease. "Stefanie, since I've seen you again tonight, I would like to discuss a couple of your classes with you." Kong led her back toward the reception room. "We have another class you might enjoy teaching."

When she glanced over her shoulder, Yuliang had already disappeared behind the closed door.

When Kong opened the door to his apartment, he found Chen Yuliang sitting in an armchair, smoking. He ignored her presence while removing and hanging his overcoat. Without a word, he came back out from his bedroom and perched on the arm of the sofa.

Yuliang blew a long column of smoke, light glinting from her glasses.

"You behaved unprofessionally tonight."

"She caught me by surprise."

"You must always be ready for surprises. You showed considerable irritation with her. She saw it. You must control yourself and hide your feelings."

She ground her cigarette out in the ashtray. "I did not realize how hard it would be to see her."

"He must have been special to you." Kong leaned back and folded his arms.

Her face paled. "What are you talking about?"

"Your American boyfriend. The one she stole from you."

She stared at him with parted lips.

"No, that was not in your *Dang An Chu* file, Chen. But I know of nothing else that makes one woman hate another as you show hatred for her. Only a man." He went to the fridge, uncorked a bottle of bai jiu, poured two glasses, and carried one to her.

"Chen, I see promise in you, but if you intend to work with me, you will control your emotions. It will grow easier with practice. You must work at it. Now I want to know how deep this animosity runs."

"He was a tutorial student. She had her own car and a big home. He took one look at her and decided she had to be his tutor."

"A tutorial student?"

She did not meet his eyes. "I needed the money."

He squatted beside her, his breath stirring the hair by her ear. "Hate her as much as you want, Chen, but she cannot suspect that you want revenge." He returned to his chair.

"Another matter. When you call her, work into the conversation that you and I have had an argument over religion."

"What?" Chen's glass hit the arm of the chair, and a little of the liquor slopped out.

"Yes, you were angry at me. I was trying to, what is it these cultists do?"

"Proselytize, evangelize, witness. Stefanie and I have had that argument a number of times. Why?"

"Because I do not have her trust, and she may resist sexual seduction. She is a born-and-bred cultist. This is the way to lead our little lamb into the tiger's lair."

"Do not underestimate Stefanie Peng. She may be a naïve cultist, but she is no fool."

"Call her tomorrow. Set up a time with her."

She paused, as if steeling herself for an unpleasant but necessary business, then nodded.

Kong raised his glass. "To the tigers, Chen. Be one of them."

Kong pushed through the unlocked doors of a Beijing church. Rows of benches stretched the length of the high-ceilinged room. A lectern stood on a stage in the front. A table with a lidded silver bowl sat in front of the podium. A large, empty, hollow feeling attached itself to this auditorium.

A teenage girl hummed as she mopped the hardwood floor. She glanced up at the sound of footsteps, then stared with wide, frightened eyes.

I've never understood why so many people immediately know I am Public Security, however I am dressed.

"Where is the priest, minister, preacher—whatever he is called?" His voice reverberated about the room.

The girl's lips moved but nothing seemed to be coming out. Clearing her throat, she managed, "My grandfather—"

"Go study now, Shan. You can finish later," came a voice from across the room.

With several frightened glances, the girl set her mop in the bucket, picked up the bucket by its wire handle, and hurried past Kong.

"What may I do for you?" The old man's silver hair gleamed like the bowl at the front of the church. He was poised but nervous.

"I have business with you." Again Kong's voice reverberated. He glanced around uncomfortably.

"My office is back here." The minister led Kong toward the side of the stage in the front. A door nearly hidden in the shadows cast by the lectern opened into a small room about the size of a large closet. It held a couple of shelves with about two dozen books, a desk, and three chairs. A Bible lay on the desk. After offering Kong a chair, the preacher seated himself behind his desk.

"My name is Kong." He flicked open his Public Security Bureau identification and extended it toward the preacher. "I am with—"

The preacher raised a hand. "I know. Three-Self or Religious Affairs, but I have been preaching only what is allowed."

Qili started to correct the mistaken notion that he was only a Religious Affairs officer, but then he realized that this part of his portfolio might have more impact with the Christian than his more important work in national security. "I know what you have been preaching. That is not why I am here."

Though the building was cool, drops of perspiration had formed on the preacher's brow. "I am careful to follow all of the Party's rules."

"That is good. Next Sunday I will attend your meeting. I will be with a young woman. You will greet me and tell me that you missed me last week."

"That is all?" The preacher watched him from narrowed, wary eyes.

"That is all."

"And the deception of this young woman . . ."

". . . is Public Security business, not yours." Kong saw no reason to let the old man save face. "You have a granddaughter to consider."

The preacher glanced up sharply. He swallowed hard and nodded.

Kong leaned back. "Tell me about your program."

As the old man described the service, Kong stopped him. "What about singing? Does everyone know these songs?"

"Most do. The tunes are usually simple."

"Teach them to me."

"I have not chosen the hymns for next week."

Kong leaned back and steepled his fingers. "Choose now and teach them to me."

Chapter 16

"THIS WILL BE FINE," the Brother told the driver.

The trucker pulled to the side of the road for Lao to climb out. Joining him at the back, the driver opened the truck's panel door and helped him get his bicycle down.

The Brother shook hands with him. "Thank you for the ride. You saved me many cold days."

"Thank you, Lao. I am going to find my wife when I return to Shanghai. I want to tell her that I have changed. Maybe she will forgive me."

"I will pray for the two of you. Remember to read the New Testament and see Brother Wu."

Mounting his bike, the Brother waved good-bye and rode east toward Dongting in Hebei Province. Enjoying the warmth of the early January day, the Brother praised God for the driver's conversion, prayed for his growth, and for his reunion with his family. As the afternoon wore on, the Brother halted to rest once and eat a small meal of biscuits. The further into the province he rode, the more the rumors that had come out of the province occupied his thoughts.

Several brothers and sisters had sent word for him to come to Hebei. After acquiring a copy of a document that promised trouble for the church, they wanted his advice. They also asked him to warn churches in other provinces what to expect. He was quick to heed this request. Hebei Christians had known some of the most intense and unrelenting persecution in China. One had to have the courage of conviction to serve the Lord in Hebei. Many did.

He especially looked forward to seeing elderly Sister Luoyi, his spiritual mother and rock. Had she not been courageous in the face of his threats, he would not have found the Lord. He would be dead now, killed in the gang wars during the Cultural Revolution or at his own hand. He had felt so hopeless in those dark years.

Sister Luoyi and her husband were both well educated. When they were arrested for speaking about Jesus and were relocated to a rural collective, the couple had immediately located other believers and organized a church of about twenty. During the Cultural Revolution, Maoist revolutionaries had beaten the pastor before his wife's eyes and dragged him away. Luoyi was the only person left in the small church who could read, so she took over her husband's ministry.

She had remarkable skill in reading the need in people's lives, and she was fearless in applying Scripture to that need. After five years, her husband had returned from prison to a church that had grown to three hundred and met in a dozen locations. Over the years, Sister Luoyi had started seventeen churches—under Beijing's nose in the very center of Hebei Province! Even before he had become "the Brother," Lao had admired this resourceful and courageous woman.

Until her eyes went bad, when Lao arrived he always found her busy sewing clothes for others or reading the Bible to someone. She welcomed the traveling evangelists, feeding both their bodies and their souls. The Brother needed to speak to Sister Luoyi now, his model of encouragement that those who gave up everything for Jesus would find abundant resources for the journey.

Deng An greeted him warmly at his tiny home in Dongting. His wife was working, so Brother Deng cooked for the two of them and Deng's twelve-year-old son. While he was cooking, the Brother read a handwritten copy of the "Work Plan of the Baoding Municipal Public Security Bureau to Prohibit Christian Illegal Activities."

Lao refrained from asking how the paper had been obtained. Either someone had been sympathetic to the Christians or someone in Baoding's Public Security Bureau had been careless around the wrong people. The document, dated August 20, 2002, called for an aggressive attack on the underground church by building a special force to infiltrate and record illegal activities. The infiltrators would "set up full files; recognize influential people and illegal meeting places."

"How successful have they been?" the Brother asked.

"They originally planned to implement it through October of 2002, but they did not stop the infiltration effort, and we continue to lose leaders in the province. Several meeting places have been closed entirely," Deng An said.

"This surely creates more than the usual suspicion toward newcomers." The Brother jabbed the document with his forefinger.

"Not only that," Deng An said, "but several of the agents we have identified have been in the body for a long time. Do we hide the new converts and make more of our network vulnerable to infiltrators who may not really have converted, or do we protect our known people by not protecting those who may be legitimate babes in Christ? Some of our congregations are divided."

"What have you done so far?"

"We have taken each individual who has requested protection on an individual basis and have allowed the church to decide. We have converts in the PSB who are trying to obtain information for us and protect us." Deng An stared for several moments at the food he was stirring. "One of them disappeared last week. The rumor is that he was sent to the *laogai*."

The Brother returned to his study of the document. Of special concern to the government were illegal activities "organized by freelance missionaries"— in other words, people like him. They wanted to stop "overseas infiltration." That would include the donkeys who brought Bibles. The next phrase sent a chill down Lao's back: "and terminate them." Did that mean to terminate the activities—or the people? No agent of the PSB would be in trouble for acting on the latter interpretation.

Lines calling for "forced confessions" and stubborn members being "severely punished" defended torture.

Shaking his head, the Brother read aloud, "The police should 'understand that freedom of religious faith does not necessarily mean freedom of religious activities.'"

"How do you separate faith and practice? How can you have freedom of one but not the other?"

The Brother set the papers down. "It is not as if they have not been practicing this anyway."

"True," Deng An said, "but it is chilling to see it all written down. Tomorrow we will meet the others at Sister Luoyi's to discuss what we should do."

"How is Sister Luoyi?"

Deng An laughed. "She cannot see, but she teaches twenty women how to read. She teaches Bible studies to women from three villages. She walks so close to the Lord that one of these days she will just sprout wings and fly home."

After eating, the Brother spent the evening teaching 1 Corinthians to the young evangelists and church workers of Dongting. As the others left early in the morning, he fell asleep on the hard-packed earthen floor of the house.

After Deng An's son left for school, the two men rode their bikes to Liucun. The heavier traffic of Anguo slowed them, so they were late and tired by the time they approached Sister Luoyi's house. But some distance away they dismounted and approached with apprehension. Cars, vans, and people surrounded the house.

"Something is wrong," the Brother said.

They reached the edge of the crowd.

"What is happening?" Deng An asked a woman.

The woman turned a worried, wrinkled face to him. She spoke softly. "Someone must have betrayed the meeting. We came late. I do not know how many they caught."

Police in their green uniforms carried Sister Luoyi's meager belongings—an armload of clothing, two chairs, a small table, a half dozen books, bedding—to the road and piled them there.

Deng An leaned close to the Brother. "She gave her Bible away when her eyes went bad."

The police shoved five people from the small house. Two middle-aged church leaders, a young male teacher, Sister Luoyi's middle-aged daughter, and Sister Luoyi staggered out. Sister Luoyi would have fallen if a woman had not stepped from the crowd and caught her.

The village cadre whirled. "Maybe you are one of them. Do you want to be here with them?"

The woman lowered her head. "She is an old woman, cadre. It is not right to let an elder fall."

The cadre shoved his face close to the woman's. "Chairman Mao said, 'Mercy to the enemy is cruelty to the people.' Would you be cruel to your neighbors, to the law-abiding citizens?"

The woman faded back into the crowd.

The cadre was enjoying his own histrionics. The Brother had seen his type too often.

The cadre surveyed the crowd while Sister Luoyi and her daughter shivered. Though the day was not cold for early January, it was too cool for thin blouses and no coats.

"Look at these criminals before you. Some of you see only neighbors. Like this other fool—" he pointed at the woman who had steadied Sister Luoyi—

"you think these are old women, helpless. You do not realize that these crimi-nals teach wicked lies. They seduce you to disobey your government. Is that good?" He glared at the listeners.

A few mumbled, "No, it is not good."

"What?" He demanded. "I did not hear you."

More people raised their voices, "No, it is not good."

The cadre advanced on the prisoners. "If you tell the people here that you were wrong to teach rebellion to the people, we will go lightly on you."

The young teacher said, "We taught no rebellion against the government."

The cadre backhanded him. Blood trickled from the man's mouth. "Liar! Do you hear how he lies? It is against the law to gather for religious worship without a permit."

"There is no church here for us to attend," the teacher said. "When we peti-tion the government for a church, they deny us."

The young brother had placed himself between the cadre's wrath and the older believers, but Sister Luoyi would have none of it.

She hobbled closer to the cadre. "You know what he says is true, cadre. I brought you the petition myself."

"Silence, woman."

"We seek only to worship God."

"You disobey the government. You subvert hearers, teaching them that they must submit to your god, rather than to the will of the people. What do you say to this charge?"

The Brother prayed silently that the tiny woman would not say what he expected her to say. His prayer was not answered. Instead, Sister Luoyi raised her voice so all could hear.

"After Jesus was killed by his country's government to pay for our sins, the rulers told His followers not to speak about Him, but they could not be stilled. They healed people and cared for them and told them that Jesus loved them and died for them. When the rulers captured them and commanded them to stop, they said, 'We must obey God, rather than men.'"

The young evangelist plunged between Sister Luoyi and the cadre's raised fist. The ensuing blow knocked him backward into the elderly woman, who stumbled. A policeman steadied her as other policemen held the other prison-ers back.

"You would interfere?" he screamed at the evangelist.

The cadre grabbed a baton from the nearest policemen. The evangelist covered his head with his arms, but the cadre swung the baton against the young man's ribs, then into his face, and against his raised arms, knocking the younger man to the ground. Several policemen joined the cadre in kicking and hitting the teacher.

Grinding his teeth at his own helplessness, the Brother wished he could block out the thuds, whacks, and groans of the beating.

The woman beside Deng An covered her face with her hands and sobbed softly. The Brother lowered his head and prayed. Sister Luoyi and the other prisoners wept.

When the cadre had spent his wrath, he turned on the crowd. His face was red and sweating. "You see what happens to rebels who teach you to obey a Western god instead of the Party. Fire the belongings. Fire the house."

A policeman doused the small pile of belongings with kerosene and lit it with a match. The flame flickered, swelled as the kerosene caught, and roared upward.

Another policeman poured kerosene along the walls of Sister Luoyi's house. He set the house aflame.

Neighbors whose own houses were threatened by the flames burst from the crowd for buckets of water to protect their homes.

The cadre glared at the crowd. He waited until the house was beyond saving to turn to his men. "Load them into the vans."

The policemen shoved the prisoners forward. Two prisoners lifted the scarcely breathing evangelist.

"Leave him." The cadre sneered at the crowd. "Let his brothers and sisters care for him."

As the vans pulled out, the Brother and Deng An joined several other preachers around the body.

"He is still breathing," one of them said. "We have to get him to some place warm."

The crowd stared at them. Finally the woman who had caught Sister Luoyi stepped forward. "My house is the third one. Take him there."

A blanket appeared out of one of the houses. They eased the young evangelist onto it and carried him to the house. The Brother stared after the van carrying Sister Luoyi. He said softly, "I hope she sprouts those wings quickly."

Chapter 17

WET SNOWFLAKES FLASHED as tiny spears of light through the glow of the army truck's taillights. The storm had driven the citizens of Xining inside. The lights of the homes reflected on the new snow lent a pristine cleanness that the city had not had in the daylight. Xining once was a rich trading post on the legendary Silk Road's southern route and a preeminent holy city for Buddhists. Now it was among the poorest provincial capitals.

The truck turned a corner, giving the wind free rein to swoop under the tarp that covered the prisoners. Ren Shaoqi shifted his wrists, hoping to ease more of his thin sleeves over the steel handcuffs binding him. Warming his hands, one at a time, inside the sack that held his few belongings, he leaned against the stiff tarp covering the back of the truck.

Another prisoner moaned. Their shoulders hunched close to their ears, the guards at the back of the truck huddled in their thick coats. However, the prisoners' thin coats did little to protect them from the bone-shaking cold.

The truck slowed. Shaoqi heard the clang of the chain on the gate behind Qinghai Provincial Labor Reform Detachment #37, although officials now called it a prison to deflect international criticism of the *laogai* system. Qili had told him the sign in front of the *laogai* said "Western China Leather Manufacturing Company."

They display a sheep's head in the window while selling only dog meat, Ren thought bitterly. Neither form nor function had changed.

Shaoqi raised his manacled hands to his wind-frozen face in hopes of warming it. After the truck stopped inside the high steel fence, the two guards at the back lowered the tailgate. One guard hopped down while the other ordered the prisoners out.

A People's Liberation Army captain strolled to the door of the office from the front of the truck. Warm from the heated cab and dressed in a thick green coat, he was not shivering like the prisoners.

Shaoqi glowered at him, pleased at the hatred that could still well up within him. He figured that as long as he kept his hatred he would never be entirely broken, he would remain a human being.

The wind off the mountains had full sweep once the prisoners jumped out of the truck. It caught the man behind and tossed him against Shaoqi, who stumbled. The captain bellowed at the guards to keep the prisoners in line.

He is like Qili. He loves the power to make others tremble. Hatred swelled.

As the captain opened the door to the prison office, the wind swept in. Shaoqi saw the papers on the desk inside fly up and swirl. The woman at the desk grabbed for them and began bellowing insults at the captain before he could shut the door. The two guards grinned at each other. Shaoqi smirked, feeling warmer in spite of the wind.

The rough cap he wore did not cover his ears. His left ear seemed frozen; it felt like it would shatter if touched. He ducked his head close to his left shoulder in a vain attempt to warm it. The ear of the prisoner in front of him was turning white.

The captain emerged from the office and ordered them to follow him. Bending his head forward against the stinging snow, Shaoqi tucked his head as far into his jacket as he could until they entered the barracks. In the comparative warmth of the unheated hallway, the prisoners sighed. At least they were out of the wind.

The guard and captain led them up a dimly lit stairway that creaked more in the wind with each story they climbed. They halted outside large steel doors while the guard pounded on the door for another guard to let them in. After passing the guard's station, they entered a large dormitory room filled with rows of bunks.

The windows were covered, making the room feel warmer. Shaoqi suspected that the guards kept them covered in the sweltering summer heat also.

Some prisoners lay on their bunks, staring at the bunk above, smoking; others sat together in little knots. Most of the prisoners were making silk flowers; some wrapping the wire stems, others gluing petals together to form the heads, and others assembling the parts into completed flowers.

Shaoqi watched each group. No one was talking. His gaze settled on a group of a dozen men putting yellow carnations together. Baskets of parts lay on one side of them, and baskets of completed carnations on the other. He followed the beginning of a carnation through the fingers of each man.

The hands of the last man made him forget the flowers. Gnarled, bony, and ancient, the fingers twisted as if someone had tried to make curled noodles of them. Yet they worked swiftly and knowingly. As the man completed each flower, he fluffed it.

Shaoqi shifted his gaze to the face. How many years did it take to erode a face into so many ditches and fissures? The old man looked up without stopping his work, apprising Ren Shaoqi with tired but shrewd eyes.

The guard bellowed, "Chu Zhurun, Chen Huaze, Peng Chongde."

A burly man with a hard face rolled from a bunk. Then a tiny man with a pointed nose and chin scurried forward from another flower-making group. Last, the old man with the twisted fingers shuffled his gaunt, hunched figure forward.

The old man fascinated him. So this was what an "incorrigible" looked like after more than forty years in prison.

After undoing their handcuffs, the captain shoved him and another prisoner toward Peng Chongde, who led them to the group where he had been working. He pointed out two empty bunks as they passed.

The room smelled of unwashed men, smoke from cheap cigarettes and the coal stove in the center of the room, and something sharp that wrinkled his nose in protest when he passed the tiny man's group of prisoners.

Chongde, his fingers again fluffing flowers, told the two newcomers the rules in a voice that was soft, high, and reedy, like some ancient flute.

Once the guards left, the men murmured among themselves. A young peasant squatted on the far side of Chongde. He laid the assembled flowers into a basket. He patted the old man's hand to interrupt. "Uncle, should I get another basket?" he asked.

"Yes, Jun. Take the basket that Rongzhen is emptying," the old man said.

Instead of throwing the basket, the huge man winding silk around the stems at the other end of the group passed it to Jun. These men differed from the coal miners. Ren wondered why.

Grinning, the boy returned to Chongde's side with the basket. "I have it, Uncle."

"Good, Jun. Put it down. You have flowers to put in."

The young man tenderly laid the new flowers in the basket like a new mother her baby. As Shaoqi watched the young man's awkward repetitive movements, he remembered a cousin who looked and acted much the same. Down syndrome, the doctor had called it, using its Western medical name.

Over the next days, Shaoqi quickly learned the basics of this work group, whose members differed markedly from one another in age, appearance, and background. Rongzhen, the factory worker who had passed Jun the basket, had petitioned the government for a trade union free of government control.

A thin young man had been a university student. He was arrested for running an underground press that printed songs for a cultic group to use when they worshiped their god. Another former student had been involved in the protests in Tiananmen Square. Two had been thieves. One rugged man of about thirty who was missing three front teeth had been an itinerant teacher in the same religious cult that used the young man's song books. Another dissident in the group had tried to smuggle a list of political prisoners out of China. Another had printed counterfeit food coupons after being laid off at his factory.

The biggest man in the group had killed his work leader. Jun, with his innocent eyes and awkward movements, told of his experience with his cadre's daughter. "She kissed me and I kissed her." Jun sighed. "Kissing was very nice." He glanced at the old man. "I did not know kissing was bad. I thought she wanted to marry me." His face crinkled. "Now my mother will have no grandsons."

"Take the baskets down now, Jun." Chongde patted his shoulder.

After he left, the old man said, "He is sentenced to be executed for rape."

Shaoqi stared after him. "I cannot imagine—"

"It was a trap," Rongzhen said. "Somebody wanted his kidneys."

Chongde bowed his head. "He does not understand that he is about to die or why."

At the tender look on the old man's face, Ren turned away to help the others pick up scraps of material.

He has disseminated foreign superstitions. He has been an agent of hostile foreign powers. He stirs up the people. I must not like him. I must hate only. I must hate.

Chapter 18

"I LOVE YOU, TOO." The click on the other end sounded final and far away. Stefanie held the phone to link her with her family for a moment longer. She cradled the telephone handset, leaned back in the big stuffed chair, and closed her eyes.

Nanai's tumor was malignant, as Dr. Liu expected, and now Nanai was putting off chemotherapy and radiation treatments. She remained closed to surgery options.

Despite spending every afternoon after classes at either the American Embassy or the Public Security Bureau, Stefanie had accomplished nothing in the week since her arrival to give Nanai the will to live. Bureaucracy, like the mills of the gods, ground exceedingly slowly.

Bo Qin, the cleaning woman, pulled her cleaning cart with its supplies across the carpet. Stefanie sensed that the plump, middle-aged woman was looking at her.

"Are you sick, Miss Peng?" Qin asked over the sounds of Edda's cello practice in the bedroom.

Stefanie opened her eyes. "I am well. I am sad because I miss my family."

The woman nodded, her eyes sympathetic. "Can I do anything for you?"

Stefanie glanced around the apartment. She had heard horror stories about cleaning women, but Qin did a wonderful job. "It looks great again. Thank you, Qin. I will try not to make a mess for you before Monday."

"Except for your books and papers, I would not know you were here. Miss Ansgar is much happier with you than with her last roommate."

When Qin opened the door, her smile vanished. Kong Qili stood there, ready to knock. Qin dropped her eyes, her mouth puckered, and she hunched her shoulders. Her reaction surprised Stefanie. Kong ignored the cleaning woman.

"May I come in?" he asked in English.

"Of course, Mr. Kong," Stefanie said.

As Kong brushed past the cleaning woman, she shifted away from him and pushed her cart through the doorway. Stefanie watched her go and their eyes met for an instant. Qin looked positively frightened, Stefanie noted as the door closed.

The man raised a sardonic eyebrow at Stefanie. Even a small silver scar on his chin did not detract from his suave good looks, although something about that scar still nagged at Stefanie's memory banks. "You've forgotten already?"

"I'm sorry. What did I forget?"

"I will have to see more of you so that you remember my name is Qili."

He seated himself on the sofa across from her without invitation, his movements manfully graceful. Again without asking, he pulled a packet of cigarettes from his suit pocket, methodically tapped it to remove one, and lit it. Stefanie was surprised. *American cigarettes. That's an expensive habit.*

He looked for an ashtray, and Stefanie pulled one that had come with the apartment from under an end table. What was it about him that kept her from asking him not to smoke in her apartment? With smoke issuing from his nostrils, he reminded her of a dragon, of the part of China she disliked, of bureaucrats with their fiefdoms and petty rules.

At the smell of smoke, Edda appeared in the bedroom doorway with raised eyebrows. She scowled at Qili before disappearing into the bedroom and shutting the door firmly.

"Would you like tea?" Stefanie asked, rising.

Edda had arranged the sofa to separate the tiny kitchenette from the rest of the apartment. Stefanie was still learning to use the hot plate that served as a stove on the counter.

Qili laid a long arm along the back of the sofa and watched her. "I'll pick you up at eight for breakfast before church. After church my mother expects us to eat with her."

Stefanie turned with the water half poured into the teapot. "That will take all day! I have other plans."

"You would not want to insult my mother by turning down her invitation. She will feel that you, as an American, think you are too good to meet her. Now, tell me how you like teaching your students?"

They talked of her classes and of education in China until the tea was ready. Some of Qili's ideas seemed vague for a man who had spent nearly a decade in Chinese education.

Maybe he depends on people like Yuliang. She has plenty of ideas.

The tea was served and drunk, but her guest showed no sign of leaving. Two hours passed. Stefanie's politely half-stifled yawns did not prompt him to leave. Not until Edda came to the bedroom door and said good night did he rise. Stefanie led him to the door. He reached for the doorknob when she did, his hand landing gently over hers. It was a smoothly executed action that again reminded Stefanie of Roger's suave, smooth moves as he inserted himself into her life.

"Yuliang told me of your grandfather. I have some *guanxi* in Public Security. I may be able to help."

Stefanie's irritation eased. "I'd appreciate your help."

He squeezed her shoulder. "You are tired. We will talk about it tomorrow."

She closed the door behind him. She needed the help his connections offered, but what if he tried to trade help for a relationship? The last thing she needed was the charming subtle pressures of a Chinese Roger, complete with the same aftershave. *Father, I've turned this over to you. Help me deal with Kong Qili.*

For a man in his home church, Kong Qili seemed ill at ease during the morning worship service. He reached for his cigarettes three times and stopped himself. He stumbled through the hymns.

Although Stefanie's grandfather had been imprisoned for refusing to join the Three-Self churches, she was glad to attend one of them. The church pastor was speaking on Isaiah and the prophecies fulfilled in Christ. The teaching seemed academic and superficial, but at least Scripture was expounded.

The other thing she noticed was that, although the church was packed, an invisible wall surrounded Kong and her. No one approached them after the service. Kong opened a way through those who were chatting in the aisles like Moses through the Red Sea. *Maybe I look too foreign. He doesn't seem to have many friends.* Stefanie smiled shyly at people who looked her way and followed Kong toward the door.

At the door the minister said, "You are back again, Mr. Kong."

"I would like to introduce Miss Peng, who is from America. She teaches at Beijing University."

She shook hands with him. "I enjoyed your message. Isaiah 56 is one of the most powerful passages in the Bible."

"You are familiar with it?" the preacher asked.

"One Sunday school teacher helped us memorize part of it when I was a child."

The preacher glanced at Kong. Stefanie wondered if she saw a scowl flash across the pastor's face to interrupt his look of benign gentleness. She gazed around. From her research she knew that the government restricted the teaching of children. Still, seeing no youngsters in the congregation was still a shock.

"It is sad not to see any children here."

The preacher stiffened. "No, there are no children here. A pleasure to meet you. Excuse me."

Stefanie's head throbbed by the time she and Kong reached the housing for the foreign teachers. Her meeting with his attractive, doting mother revealed where he had picked up his charm. Tall, slender, and poised, she dropped hints constantly about Qili's girlfriends and her desire for him to marry and give her a grandchild. Her shelves contained knickknacks from India, Japan, San Francisco, Paris, and New York, though both Kong and his mother protested that they had never been outside China.

Stefanie had enjoyed their kindness, but she just could not relax her guard. Finally, the tension had spilled over into a raging headache. At least her apartment building was in sight. Instead of walking her to her apartment, however, Kong blocked her way when he reached his apartment, fussed with the door, and invited her in.

"Qili, thank you for a very nice day, but I need to get back." Stefanie rubbed her forehead.

"We have not talked about your grandfather yet."

"All right. For just a few minutes." She hesitated, glanced through the door, and preceded Kong into the apartment. Its carpeting and furniture were similar to hers, but the layout was slightly different. His location near the front door gave him access to the comings and goings of the foreign teachers he was overseeing. The bathroom and bedroom doors were closed. An expensive computer sat on a desk near the end of the sofa.

He guided her with a hand on her arm into the living room, noticed that his door had stuck, and returned to close it. When he joined her on the sofa, he casually put his arm on the back of it behind her. Roger had made that move early in their dating.

"Tell me about your grandfather."

"This may take some time." She rose to remove her coat. Before he got to his feet, she tossed her coat on the sofa where she had been sitting and seated herself in the armchair. His eyes twinkled. She told him the story briefly, describing her family's frustration in trying to get some response from the system.

"Stefanie, you can't accomplish anything in China without knowing the right people. The children of the party leaders, the princelings, get rich by providing the connections. If your father is in the Congress, all you have to do is buy a suit, a briefcase, and some business cards. Then you offer to make contacts for the eager businessmen for a cut or a place on the board."

Stefanie pondered that. Her headache screamed at her. "I do not have the re-sources to buy my grandfather's way out of prison. I borrowed money from friends and sold my car in order to make this trip." She pushed herself back in the chair.

"What did your grandfather do to get into prison?"

"He preached against joining the Three-Self churches."

"I wondered. He is *that* Peng Chongde?" He shook his head. "This is amaz-ing." He leaned toward her. "My grandmother heard him preach years ago, but I had no idea he was still alive. Through him my grandmother became a Chris-tian, and through her I did."

Stefanie relaxed. Qili's face glowed with animation as he described his close-ness to his grandmother. Their relationship resembled hers with Nanai.

"She was especially concerned about my mother. We prayed together for her all the time." He lowered his head and spoke softly. "Sometimes I just wish I could talk to her. We could talk about anything."

"What happened to her?"

Kong brushed at his pant leg. "About six years ago she died of breast cancer."

"Oh." Stefanie blinked back the tears. Helplessness against Nanai's cancer swept over her.

"Are you all right, Stefanie? I am most sorry if I said something to upset you." He rose and placed his hand gently on her shoulder. "Let me get you something."

She shook her head. Kong pressed his handkerchief into her hand. The strong scent of aftershave on the handkerchief and his hand on her shoulder both-ered her. Fear swelled inside her, and she inched away from Kong to ease her panic. Had Roger made her paranoid toward any man who wore his cologne? She wiped the tears away and swallowed hard to clear her throat. "I am sorry. You took me by surprise. My grandmother has breast cancer. That is why it is so important to take my grandfather home with me." She told him of Nanai's fears and of her dream to see her husband again.

Kong sat on the edge of the sofa near her chair. He spoke slowly. "Let me see what my connections can do."

"I cannot pay you."

"I am not looking for money. I want to do this for my grandmother. It would have meant a lot to her—and I am doing it for you. I am not often in a position to help a friend."

"I appreciate your friendship, Qili, and I can really use your help. But please understand that I have just had a painful end to an engagement. I can offer only my friendship."

"You are tired. Let me walk you to your apartment."

When he returned to his apartment, Kong's somber expression slid into a grin. Reaching for a cigarette, he laughed softly. Through the smoke of his cigarette, he saw Yuliang leaning against the bedroom door. He tossed her the pack of Marlboros.

"You could at least smoke Chinese cigarettes."

"Testy today, Chen? How long have you been here?"

She threw the pack of cigarettes on the table and lit hers, the flame of the lighter glinting in her glasses. "I heard the whole disgusting Ming opera. 'My poor grandmother and I could talk about everything.'" She dropped onto the sofa.

"The problem with you, Chen, is that you have a stone in the place of a heart, so you think everyone else does too."

"She received two letters today, one from her grandmother and one from her best friend. I made copies and resealed the envelopes."

Kong ignored her. "With Americans, love trembles always in the heart. They would sell their country to prevent a child or an old person from coming to harm."

She blew a column of smoke at him. "I repeat my warning that Stefanie is not stupid."

Kong dropped into the armchair and propped his feet on the sofa. He breathed in the smoke, then let it out slowly. "Stefanie is a sweet and delectable lamb for the Tiger."

Yuliang leaned forward and slammed the ashtray onto the end table. "Underestimate that lamb, and the Beijing Tiger will have the worst case of heartburn he has ever known."

Chapter 19

TROY HARDIGAN DUCKED under the kick that was aimed at his head. Dropping to his hands, he swept his leg out, knocking his attacker's foot out from under him. The man sprawled onto the mat and lifted hands in surrender.

"That's it for me."

Hardigan offered Jerry Kantaro a hand up. Jerry slapped Troy on the back. "Good match. Thanks. Man, I'll be sore for a week."

Hardigan stopped at a soda machine before answering. "I'll be lucky if I can move!" It was an exaggeration. Both men knew it, and Kantaro grinned appreciation. The two men sparred when they had the opportunity.

"Some of us are going out for a drink. Come along?" Kantaro asked.

"Thanks, Jerry, but I've got some things to do."

"All work, no play . . ."

". . . keeps Troy employed." He followed Kantaro from the hotel recreation room. The exercise had eased his inner restlessness a little, but he felt lonely. Joining the guys was tempting. He knew himself well enough to recognize the mood that could lead him to a blowout like the one in Japan a couple years before. The guilt had been worse than the hangover, and the hangover had been intense. When he accepted Christ he vowed to avoid temptations to binge. Alone and far from home, the temptation could be severe. *Who would know? Who would care? God would. Nanai would. Stef would. Ultimately, I would.*

His hotel room looked like hotel rooms he had slept in from Washington to Sydney—neat, clean, impersonal. Only a recognizable jumble of clothes and bags personalized this space. No one welcomed him. No one wanted him. Hardigan leaned against the window frame to watch the flow of life in Manila stream past his hotel. Night life people were coming out—people going shopping, to restaurants and bars, to a concert, or a dance; maybe to a kid's performance or a sports program. People were coming out to have a good time.

At least it was a change from India, which was becoming all too familiar by the time the technicians had satisfied Sur Dalal. They had not really "satisfied" him, but he was willing to accept Troy's departure from the country.

I wonder if Jerry's left yet. He reached for the phone. He ran his tongue over his teeth thinking of an exotic and potent Philippine rum. The thought scared him. He had been wanting a drink too often lately. His older sister, "Maggie the Mouth," always said he was just like Dad. What if she was right?

Oh, God, I'm so tired. He could not remember the last time he had prayed on this trip. *I'm tired of ego-swelled diplomats, empty-headed bureaucrats, planes, customs, and hotels.*

He raised his eyes to the sky and wondered when he had last seen a star that was unobscured by lights. *And I'm tired of cities,* he added to his prayer.

He pictured the two-story white Colonial he had spotted for sale on the way to the Pengs' home, with red shutters and trim, and a white picket fence. It just breathed in his ear, *"Settle down here and mow the grass."* He had come close to making an offer on it after Stefanie broke up with Eddington.

I want to come home every night to Stef with supper on the table, even fish sticks. I want to feel my kids move in her belly, and watch them grow up. I want to go to church every week with my family and put dollhouses together at Christmas and move bikes out of the driveway. I want to hold Stef when she cries, and laugh at her jokes when she messes up the punch line.

"No, Maggie," he said aloud to the world out the window, "I am not Dad. I want more than empty intrigue and passport stamps."

Troy could analyze his own neuroses well enough to know that part of the reason he was depressed was that he hadn't heard anything from Stefanie. No snail mail letters through the home office. Not even an e-mail for over a week. That last one had seemed guarded, as if Stefanie was hiding something.

As if I don't hide things from Stef. I guess I don't like it when she acts the way I do.

The bright inviting lights were starting to come on. Traffic in the streets along the Manila Bay waterfront was picking up. And God didn't seem to speak to him out of the cityscape. Troy had not given God much opportunity to say anything since he'd left Chicago. He had not been to a church or cracked his Bible more than a half dozen times in three weeks. That had to change. He dug his Bible, his tape recorder, and a couple of cassettes out of his suitcase, kicked off his shoes, popped the top on a soda can, and settled on the bed to listen to a cassette of Stefanie playing hymns on the violin. He had lost track of time with his Bible reading when the front desk called with a package.

Letters from home. It has to be.

He tipped the bellboy who delivered them, then hefted the package. "Eleven," he guessed.

He tore the packet open with the pleasure of a kid on Christmas Day. Sitting on the edge of the bed, he counted the letters. "Ten. Not bad." It was about time they caught up with him.

He set the personal letters aside to read the two letters from Frontiers Technology. They updated his background information, urged him to push harder on a couple of contracts. The company still used surface mail for formal instructions, information that could be intercepted and read without harm. Encrypted e-mail messages covered more sensitive topics and information needed in seconds instead of days. Some information still came in code form, however it was sent. This mailing included a bit of that. Troy memorized some instructions, tore the letters into tiny pieces, and dropped them into the trash basket.

He changed the cassette to one of Stefanie singing Chinese songs. With Stefanie's voice in the background, he pondered the order of letter reading. *Two letters from Stefanie. It's odd she used surface mail. Should I read them as dessert or as the appetizer, or will they give me indigestion? None of the postmarks are from the past week. Wonder what she's doing now? Going out with someone? Quit your mooning.*

He decided to approach the letters chronologically. He opened the letter from his little sister Patty first. She had just found out that she was pregnant with her first baby. Her letter exuded joy. He was glad for her.

Stefanie's first letter was disappointing, probably written the night he'd flown out. It was friendly, wishing him well and promising to pray for him, but it was something she would have written to "Uncle Troy." *Maybe she's telling me that things will stay that way.* This was written before her e-mail and also seemed a little guarded.

Stefanie's second letter was written a week later. It included a check from her friend Laura, repaying him for a loan so that she could buy tires for her car. There was a little family news, then his eyes riveted on the next item.

> By the time you receive this, I will be across the world from Chicago on an adventure—to China! I won't say anything in my

e-mails to you right away, frankly because I'm in no hurry for you to find out. I'm not sure you'll approve, any more than Father did. I'll have to tell you sometime how Madre got around him. My friend Chen Yuliang has learned a great deal about Grandfather, including the fact that he's up for release soon. He may be released and allowed to leave the country if a family member is at his hearing.

Troy felt ill. *Stefanie in China? Why did Andrew let her do this?* He ran his fingers through his close-cropped hair and continued reading.

So I will be there. I will actually be employed by the Chinese government for awhile, teaching English grammar and maybe some writing. I will even get to write the articles I intended. Then, if all goes well, I will take Grandfather home. I will be at Beijing University under Yuliang's boss, a very friendly man named Kong Qili.

Kong Qili? Troy's breath came faster as he reread the last paragraph. He paced the room, pounding his fist against his hand. He would have been concerned simply knowing that Stefanie was in China. But with the name Kong Qili . . . what were the chances?

There must be millions of Kongs in China. It has to be only a coincidence. But something told him it was not. He already suspected that the Kong he had dealt with at Frontiers was a government agent, and if by chance it was the same man . . .

Stef, you are walking into a trap. He quickly scanned the rest of the letter as he continued to pace.

Please don't worry about me. As soon as I get settled I'll write. I think I will have an e-mail account through the university, and I'll send that as soon as I get settled and have a connection.

I can't tell you how much I'm missing you. I suppose it will be worse in Beijing.

Troy's heart sank. If only she knew how much worse it could be in Beijing if this Kong was a government agent. He felt suddenly very helpless. He couldn't even warn her. Delores Peng no doubt had contact information for Stefanie by now, but if Troy's fears and suspicions were true, any connection would likely be monitored. He folded the letter carefully and placed it back in the envelope. Turning again toward the window, he prayed, "Lord, confuse the plans of the wicked. Keep my beloved in your protection. Help me know what to do."

Chapter 20

THE MESS HAD BEGUN innocently enough. Two girls in beginning conversational English class were going shopping downtown. Would Teacher like to come?

The still cold pinched Stefanie's cheeks as she emerged from the library with her bag of study books and her two young student friends. It sounded like a nice break from her daily routine, and soon she was crowding a bus seat with them, enjoying their chatter and answering a stream of questions about American dating customs.

She wasn't sure where the bus was going; she didn't care. Anyplace different would lift her mood. It was funny how she melted into a crowd in Beijing, when she always stuck out on the streets of Chicago. Yet she couldn't remember ever feeling more displaced and lonely than she did today. Edda's cool politeness in the apartment would not help much.

When it came down to it, Stefanie felt too depressed to go shopping. So she did not get off with the girls at the lively and glittery neon shopping district. Who wanted to carry a half-dozen books around all of those shops and stalls anyway?

She wondered what Lani and Laura might be doing and where Troy was.

The girls got off and one of the three young soldiers standing in the aisle quickly slid into the seat beside her. She ignored his leering grin, to his discomfort and his buddies' chortles. The bus had reached the Tiananmen area, and she watched the lights playing on the vast expanse of the square and all the people who were out in the late afternoon cold.

The soldier's body now pinned her against the side of the bus as he slid over to give ample room for a middle-aged woman to sit on the edge. His two friends laughed at their friend's attempt to get her attention.

"Are you from Beijing?" the soldier asked. His accent was neither from Beijing nor Shanghai. He was a country boy in uniform, turned loose and out for a good time in town. By the smell of his breath, he had already been enjoying some strong refreshment.

"No, I am from *Mei Guo*."

He laughed and slapped his knee. He was at most twenty-two, probably younger.

"Good joke." He turned to tell his friends about the little piece of fluff who said she was from America. For some inebriated reason, they found this hilarious.

Stefanie welcomed the relief from the liquor on his breath. His breath hit her again as he leaned back toward her to lament the hardships of military life. He was to be transported to the Uygur Autonomous Region in Northwest China. He would be lonely in such a barren place, and he might be killed in a rebellion of the backward and superstitious Muslims. He wanted a few dances with a pretty girl before boarding the train. "We are going to a hot disco. We could get you in without anyone asking your age. It would be fun."

At least she had not heard this pick-up line before.

"No, thank you. I have other plans."

The middle-aged woman stood at the next stop, but one of the soldier's buddies quickly took her seat. He drank from a bottle and passed it to his buddy, who offered some to Stefanie. "It is good stuff."

"I do not drink."

The other soldier leaned around his buddy. "Do not be afraid. You are not too young for a good time. Try some."

Several rows ahead of her a small woman with silver hair held a poster open to read. All the passengers in the back of the bus could read the large characters: "God loved the world . . ."

Stefanie straightened. *John 3:16.*

The woman began to fold the poster. When the man next to her asked about it, she passed it to him. The woman stepped into the aisle as the bus slowed.

Stefanie pushed the soldier's beer bottle aside and rose. "Please let me out. This is my stop." She riveted her attention on the small, elderly woman making her way down the aisle of the bus.

Still making offers, the two soldiers grudgingly gave enough room for Stefanie to squeeze past.

"Come on. We will change her mind," the pushy soldier with the bottle said.

Out of the corner of her eye she saw that the drunk had gotten up and was following. The other two soldiers got up to join him. A lot of people were exiting here. Several bodies in the aisle separated her from the soldiers, but others separated her from the woman who already was stepping to the street. The crush to get off was moving at a glacial pace. She rose on tiptoe to catch a glimpse of the woman, and when she finally got down the steps, she walked briskly in the direction she had seen the woman go. The soldiers reached the door and were leering at her.

"Leave the little sister alone, Haoquan. You want a woman, not a kid," one of them called.

Night was falling, and the streetlights and bright neon signs were not so plentiful here. Fearing to look around to see if the drunken soldiers were still following her, she wondered if she had made a serious mistake. But the elderly woman might be Stefanie's only chance to get to know someone from the underground church. She wanted to understand the church of her grandfather, the cause for which he had left his wife and son to spend most of his life in prison.

Yes, two soldiers were walking in her direction. The third must have stayed on the bus. Stefanie hurried to join a knot of scurrying pedestrians. The air was so cold and still that a perpetual fog seemed to puff from their mouths and noses. *Lord, I'm sick of being so small that men think I'm an easy mark. And where did that woman go?*

The street seemed vaguely familiar and she realized that she had seen the intersection ahead only the day before. It was where she and Qili had exited a taxi to go to his church. That church must be just around the corner. She ducked out of the crowd at the corner and broke into a near trot, hoping to lose the soldiers. As she approached the church she had attended with Qili, she glanced back. The soldiers reached the intersection and saw her before she could find a place to hide. They were not gaining on her, but they were still coming.

She sprinted toward the sanctuary door. *I'll bet it's locked for the night. How did I get myself into this trouble?*

The soldiers' walking was a little uncoordinated for efficient speed. Stefanie reached the church door and tried it.

Unlocked. It opened with a hard pull, and she slipped inside.

Two women knelt beside pews, praying. One sobbed softly.

Stefanie knelt at a pew in a shadowed corner. Removing her coat, she reversed it so that the red plaid showed. She searched through her purse until she found one of her grandmother's little surprises, a packet containing a pink rain hat. Quickly, she donned the rain hat and set her books under the pew.

The two women left, and Stefanie's prayers turned to thanks that no one had entered the building. Then the other end of the pew creaked. Afraid she would see one of the soldiers from the bus, she nevertheless looked up. The minister was smiling at her.

"You are back, Miss Peng. Did you come to see me?"

She sighed with relief and stood. "You remember my name? No, I did not really intend to make this visit, but I needed a refuge." She explained about the soldiers, although she tried to be vague about why she wanted to speak with the woman with the poster. "I hope you do not mind my coming in."

"No, the church should be a refuge, even to young women escaping celebrating soldiers."

"Do you know the woman with the poster, sir?"

He glanced over his shoulder at the door. "Perhaps we should talk in my office."

The room was small and stark. Back home, Pastor Avery's scarred desk was covered with books he couldn't cram into the ceiling-to-floor shelves on one wall. This preacher's desk held a Bible, a pad of paper with scattered notes, and a pencil. Perhaps two dozen books stood neatly on the two shelves behind his chair.

He folded his hands together on his desk. "Tell me about yourself."

Stefanie wondered if government pastors were agents, but this man seemed to be someone she could trust. She spoke of her family, including her grandmother and father's reasons for leaving. Then she told about her grandfather and her reason for being in China. Aside from a few friendly questions, the pastor said nothing.

"You know, I remember your grandfather. I did not really meet him, but I heard him speak. So long ago. It must be over forty years. He urged us not to join the Three-Self Patriotic Movement. Wang Mingdao and Watchman Nee led the opposition to Three-Self, but your grandfather was known."

"The man I was here with yesterday, Mr. Kong, said his grandmother also heard my grandfather speak."

A shadow crossed the pastor's face.

"Sir, because of my grandfather, I am struggling to understand the differences between the churches. Why did you join the Three-Self church?"

He steepled his fingers, reminding Stefanie of her father.

"It seemed more Chinese. Many of us resented the West. We hated the West for the Opium War and their smug policies to divide up Asian land any way they saw fit. I was only a child at the time of the Long March and the Revolution, and I believed in the Christ I learned about from my parents. But many of us grew up thinking that the church would grow more without foreign intervention."

He paused, staring at nothing that she could see. "W. T. Wu, who had been involved in the YMCA, was the first chairman of the Three-Self. We trusted him. The government promised freedom to preach."

"Did they keep their promise? Are you allowed to preach freely?"

He planted his elbows on his desk and leaned toward her with a frown. "How can you understand? You in the West do whatever you want. You live in luxury and vice, and then you criticize China. Your country has not been rent by famines, war, and poverty. It has been so easy for you."

His vehemence startled her.

"Forgive me. I was not criticizing. I want to learn—to understand why my grandmother has not seen her husband all these years."

He patted his fingertips together. His voice softened.

"Your grandfather and I both had families, Miss Peng. I was afraid to make the sacrifice. I was afraid that my wife would be like your grandmother. He made one decision, and I made another. I am sure God has used your grandfather's decision. But I believe God has used me also. I have seen many people come to Christ. I think for me this was the right choice. I could be of more use outside a prison camp instead of inside one.

"We do have much freedom. You heard my sermon in the worship time. It was from Scripture, not a government censor. I cannot teach or baptize children. The government still hopes to win them to atheism. I cannot criticize policy. There are forbidden subjects, such as the second coming of Christ and abortion."

"How difficult is life for Christians?"

He thought about this for several moments. "For us, the situation is quite good. We are watched, of course. Some of our children are allowed into the universities, though it is harder than for a Party member's children. Some Christians hold good positions.

"Christians in the underground churches are persecuted. The extent depends much on their location. Some parts of China are relatively unconcerned about such matters. Their situation can be more difficult if local Party leaders want to make a name for themselves. Christians who make themselves more visible are in some danger, and, current policies change . . . many factors. There still are threats, arrests, beatings, and worse. I know someone in an underground church who believes that the persecution in provinces close to Beijing is as bad now as it was during the mistakes before."

"Mistakes?"

"The Cultural Revolution, when your grandfather was arrested." He glanced at the clock behind Stefanie. "The next bus will arrive shortly. Let me walk you to the bus stop."

"The woman with the poster?"

"I have seen her, but I do not know her. She rides the buses with tracts or posters, then gives them to whoever seems interested."

The cold seemed harsher after being in the warm building. Few people were on the streets.

"May I ask something more?" Stefanie asked.

The preacher nodded.

"What effect does the underground church have? How does it affect things?"

"Many rural regions have no established churches, and the government is in no hurry to allow new ones when the old ones are supposed to be only temporary, until everyone grows past superstition. Underground churches are doing well. They provide worship, growth, fellowship, teaching. TSPM churches are growing, but no one knows how many are converting through the unregistered churches. Some say five thousand a day; some say fifteen thousand a day. Not a lot in a nation as large as China, but a lot in a society under attack."

"Fifteen thousand seems a lot." As they approached, Stefanie satisfied herself that the soldiers were not in the knot of people at the bus stop. She turned to study the preacher's wrinkled face.

"Miss Peng, you must understand the government's frustration about the unregistered churches. We Bible-believing Christians tend to confound the simple predictions of Marx and Trotsky. Underground churches in particular stand aloof from the state, and they cannot be controlled. Anything outside Party control frightens those in charge."

He stopped several feet from the handful of those waiting for the bus. He turned to her and lowered his voice. "I have a lovely young granddaughter, Miss Peng. May I give you a grandfather's advice in confidence?"

A cloud of steam billowed from his mouth. Stefanie's nose tingled from the cold. She nodded as the bus roared up.

"Do not give your heart to Mr. Kong."

Chapter 21

"Halt!"

A line of sweat formed instantly on the Brother's back. Praying, he turned slowly. The policeman, eyes fastened on Lao, had a hand on his holstered gun.

"Were you speaking to me?" the Brother asked. The train car that he had just stepped down from was filling for its return trip toward Beijing from Jilin, the northeastern province bordering North Korea.

"Yes, let me see your papers. What is your business here?"

The Brother pulled his identification papers from an inside coat pocket. "I was here many years ago, *xiansheng* [sir]. I wanted to see the beauty of the snow on the mountains again."

The young policeman removed his hand from the gun to look at the papers. "What is your job?"

"I have had many jobs, but I need work now. Are there places for day laborers?"

"We do not have enough work for our own people," the policeman said as he handed the Brother's papers back. Lao slipped them into his coat pocket.

"I do not remember so many policeman when I visited before." The Brother leaned closer and lowered his voice. "You must be having someone important visit. The premier must be visiting."

The young policeman laughed and shook his head.

"A movie star or singer?" The Brother stepped closer. "It must be that pretty Hong Kong singer you young people all like."

"I wish it were Leslie Cheung. We are looking for people who help illegals from North Korea to enter the country."

The Brother stepped back and looked around. "So many policemen. It must be a big problem."

This time the policeman stepped closer. "It is such a big problem that the government is now paying ten times more to find people who are aiding the economic migrants than for the migrants themselves." He glanced around, his authority dropping as his youthful enthusiasm grew.

"Is it so bad in North Korea?"

"People are starving. They want a better life here, but they are not *refugees*. The government is very precise that they are *economic migrants*."

"Why?"

"The United Nations tells us that we have to take in refugees, but not illegal migrants."

"The word used is so important?"

"You are here looking for work, but you will not find much. One reason is that Korean illegals take the job you should have." The policeman turned away, then back to the Brother. "A good job here is to hunt for migrants and the criminals who hide them. My brother made over 5000 yuan for turning in a neighbor who was hiding the illegal economic migrants."

"They must have been very dangerous."

The policeman glanced at his shoes. "They were children." He resumed his authoritarian role. "The important thing is enforcing the laws among our people." He turned away from the Brother toward the train. "You—Halt!"

Heavyhearted, Lao trudged away. *Probably some kindhearted farmer gave hungry North Korean children a bowl of rice. For that he will be imprisoned and maybe tortured to give up the names of others.*

No one paid attention to the vagabond as he left the station, and his mind was occupied. *How can churches in China do more to help the starving Koreans?* Poverty-stricken themselves, the churches he visited had collected 1200 yuan to send to one hidden orphanage in Jilin Province.

Two hours' walk brought the Brother to a market district. Enjoying the scenery sparkling with snow, he pulled his coat more tightly around him. He had not seen a Jilin winter for eight years and had not lived there for twenty years.

The faces of many people on the road showed Korean or mixed Han Chinese and Korean ancestry. The Brother heard scraps of Korean conversation as he continued along the road, occasionally picking out a word he knew. Perhaps 40 percent of Jilin was all or part ethnic Korean. That had made it easier for three hundred thousand North Koreans to slip into China since 1995, when a disastrous drought combined with President Kim Jong-Il's egocentric policies initiated a permanent state of famine. One-twelfth of North Korea's population had starved to keep 1 million men, about a sixth of the adult male population, in the military.

How can one man be so selfish as to consider his own power more important than the lives of 2 million of his men, women, and children who had starved?

Shortly before dark, the Brother entered the front door of a small shop below an apartment. The scent of frying onions reminded him how hungry he was. From behind a curtain he heard the sounds of vegetables being chopped and heard a pot set loudly onto a stove. On the shop's counter were knitted caps, mittens, scarves, and socks. Jackets, sweaters, and coats hung on a rack near the wall. Weary, he eased himself onto a bench. In the warmth of the room his feet started thawing.

He must have drifted to sleep because a gasp awakened him. A small brown face peered at him from behind the curtain, then disappeared.

Son-kyong, Cha Chul Min's wife, her face pale with fear, drew the curtain back. Her shoulders relaxed, and she smiled. Her obvious ethnic background was Korean but her voice was a lilting Mandarin. "Lao, we did not hear you come in. We were careless."

He shook her hand warmly. "I understand that the government is paying over five thousand yuan to informers. I could have been one."

"You are right. When things become quiet, I start to hope that we can give the children a normal childhood. You see that eyes are vigilant once again. Our neighbors help protect us, but I became negligent today." She drew the curtain back. "Come in. The evening meal is almost ready."

The Brother rounded the counter while Son-kyong put a sign in the window, closing the shop for the night.

Six children stared at the Brother with distrustful faces. He smiled at them, but none smiled back. Son-kyong closed the curtain behind her.

A small woman with black hair, dark brown eyes, and thick eyeglasses, Son-kyong said something to the children, but only the words for "friend" and "Brother" were recognizable.

The children, who looked to be from five to ten years old, still did not smile or greet him. The oldest girl, perhaps ten or eleven, began stirring rice at the stove.

"I wish I could take the fear and hurt from them, at least heal their souls," Son-kyong said, her eyes tearful.

She described each child's background. The oldest girl was actually sixteen. She and her brother had seen her grandparents and two younger siblings die of starvation after her father disappeared into Kim Jong-Il's prison camps. Her mother had died in childbirth, taking her tiny newborn with her. The girl and her fourteen-year-old brother, who appeared to be seven or eight, had been shot at by soldiers as they stumbled across the frozen Tumen River toward China.

The other stories were similar. The youngest girl, a nine-year-old who appeared to be five, had been found by brothel pimps, who had reached the girl and her sisters before Son-kyong or the police did. Thinking she was near death and not worth their investment, they took the sisters but left her in a barn.

"It is a three-way race with the brothel owners and the police to reach the refugees," Son-kyong said. "Many parents send their children across the border, thinking that even life in a Chinese brothel is better than slow death in North Korea.

"Sometimes brothels and police work out deals. One brothel that did not have a police protector was raided a few weeks ago. The girls were sent back to North Korea. We heard word from a friend whose cousin's husband was one of the policemen. He said that a pregnant girl was forcibly aborted by the North Korean guards. All the girls would go to detention camps for seven years. They were all just hungry, frightened children."

Son-kyong laid her chopsticks down. They ate quietly and the children ate very quickly, lest the food disappear before they had some. Not wanting to take from the children, the Brother ate only enough to still the ache in his stomach. After dinner the children washed the dishes and straightened the room. The oldest boy brought coal up from the basement to add to the stove. Then they brought out books, papers, pencils, and slates for schoolwork.

"I teach them here, of course. They are doing well in their studies." She repeated the last statement in Korean for the children with a smile. For the first time, the Brother saw their small faces beam back.

"Where is Chul Min?" the Brother asked.

"He took two children north to a farm. Some Christians there could use the help and offered to raise them with their own daughter. He should be back the day after tomorrow."

The Brother leaned his arms onto the table. "How is Chul Min's ministry to adults?"

Son-kyong shook her head. "Fifteen more have come to the Lord since your last visit. So few people here have even heard of Jesus!" She bowed her head. "Do you remember Rodong Yong-tae and his wife?"

The Brother smiled. "Just watching them learn made the Word fresh again."

"That is how they affected us all." Son-kyong wiped a tear away. "They were so excited to know Jesus that they went back to North Korea to teach the people. The border guards caught them, and when Yong-tae tried to tell about Jesus, the guards marched them to the nearest village square and shot them. Another couple who was with them escaped."

The Brother felt as if an electric baton had been pressed to his heart. He could not speak for a long moment. *Such beautiful and alive young Christians, with such zeal for the Savior. Faithful even to death.*

"Now they wear a crown of life, Son-kyong." He pulled an envelope from his coat. "This is not much, but the churches want to help. They want you to know that they pray for you daily."

Son-kyong's eyes filled with tears. "I know that this was given out of great need. It is a sacrifice of praise that I hold in my hand. Please thank them for us, for the children. We have received some help from a group in South Korea called Helping Hands Korea. They send a ton of grain each month into North Korea for the orphans there. But there are so many hungry people that it is hard to make ends meet."

Someone pounded on the door. Son-kyong glanced at the children, but each was already gathering materials and heading down the passageway in the floor that led to the coal cellar. The oldest boy closed the door over him.

Son-kyong glanced around to make sure that everything that would betray them had disappeared. The Brother waited silently at the table.

The door on the other side of the curtain could be heard opening and then closing quietly. He heard a woman's whisper. Son-kyong came to the curtain. "Brother, could you help me? Three girls came to this woman's house out in the country. Her husband has gone to get the brothel owners. A neighbor who will inform the police probably saw them. We have a chance to get there first, but I cannot carry all three. Could you ride Chul Min's bicycle and help me?"

The farm woman drank some tea and warmed her work-roughened hands over the stove while Son-kyong and the Brother dressed. His hostess insisted that he wear a pair of socks from her shop over his regular pair to prevent his feet from freezing.

Son-kyong locked the door and led them to a shed out back. She brought two bicycles out and put a backpack on.

The still cold was making the Brother's nose run before they had gone far in the darkness. He followed the two women by sound more than sight. Twice the bike slipped in the snow, sending the Brother tumbling onto the ground. Even with mittens and the extra socks, he was cold. He prayed that they would not be too late.

The bike tires crunched through the snow. Three times they heard vehicles coming and hid in the bushes. Once, they could find no bushes so they dropped onto their bellies in a ditch. The snow melting beneath his face seeped deep into the Brother's pores, making his face stiff as he wiped it on the tail of his scarf.

Then the farm woman led them into a small grove of trees.

"Leave the bicycles here," she ordered. Son-kyong left the backpack too.

As quietly as they could, they crunched through the snowy grove. The woman stopped at the edge of the grove near a small farmhouse with some sheds for animals.

"The brothel owners are here," Son-kyong muttered, as they watched two men get out of a car. The small woman rose to step forward, but the farm woman pulled her back. A police car pulled up behind the car from the brothel.

They moved more quickly through the grove until they reached a spot near the back of the house. They ran across the empty space, crisscrossed with tracks in the snow. Heated words were coming from the road.

The woman led them into the house to a small room where three girls huddled together on a pile of straw, their eyes large in their skulls.

"Come," Son-kyong whispered. "Bad men. Quiet."

Though weak, the two larger girls rose. The smallest one could not stand, so the Brother picked her up. He didn't know her age, but she couldn't have weighed over fifty pounds.

They could still hear loud voices. As she let them out, the farm woman wiped the floor with a rag to cover signs of their presence.

"Will you be all right?" the Brother asked her.

"My husband will beat me for letting them escape." She shrugged. "I will tell him I was sleeping. He does not hit hard. Hurry."

Praying every step of the way, the Brother followed the two girls and Son-kyong across the empty space to the trees. From the tone of the voices, the men were nearing a bargain.

Already weary, the two girls sat down to rest on a fallen tree.

Lights went on in the farmhouse.

Son-kyong urged the girls on.

Now loud voices were coming from the house. He heard the wife yell back: "They were there when I went to sleep. They must be here."

Men with flashlights emerged from the house to search the ground for their trail, but the mishmash of tracks would slow them.

The two stronger girls pushed on after Son-kyong. The girl in the Brother's arms whimpered.

"It will be all right, little one," the Brother murmured. "Jesus loves you. He will keep you safe."

Behind them, men crashed through the brush, their flashlights reaching out for their prey. A car raced along the road.

What if they find our bicycles? Blind their eyes, oh, Lord, for the children's sake.

No one was near when they reached the bushes where they had left the bicycles. The largest girl sat on Son-kyong's bike seat while the younger of the two sat on the Brother's. Son-kyong tied the smallest girl to the Brother's back. She pulled warm woolen robes from the backpack to wrap each child.

Son-kyong led out. The Brother marveled at her courage and endurance. The night was cloudless, so the air was becoming even colder. They hid from vehicles seven times in ditches, behind buildings, and in bushes.

Pumping hard to beat the morning light, the Brother's face stung in the cold. His lungs ached.

As light touched the sky in the east, he and Son-kyong returned their bicycles to the shed. With the Brother still carrying the smallest child, they hustled the girls inside near the stove. Son-kyong stoked the fire with coal and drew the two older girls closer to it.

As the Brother untied the rags holding the smallest child to his back, Son-kyong lowered her onto the table. The little girl did not move.

Rubbing the child's hands, Son-kyong bent her cheek next to the girl's mouth. She slowly straightened, her eyes filling with tears. She looked at the two girls by the stove and then turned to the Brother. One girl came over and put an arm around the still form of her little sister.

The Brother stared at the gaunt little frame on the table. Though little more than skin and bones, she seemed to smile. He stroked her hand and wept.

The oldest sister stepped beside him. Gazing into his face, she said something.

Son-kyong stooped to her knees and wrapped the two girls in her arms.

"What did she say?" the Brother asked.

"She said, 'Do not cry. Sun-ae had a full belly,'" Son-kyong said softly. "This little one probably knew more happiness and care in that farmhouse than she had ever known in her life. Now, Brother, let us move her so that we can think about the living."

Chapter 22

"I HAVE SEEN TIANANMEN," Stefanie said.

"You have not seen what I want to show you," said Pete Weston in his easy Australian drawl. "Just settle petal. We're mobile and show time approaches."

Pete had a few days off between photographic assignments and he and Stefanie were taking the sightseeing tour he had promised on the plane. Stefanie appreciated being able to call this new friend with the Australian accent and a native's knowledge of Beijing when she felt lonely.

Pete paid the cabby, and the two began strolling across the world's largest public square. He described what he had seen of the Tiananmen Massacre from the Beijing Dongjiaominxiang Hotel nearby. As he lead Stefanie to the Monument to the People's Heroes in the center of the square, he described the burning of the students' Goddess of Liberty. They continued around the monument until they could look back across the expanse they had just crossed. The figures in relief seemed to stare down at her.

"Here's our show pony. Do you see the man in the brown jacket wandering this way? The aesthetically challenged one."

"Oh, I've seen him before." He wore no hat. Though not as tall as Pete, the man outweighed him. Now looking around, he bulled past several clumps of people, his Fu Manchu mustache bristling.

"I fancy you've seen him a mite. He's your tail, darlin'." Pete turned toward the Gate of Heavenly Peace where Mao's huge portrait smiled benignly. "Now turn away so he doesn't spot you spottin' him."

The two began strolling away.

"You're sure? I'm an English teacher. Why would they be watching me?"

"Oh, there are any number of reasons they might have taken an interest in a pretty Yankee sheila. Don't know the why, but I've been around here long enough to have a mate here and there. What you said about your grandfather made me a bit curious. I called a bloke who knows this sort of thing. Sure enough, your name is on the watch list."

"That's a little frightening."

"Around here you keep this sort of thing in perspective. Look at it this way: You're giving that fellow a job, puttin' the rice bowl in front of his kid. I bought lunch for a tail one time, but he didn't seem to appreciate it. I disappeared then tapped his shoulder and popped the kit into his hand. I really hate to make life any harder for this one, but it's time to slope off. Three's a crowd today."

Pete and Stefanie stopped to have their picture taken by one of Tiananmen's numerous photographers. Pete gave Stefanie's name and address for sending the picture.

"That photographer was a cop, you know."

"How do you know?"

Pete laughed. "Little sheila, we've got to do something about your innocence. They're all cops. It's how they keep track of who comes to Tiananmen."

As they walked under the portrait of Chairman Mao on the vermilion Gate of Heavenly Peace, Stefanie could not stifle the resentment she felt every time she saw the heroic-sized images of Mao. He and his followers had done so much evil to her grandparents and to many millions of others.

Amid the crowd of red-cheeked tourists, Pete paused and loudly pointed out more items of interest. They turned north along the west wall of the Working People's Cultural Palace. When they turned east along the moat, Stefanie peeked over her shoulder. Her tail was about a hundred yards behind with his coat collar turned up, his head turtled into his collar, and his hands stuffed into his pockets.

"I hope he freezes," she muttered.

They followed the sidewalk south and then east. The Cultural Palace blocked the wind.

"See the path coming up on the left?" Pete asked. "We're going to stroll along it. Then when our friend thinks we're headin' back, we slope off through the gate there. I have a car waiting."

Stefanie caught another glance of the tail, who was trying to bury his chin even deeper into his collar. As they dashed toward the gate, the tail's chin suddenly came out of his coat, and his mouth dropped open.

Pete shoved her into the waiting cab. He said nothing but the cabby drove them to Dongdan Street. They got out next to an old white Fiat without paying the cabby.

"Get in," Pete said.

Pete drove off. At the intersection of Dongdan and Guluo Street, a red Yugo pulled out behind them.

"Get out," Pete said, opening his door. Bewildered, Stefanie just followed his lead.

The man and woman in the red Yugo traded places with them.

Stefanie watched the Fiat take a side street. Her eyes were big, and she was speechless. Pete grinned at her.

"Now for the grand tour-a-rama."

They drove through the municipal district. Pete pulled over and pointed at a large building. "That used to be a prison."

The sign read Scientific Experiment Instrument Works.

Outside the Qinghe Knitting Mill, Pete said bitterly, "Beijing Number One Prison. You can earn your way into here for three years without a trial. It produces Jinshuangma socks, which are sold at home and abroad. I'm sure I have a few pairs from there. There's a plastics factory here too, and who knows what else. It's a showplace. Two of your Congressmen visited in '91."

He also pointed out factories. "That one's owned by a Hong Kong outfit. This one's state owned."

"It looks closed."

"Now that depends on what you mean by 'closed.' The state factories are just about one step more active than if they were closed entirely. It's the old 'iron rice bowl.' The work unit takes care of your housing, medical, your kid's schooling, everything, and they can't fire you, whether you work or not."

"So some hardly work?"

"Welcome to the workers' paradise, with full employment, assigned jobs, and all that. China's got such an employment crunch that in some factories mandatory retirement is forty-two for women."

"How can they afford it?"

"The people can't. No safety net to speak of. Suicide, crime, prostitution, AIDS, drug rates—everything's up."

They drove past an open-air bazaar. Pete parked outside a series of cookie-cutter concrete apartment buildings. He helped Stefanie out and swung a knapsack from the back seat over his shoulder. They passed two buildings. Outside the third, Pete turned Stefanie so he could look over her shoulder through the dirty glass into the lobby.

When the elderly woman who operated the elevator had taken it up, he nodded to Stefanie. They trudged up the stairs to the fifth floor. A few light bulbs hanging from the ceiling lighted a hallway cluttered with boxes, bikes, and clotheslines.

Stefanie glanced into an open doorway as she threaded her way through the hall. A young man sat in a straight-backed chair in his pajamas, watching a black and white TV. His dark, empty eyes met hers. Blushing, she lowered her gaze and caught up with Pete.

Pete stopped at a closed door and knocked. The door cracked an inch. A man's eyes appeared above the door chain. Pete slid a package of Panda cigarettes through the opening.

"I have cigarettes, but I have no matches. Can you spare a match?" Pete asked in perfect Mandarin.

The eyes in the doorway shifted toward Stefanie.

"I think I can find matches for you," the man behind the door said. He unchained and opened the door.

Stefanie followed Pete into a small two-room apartment. Two narrow cots were placed on either side of a green table. On the table, a small electric plate served as the stove. Above the table, a half-empty bag of rice, a bowl with a few potatoes, and an onion were stored on a shelf.

Their host turned on the TV in the corner so that the Chinese news commentators' voices blared. He rechained the door.

"Is this the reporter?"

Pete nodded. "Peng Stefanie. Chang Ling."

"She is so young. Are you sure she can help us?"

"I think so. She is American. Everyone knows American journalists like to make governments look bad. They like the big exposé. Isn't that right, luv?"

"That depends," Stefanie said.

Pete pulled a manila folder from inside his coat. He dropped the knapsack on the table and took his coat off. "We'll be here awhile."

Chang took the coats into the next room. When he returned, four others accompanied him. A pretty girl, younger and smaller than Stefanie, was holding hands with a young man who was missing two front teeth. He had a black eye.

170

A rugged, blocky man limped in with a badly bruised face and his left arm in a sling. A slight young man who resembled the girl followed.

"For our purposes, we will call our friends Chang Ling, Yi, Er, San, and Si," Pete said.

Like John Doe one, two, three, four, and five.

"You can call me by my real name—Chang Sitong," the bruised broad-shouldered man said. "I will not wear a number until they put one on a prison uniform for me. And they have to catch me first."

The girl looked at Stefanie with big, pleading eyes.

"My name is Stefanie, and I want to help if I can."

The girl smiled shyly and said something in a strong rural dialect. It took Stefanie a moment to recognize the common rural greeting, "Have you eaten?"

"No, we have not eaten," Pete said. He shoved the knapsack across the table to the girl. "This should help out."

The girl hesitantly opened it. She smiled her gratitude as she pulled out a large bag of rice, fresh bamboo sprouts, beans, and other supplies. Stefanie rose to help the girl with the meal, but Pete pulled her back onto the cot that served as a bench. "I think you'll find this interesting."

He opened the manila folder he had brought and pulled out several black-and-white eight-by-ten-inch photographs. He slid them across the table to the three men. When they had finished looking at them, they passed them to Stefanie.

In the pictures, a group of people were watching two men hold a third, while a fourth man beat him. Machinery in the background showed that the beating was taking place in a factory. Pictures showed various stages of the beating. In the last photograph, the bloodied victim held an arm over his head while the beater swung a cant hook at him.

Stefanie drew in her breath. "This is you?" she asked Chang Sitong.

He nodded.

"Why?"

"I presented a petition to the government on behalf of the workers." He rubbed a scabbed knuckle across his mouth.

Chang One, who had opened the door, leaned across the table toward her. "Sitong is the union representative for his plant, which is foreign-owned."

"I have complained to the management from the start about the conditions," Sitong said. "They have brought migrant workers and peasants in from the countryside and offered them 1200 yuan per month to work."

"Is that a good wage?" Stefanie asked.

All four Chinese men nodded. The girl's brother said, "We were driven off our farmland for the Three Gorges Dam to be built. The government paid us 180 yuan for resettlement."

"We could not buy good farmland or a house for that." The girl paused her stirring of rice in the wok.

"In the six months we have worked here, I have been paid 200 yuan and my sister 180 yuan," the brother said.

"Why? You should have had . . . over eight thousand yuan each," Stefanie said.

"The factory sets rules they do not tell the workers about. When the workers break the rules, their pay is docked," Chang Sitong said.

"What kind of rules?"

"No talking during work or even during lunch," Sitong said.

"We cannot use the toilet more than twice a day, even if we work twelve hours," the girl's brother said.

"We cannot talk love," the girl said, gazing at the young man with the black eye.

"She means they can't date," Pete explained at Stefanie's raised eyebrows.

"The security guards carry electric batons and beat you if you break the rules," the young man with the missing teeth said.

"The health and safety situation in many foreign-owned factories is very bad," Chang Sitong said. "Fire exits are locked. People have died or been badly injured because of the fire exits. Some worked over 100 hours of overtime last month without overtime pay."

"Does the government know about the conditions? Can the union do nothing?" Stefanie demanded.

Sitong's bitter laugh grated on Stefanie's ears. "The unions are appointed and controlled by the government. We are not allowed to strike. I took my petition to my supervisor in the government. The next day the security guards at the factory burned it in front of everyone before they beat me."

Seeing Stefanie's stunned look, Pete said, "Collusion, luv. Kickbacks. A piece of the pie. The regulators are bribed not to regulate by puttin' them or their Uncle Henry or Sister Jane on the board."

Stefanie stared at the table, digesting the information. When she looked up, the others were watching her.

"Why have you not gotten someone to write about this?" she asked Pete. "If this got out, unions around the world could push their governments to pressure China to improve conditions."

"To stir the 'possum, you mean?" Pete slid the photos to her. "I think I just did."

It was after ten when Stefanie and Pete entered the faculty apartment building. Discussing her stubborn bathroom door, Stefanie waved the screwdriver she had purchased during their outing. "I hope I can use this well enough to work myself out of the bathroom. Can you believe that the door never sticks on Edda?"

"You just weren't here when she first moved in," Pete said.

The elevator had closed for the night. Ahead of them Kong Qili's door opened. Qili stepped out and into their path.

"May I speak to you, Stefanie?" Qili's mouth smiled toward Stefanie, but his dark eyes glittered as they took in Pete.

"Of course, Qili." She waited.

"Alone."

"No need to get maggoty, mate," Pete said.

She turned to Pete. "Thanks, Pete. I'll see you next Tuesday."

He winked at her and left.

Qili waved her into his apartment, which she entered reluctantly. "You are coming in late tonight." He towered over her.

She drew herself to her full height, which didn't help much. "I didn't know I had a curfew."

He strode to his computer. After shutting it down, he said, "You came in late last night also." He seated himself but did not offer her a chair.

"Did I keep your tail out past his bedtime?"

"Who was the man?"

"A friend I met on the plane from Hong Kong."

Kong examined his nails. "What is your relationship with him?"

"He's a photographer. I'm a writer. We're working on some articles together."

"Nothing personal then?"

"That would be my business."

"He is a foreigner."

"So am I."

He smiled slowly. "You are *huaqiao*, a Chinese from abroad."

"And the next time I am in Mexico City, I guess I will be a Mexican from abroad. No, Mr. Kong, I am not *huaqiao*. I am an American whose father comes from China."

Kong visibly relaxed. He strode across the room and put a hand on her shoulder. Stefanie stiffened and craned her neck so she could continue to glare at him. He caressed her arm and smiled. "It's only natural that I'm interested in the men you bring into our faculty apartments."

She blushed at the implication. She plucked his hand from her arm and dropped it. "Pete was merely walking me to my door while we discussed our work. You have no right to imply that I would do anything to shame the Lord, my family, or Beijing University. Now what about the man who is following me?"

Kong waved a hand. His self-satisfied smirk infuriated her. "Who knows who the government watches? Employment is a problem. It provides jobs. Today they follow you or perhaps your friend. Tomorrow someone else."

"That's the same reasoning Pete gave. I find it unacceptable. You didn't order me followed?"

"I'm an educator. What kind of power do you think I have?"

She stared at the scar on his face. She did not believe him, and now she knew why. This man who had never been outside of China had gotten out of a Chicago taxi. It wasn't that he reminded her of someone. She had seen him before. And the aftershave—the man who had hit her in the dark office had worn Roger's aftershave as well.

Raw fear knotted her stomach. She edged backward toward the door.

Qili inserted himself between Stefanie and her exit. He folded his arms across his chest, his voice and manner dripping with easy, intimate charm. "With your friend around, I would be tempted to follow you myself."

"Friends don't spy on friends, Qili. If that's all, I'm tired." She turned to the door.

"We leave in three weeks for Xining."

"What?" She took her hand off of the door knob and turned toward him.

"My friend arranged permission for us to see your grandfather in three weeks."

Stefanie put a hand to her mouth and stared at him.

"The Lawrences have agreed to take your classes through the following Monday. We fly out three weeks from tonight at 6:15. Dress warmly, because we'll take the train from Xian in Shaanxi Province to Xining." He laughed. "You should see your face."

"I don't know whether to laugh or cry. I cannot believe it." She brushed at tears that were forming. "Thank you."

Qili smiled. "Having you and your grandfather together will make me very happy."

Chapter 23

"Unless you want us to shoot your bird out of the sky and take it apart piece by piece, General, we just don't have any more tests to run," Kurt Boley told Rafik Macopagal. "The problem is not—I repeat, is *not*—the technology or the software."

Troy Hardigan winced at Boley's defensive tone. Boley respected technology more than people, especially people in authority who questioned "his" technology. When Boley and Dalal met in India, Troy was certain that the United States and India would be at war with each other in about five minutes. Instead, after they had finished screaming at each other, Boley and Dalal settled into a confident friendship of perfect mutual understanding.

But now Boley was doing his best to offend a general in the Army of the Philippines. What Boley wasn't telling the general was that the Indians were having the same problem: The Chinese were trying to gain access to both military communication satellites.

The technician who had worked beside Boley leaned forward. "He is correct, sir. There's nothing else we can do."

General Macopagal, stiff-backed and sternly starched, nodded. "Then what do you suggest?"

"New passwords and codes," Boley replied.

General Macopagal studied his hands. He looked at Hardigan and his partner, Alan Foo, and again nodded. "Foreseeing this possibility, we've prepared alternative passwords and codes. I have them here. We'll leave them in my safe until Monday morning, then install them. This time all of the coding will be kept in top priority security. None of it will be available to your company unless there is an emergency."

"Agreed."

The general closed his folder of materials and carried it to the office safe, unlocked it, and placed it inside. "You are dismissed."

Macopagal's staff and the technicians filed out. "Please close the door behind you, Bernice," he said to his secretary. The plump, middle-aged woman carried her notepad out and closed the door behind her.

Hardigan and Foo remained seated on either side of Macopagal's table. The two men waited for the general to speak.

"I think that went very well, General," Troy remarked quietly.

"I still don't want to think that it could be any of my people. I have worked with most of them for years."

"We understand, General, but you can see from the tests that we never had some of the passwords that were compromised. It has to be someone at this end," Foo said.

Macopagal thumbed through the pages of test results that Boley and his own Filipino technician had provided, occasionally stopping to read. "I suppose there's no other conclusion."

"None that we can think of, sir. If the Chinese have discovered a way around the access codes, it just doesn't seem possible," Hardigan said.

"And you think your plan will work."

"We think it has a decent chance of working," Foo said. "It is built on a solid premise. Whoever has stolen your codes has access to the safe."

"Your code thief may be on vacation or sick leave, but if he was here today, he knows he has a limited time to get this information," Hardigan said. "You can be thankful, sir, that you didn't have all of the codes in one place, or we would have more serious problems."

Macopagal stood. "Very well, gentlemen."

At dinner with Hardigan and Foo, Kurt Boley continued his favorite tirade: technology as scapegoat for human failings. Hardigan excused himself from the table.

Foo interrupted Boley. "What's up?"

"I need to make a call." Hardigan headed outside into the balmy air of Manila's early evening. He needed the distraction of hearth and home. He punched in a number on his cell phone. When Delores Peng answered, he thought of how much Stefanie sounded like her mother. "Hi, Delores, this is Troy. How is Nanai?"

"Her blood pressure dropped after the surgery, so they kept her overnight.

Andrew stayed at the hospital with her. He just called with an update. He expects to bring her home later today or tomorrow."

"I'm surprised that she went through with the surgery."

"I don't think she would have if Stefanie hadn't called and shamed her into it. She still doesn't know that her grandmother had the surgery today. We'll tell her on the weekend. Grace should be stronger then, and Stefanie won't worry about her being in the hospital.

"It's so sweet of you to call. Where are you?"

"Manila. I don't know how long I'll be here." He paused, unsure about asking about Stefanie.

"Troy, what's going on between you and Stefanie? Did she do something to upset you? I'm her mother and almost yours, so I'm claiming the right to know."

He searched for words.

"I'm not . . ."

"Of course, you don't have to tell me. I am not one of those mothers who intrudes," Delores said with a chuckle that sounded positively malevolent. "Just remember who pours the hot sauce on your enchiladas next time you sit at my table."

The last time Troy had offended Delores, a tortilla had nearly ignited in his mouth, and she had innocently asked if something he needed to apologize for had brought tears to his eyes.

He took a deep breath. "Delores, I'm in love with your daughter."

"This is supposed to be new information?"

"You know?"

"You are pretty obvious when you take out your heart and gnaw on it. About the only ones who don't know are Andrew and Stefanie. Those two are equally dense. I had no end of trouble getting Andrew to notice that he was in love with me. Now I will even intrude enough to say that Stefanie feels love for you far more deeply than she ever did for Roger."

"Then she's good at hiding it."

"Yes, she is, especially from herself."

"She keeps pushing me away. She hardly even writes to me, and I haven't received so much as an e-mail since she reached Beijing. She promised to send her e-mail address, but she hasn't."

"She is having connection problems getting on the university Internet system, so we haven't received any e-mails yet either. I don't know much more than that. But she told me of at least three letters she's written to you since she arrived in China and complained that she hasn't heard from you."

"I've written to the only address I have. I think it's correct. Anything she sent would have passed through Nancy, my secretary. She's received nothing as of today. I asked."

Delores was quiet.

"Delores, have you had any indication that something is wrong?"

"I'm so worried about her. I don't dare mention it to Andrew. He feels guilty enough about her going."

"What's wrong?"

"The letters we receive look like they've been opened and resealed. Lani noticed the same thing, so it's not just my imagination. Then I developed some rolls of film here, including one of Steffie's. There were two photos of Roger in the bunch. I considered not sending those two, but I did. I sent all of them. I know I did."

"And?"

"She got all of the photos but not the ones of Roger. I asked her if I should have left them out, but she said I must have, since they weren't there. But, Troy, I searched. I sent those pictures."

Hardigan processed these thoughts with the nagging questions already on his mind: *Why did the Chinese go out of their way to invite Stef? Did Kong find out about me? Is he going to use her against me or her father? What else could it be?*

He must have been silent too long, for Delores burst out, "You think I'm just being a foolish mother?"

"No. No, I don't. Give me her address again and her phone number."

General Macopagal's nephew unlocked the underground entryway and led Hardigan and Foo through the tunnel into the Defense Ministry's basement and up the stairs to the main floor. Checking his watch, he punched numbers into an entry keypad.

He held up two fingers. They had to wait two minutes to get past the cameras.

The heavy door slid open. The young man strode out and approached the guard at the main desk.

"Everything's fine down there," he said. "I thought I'd check the cameras on each level now and do a quick diagnostic."

"That sounds good to me." The other guard pushed himself back in his chair and propped his boots on the desk.

The two men hidden in the basement entryway counted silently down. They took a quick look at Macopagal and the other guard. Hardigan, dressed in black with his face smeared with black makeup and his red hair covered by a wig, stepped across the hall to the stairwell. He eased the door open and slipped inside. In two seconds, Foo joined him.

Hardigan adjusted the backpack he carried as Foo counted down, then inched up the stairs until he could see the green light go out on the second-floor stairwell camera. They darted up the steps, past the camera. The light on the third-floor camera flicked off as they rounded the bend in the stairs below.

Ten seconds after they reached the fifth floor the hall camera went dark. Although they were in shape, the five-story race up the stairs had both men a little winded. Now they would have one minute to reach the general's door, punch in the access code, and enter the office.

Hardigan pulled the door open and was about to step through when he heard someone approaching with a radio blaring. He jumped backward into Foo.

A man about sixty years old ambled around the corner of the corridor, carrying a radio and mop and pulling a wheeled bucket. He entered the women's bathroom.

Hardigan slipped through the stairwell door into the hall and darted toward the women's bathroom. Peeking around the corner of the door, he saw the janitor at the other end. As Hardigan eased the bathroom door shut, Foo was punching in the access code to the general's office. Suddenly the light on the surveillance camera flashed green. The camera started its rotation back toward them.

"Got it." Foo shoved the door open. Both jumped inside. Hardigan crossed behind the secretary's desk to punch in the general's access code while Foo reset the lock on the outside office door. Hardigan swung his backpack onto the carpet and removed a small electronic box from his belt. He circled the room, pointing the box here and there to check for electronic microphones and transmitters. Opening his backpack, he pulled a telescoping rod out and attached it to his bug sweeper. He wanded the ceiling and floor.

Foo opened the general's closet door and wanded it for bugs. The two men returned their equipment to their belts and packs.

"I thought the janitorial staff was supposed to be done by now," Hardigan said.

Foo shrugged. "Maybe he's our man, and this will be over quickly."

"In your dreams."

"The janitor looks to be working this way. Let's stow in the closet and put some ears on."

Hardigan placed a listening device on the door and tuned it to his earpiece's frequency. That would warn them of activity in the outer office. As Hardigan carried his pack to the closet, Foo was already assembling a movement-activated camera to attach to the closet door's keyhole. Hardigan opened the tray of listening devices again and chose another. He swung aside the large painting covering the general's wall safe and attached a bug to the upper left hand corner of the back of the frame. Shadows from the frame would obscure it.

Just as he pulled the general's safe code out of his pocket, the door from the corridor to the secretary's office opened. The rumble of a vacuum cleaner immediately sent a deafening blast into Hardigan's ear set. Closing the frame, he yanked the earpiece out of his ear and turned it off. He grabbed his back-pack on the silent dash across to the closet. Foo closed the door behind them and locked it.

The janitor took several minutes to get to the general's office. Inside the closet, Foo continued to set up surveillance equipment as Hardigan held a penlight.

The vacuum cleaner neared the closet door. The janitor tried the locked closet door handle, then ignored it.

Before the janitor vacuumed to the safe on the other side of the room, Foo turned on the computer that would allow them to record all three cameras once they were placed. The computer transferred the images to the general's secure ready room. The vacuum cleaner's roar covered the soft beeps of the computer boot-up.

The display through the keyhole camera showed the janitor approaching the far end of the room with the vacuum cleaner. If he knew the safe was there, he ignored it.

After several minutes, he turned the vacuum cleaner off, surveyed the room, and dragged the vacuum cleaner out, leaving the door to the outer office open.

After five minutes with no movement, the keyhole camera shut off.

Hardigan reinserted the receiver into his ear. With no noise from the outer office, he eased the door open. Then music roared into his ear as the janitor opened the outer office door. Hardigan grabbed at the earpiece once again and rubbed his pained ear as he settled back onto his haunches.

The keyhole camera turned on as the janitor set his radio down in the door-way of the outer office and began dusting his way around the room.

Foo pointed at the screen as the janitor dusted the painting covering the safe. Hardigan held his breath. But dusting the painting was the closest the janitor came to the safe. After cleaning the private bathroom, he left, locking the door behind him.

Hardigan and Foo placed a tiny camera inside the safe. The general had connected the folder to a magnet on the inside of the safe with a thread. It had not been disturbed. Once all of their equipment was in place, they settled into the small closet between the general's golf clubs and his extra clothes to wait.

Foo and Hardigan took turns catnapping. Morning arrived to end their night vigil. It was almost eight in the morning before Hardigan's earpiece announced the secretary's arrival. He heard the computer start and file cabinet drawers open and close.

It's Saturday. Why is she here?

Bernice Arroyo had been married to a staff officer. She had accepted the general's offer of work after her husband's death twelve years before. When Hardigan heard the secretary punch the general's code into the door, he nudged Foo, who straightened without a sound.

The camera turned on as the door swung open. A plain woman with short curled hair entered, glanced around the room, and relocked the door behind her. She crossed to the painting covering the wall safe. Wiping her hands on her skirt, she pulled on a pair of rubber gloves, then swung the painting out. She opened the safe more quickly than the general had, removed the file, set it on the table, and opened it.

After thumbing through the pages, she pulled a cell phone from her pocket. She punched in a number. One of the cameras picked it up

"Chunshan, I have the code and passwords for Kong."

"Kong," Hardigan mouthed.

Foo gave him the thumbs up.

The cameras recorded every movement and the microphones captured every word as Bernice Arroyo read all of the planted information to Chunshan. She returned the folder to the general's wall safe, then turned to leave. But a large, dark figure suddenly loomed in the closet doorway behind her with a fierce-looking smeared face. As she turned, the woman's eyes widened and her mouth burst open.

"You can scream if you like, Mrs. Arroyo," Hardigan said. "The general will be here shortly."

Chapter 24

Ren Shaoqi pushed the dolly while Rongzhen, the free-union prisoner from his work group, loaded piles of tanned and dried lambskins. Shaoqi's back already throbbed at the thought of loading the crated skins into the truck.

The two guards chatted amiably, but the prisoners were not allowed to speak.

The old man, Peng Chongde, and young Jun were piling filled crates onto another dolly. The old man looked frail, but he worked steadily. As much as possible, Shaoqi avoided him. The man had an innocent goodness that was so out of place here. It was almost that he had an inner glow, and it left Shaoqi feeling more alone and hungry for something—he knew not what. This was the man that he was to betray?

Rongzhen packed the last skins onto the dolly, then stood beside Shaoqi to stretch. As he did so he whispered, "Chu Zhurun has been talking to the guard. Be careful."

Ren appreciated the warning, knowing that Rongzhen risked punishment for giving it. He had recognized Chu Zhurun for what he was within twenty-four hours of arriving. The big workleader of the packing crew was an enforcer and spy who served the guards. In exchange, he ruled this dirty little kingdom. Ruthless and hard, he and his friends bullied the others. When the guards wanted someone persecuted or dead, they went to Chu. Even if a foreign human-rights organization got wind of it, Chinese officials could simply say that every prison in the world had conflicts that could turn deadly. No one could blame the government or prison administration.

Jun's face was still swollen from a beating two days before. Old Chongde had thrown himself across Jun's body as Chu's bullies kicked him. That had caused a remarkable reaction in the guards. Instead of laughing at Chongde's ridiculous and stupid action, they had stopped the beating.

Shaoqi pulled the dolly of lambskins to the long table where packers crated them for shipment. Two men from his crew unloaded the dolly. At the other end of the table, Jun and Chongde were finishing loading a dolly of filled shipping boxes.

Now Shaoqi stretched to relieve the day's aches in his back and shoulders. *Just a couple more hours.*

After pulling an empty dolly near Chongde and Jun, Shaoqi dragged the loaded cart through the workroom, past a naked man stirring the tanning solution with his body in the large tanning tank. Shaoqi's nostrils tingled as if the fumes from the tanning acids were eating his nose from the inside out. Tanning solution discolored the arms of the two men who fished the treated lambskins out of the tank as two others put fresh ones in.

One of the guards at the door to the loading bay smirked at Shaoqi. He tossed his cigarette onto the floor to join the hundreds of other butts. "I will get the door for you."

Shaoqi stopped, stunned. The guards rarely helped in any way. The guard opened the door. The cold wind stirred the discarded cigarette butts. Still trying to understand this sudden courtesy, he pulled the dolly through the doorway. The guard slammed the door closed behind him.

"Ren, you have not been doing your job," Chu Zhurun said.

As Shaoqi turned, Chu hit him in the mouth. He fell against the steel handle of the cart. Shaking his head to clear his vision, he dodged Chu's kick, so that it hit his left shoulder instead of his head. His arm shrieked with pain.

Two burly men grabbed his arms and dragged him to his feet. He lost track of the blows against his belly and face. Chu's laugh faded into blackness.

When he awakened, Shaoqi blinked and stifled a moan. He could not see from one eye, and his vision blurred in the other. He closed his eyes to try again. His throat felt dry, his tongue swollen. He tried to breathe deeply but could not.

Voices murmured nearby. Turning his head, he saw two blurry forms.

"As long as he does not develop a fever, he will be all right. If he gets feverish, call me."

"Jun is my concern. I have tried to prepare him, but he is only a child." Shaoqi recognized Chongde's voice, which was tinged with pain.

The doctor sat down at a desk. "What have we come to when old generals seize life by killing children?" Neither man spoke for some time. Shaoqi, remembering his own ordeal, ached inside as badly as his body hurt. "I have heard a rumor in the office," the doctor said. "They had another match for the general. Somebody from the coal mines. I do not know what happened."

To Shaoqi it seemed that Chu had again kicked his ribs, for he could not breathe. *No, Jun cannot be the one, can he? But he must have been sentenced before I was selected.* It was becoming clear that the government, personified by Kong Qili, was throwing the *shik tsai* dice with all of their lives. It was also probable that Jun would not be receiving a bullet to the base of his skull if Shaoqi's guard had pulled the trigger on schedule. His vision blurred with tears. He tried to get his breath. A moan escaped. The doctor and Chongde hurried to him.

The doctor checked his pulse. "Are you in pain?"

"It is difficult to breathe," he whispered.

The doctor turned the heavy woolen blankets down and tugged the bandages around his body. "You have two cracked ribs. We wrapped them. Relax."

"You have nothing to be afraid of." Chongde's twisted fingers patted Shaoqi's shoulder. "I will sit up with you tonight."

The doctor gave him something that eased him into forgetfulness, but when he awakened during the night, his body throbbed. To distract himself, he glanced around the clinic until he found Peng.

The old man knelt on the floor, his elbows on a chair. His pale skull reflected the light through the sparse white hair. The dim lightbulb gleamed on the twisted broken fingers that Peng clasped.

Shaoqi's eyes filled with tears from a feeling he could not name. Had anyone prayed for him as he was led away? Did anyone care for him as old Chongde loved Jun? The old man and the medic would be happier if he had died instead of Jun. He could not blame them.

A spasm of pain rocked his frame. To steady himself, he returned to the one emotion he had nurtured for a decade. He added Chu Zhurun's face to Kong Qili's.

"That was a good meal," Chen Yuliang said. "Now I want to show you my favorite place." She rose from her seat when the bus stopped at Tiananmen Square. Stefanie followed her and stepped down onto the pavement. Today the small man she called "Fox" was following her, instead of the big one she had nicknamed "Thug." Naming the agents who followed her made the menacing implications of their presence a little less frightening.

Instead of turning toward the square, Yuliang turned south. Stefanie followed her into line at the Mao Zedong Memorial Hall, the mausoleum that held Mao's embalmed body in a glass case.

Stefanie's lunch turned over in her stomach. The day was cold but pleasant, though the air smelled of diesel fumes and coal smoke, as usual. The bright days seemed much brighter at home. Maybe it was just that she was wondering how Nanai was and why she had heard nothing from Troy.

Yuliang, her face full of anticipation, smiled. "Have you been here yet?"

"No." She could have added that she didn't want to see the dried up dictator, but Stefanie did not want to disrupt the bonhomie of a pleasant outing with her friend.

"On holidays and Sundays so many people come that you can hardly get in."

Stefanie wished this were a holiday or Sunday so that she could excuse herself. Just the thought of Mao's persecution of her grandparents and the millions who died during his rule angered her. She had no desire to see his preserved corpse.

The building was elegant. People spoke in awed whispers, reminding Stefanie of a church service.

"When I think of how great Chairman Mao was, how much we owe to him, I wish we could bring him back," Yuliang said.

Stefanie had seen Yuliang so pleasantly animated only once before, about a young man she had met at college. She had never told Stefanie his name. Now Yuliang looked at Stefanie, as if expecting her to join in the spirit of the occasion. When Stefanie didn't respond, she said, "You know what he did for China?"

"Yuliang, we are not going to see things alike regarding Chairman Mao."

"If you would just throw out those bourgeois ideas that the West taught you. They do not want Chinese in America to realize how they wronged us, how they forced opium onto us, and how they ripped us apart into tiny pieces that they controlled."

"I know about the awful things the West did. All the West should feel shame for what happened in the Opium Wars. All of that was wrong, and the people were justified for anger against the West and the emperor. But that does not justify the millions who died or the millions more who were tortured and imprisoned unjustly."

"Chairman Mao unified us. He gave us our dignity and our country back. He unified our language, built roads and railroads, simplified our written language."

"Yes, he did much that helped the nation."

"He gave us order from anarchy, a unified government." Yuliang stopped at the case holding Mao's preserved body. "He did what he had to do for the country. If people would not have disobeyed, everything would have been all right. Of course, the Gang of Four took advantage of everyone when Chairman Mao was too old to protect us."

As she looked at the body, Stefanie's anger drained into sadness. This was just the stiff, pale body of a dead man. Yes, he had destroyed the lives of millions, but he had answered to the Judge, whose children he had tried to destroy in the name of atheism.

Behind her in line, a chubby Chinese man whispered to the man and woman with him, "The dirty, little secret is that the embalmer did not do a good job. Mao is shrinking."

Stefanie hoped that Yuliang had not heard the man. Tears filled her friend's eyes as she looked at Stefanie. "How can you look at him and not see what a great man he was?" Yuliang brushed tears from her eyes as she stared at the body. "We need him more than ever, instead of weaklings who would betray us to the West again." Yuliang stalked out.

Stefanie overheard the man behind her tell his companions, "Now you've seen a peasant under glass." The three chuckled.

Stefanie hailed a cab home. Neither she nor Yuliang said much until they were halfway back to the student village.

"What is Roger doing now?" Yuliang asked.

"He is working for his father's firm in New York. And, as always, he has been enjoying the privileges of the wealthy and wicked." Though she thought of Troy daily, Stefanie realized that Roger had not crossed the threshold of her mind in at least two weeks. She was on the road to getting over him.

"Position brings privilege. You could have shared that privilege if you had not been so puritanical."

Stefanie couldn't understand Yuliang's attitude. "It is no privilege to be cheated on, though at least I've had the privilege of avoiding a terrible mistake. Roger knows a lot about China, but he glories in the rich Western attitudes you despise. I would think you would find him more despicable than I do. If you had loved someone and been betrayed, you would understand," she said gently.

"What makes you think I have not?"

The taxi stopped outside the gates of Beijing University. Before Stefanie could answer, Yuliang stepped out and slammed the door. Stefanie paid the driver.

Yuliang strode off, then stopped. Stefanie trotted to catch up. "Yuliang, I am sorry. I did not know. Please forgive me."

Yuliang shook her head. "It was my fault. I am touchy, and after such a nice day. I should not let these differences come between us. I imagine you have someone else. I would like to hear about him." Yuliang's smile did not reach her eyes.

"No, there is no one else. It's still too soon after Roger." But even as she said this, Stefanie thought of Troy and blushed.

"It is Mr. Kong. I see it in your face."

"No, I was just thinking of someone else, a man who is a little older. He is a long-time family friend. You might remember meeting an ex-Marine with bright red hair named Troy Hardigan?"

"Red hair? Did he have long arms?" Yuliang winced. "I remember. He was not very handsome."

"Not very, but he is a good man. He and Nanai have been my supports through bad times. Maybe he is becoming more . . ."

As they paused outside the residence hall door, a man waiting by the door glanced at a photograph, then stepped toward them with a bouquet of flowers.

"Miss Peng?"

Stefanie glanced up in surprise. "I am Peng Stefanie."

"I was asked to deliver these to you."

Stefanie opened the card, which was written in Spanish:

Stef, if you need to reach me or are in trouble, see the carrier of this, Hu Youmei, at the Tiananmen taxi stands. Destroy this after reading. Missing you. Love, Troy.

Stefanie felt her face burn. The deliveryman and Yuliang both watched her. Trying to collect her thoughts, she tipped the deliveryman and thanked him, memorizing his face and wide-shouldered build. He held his left arm stiffly.

"A secret admirer?" Yuliang asked.

"Perhaps not so secret. They are from the man we were just discussing."

Chapter 25

"THERE IS SIN in our midst." The Brother leaned down to hear the old woman's thready voice. When he said nothing, she squeezed his hand and pulled him closer to where she lay on the *kang*. "God cannot bless us."

"What is this sin, Sister Ling?" he asked.

"I do not know. But when they took me to church two weeks ago, the preacher had no power, the Spirit had no access to the people. People are no longer being saved and some have backslidden. It is sin, the sin of Achan." Gaunt and fragile, the old woman lay on her side in a fetal position, her blind eyes closed.

It was hard to imagine that this woman had started seventy churches in Shaanxi Province. A beating by police had left her blind and nearly crippled.

The Brother raised his eyebrows in question to Brother Nian, one of the pastors in this assembly of Christians in Xian.

Nian nodded. "Sister Ling is right. We have sin in the church. We have had only three conversions in six months, and one of those fell away promptly. Three of our evangelists have disappeared, perhaps converted to Budding Rod. Two unmarried girls in our assembly have become pregnant. One of them married the father of the child; the other aborted the child and has not repented."

The Brother rocked back on his heels. Sin could destroy the church more effectively than could the communists.

Sister Ling squeezed his hand. "We must fast and pray that the wolf will be revealed and that God's power will crush the power of Satan."

"Sister Ling is right," the Brother said. "We will fast and pray tonight for tomorrow's service."

Nian and his wife knelt beside the *kang*, the fireplace's warmth welcome in the small hut. Sister Ling struggled to sit upright.

"Sister Ling, you should stay in bed," the Brother protested.

"When Satan is after my lambs? I can still fight a little longer on my knees. When I see Jesus, I want to bring his lambs with me."

They wrapped a blanket around the frail woman and eased her to her knees.

They prayed for hours. Others joined them, kneeling alongside the *kang* or prostrating themselves before the Lord. They prayed for forgiveness for their own sins, for the problems in the church, for the missing evangelists, for Xian and China. After hours of prayer, the presence of God descended on them and they poured out prayers, praise, and hymns of love. Tears rolled down the Brother's face as his own recurring fears and burdens were lifted. After praying through the night, the Brother felt clean and loved. He knew the power of the Spirit would fill him with the words to say.

With the morning light, they rose from their prayers with stiff knees and joyful spirits. The men had to lift Sister Ling onto the *kang*, for she could not rise.

"You will preach, Lao," Nian said. The others nodded their agreement.

Sister Ling grasped his hand and pulled him down to her. "Pull Jesus' lambs from the wolf's mouth. You fight from the pulpit. I will fight here."

Separating himself from the others, he seated himself at the table near the corner of the room and studied his Bible. He had sensed the passage that God wanted him to use, but he prayed that each word would honor God and would minister with the Spirit's power.

The others whom the Spirit had drawn to prayer filtered out. Nian's wife and son left.

"It is time to go, Lao," Nian said.

The Brother nodded, but his heart was too full to allow him to speak.

"Lao." The Brother glanced back at Sister Ling's call. She nodded. "The Lord's will be done."

Nian and the Brother made their way silently into a warehouse on the outskirts of the city. Lao followed Nian through a door to the office. People were already singing and a few stragglers were finding their places.

Nian looked out over the hundreds who had gathered in the warehouse. His eyes welled with tears. "God has heard us. Praise His name. Some of those who dropped away are here."

Nian bowed his head in silent worship, tears rolling down his face.

Four church leaders joined them in the office. "Something happened at the home of Brother Chin Muhang this morning. Strangers were there," one of the leaders said.

"A raid?" Nian asked.

"It did not seem to be. I wondered if it might be something about Zilin." The leader turned to the Brother to explain, "Brother Muhang's daughter is one of the missing evangelists."

The six men knelt while the people sang. When the other church leaders rose, the Brother remained kneeling to beg for the Spirit's power on the preaching. The people continued singing, praying, and sharing testimonies and prayer requests.

Moments before the last prayer ended, the Brother knew it was time. He rose and seated himself on a chair in the office. He stretched, eager for battle.

The brethren had made a platform of old pallets. When the Brother stepped onto their heavy pine slats, his gaze swept the crowd of nearly four hundred. One face captured his attention. One face paled, then lowered. The young man hunched his shoulders as if to ward off a blow. He sat in the midst of the crowd. To rise would have drawn attention.

My son, my son, you have lamb's wool, but wolf's fangs.

"The Spirit recorded these actions of the early church in Acts 4. . . ."

The Brother read the chapter about the arrest of Peter and John for healing the lame man in the temple. Then he explained the persecution of the infant church under the Jews. Next he returned to Peter's response in verses eight through eleven. Scripture's words rolled across the crowd with authority.

". . . by the name of Jesus Christ of Nazareth, whom you crucified, whom God raised from the dead. . . . And there is salvation in no one else; for there is no other name under heaven that has been given among men, by which we must be saved."

He let the words linger on his hearers' ear. Some eagerly awaited his teaching; some squirmed; one would not look up.

"In this short answer to the Sadducees, Peter gives the basis of our faith, Jesus Christ, crucified and risen.

"Some have come among us with false doctrines, denying Jesus Christ, denying the Holy Spirit's word through Peter that *no other name brings salvation under all of heaven.*

"In the name of a false and lying religion, Budding Rod, wolves come among our flocks, telling us to ignore Jesus, the Jesus who died for us and rose again. They say there is a new Christ, a woman Christ. This false Christ was not crucified for you but has killed and maimed and perverted your brothers and sisters."

Squirmers had stopped squirming. Even the small children listened, transfixed. One man still did not look up.

"The followers of Budding Rod believe that Jesus is not God, that there is no Trinity. Now, they say, we live in the Kingdom Age, where there is no grace—only judgment.

"Instead of trusting in Christ's resurrection, they promise you reincarnation until you get it right.

"The false prophet of Satan who started this cult, desired power. We know because he gave himself the title 'Worshipful Master.' Instead of submitting to the wooing of the Holy Spirit to win converts, he has offered money and immoral temptations."

The Budding Rod infiltrator glanced up sharply. His eyes met the Brother's direct and steady gaze.

"They brainwash our people. They have beaten and seduced our evangelists. They have drugged our preachers to take photographs of them in immoral situations to blackmail or shame them before the people. And when this has not worked, they have beaten them or broken their kneecaps or killed them.

"They twist the Scripture to their own damnation and to that of their hearers. They put together Ezekiel 7: 9-12 which speaks of the time of judgment being a rod that blossomed and I Corinthians 4:21 where Paul asks the Corinthians if they want him to come with a rod to discipline them or with love. Paul rebukes the Corinthians for the very things that Budding Rod promotes—divisiveness, fornication, following those who are not Jesus."

"One name," someone called.

"Jesus," others called.

"The Apostle Paul spoke of groups just like Budding Rod that were trying to subvert the church in his day. He warned us in 2 Corinthians 11:13–15 about them."

The Brother stepped off the platform.

"What did he say of them? 'For such men are *false apostles.*'" The Brother stepped forward. The listeners seated in front of him wiggled to the side to let him through.

"*Deceitful workers.*" He stepped again into the midst of the congregation. "Disguising themselves as apostles of Christ."

Another step.

"No wonder, for even Satan disguises himself as an angel of light."

Two more steps through the crowd took him to a handsome and promising young believer named Ming Dongxing. He looked down at him with a heart that was both heavy and angry.

"What else does Paul write of them? He promises that their 'end will be according to their deeds.' Their works are totally evil."

The Brother noticed a young woman come through the doorway of the warehouse. She was leaning on the arms of the preacher, Chin Muhang, and his son.

"Zilin!" Nian rose in the front of the room. As people scooted aside to allow her to pass, Zilin limped forward. Her face was swollen and badly bruised.

She stopped beside the Brother and pointed down at Ming Dongxing.

"You betrayed us. You deceived us."

"You do not know what you are saying," Dongxing remonstrated loudly. "I am one of you—converted under the Brother's preaching years ago."

"That is not what you told us," Nian said.

"You told us you were a new convert," Zilin said, her voice strained by pain. "You convinced us to meet friends of yours. When we got there, they separated us. They told us they had too many groups who wanted to hear about Jesus, so we separated so that we could talk to more people."

Zilin's name might mean "gentle rain," but her words fell with the power of a monsoon. She looked at the congregation.

"While I was at a meeting speaking, they brought in a woman that they said was near death and asked me to pray for her. Nothing happened. The next day one of their leaders came and healed the woman, and everyone believed."

Dongxing sneered at her.

"They tried to convince me that Budding Rod was true and had power that Jesus did not have. Someone talked to me constantly for days. I was allowed to sleep only a few hours at a time. I prayed and tried to remember Scripture."

She put a hand to her head. "They would not let me go. When I refused to convert, they beat my legs so that I could not run away. They tried to tell me that it was God's will that I sleep with the leader of their group. When I refused, they again beat me. They thought I was so badly beaten that I could not get away, so they left me alone. That is when God helped me to escape."

Zilin wept.

Her father and mother helped her from the room. With clenched fists, her brother glared at Ming Dongxing. "What will we do to him, Lao?"

Every eye turned to the Brother. "Your church leaders and I will discuss it."

He raised his voice. "Remember what you have learned here today. Those who say they are converts must be questioned closely and must show fruits of righteousness. Evangelists must travel in twos and not allow themselves to be separated from each other. You should go to your homes now and pray for your body, that it will not be seduced and that its evangelists will be protected from the evil one. You are dismissed."

The congregation exited slowly with one ear turned back to the room.

"Why, Dongxing? Why did you sell out to Satan?" Lao asked.

The young man glared at the Brother, then dropped his gaze to the floor. "If you truly knew our teachings, you would know they are true. The Scriptures tell of Budding Rod and the Kingdom Age."

"You take these words away from the rest of Scripture and pervert their meaning when you preach them," the Brother replied.

"We save people that you are damning with your preaching of Jesus! It is time for judgment!"

"But not judgment for fornication?"

Dongxing flushed and looked away.

"They did not need drugs or beatings with you, Dongxing. One of their women seduced you."

"Someone showed you the pictures."

"No one needed to show me anything, Dongxing. I remember you from the night you confessed Christ. You admitted your love of pornography. I imagine that you stood faithful for a time. Remember that I warned you that your weakness would be women. These people have played on your weakness about sex."

Dongxing turned toward the door, but other preachers were blocking his way.

"If you repent, Dongxing . . . ," Nian began.

"I do not need to repent for believing the truth. I am leaving." He shoved his way through the men and paused at the door. "God rewards faithful service with joy and pleasure."

"And Satan rewards faithful service with counterfeit joy and pleasure that stings back," the Brother warned.

The heavy metal door clanged as it slammed behind him.

"What will we do?" Nian asked.

"Budding Rod followers are wanted by the police, even more than we are," the Brother said. "Do you know any honest policemen?"

Nian and the others exchanged glances. "We have heard that some of the local officials have Budding Rod mistresses."

"And others are being paid by them," another preacher said. "Where do they get their money?"

"We do not know for sure, but we cannot allow that handsome young wolf to maul more lambs," the Brother said. "Are there any honest federal officials in Xian?"

Chapter 26

PENG CHONGDE WAS NOT SLEEPING tonight. The old man's tossing and turning kept Ren Shaoqi awake, but Shaoqi couldn't blame him. None of the prisoners remembered when anyone had visited the old man. As they worked on artificial flowers that evening, the prisoners speculated about who she might be.

The old man rolled over and sighed, jiggling the iron bunk bed.

Shaoqi listened to the snores and murmurs of the sleeping men. After glancing around to be sure no one was awake, Shaoqi slid over the side of the bunk. The metal of the bunk below chilled his foot. He lowered himself to the edge of the old man's bed.

"You are not sleeping tonight, Uncle," he whispered.

"I keep you awake. I am sorry." The old man leaned on his elbow.

"You are excited. I would be too." The old man's care during Shaoqi's recovery from Chu Zhurun's beating had awakened a dormant affection. He had not known human kindness since Qili's betrayal.

"Could it be your wife?"

"I pray it could not be Dehong." His voice sank. Shaoqi leaned closer to hear him. "Knowing that she is safe, she and my son, gives me strength. I am afraid that it is her sister who has come to tell me that she has died. I have always hoped . . ."

Again silence. A tear splattered on Shaoqi's hand. He squeezed the old man's frail shoulder. *Why does someone good like this have to suffer?*

"I am a weak old man. I would find it hard to finish my work here if she has gone on ahead."

"I think it will be good news. I feel it."

"I am a foolish old man to worry. It is in the Father's hands. Though he takes my life or Dehong's, I will trust Him."

Shaoqi did not understand the old man's ramblings, but he patted his shoulder. "That is right, Uncle. Try to sleep." He tucked the blanket gently around the old man's shoulder, as Chongde had done for him.

A few minutes later, the old man's breathing had settled into his regular whistling snore, but Shaoqi stared into the darkness wondering who it was the old man could trust that gave him such peace.

Kong Qili's hand closed over Stefanie's drumming fingers.

"You are nervous."

She pulled her hand free and pushed a strand of hair back. About two dozen people huddled in little groups around the stark waiting room. In one corner an elderly couple stared at a couple of sacks of food at their feet without speaking. A thin young woman nursed a baby a few feet away. A man with a lined face and heavy jowls chain-smoked and stared at a blank wall. Three men who looked like brothers talked softly among themselves and occasionally eyed a young woman in a short skirt and purple and green dangling earrings who was puffing on a Panda and pacing.

They're all probably just as nervous as I am, Stefanie thought.

Kong leaned over and murmured, "I asked them to check with the Public Security Bureau for some special arrangements. I'll see what they have found out." He squeezed her shoulder before leaving.

She watched him stroll away in his expensive suit. The suit reminded her of Troy's expensive suit on the day of the international sales meetings at Frontiers Technology. Troy had dressed so expensively for the important international sales meeting. The thought of Troy warmed her. She wished that he were the one who had come with her.

Her mind drifted to the more unsettling memory that she had first seen Kong Qili on that day in Chicago. She hadn't confronted him about it. She doubted that he would admit he had lied, and she hoped to ask Troy what he knew about the educator turned satellite technology buyer. Stefanie's Hispanic side wanted to pin the man to the wall and get the truth. Her Chinese caution was willing to watch and wait.

Now that he was helping her contact her grandfather, Kong's attentions had been more of a problem. During the flight to Xian, their wait for the train, the train ride to Xining City, and while arrangements were made to see her grandfather, he had become casual about touching her—taking her hand, drawing her arm through his, or putting an arm around her. On each occasion she had busied herself or moved away, trying to find a subtle way of giving the message that his gestures were not welcome.

The truth was, Kong's smooth manner was turning almost possessive. His touch felt too much like Roger's. She must not openly criticize or he could lose face. But it was difficult to protect his Chinese sensibilities when his actions would seem boorish even in the West. She was ready to lash out and tell him once and for all to keep his hands to himself. Maybe she was too sensitive because of Roger.

Kong returned to interrupt her thoughts. Picking up one of the sacks of gifts she had brought, he nodded toward a door. "You can meet your grandfather in there. Because you have come from *Mei Guo*, they want you to have a good impression of the system."

She carried her gifts and her violin into the room. It was smaller than the waiting room, with a mirror on the wall, a table with two chairs, a bench, and a couple of nails to serve as coat hooks. Kong hung up her black leather coat while she set the gifts and her violin on the table.

"You remember the regulations?"

"I think so."

"I will wait outside. Someone will bring him in for you."

She nodded, too preoccupied to speak or notice when he left. She thought of doing some stretches to relax, but who knew what the men behind the two-way mirror would think? She had to assume someone was watching.

She unpacked several pairs of warm socks, mittens, long underwear, fleece-lined boots, two flannel shirts, a heavy coat, crackers, cheese, sausage, and chocolates. She had smuggled some money into the socks.

She took out her violin, set it to her chin, and adjusted the strings. To calm herself, she played "Amazing Grace," but fears still tumbled though her mind.

What if we don't like each other or he won't come to America or won't approve of me or . . .

At the opening of the door, Stefanie glanced up. An ancient man, gaunt and stooped, stared at her through bleary eyes. He stared at her, then squinted, and raised a hand.

"Dehong? Is it you?"

Smiling, she set the violin back into the case and rose.

He squinted again and tipped his head. "I do not know you. It is Dehong's face, but not her smile."

Her eyes welling with tears, she advanced slowly, searching the fissured face.

"But I know you. I have waited all my life to see you. I am Peng Stefanie Dehong. I am Andrew's daughter—your granddaughter."

"My Andrew?"

"Yes, Grandfather, your Andrew." She stopped in front of him, then threw her arms around the thin frame. "We have prayed for you so long. I was afraid I would never meet you."

His arms closed around her. "You should not be here. They will arrest you." He stepped back, tears rolling down the wrinkled face. "You have to leave." He pulled her toward the door.

"No, no, it is all right, Grandfather. I am an American. I teach at Beijing University, and soon you can be released to go home to America with me."

"To America?" He stared at her.

She smiled through her tears. "To live with Nanai, and Father, and all of us." She grasped his hand, then stared at it in horror. The long, slender fingers that had played the violin to stir Nanai's heart were twisted and gnarled with large swollen knuckles. "What have they done to you?"

He gently squeezed her hand. "It was many years ago. It does not bear speaking of. Tell me of Dehong and Andrew. Has he been faithful? So many temptations in America."

"That was his message to you, Grandfather. He has faithfully raised us in the nurture and admonition of the Lord." She quelled her horror to lead him to the table. She picked up one of the photographs she had brought. "Come see your family."

He picked up one of the photographs of the family she had laid on the table. He peered at it, then lifted his eyes. "My Grace is so beautiful. Tell me about them, all of them."

Ren Shaoqi twisted the green silk around the wire to make the stem for a red rosebud. He glanced at the old man across from him whose sparkling eyes kept turning to the pictures on the bed beside him.

"Did I tell you that my grandson Chongde plays a game with a ball and stick that is called baseball at school?" the old man asked, picking up the picture of his family.

Rongzhen grinned at the others and asked, "What position does he play?"

"He is a pitcher. That means he throws a ball, and someone hits it with the stick." He laughed and waved a hand at his work crew. "You are good to an old man to put up with his ramblings." They all laughed. He had told them three times already.

The old man's bliss enlivened the whole work crew. Not only had the warden allowed him to keep the pictures the girl had brought, something nearly unheard of, but the warden had told him that he was going to be transferred close to Beijing. From there he could be released to go to America. If it happened, Shaoqi thought, the old man would be beyond Qili's power. He could barely remember such happiness as he felt tonight.

But Qili's hand is in this. The old man will certainly not leave China alive. And what will happen to his granddaughter?

"Shh," one of the men facing the door whispered.

Their smiles disappeared. Each bent his head to the silk flowers they were making.

From the corner of his eye Shaoqi saw the thin, arrogant guard approach with Chu Zhurun and two of his thugs. A cigarette dangled from the corner of the guard's mouth. The muscles in Shaoqi's back and neck tensed. *Being happy means trouble.*

"I hear you had a visit with a beautiful woman, Peng," the guard said. He tapped the electric baton against his leg.

Chongde offered the guard a chocolate from the large box his granddaughter had brought. The old man had shared the top layer of chocolates, the crackers, sausage, and other treats with his crew, making his good fortune theirs.

The guard, Chu, and his two buddies ate the next layer of chocolates by themselves. Peng's work crew scowled as Chu and his friends emptied the rest of the chocolates into their pockets.

A stocky, pleasant guard strolled over. "You are happy tonight, Peng."

The old man nodded.

"I hear you had your picture taken with your beautiful granddaughter."

Peng handed the picture over reluctantly.

The other guard, Chu, and his friends crowded behind the stocky guard.

"It is a good picture of you and her. She is very pretty," the stocky guard said.

"My girlfriend is a piece of sweetbread compared to that," Chu boasted.

Chongde ignored the burly prisoner. "My granddaughter teaches English at Beijing University."

"What is her name?" the friendly guard asked.

"Dehong is her Chinese name, but she has a strange American name too." *Dehong means virtue.*

"She would have had to find a new name if I had been with her behind closed doors," Chu said.

Shaoqi gritted his teeth and reveled at the thought of killing the man. Old Chongde said nothing, but his twisted hands knotted.

"If Chu worked as much as he blew wind through his mouth, his work crew might be able to meet its quotas," Shaoqi said.

"Get back to your crew, Chu," the stocky guard said.

"Maybe I will take this with me," Chu said, snatching the picture from the stocky guard's hand.

Shaoqi launched himself at Chu's back. His mending ribs seemed to tear loose. Chu hit the floor beneath him on his belly. The air whooshed out of him. The picture slid from the big criminal's grasp.

Shaoqi gripped the wrist of the arm he had slung around the big man's throat and tightened. Chu flailed his arms and tried to roll.

The jolt of the electric baton shocked Shaoqi's arms loose. The guards pulled the two men apart.

Chu tensed to throw himself at Shaoqi.

"If you want a taste of this, go ahead, Chu." The stocky guard held the baton ready. "You two hotheads need some time in the box to cool yourselves off."

Two things pleased Shaoqi as the guard marched them to the punishment boxes: The old man had his picture back, and the box would feel tighter to the big criminal than it would to him.

The confinement cell stank of human waste. The guard unlocked the grilled door and ordered Ren Shaoqi inside. Shaoqi could lie down in its two-meter length, but the concrete floor chilled him. To avoid the cold, reeking floor, Shaoqi squatted in the box, which was under a meter high by a meter wide.

He squatted until he could stand no more. Then he sat on the floor with his legs begging to stretch out, his feet propped against the opposite wall.

Chu cursed, groaned, and threatened from a box nearby. "I will not forget this, Ren, and neither will you."

Shaoqi ignored Chu's curses. *You should know better. What have friends ever done for you?* But as he dozed he remembered Chongde's kindness. The click of the lock and slide of metal against metal awakened him. The grill's perspective changed as it opened. Someone grabbed his arm.

He crawled from the box and found it hard to straighten. With a hand to his mouth for silence, the guard pointed to the door opposite the one he had entered. Shaoqi staggered toward the door as quietly as he could.

Chu Zhurun moaned in his sleep.

The guard prodded Shaoqi to a small interrogation room. His mouth going dry, Shaoqi glanced between the guard and the door. The guard shoved him forward.

At the sight of Kong Qili leaning arrogantly back in a chair, he felt nauseated. Qili knew. The old man would not go free.

"What do you have for me?" Qili asked.

"Not much yet. It takes time to earn someone's trust. I protected him tonight, and that may help. He has mentioned names. I have memorized them, but I am not sure that they will help. What are you doing here?"

Qili flashed the handsome, arrogant smile that made Shaoqi want to hit him. Tonight after the shock and the box, he could hardly lift a hand against Qili. Qili could thrash him without raising a sweat. Shaoqi forced his fist to relax.

"Enjoying a smoke and a beautiful woman."

Shaoqi's nausea grew. *Poor old Peng.*

"You are going to destroy that poor old man."

Kong blew smoke from his nose before tapping his cigarette out in an ashtray. "I care nothing about the 'poor old man.' He can rot here or in America. Once you get the information I want, Hu can stick him on the first plane."

"And the girl?"

Kong smiled slowly. "The girl is my concern."

Stefanie was unable to sleep. She wrote to Nanai and the family, to Laura, and to Troy.

Lying under the bedding in her cool hotel room, she had read her Bible until the words blurred, then picked up the book of Chinese poetry that Troy had given to her. He had made notes and asked questions about translation in places.

When she came to Wen Yi-Tuo's "Forget Her," she wondered how Troy could have scrambled the translation so badly. Wen Yi-Tuo had started it, "Forget her as a forgotten flower."

Troy had written, "I cannot forget her as last spring's flower, removed and tossed away."

As Stefanie read on, her eyes teared. *This isn't a translation. Troy is answering the poet in his own poem.*

Not that Wen's place in literary history was threatened by Troy's efforts. He had written to promise undying friendship.

Someone was knocking softly on her door. She brushed her eyes, pulled on furry red footies, and tossed her coat around her. She glanced at her watch. It was after one o'clock.

"Who is it?"

"Qili. Stefanie, let me in."

She cracked the door but left the chain fastened. She peeked around. "Is something wrong?"

He leaned against the door frame. Through the opening in the door, Stefanie could smell liquor and smoke.

"I cannot sleep. Go dancing with me."

"At one in the morning?"

"You are a beautiful woman. I want to show you off." He reached through the doorway as if he would caress her cheek.

She stepped back.

He frowned.

"That's sweet, Qili, but I do not dance."

"If you are not sleeping well, a few drinks, a little dancing would make you feel like a different woman. I can wait out here while you change."

His insistence irritated her. "Thank you for your invitation, but I am tired. I will see you in the morning." She tried to close the door, but he pushed it to the extent of the chain.

"I thought you would be grateful for all I have done. Maybe you show gratitude only to white men."

His accusation and his sneer stung her. "Qili, I had a cheating white fiancé. If you insist, I will give you just what he got."

Qili leered at her.

She shut the door in his face and made certain the lock was secure.

Chapter 27

Two contacts aboard the train from Xining to Xian would complete the Brother's delivery of Bibles. The young brother who had purchased them had discovered that he had been followed from Beijing. Apparently the police wanted his contacts more than they wanted him. The young man had signaled his contacts away before they could be caught. As the train slowed for Xining City, he had jumped out with the bag of Bibles, hidden them, and passed word to the church.

Though buying Bibles was legal in some large cities, including Beijing, those from the country who came to buy several Bibles were frequently arrested after giving up hard-earned yuan. Then the Bibles were confiscated. Depending on the government's current attitude toward Christianity, the hapless purchaser might be released, beaten, or sent to the *laogai*.

If the police caught the Brother with the Bibles, they would make him dance at the head of an electric baton before killing him or throwing him in the *laogai* for the rest of his life.

The Brother strolled through the car where Nei Jizhong entertained her tiny grandchild. A bag with whatever women carried for toddlers sat on the seat beside her.

He passed two plainclothes police. He had never been on a train with so many police. He sat down in an empty spot to study them, his stomach hurting, the old familiar fear mocking him.

The police did not seem interested in Nei Jizhong or any particular individual. They were looking over the passengers. One nodded to the other. They separated. One left the car while the other found a seat and a magazine.

The Brother watched the other passengers. People of all ages munched peanuts, chatted with seatmates, strolled to the dining car or restroom, read, or slept. He had developed an intuition about police, or perhaps the Lord was warning him.

He waited for several minutes before rising. The policeman did not glance his way. He stretched. No one paid any attention. Ordinariness again was his camouflage. He carried the bag of Bibles and clothes to Nei Jizhong where he squatted to ask about the baby. A few people nearby glanced up, then returned to their occupations.

Nei Jizhong lifted her bag from the seat next to her and set it on the floor. Her granddaughter, perhaps a year old, stretched and tried to break loose from her grasp.

The Brother sat down and placed his bag beside hers under the seats.

"Babies this age are hard to travel with," Nei Jizhong said. People nearby ignored her. "This is my third grandchild. Do you have children?"

"No, I have never married."

"That is sad. Here. You can hold her while I get her something to eat."

The elderly woman thrust the tiny child into his arms before he knew what to expect. He must have looked foolish, because several people looked up and tittered. The tiny child wiggled, jumped, and threw herself backward, arching her back. What better distraction could Sister Jizhong have thought of than a man who knew nothing about babies holding an active one?

"What do I do with her?"

Nei Jizhong bent over the bags. "Just hold onto her. Do not drop her. I know I put that fruit in here."

The baby stomped on his knees and lunged for her grandmother. Her flailing fists pulled his glasses off one ear. She wailed.

"What do I do?"

"Just one more minute," Nei Jizhong said. "Here it is." She straightened with a pear and knife in her hand. She extracted the child from his arms. The baby continued wailing. "She does not seem to like you."

The Brother righted his glasses. When he picked up his bag, lighter by three Bibles, a few people grinned at him, but no one stopped him. He settled down in his former place, out of the baby's sight.

The pain in his stomach eased. One more contact, but he could not make that for another hour. He closed his eyes.

For his final rendezvous, the Brother went to a soft travel compartment, a small room with bunks and chairs for more comfortable traveling. A Christian conductor had obtained the tickets for him and the young peasant he was meeting.

A tall man in an expensive suit smoked at the compartment's small table. He glanced up from his paper, turned away, and glanced back.

An attractive young woman was curled up on the lower bunk, writing. She smiled at him as he entered. The third man, his contact, lay on the top bunk opposite the girl. He looked scared.

In most soft carriages on a long trip people were friendly and talkative. The sternly handsome man reading the paper controlled the atmosphere of the compartment. He neither spoke nor acknowledged anyone in the room, though the Brother matched the girl and man in his mind because they both had fine clothes.

The Brother sank onto the lower bunk beneath his contact rather than take a chair at the table with the young man. He would not thrust himself into the attention of the policeman, for that was what the man's air and self-confidence announced loudly.

The girl laid her writing tablet aside. She dug through her carryall and pulled out a book of poetry. She then opened a can of peanuts.

"Qili?" She held them to her companion.

"No, thank you," the man said coolly.

"Would you like some peanuts?" She held them out toward the Brother and his contact. The young peasant nervously refused, but the Brother thanked her. Opportunities like this saved him money for meals, stretching his subsistence on the church's meager offerings. He lay down, nibbled peanuts, and prayed. The rhythm of the carriage rocked him to sleep.

The young man whom the girl had called Qili awakened him by speaking to the girl. Though he spoke in a foreign language, she answered in Chinese.

"Thank you, but since eating all these peanuts, I am not hungry. You go ahead."

Qili nodded and left. Again the Brother sensed his anger. He tried to think of something to say to the girl. He wished she had gone too, so that he and his contact could make their exchange. *Now what should I do?* Through the window he saw that it was snowing.

"Please finish the peanuts if you would like," the girl offered. He accepted them and passed the can up to his contact.

"Your husband does not like peanuts?" the Brother asked.

"He is my work supervisor. Right now he dislikes me more than he does my peanuts."

"Where do you work?"

She told him that she was from *Mei Guo* and taught English at Beijing University. Her large smile warmed him. But the Brother would have staked his life on the belief that Qili was no supervisor of education. Perhaps he was military instead of police, but he definitely was an official accustomed to authority.

Minutes ticked by. The man would return soon. He had to find a way to get the Bibles to his young contact. He prayed that God would open a way.

"Would my playing the violin bother you?" the girl, who introduced herself as Dehong, asked.

"No, it would be very nice."

The Lord soothed his burning stomach with the peaceful strain. His young contact leaned over his bunk. The Brother beckoned him to come down. They sat together on his bunk, their traveling bags between them. His companion stared at the girl.

The Brother did not recognize the music, but the girl closed her eyes, losing herself in the strains. Perhaps they could make the exchange while she played the violin with her eyes closed. The Brother nudged the peasant beside him who seemed bewitched by the girl and her music. He stared at her as he fumbled the bag open for the Bibles. The Brother nudged him harder. Others would soon hear the music and come.

The girl opened her eyes just as he held two Bibles in full sight. She must not have realized what they were for she immediately closed her eyes again. Or perhaps she would wait until her associate came in and inform on them. The pain in his stomach was eating its way through his belly. A bead of sweat rolled down his face. He shoved the last Bible into his companion's bag. He thought of leaving the car and losing himself in the crowd on the train. He stood, but a uniformed policeman suddenly stood in the doorway with several travelers.

"Is my violin bothering anyone, sir?" the girl asked the policeman.

"No. Do you mind if I listen?"

She merely smiled.

The Brother waited for her to turn them in. Trying to leave now would draw more attention to them.

The next song sounded familiar. He should know it. "Blessed Assurance." He stared at her. Was she telling him that she too was a Christian? She played a Chinese folksong that some of the peasants in the doorway clapped to. Then

"Amazing Grace" sent the Brother's heart soaring. She finished and flashed a knowing smile across the car at him.

"What is going on here? Let me through." Qili shoved through the crowd. "What do you think you are doing?"

The girl's eyes widened in innocence. "The policeman said it was all right."

"Get your things together. We will be in Xian soon."

The peasants grumbled back to their seats. The officer left without meeting Qili's eyes.

"I did not mean to upset you, Qili."

He glanced at the Brother and the young peasant. "We will discuss it later."

Qili carried an entertainment magazine from Shanghai with chorus girls on the cover. He returned to his seat at the table, held the magazine open so that the girl could see the chorus girls. She watched him, her face sober, before putting her violin away.

When the train stopped, the Brother's contact rushed away, but the Brother lingered, hoping for a word with Dehong. The stern Qili did not help her with her luggage, but she rolled a suitcase out on little wheels, carried her bag, violin case, and purse, and wore a handsome leather coat. The Brother watched her, wondering about the meaning of the two hymns.

As he picked up his sack, he noticed a photograph lying on the girl's bunk. She must have left it. He picked it up. *An old man with the girl. So much older, but it almost looked like. . . . No, it could not be. Could it?*

Xian's fresh blanket of snow disguised the city's dinginess. The cab driver stayed in the tracks of the vehicles that had gone before him on Huancheng Bei Road. When the Brother wasn't watching the girl's cab kick up snow ahead of him, he stared at Xian's ancient wall south of them and wondered how many peasants had labored on the ancient capital's wall. How many of them were prisoners like Peng Chongde—if the man in the photograph was Peng Chongde? He prayed for a chance to speak to Dehong alone.

The girl's cab stopped at the airport entrance.

The Brother paid his cab driver from the money he had saved for meals. He did not care about eating now.

The other cab driver set out the girl's baggage.

As the Brother neared the other cab, Qili was saying, "I will be back before the flight leaves."

The Brother stepped back, hoping the girl's companion would not notice him, praying that his ordinariness again made him invisible. Qili glanced back but several people surged past the Brother at that moment, effectively screening him. The cab's leaving eased his fear.

The Brother rushed toward the girl. "Would you like some help?"

"Why, thank you. Are you taking the plane also?" For a moment, he thought she did not recognize him. She lowered her voice. "I will not say anything about the Bibles. I am a Christian too."

Why is she saying that? To trap me? He glanced around, but no one was interested.

She tipped her head sideways, the snow drifting down catching in her hair. She had such wide, trusting eyes, such an open, honest manner.

"You are getting wet, but I would like to talk to you," she said.

He followed her into the airport. She left her bag at a counter. Perhaps because of the snow, the airport was not as crowded as he had expected. She led him to a corner of a dining room. "You have eaten only a few peanuts. Would you allow me to buy you a meal while we talk?"

"I did not . . ."

"'As to the Lord.' Besides, I hate to eat alone. It is such a blessing to talk with other Christians. I get so lonely."

He nodded. He pulled the photograph from his sack. "You left this on your bunk."

She looked surprised and her cheeks reddened.

"This picture means much to me. I was careless and would have hated to lose it. Oh, thank you. This is my grandfather. Did you make a special trip to return it?"

He thrust his hands under the table to hide their shaking. The waitress brought soup for them. The girl openly thanked the Lord.

She told him of coming to China to find her grandfather and to take him home to her ill grandmother. She introduced herself. His heart quickened at the name Peng.

"Then this is Peng Chongde, as I thought?" He said as he leaned across the table toward her.

"You know my grandfather?"

"I knew him years ago, during the Cultural Revolution." He sipped the soup, but the old memories made it hard to swallow. Dehong finished her soup first.

"Were you a student then?"

Were you a Mao-crazed youngster? Were you one of those who persecuted my grandfather? Is that what she is asking? He placed the chopsticks in his bowl and set the bowl on the table. *I have to tell her.*

"My brother and I led the mob that captured your grandfather." His eyes filled with tears. He swallowed hard. "His face has burned in my memory, but I have not seen him since those awful days."

He looked into her eyes and found gentle understanding at his shame and pain.

"Yet now you smuggle Bibles, knowing that you could end up in prison with him."

"We were taught that all good things came from Mao—our food, our clothes, everything. But Peng Chongde would not confess Mao, only Jesus. Jesus was too strong for Mao and for me. I saw the power and mercy of Jesus in Peng Chongde."

She placed a soft hand over his. "When my grandfather goes to *Mei Guo* with me, he will want to know who you are and how God is using you. What should I tell him?"

The Brother licked his lips. "Tell him his old persecutor Chang has served Jesus these twenty years because of him."

Qili told the driver to wait outside the police station. Inside, he passed the note he had received at the train station to a policeman, who led him promptly to a police captain. Working with provincial police required tact, because the structure of the government allowed a great deal of independence in the provinces.

"It is good to see you again, Mr. Kong. No prisoners this time?" the captain asked as they shook hands.

"Not this time, Captain. Not yet anyway."

The policeman ushered him to an interrogation room, where a young, good-looking man with a bruised and haggard face sat. Kong took the papers handed him by the captain. He skimmed through the papers.

"Your name is Ming Dongxing, arrested for being a member of Budding Rod. You think you can make a deal with us, and someone from the Religious Affairs Bureau agrees that what you have may be worthwhile. If I agree, you will be given a reduced sentence."

"I can give you one hundred fifty people who are members of illegal house churches here." Ming leaned forward, his bruised face bitter.

Kong folded his arms and sat on the edge of a desk. "Do one hundred fifty church members interest you, Captain?"

"I am sure that we already know them."

"However," Kong said to the man, "I have been putting out inquiries to the police departments about a sect leader called the Brother. I have come because I heard that you mentioned this Brother. Do you know where I might find him?" Kong could feel that vice ministry growing closer.

"He was here in Xian a few days ago, but he never stays in one place long."

Kong rose and turned to the door. "You are of no help to me then."

"Wait!" Ming licked his lips. "Do you have an artist? I can describe him. I can give you names of people who know him if you will release me."

"I am authorized to lessen your time. You will not be released. I will see that your time is cut by half, if I like what you tell me. I will make your time far more unpleasant if I do not. Make up your mind."

Ming chewed on his lip as Kong grasped the doorknob. "All right."

"Very well. Describe him."

"He is a small man with glasses, late forties or early fifties. He has gray hair and usually wears peasant clothes, but he has an authoritative voice that carries."

"We already knew that. Any identifying scars? Anything that stands out about him?"

"Not that I know of."

"Would you send in the artist please, Captain?"

The captain issued an order to one of the men guarding Ming and followed Kong from the room. Kong sat down in a chair near the desk.

"What is wrong, Mr. Kong?"

"Something about the description reminds of someone—someone I should remember." Stefanie's rejection had stung him the night before. He was allowing anger to interfere with his thinking.

"Captain, when you have a finished drawing, I would be very grateful if you would fax me a copy." He handed the captain a business card. "I hope soon to be in a position where I can repay favors." They shook hands.

"What do you want me to do with Ming?"

"Whatever you want, Captain."

Chapter 28

STEFANIE CHECKED HER WATCH— still an hour before her only class for the day. Then she could come back to the apartment to sleep. Qili's contempt had allowed her freedom from his incessant talking, so she could sleep on the flight from Xian. Still, she needed more rest.

She knew she should finish grading the last three papers from her journalism class. Then she could return the papers, explain the need for documentation and revision, and lecture on conducting interviews.

She glanced up at the click of the lock.

Bo Qin pulled her cleaning cart in.

"*Ni hao*, Qin. How are you?"

The middle-aged woman smiled. "I am fine. When did you get back?"

"This morning."

"Did you see your grandfather?"

"Come see my pictures. Here are two of Grandfather." Stefanie thrust them into the woman's hands.

"He is a prisoner?" She drew back with a strange look. Maybe ordinary Chinese would be offended because of Grandfather's prison record, but Stefanie was proud of him.

"Yes, he is a Christian. He has been imprisoned for a long time because he preached about Jesus and because he urged the government not to attack the students during the June Fourth movement at Tiananmen."

The cords in Qin's throat stood out with tension. "What is his name?"

When Stefanie told her, she said, "I do not know the name." She changed the subject. "Is your computer working again?"

"I have had problems sending messages back home, but that may be the telephone line. Did it get knocked over?"

Qin scowled. "No, I am very careful around such things. I asked because your friend came with a man when I was dusting your bedroom last week. I thought that he must be a repairman. They worked on it."

"My friend with glasses?"

"Yes."

Stefanie felt a tingle run up her spine. Could they have broken the passwords that Troy had installed to keep Jamie from exploring too freely? If so, they could have found out about the union man, Chang Sitong, or read her interview with pastors of legal churches.

"Was Edda here then?"

"She was not here."

Stefanie opened the laptop. "What were they doing, Qin? Did you happen to see what the screen looked like?"

"There was just a box on it."

Stefanie started the machine. A warning box, Troy's idea of a joke, flashed up. "All hope abandon, ye who enter here." Beneath it was the password request.

"Did it look like this?"

Qin squinted at it. "I just peeked from the bedroom, because I did not want your friend to see me. I think it looked like that."

"What did they do?"

"They put something black into the machine."

Stefanie went to the bedroom and found a floppy disk in her dresser drawer. She brought it out. "Was it like this?"

"I think so."

Stefanie inserted the floppy.

"That is what they did," Qin said. "Is everything all right?"

"Probably. But thank you very much for telling me, Qin. If you see anyone else near my computer, please let me know."

She stared at the computer, wondering what Yuliang was doing with it. Yuliang had been acting oddly, even for her. She was angry one minute, then unnaturally sweet the next.

Stefanie typed her password, "Psalm 46:1," in the space. After the computer came on with no problem, Stefanie called up her file on Chang Sitong's beating. Everything seemed intact. She decided to take the computer with her to class. She did not want to lose sight of it.

Stefanie pushed back from her chair and rubbed her eyes. Her head felt stuffed with dryer lint. Careful not to awaken Edda, she went to the bedroom for her purse. She wanted to check a quotation of the man she had met on the train for an article about the illegal house churches. That visit must have been God's blessing, for she could not make contact with the house churches in Beijing.

Yuliang, the tail, Qili—why should a place as big as China feel as if it is collapsing in on me?

Wondering what Yuliang had been able to copy, Stefanie had tried during the afternoon to copy and bring up files without the passwords, but she could not. Of course, she was no computer whiz. *If Troy were here . . .*

She leaned her forehead on her arms. She hadn't realized how much Troy's presence and e-mails meant until she did not have them—his insight, his humor, the safety she felt with him, and his intense, masculine perspective on life. A wave of loneliness swept over her. She missed him as much as she did her family, sometimes more.

Who else could she even talk to about the tail and this tampering with her computer? Obviously Yuliang was out. She didn't trust Qili any more than she did Yuliang, and he no longer spoke to her anyway. Pete Weston would simply dismiss her concerns as "just how things are." Her parents and Nanai would insist that she come home immediately, without her grandfather. Even her grandfather wanted her to leave China. But she wouldn't leave him. She couldn't face Nanai without him.

Neither her brother nor sister could keep a secret from Madre, nor could Lani from Mrs. Avery. And Laura tended to blurt out the worst things at the worst times.

That leaves Troy. Tomorrow I'll find his friend the cabby.

Kong glanced up as Yuliang unlocked his apartment door. He noticed the stiffness in her shoulders, the tight line of her mouth.

To concentrate on the voice at the other end of the poor connection, he turned his back on her. "Then Dr. Z saw me with Dr. Po. He looked at us strangely, but I do not know that he recognized me. Once Dr. Po saw him, she would no longer speak of the research."

"Let us be careful as we speak over this line. Remember that it is monitored at your end as well as here. This is our most promising contact. If we cannot get past Z in your 'negotiations,' you must remove this obstacle. We need those plans," Kong said.

"But when I brought up this matter before, you stressed the drawbacks in acting with finality." Tsu sounded worried. "You said that Z. . . ."

"Conditions have changed. We have had limited and short-term success through other means, and we need to get on with this project quickly. Since I am on another project, you are in charge of that field office. But my advice is to proceed immediately."

The other end of the line remained silent.

"If you cannot do this work, Tsu, subcontract it."

Tsu answered quickly, "I can do it, but it may take time. He is cautious."

"This is not something you can leave to your descendants. Do it."

"I understand. On the matter of our former associate and her contacts, we have narrowed the possible list. Unless we reconsider Foo and Hardigan, we have to consider the possibility that she was meeting with someone unknown to us."

"Follow up on the two of them, but keep the other option open." Without a good-bye, Kong hung up. Rubbing his hands together, he turned, still planning his next steps toward breaking through Frontiers Technology's safeguards on the satellites.

By locking onto the new generation of Frontier satellites, which seemed to be vulnerable, and targeting other satellites with lasers from China's own killer satellite, which was now on the drawing board, Qili and others in the intelligence community were certain that China could take control of much of the world's communications system. The West would not retaliate with their remaining birds at risk, and their ability to react and carry out operations would be diminished. China would become the preeminent superpower. China would recover the glory stolen by the colonials. Her destiny lay in technology, and Kong had dedicated himself to seeing that she had it.

China and Kong would rise to glory together.

Yuliang swung her briefcase onto the table. "You will not be so pleased when you see what your darling Stefanie has been up to."

"Did that drawing of our cultist come from Xian?" Kong strode to the door. It had stuck again. He wedged it shut.

Yuliang removed a paper from her briefcase and passed it to him. He studied it, then seated himself on the arm of the sofa. "Hmm." The drawing reminded him of—who? He couldn't quite place the features, but he had seen this face before.

Yuliang pulled a file from her briefcase. She slapped it onto the sofa beside him.

Reluctantly, he set the drawing aside.

He lowered himself onto the sofa cushions, stretched his legs out, and leaned his head back against his clasped hands.

Out of the file he removed four manuscripts. "From the computer?"

"All of her programs are guarded. Our programmers said they could get in, but they might leave tracks. You said no sign of invasion. These are from the fax machine."

He nodded as he scanned them. Ordering that the teachers use a single fax machine at the library had been a brilliant stroke. The machine not only sent out faxes to the intended recipients, but it also sent a copy to Kong's computer receiver.

"Our little friend has been busy." He tossed an article on Chinese restaurants aside. He skimmed the next article about Stefanie's teaching experiences. *Nothing here.*

He read the cover letter for an article on legalized Christianity in China with a smile. *More like it.* Plus it was being sent to a noted human rights group. He licked his lips. That could be used in charges against her.

Setting the article down carefully, he turned to the last article on the plight of rural laborers being cheated in foreign-owned factories. He chuckled. *Very good!*

"I do not see what is so funny!" Yuliang's eyes glittered like burning coals behind her thick glasses. "How will China look when those articles come out?" Her mouth puckered.

"Did you get her documents?"

Yuliang returned to her briefcase. She tilted a manila envelope until a blue American passport slid out, along with several letters.

"Are those the letters to and from her romantic interests?"

"Just one interest. All her letters, incoming and outgoing, have been checked. We kept the ones from Hardigan . . ."

"Hardigan? Did you say Hardigan? What Hardigan?"

"His name is Troy Hardigan. You said to keep any that indicated a romantic interest."

He sorted through the materials in the manila folder until he found the letters. *How could Stefanie consider that red gorilla more attractive than me?* "What do you know about this Hardigan?"

"He is a family friend with red hair and long arms." Yuliang lit a cigarette. "A salesman of some sort."

An interesting development. He tapped the letters against his left hand. He might be able to exploit their relationship.

"What are they saying about not hearing from each other?"

"Perhaps each thinks the other is angry. There is a strain between them, but Hardigan sent flowers two weeks ago." Yuliang removed her glasses and wiped them on a handkerchief. Without them she was quite attractive.

Kong leaned back again, staring at the room without seeing it. "He is trying to get her forgiveness after he cheated on her."

"What are you talking about?"

"She told me her fiancé cheated on her just before they were to be married."

"That was not Hardigan," Yuliang said. "She was engaged to a rich diplomat's son who owns an import–export firm. The son works at the firm now, but he is being groomed to work at the American embassy here. The father is an American princeling, so it is not to be doubted that the son will end up here."

"What is his name? When will he be here? Do you know him?" Kong lowered his legs to the floor and straightened.

Yuliang looked away. "I tutored Roger Eddington in Chinese for a short while. Stefanie neither knows nor cares when he will be here." Kong noticed a tone of bitterness that might answer his question about why Yuliang hated Stefanie. Though Stefanie might not care when the diplomat's son arrived, Yuliang did.

"You have given me helpful information. Continue listening to conversations in the apartment, as well as all correspondence—and especially phone calls."

"What about these?" Yuliang backhanded the articles. "China has lost face because of her writing."

Kong placed a soothing hand on her arm. "Patience, Chen," he said softly. "Even I cannot arrest an American citizen for selling Chinese state secrets without evidence. I trust no one but you to find every legal violation in every article."

Yuliang's morale had lifted before Kong carefully closed the door behind her. He sat several minutes longer thinking of the two cases on which he was working. He glanced around the drab room. He would be glad to finish this and get back to Hong Kong and the West. One could love China and still appreciate the comforts of the more decadent West.

He picked up the phone and dialed a number.

"Good work so far, but I need more," he said.

"Anything in particular?"

"Do you have any contacts with unregistered cultists? Christians?"

Chapter 29

A STORM WAS COMING. Ren Shaoqi could tell because Peng Chongde tossed and moaned on his bunk below. He wished he could ease the old man's suffering. Uneasy that he might add to the suffering through betrayal, he rolled over. If he could find the man called Lao, Kong Qili might let the good old man and his granddaughter leave China. Shaoqi considered this possibility while tossing and turning nearly as much as Peng Chongde.

It is my only chance to help him.

Shaoqi slid over the edge of the bunk. The cold metal of the bunk streaked through his bare feet. He sat on the edge of the lower bunk beside Peng Chongde.

"You are in pain, Uncle," he whispered.

"I keep you awake."

"I do not mind."

Peng Chongde leaned on his elbow. "I worry about my little Dehong. God has shown me that she is in trouble."

Shaoqi, thankful for the darkness, ducked his head. "What kind of trouble?" *Qili trouble.*

"I am not sure, but I think she faces great danger, and I cannot warn her."

Shaoqi sat silently, unsure of what to say. Finally he patted the old man's arm. "She is a very pretty girl. You are just having grandfather worries."

"I do not think so. Did you want something?"

"I remembered something I wanted to ask you about. In the other prison camp someone mentioned hearing a preacher called the Brother."

"Just the Brother? Christians call each other 'brother' and 'sister.'"

"Well, this one was just called 'the Brother.' Nothing else. I thought you might know something about him."

The old man stared at the bunk above him, then shook his head. "I know nothing of him."

"Thank you anyway, Uncle." With a heavy heart, Shaoqi climbed back into his bunk.

The young man stood. Blushing, he tossed the ball from hand to hand, dropped it, retrieved it, and glanced at Stefanie. Some of the girls in the English class giggled.

Stefanie nodded. "Take your time, Dosheng."

"My name is Dosheng. I study Chinese literature." Dosheng stared at her as if she held a lifeline for him alone. "My father is engineer. My mother is teacher." He dropped into his seat.

"Where are you from, Dosheng?" Peijun, the girl who had tossed him the ball, asked.

Dosheng winced at his forgetfulness. He rose, opened his mouth, and stared at the door.

The other students facing the door rose. Then those opposite scrambled to their feet. Stefanie turned.

Kong Qili entered the room, carrying a package wrapped in red paper under one arm and a notebook in the other hand.

"Welcome to our class, Mr. Kong. May I help you?" She asked in English as she rose.

"Thank you, Miss Peng, but I am observing several classes today," he answered in perfect English.

"Please join our circle if you would like."

"Thank you, but I will watch from here."

The students did not return to their seats until Kong sat down.

"Where were we?"

"Dosheng, where are you from?" Peijun asked. She was learning English quickly while Dosheng, a promising scholar in Chinese, struggled.

Dosheng rose again. He stared at the floor. "I am from Hangzhou."

"Good, Dosheng," Stefanie said.

He tossed the ball to another student and sank into his seat as if he wished he could sink beneath the carpet. The next student went on.

After fifteen minutes, Stefanie stopped the game. "You are making good progress. Continue to learn the list of kinds of work. We will discuss tools the workers use next time." The bell rang. "You are dismissed."

The students pushed their chairs into place behind their desks before leaving. Some shot nervous glances at Kong Qili. Others sauntered past as if unaware that he existed. Peijun and two of her friends loitered at their desks.

Kong waited until most had gone before he joined Stefanie and set the package on her desk. He stared at Peijun and the two other girls until they ducked their heads, grabbed their books, and left.

Stefanie had not seen him since their return from Xining, two weeks before. If he felt as uncomfortable as she did, he did not act it. He moved with his usual feline grace.

"You did not have to send the camera. It was my pleasure to see you united with your grandfather."

"My family and I wish to express our gratitude. The camera is certainly nothing compared to what we owe you."

Kong pushed the package across the desk. The red paper, a wish for happiness, rose from the rounded base to sweep upward toward a central rounded peak topped with a red bow.

"We do not offer olive branches in China for regrettable incidents."

It was not much of an apology, but perhaps it was the best he could do. She had to give him the opportunity to save face. She unwrapped the package to find a basket of peaches.

"Thank you, Qili. They look delicious."

"I think my second offering will be more welcome than peaches."

She waited. His eyes sparkled with a sardonic gleam.

"Your grandfather will be transferred to Beijing in two weeks."

"Two weeks!" Stefanie steadied herself by grabbing the edge of the desk.

"I'll take you to see him after he comes."

"What happens then?"

His smile pricked her. She wanted to squirm, but did not know why. "The officials schedule . . ."

"Stefanie?" Edda looked into the room. "Time to eat."

Since Stefanie's return from Xining, Edda had become friendlier—or perhaps Stefanie herself was more open to friendship. Now that she had met her grandfather, Stefanie was much less worried and was even letting Edda teach her some German as Stefanie helped her with her Mandarin..

Edda's eyes brightened. "Ahh, peaches. My favorite!"

"They are lovely. Mr. Kong brought them. Come have one." Stefanie welcomed Edda in.

Edda carried the television remote control that Pete Weston had given them. They rarely turned on the television, so they had agreed to lend it to Mr. Osaka, a neighboring teacher who had fallen on the ice and broken an ankle.

Stefanie offered the peaches to Edda who took one and turned it over in her hands. "Thank you," she said to both Stefanie and Kong.

Stefanie grinned and nodded. "Edda, Mr. Kong says Grandfather, umm *Grosvater,* will come to Beijing in two weeks." She held up two fingers. "Umm, *zwei Wochen.* Edda has been teaching me German," she explained to Mr. Kong, "so I practice the little vocabulary I remember when she's around."

"What do you have there?" Kong asked Edda, nodding toward the TV remote in her hand.

"We are lending our remote to Mr. Osaka," Stefanie said. "We have not had the television on more than three times since I have been here. We thought Mr. Osaka could use it while he is laid up. Take him some peaches, some *Pfirsiche.*" Stefanie extended the basket to Edda.

She turned to Kong to thank him again, but his lips were set in a firm line of disapproval. As he caught her eye, his lips relaxed into a subdued smile.

Edda gathered several peaches. "Thank you."

She joined two other teachers who waited in the hall.

Kong's smile lapsed into sternness. "Perhaps Mr. Weston would not appreciate your taking his gift so lightly that you give it away."

Stefanie stepped backward. "I really love your peaches, and you know that it is our Christian custom to share such special gifts with the sick, Qili. I am sorry. I did not mean to hurt your feelings, and I will enjoy the rest."

He waved her apology away. The tightness in his shoulders relaxed. "That is fine. I will be gone for several days. I will call you about your grandfather when I return."

Stefanie watched him stride away. So much about Qili did not ring true. He had no Christian background and was not as good as Roger at concealing the fact that he had no real Christian faith. Nor was he good at lying about never being out of China. Even if she had not seen him in Chicago, his manner breathed exposure to a sophisticated and self-assured Western materialism.

Suddenly a new thought struck her:

I said nothing to Qili about Pete. How did he know about the remote?

Chapter 30

BECAUSE THE WARDEN HAD LEFT early for a conference in Beijing, his assistant read the warden's prepared statement urging the prisoners about to be released or transferred to remember what they had learned in the *laogai*. They should become good citizens of the socialist state. They should refrain from companions who would drag them into their previous errors. They should dedicate themselves to the welfare of all.

Ren Shaoqi restrained a yawn. He had heard such speeches before.

The guard read the names of the transferees first. Shaoqi watched Peng Chongde quivering in rapt attention. He had been as tense as a Tartar's bowstring for the last several days, easily startled, his mind elsewhere.

". . . Those were the prisoners to be transferred," finished the young administrator.

Did I miss it? Chongde should have been on the list.

When his name was not called for transfer, Peng Chongde's head drooped, and his shoulders slumped. Shaoqi's mouth tightened, angrier for the old man than for himself.

They play with you, tell you one thing to get your hopes up, then do the opposite.

The guard finished his final instructions to the transferees.

"These are the prisoners who will receive unconditional release: Chu Zhurun . . ."

At least we will be rid of him.

". . . Ren Shaoqi . . ."

Released? That is not right.

". . . Peng Chongde . . ."

The old man bowed his head. His twisted fingers trembled.

After dismissal, one of the transferees complained bitterly that he was certain his name was on the release list. Peng Chongde's work group clustered around him, hugging him, shaking his hand, patting his shoulder in congratulations. Christians from other work groups congratulated him.

The big union man shook Peng Chongde's hand wildly but spoke softly. "This is even better than we thought."

"Somehow they switched the lists. It is a mistake," Shaoqi mumbled in wonder.

One of the Christians was standing next to him and grinned. "Yes—a wonderful divine mistake. It makes one wonder *who* really is in charge here, Shaoqi."

The man left Shaoqi's side and walked toward the circle of Christians with a giddy laugh.

"Pray for my little granddaughter," Chongde was pleading nearby to the others.

Something rammed Shaoqi. He hit the concrete floor and grabbed his healing ribs. He huddled on the floor, rocking in pain.

Chu Zhurun stood straddle-legged above him. The big man snarled, "Stay out of my way, Shaoqi, or you will be released in little pieces."

Bah, it is no God who brings happiness.

Part Three

Kill the chicken to scare the monkey.

—Chinese saying

"And now, Lord, take note of their threats, and grant that Your bond-servants may speak Your word with all confidence. . . ." And when they had prayed, the place where they had gathered together was shaken, and they were all filled with the Holy Spirit, and began to speak the word of God with boldness.

—Acts 4:29, 31

Chapter 31

THE FACE OF THE TALL, thin man paled. He looked both ways and behind him before approaching the Brother on the busy Nanjing street.

"What are you doing here?"

"I had to see you, Brother Jian," Lao said, pulling his coat more tightly about him to block the drizzle. He had waited at a spot that he expected Nie Jian to pass on his way home.

Nie Jian again looked in both directions and behind him. Taking the Brother's arm, Nie led him into an alley and stopped when they were out of sight beneath a staircase. "The authorities are looking for you."

The Brother shrugged. "We all live with that knowledge."

"No, I mean they are looking for you *specifically*. They have a fairly accurate sketch. Copies are all over the seminary, with the warning that we must notify them if we have seen you."

Professor Nie Jian taught biblical languages at China's sole graduate-level Protestant seminary, the Nanjing Union Theological Seminary. Though the Three-Self Patriotic Movement controlled the seminary, some of the professors, Brother Nie among them, loved the Lord fervently and did what they could to faithfully teach future preachers.

Professor Nie peered down over his horn-rims at the Brother and pushed his coarse salt-and-pepper hair back from his forehead.

"What does the poster say?" the Brother asked calmly.

"Relatively little. A brief description. But they offer a reward of twenty thousand yuan. It was signed by the assistant to the director of the Religious Affairs Bureau."

"So Chang Rongwen wants to see me, does he?"

"He is the anointed heir to the director's throne, a doctrinaire Party man with a reputation for cruelty."

Lao shivered in the dampness. "Yes, I know him."

"You know him?"

"Long ago. We grew up together. But that is not why I came to see you." He pulled a computer disk from his coat pocket. "We need your help."

Professor Nie grimaced at the disk and drew back. "What is that?"

The Brother forced back a chuckle. "Come, Brother Jian, even I know that this is a computer disk."

"But what is on it?"

"It contains concordances and commentaries and works of history. You know the trouble that we have with cults." He tapped the disk against his hand.

"Even the government recognizes the gravity of the cults."

"It is written in English. We need it translated."

His mouth open, Jian stared at him. He shook his head as if to clear it. "Do you know what you are asking?"

"I am asking much."

"If that disk is found in my possession, the least that will happen is that I will lose my job. The bishop already distrusts me. He has forbidden us to teach anything from the Bible that does not support socialism. He will not allow us to teach from Revelation or Romans. I must sneak around to teach justification by faith or the Last Judgment."

"I know you are doing a great work here and that you face danger if you accept this disk. Perhaps it is not worth the risk. But I see thousands who will never sit in your classes, and their churches face attack by cults. Many of these people are well meaning, but ignorant. They misunderstand obscure phrases and those misunderstandings breed great errors. Then there are the groups such as Budding Rod that deliberately undermine faith. Until we have more Bibles and study books, the churches' dangers grow."

"I counsel young preachers. I teach illegal Bible studies. My wife teaches children about the Lord. We hold illegal communion services for young people. I do my best."

"If you did not, I would not come to you."

Professor Nie wrung his hands. "Brother, please recognize my position. It is not that I do not want to help, but I feel so alone with such a great burden. You know how hard it is always to be in danger of arrest. And it seems selfish, but if they fire me, my son cannot go to the university. We could be banished to the countryside without a pension."

"Brother Jian, you must decide. I will respect you no less if you cannot do this. We have had offers from young people who are still learning English, but we are concerned that these translators know nothing of the biblical languages. You know both and good doctrine and have access to computers."

Leaning against the wall, Nie Jian bit his lip. He bowed his head for what seemed long minutes while the Brother silently prayed.

"I cannot think of anyone else," Jian said.

"Neither can I."

"The work will be tedious, time-consuming."

"We are asking only for the most important parts."

"Does it have commentary on Romans?" Jian held out his hand.

The Brother gratefully passed him the disk. "I believe so."

"I will at least do Romans."

The Brother nodded. "Thank you, Jian." The Brother marveled again that he had passed his friend a whole library with one hand. Both stared at the disk. Then Jian slipped it inside his coat.

"We should separate now. Sometimes I am watched," Jian said. He held out his hand. "God go with you, Brother, and be vigilant. Why, I do not know, but Chang Rongwen wants you very badly."

Passersby thought the old man on the bench of the packed train was dozing. Ren Shaoqi assumed that Peng Chongde was praying. Shaoqi was not inclined to pray, and he was too excited to sleep. He watched the mountains grow dark in the west. *To be free*—He could not yet comprehend it. No guards glared at him. He was wearing regular clothes instead of a prison uniform. With his hat on, no one could see his prison-cropped hair. Qili could not force him to betray the old man, unless . . .

Shaoqi watched Chu Zhurun at the other end of the car, talking, braying his loud, obnoxious laugh, and watching them. *Yes, that would be like Qili.*

Chongde stood uncertainly as the passenger car swayed. Shaoqi steadied him until he had his balance. After smiling his thanks, the old man made his way out of the car toward the toilets, clutching the warm coat that his "little Dehong" had brought him.

The high plains weren't windy tonight, but cold seeped through the car.

Shaoqi scratched some frost from the window to resume watching the stars. He wiggled his feet for warmth.

Most passengers were sleeping. Even Chu could no longer be heard.

Shaoqi glanced over. *He is gone!*

Shaoqi tried to look casual as he rose. His heart pounding, he looked for a weapon as he walked but found nothing amid the sleepers, smokers, and quiet talkers. He increased his speed. Though the train was full, no one was moving near the toilets.

As he opened the door, the cold rushed up from the squat toilets, holes in the floor of the car inside stalls. The odors of urine and feces that had missed the holes struck him. Then he heard a cry.

Shaoqi bowled past the stalls.

The back door of the car was open, blocked by a bulky figure.

White twisted fingers clung to the doorway while the bulky man shoved.

"No!" he yelled.

Grabbing Chu's collar and the wrist behind the clinging fingers, he lunged backward.

Chu stumbled after him, landing against the wall of a stall, which buckled beneath his weight. He forced himself upright and shook himself. Glaring at Shaoqi, he growled, "You! Good!"

Shaoqi leaped to his feet. Peng Chongde lay just inside the open door, unconscious or dead. Squaring himself with Shaoqi, fists raised, Chu kicked up clumsily.

Shaoqi caught the foot before it reached his groin and twisted.

Chu landed heavily, shaking the floor.

Wanting to avoid getting close enough for Chu to grab him, Shaoqi shot a side kick at Chu's head, but the big man caught it on his shoulder. Pain streaked up Shaoqi's leg and back. It was like kicking a brick wall.

Now the ox was back on his feet, his hands raised to hit. The smaller man slid under the fist directed at his face.

He drove his fists into Chu's belly. The big man grunted but did not double over.

Shaoqi struck upward toward Chu's throat, but his aim was off. The blow to the chin snapped Chu's head back. Shaoqi's hand hurt so badly that he wondered if he had broken it.

Chu stumbled backward two steps before catching himself. When he shook himself, his eyes were crazed. He feinted with his right.

Too late, Shaoqi realized that he was moving into range of a left to his sore ribs. A moan slipped out. He fell backward, his head striking a stall. He shook his head.

Chu lunged at him.

All Shaoqi could do was kick upward blindly from his prone position, just as Chu came down on him. Caught squarely in the chest, Chu stretched upward and stepped backward to get his bearings, but Chongde's body lay in his path. Tripping over the old man, he pumped his legs backward to right himself but instead propelled himself through the open door of the car.

He almost managed to recover his balance on the low railing. He swayed for an instant, but the momentum was too great. He groped upward but there was no support within reach. In the dim light, he seemed to hang for a moment in midair, his mouth opened wide. Then he disappeared.

Chapter 32

Troy Hardigan watched the Beijing traffic rush by. Glad he wasn't driving amid the swarm of bicyclists, he listened to the taxi driver, Hu Youmei, speaking softly in English beside him.

"The secretary to the director of the Public Security Bureau told her sister that the Beijing Tiger officially has been pulled off the satellite job. Maybe he tried to bed somebody's mistress, I don't know."

"Beijing Tiger? Do you mean Kong?"

The driver shrugged.

"Yeah, Kong Qili. I understand he is quite full of himself. He probably started the Beijing Tiger thing himself. But he has been fairly high profile in intelligence circles. He evidently has a talent for tracking down government enemies. Then he branched out into technology. Managed a degree in the mid-nineties from an American university. He has been on the golden boy spy track."

He hit the turn signal with what should have been the inside of his elbow but was actually the end of his arm. He had lost his lower arm and his brother in the Tiananmen Square massacre.

"Some of the young secretaries talk about him. He considers himself a lady-killer. I would not recognize him."

Hardigan leaned back. "I would. Anything else?"

"Military procurement is up. There is debate among the old-timers whether to maintain troop levels or push for more specialists, pilots, submariners, missile experts."

"Who's winning?"

"With the economy slow, I don't think they will cut troop ranks much. It would dump too many into the job market. On the other hand, the hard-liners are salivating over the wealth of the 'economic tiger.' There is a theory that some radicals want to make a high-stakes gambit. Move fast and sudden to reunify China and Taiwan militarily before anyone knows what is going on. Since the old nationalists lost power in 2000, China might think the new Taiwan government could be a bit more pliable—as long as a gun is pointed at its head."

"Wouldn't that lose China the economic goodwill they have managed to forge?"

Hu hesitated. "The government wants to compete with the United States in everything. They promise to have superior airpower and to take the United States on in Internet warfare. They use the rhetoric to unite us, to make us proud of China."

Hardigan listened carefully. His companion would have made a good analyst. Several years before, the two had become friends. With his cab route near the government's central offices, Hu overheard interesting tidbits from those with access to the powerful. He still harbored much bitterness about Tiananmen and had no problem with the ethics of augmenting his income by selling what he heard to another country.

Hu had told Hardigan of the many lives devastated by the June Fourth Massacre. He had lost part of an arm, his brother, and his opportunity to study political science. The government had denied the injured and their families any compensation. Force had been needed to put down a treasonous rebellion, they said. In fact, Hu's family, as others, had been charged for the bullets that had struck down their activist family members.

Hardigan glanced at the cabby's arm. He was not wearing the prosthetic arm that American friends had procured for him. Hu Youmei caught his glance.

"I do not wear it when I work near the government offices. It makes a good disguise for my other activities. By the way, an old friend asked me to give you his regards."

Hardigan made idle talk after receiving this message, but his fingers slid under the seat cover by his knee. He probed the edge of the seat until he found a slit. He pulled a computer disk from the slit and slipped it into his coat pocket. Hu, who had become the go-between for Hardigan and his most important Chinese contact, acted as if he did not notice.

They stopped at the gates of Beijing University. Hardigan paid the cabby, tipping him a large amount in Foreign Exchange Credits. Hu grinned at him. "She's very pretty."

Hardigan grinned back. "Yes, and she's going to be my wife. She just doesn't know it yet."

He jogged up the stairs at the address Delores Peng had given him, then paused at Stefanie's landing. The eager thudding of his heart made him feel foolish, like a kid with his first crush.

Back off. You'll scare her if you come on too strong.

He pulled a business card from his jacket under his heavy leather coat. He straightened his clothes and peered into a window to finger-comb his wild red hair.

What if Kong is there? What if she's found somebody else?

He composed his face into cool irony before knocking. His breath puffed out in little clouds.

"*Ni hao,*" the middle-aged Chinese woman who opened the door said. She stopped as she caught sight of his hair. She covered her mouth with her hand. Then her eyes widened. "You are the red man in the picture."

So Stef has my picture up. He felt a grin stretch his face. "Yes, I am. This is Miss Peng's apartment?"

"Oh, yes. She is working on her computer. Sometimes she and Miss Ansgar do not hear anything when they work. I will get her."

"I would like to surprise her."

At the other end of the small apartment, Stefanie, her lips pursed, stared at her computer screen. She wore pink sweats, furry red ear muffs, and gray slipper socks inside running shoes. Her breath hung in the air. A middle-aged woman with fading blond hair glanced up from another computer desk. Her vacant glance focused. She smiled and nodded.

He pulled his gaze away to check out the apartment—small, two doors to the left, probably the bath and bedroom, no windows in the main room, a small fridge, a heating element, and a table at the far end. A green sofa and armchair bisected the room to form the living room. A vacuum cleaner sat in the middle of the floor with a cleaning cart.

He tossed his brown leather coat over the sofa back. Stefanie did not notice, but the cleaning woman and Stefanie's roommate now watched intently. He walked up behind Stefanie.

She deleted something and typed in a replacement.

He leaned over her shoulder and read a few lines of an interview with a human rights activist who had gathered the names of hundreds of victims of the Tiananmen Massacre. He inhaled her perfume, and now her nose twitched at the scent of his aftershave.

"I don't think Hu Jintao is going to want you for his press secretary," he murmured next to her earmuff.

Stefanie almost launched herself over her computer. Already her friends were laughing heartily, as she turned. Her eyes widened. "Troy!" She threw herself into his arms for a bear hug, which he happily returned. Suddenly she remembered herself and pulled away, blushing. He caught her hands.

"I can't believe you're here."

He handed her his business card. "Frontiers Technology representatives go to the ends of the earth to please."

Her gaze turned tender. "I never expected you to come." She held a hand out to the other women, who were finally bringing their own excited laughter under control. She switched to Mandarin. "Edda, Qin, excuse me. Please meet my friend, Troy Hardigan. Troy, this is Edda Ansgar and Bo Qin."

Troy said something meaninglessly polite. He found it hard to keep his eyes off Stefanie. She had lost weight, making her big eyes seem larger.

"I talked to your mother, but did not get the entire story. How is Nanai?"

Pulling her ear muffs off, she led him to the sofa. He sat beside her and took her hand. "Dr. Liu thinks she got all of the cancer. She said that Nanai's lymph glands look good, but they want her to undergo chemo and radiation."

He interlaced his fingers with hers, her slender fingers softly fragile between his wide ones.

"She agreed to everything because I am here, because of her hope to see Grandfather." Stefanie jumped up, retrieved a picture frame from one of the two shelves on the wall, and returned to the sofa. She curled her legs underneath herself, resting her arm against his. "Here is a picture of my grandfather."

"Tell me about him."

As Stefanie spoke, Troy watched her face light up with excitement. She paused, then stopped, staring into his eyes. She licked her lips. With lowered eyes, she shifted away from him. "You are looking at me strangely."

He reminded himself that she still was not ready to hear that he loved her. "You look like a dragon at New Year's. Don't they heat these apartments?"

Stefanie relaxed. "The furnace is down. It is supposed to be fixed tomorrow."

"Do you think there's a warm restaurant in town? I'll treat you to supper so we can warm up before we look at your computer to see why you haven't been getting my thousands of e-mails."

"I'll change." She scurried away, stopped at the bedroom door, and turned back. "What do you want to eat? Beijing, Shanghai, Canton, or Sichuan?"

"You pick."

"McDonald's? I've been so lonely for home."

"Burgers sound great, babe."

To distract himself from his romantic hopes, he saved her article, returning it to her coded file. He checked her other files with code words he had programmed for her. The articles listed troubled him: Chinese New Year in Beijing, restaurants, teaching, human rights activists, the legal church, foreign-owned sweat shops, illegal house churches. He winced. She had written several articles that could get her in big trouble with the Chinese government.

The cleaning woman, smelling of furniture polish and holding a polishing cloth in her hand, stopped beside him. Her brow was furrowed. "Miss Peng does not like anyone to use her computer," she said.

"Thank you for looking out for Stefanie, Mrs. Bo. She asked me to work on it."

She did not look convinced, nor did she leave until Stefanie stuck her head out of the bedroom door.

"Qin, would you please help me for a minute? I cannot quite zip this." Quickly she shifted to English. "Troy, you don't have to start on that now. I will be right out."

Troy smiled at Qin as she lowered her eyes. "Do not be embarrassed. She needs people to . . . watch for her," he said, searching for the Mandarin words.

Qin nodded. "I am afraid for her."

Stefanie emerged from her bedroom in the red dress she had worn to the Valentine's banquet with him. Even with the clouds billowing from her mouth, she took his breath away. He wondered if she had any idea that he associated that dress with falling in love with her. She looked as lovely as she had that night. She smiled and switched back to English.

"Too dressy for fast food?"

"No, no, you look great."

"It's so good to have you here that I feel like celebrating." She paused to correct herself. "I've missed everyone from home."

Okay, Stef, but I'm the one you're wearing that dress for.

In the cab and at the restaurant, Stefanie took over the conversation. It was as if someone had overwound her voice box and she had to get it all out. He watched the animation of her expression and the sparkle in her big dark eyes to the point of occasionally losing the thread of her conversation. He reminded her several times to eat.

Suddenly she stopped with a jolt. "I've bored you silly. Now tell me all about your trip. You should have been home two or three weeks ago."

"Some technology caused a problem in India, holding me up for three weeks. I had to rearrange my schedule. My last meeting is scheduled for Hong Kong next Tuesday evening."

Her smile faltered. "Then home."

"Actually, no. I have some free time coming. I would like to spend it seeing some of the sights of Beijing." He helped himself to a couple of her fries, while she looked like she might begin to cry.

"You shouldn't do that for me."

"Who says it's for you? I love to travel and see new places. You just happen to be in one of them."

"Troy, you don't know how much this. . . . Tell me more about your trip."

He told her the parts that he could. Twice he found his words fading as her gaze consumed him. Tomorrow, he would scold her and tell her about the awful chance she had taken and how afraid he had felt when he discovered she was in China, but tonight McDonald's held a magic he did not want to destroy.

The weather had turned mild, summoning crowds to Tiananmen Square. It seemed warmer outside than in Stefanie's apartment. Twice, other strollers separated him from Stefanie. After the second separation, Hardigan pulled her arm through his. They spent two hours strolling through the square, admiring a group of waltzers, watching an artist in a wheelchair paint the Monument to the People's Heroes, and chatting with students in the English corner. They were looking at the relief work of the monument when Stefanie's arm stiffened.

"What's wrong, babe?"

"That man to our right. The one in the brown coat who's taking our picture. He follows me. I haven't seen him until now."

Hardigan nonchalantly switched sides with Stefanie and gestured toward the monument as he studied the big man who was pointing a camera in their general direction.

"Are you ready to tackle the computer? It'll be getting dark and cooling off soon."

They sat close together in the cab with Stefanie's arm through his. They said little to each other on the trip across town and spoke in Spanish. They talked of nothing important.

At the apartment he tossed his coat over the back of the sofa, then he settled at the computer, more concerned than before. "Did you see the man on your trip to see your grandfather?"

"No. Someone else may have followed me. He isn't the only one."

He checked the frame of the computer carefully. He inserted his key in the padlock to be sure that no one had replaced it with a different one. No one had forced open the back of the computer. "What about your backup floppies?"

"I took them with me."

"Good thinking."

Stefanie set two pots of hot water on the hot plate. "Actually it was accidental. I just happened to have them in my purse." She opened a jar of coffee from a shelf and spooned coffee into one pan. She went into the bedroom, where her roommate was playing the cello.

Edda came out to check the coffee. "Stefanie cannot make coffee," she said.

Troy grinned over the computer. "I know."

The woman rotated the pot over the heat while Hardigan typed instructions into the computer.

"You have loved her long?" Edda asked.

"About a. . . ." He hesitated when he realized what she had asked. Appraising the shrewd blue eyes, he decided to answer. "I met her when I was nineteen. I have loved her for a year."

Edda's eyes narrowed in humor. "She speaks of you often when she is not choosing her words carefully. She likes Chinese poetry from one book."

His pleasure must have shown, for she smiled back.

"Oh, no!" Stefanie said from the bedroom. He and Edda turned toward the room. No light showed under the door.

"It isn't enough that we have no heat. Now the bulb blew again. It's so hard to change them."

Edda rummaged around on the shelf in the kitchen area and produced a bulb. "We are required to report to the janitors, but they aren't always prompt."

Hardigan glanced at the high ceiling. "I can do that for you."

"Thank you."

Stefanie, in her sweats and earmuffs, lit Hardigan's way into the bedroom with a flashlight while he carried a chair. He removed the old bulb, scraped it across a screw that stuck out too far, and handed it down. Wanting to avoid breaking the new bulb on the screw, he asked for the flashlight.

He checked it to see what kind of screwdriver he would need to screw it in, but the screw had no opening to fit the screwdriver. He frowned and changed position. This was no screw. He had similar transmitting microphones in his kit.

He held his hand out for the bulb. Edda passed it to him. "There. Good as new."

Hardigan stepped down from the chair, and leaned close to Stefanie's ear to whisper, "Keep talking as though everything's fine."

"Thank you, Troy. We always have such a hard time with that."

"No problem," he said.

Edda tipped her head, her eyebrows drawing together in a question.

Hardigan carried the chair to the living room and mounted it under the light. Stefanie stammered. He beckoned her to continue talking. He found the microphone immediately.

Stefanie and Edda followed him into the bathroom where he checked the light. He found nothing. He ran his fingers around the mirror above the sink, searched the vanity and toilet, and stepped into the tub to reach the window.

"What is he doing?" Edda asked.

"I don't know," Stefanie said, "but he must have a good reason for it."

He stepped from the tub and turned the water on full. Then he closed the bathroom door and ran his hands along the baseboard with the women staring at him. Finished, he stepped close to them.

"Did you see the screw that hangs down in the lights?" he asked softly.

Edda thought. "Yes, I noticed it when I changed a bulb in the living room two weeks ago. It was not there first semester."

Stefanie shook her head.

"It is a bug,"

"It is not alive," Edda said, knowing only one meaning of the word "bug."

"A listening device," Stefanie explained, "but why would anyone care what we say?"

"Are you sure you did not see it long ago?"

"Yes."

Hardigan put a hand on each of their shoulders. They leaned closer. "I think there are two possibilites. It could be that a paranoid government watches all foreign teachers."

"No, I think not. I changed Mr. Osaka's bulb for him a few days ago. He had no screw sticking out."

Lines deepened around Stefanie's eyes. "What is your second thought?"

"They watch one of you," Hardigan said.

"I thought that photographer would bring you danger," Edda said, her lips pursed.

"Someone has been following her and opening her mail," Hardigan said. He turned to Stefanie. "Nancy did not get the letters you sent, and you did not get my three."

"Do you think they are after my contacts?"

Hardigan watched her, the conviction growing that his friendship with her had endangered her. Why else would Kong be involved?

The telephone's ring jolted them all. They stared at one another as if their conspiratorial whispers had been found out. Hardigan shut off the water while Stefanie ran to answer the phone.

Edda squeezed her long hands together. "I do not like this."

"If that is Qili, he is going to hear an earful," Stefanie said. Troy grabbed her hand. "Say nothing!" he whispered sternly.

She reached the phone in the main room of the apartment. "*Ni hao.*" Her voice lost its belligerence. She switched to English. "Madre, what's wrong?"

Nanai. Hardigan joined Stefanie. Her face paled.

"Hit and run!"

She reached behind her for a chair. He put an arm around Stefanie to steady them both. "But he'll make it? He's going to make it?" Stefanie's voice cracked.

Jamie. Picturing the twelve-year-old laid out by a hit-and-run driver left him feeling wobbly. Edda joined them by the phone.

Stefanie brushed tears from her cheeks. "Just a minute, Madre." She handed him the phone before sinking onto the sofa. She wrapped her arms around herself, lowered her head, and pressed one fist against her lips. Edda patted her on the shoulder.

"Delores, this is Troy. Is Jamie all right?"

"Troy?" Her voice was shaky. "Thank You, Lord," she murmured. "How's Steffie?"

He glanced at her. She was staring at the floor, her body stiff, her hands clasped in front of her. He switched to Spanish, suspecting that the phone would be tapped too.

"She is taking it hard. *Jamie esta lastimado?*"

She followed him into Spanish. "*Ningun.* Dr. Jim was hit by a speeder yesterday on campus."

"It was not an accident?"

"They do not think so." She told him what she knew. Dr. Jim was in critical condition after saving the lives of two students. An ethnic Chinese man had rented the car used in the attack and later abandoned it. The police were looking for the driver, but the car had been wiped clean of prints. FBI agents had come for Andrew at Dr. Jim's request. If he did live, he would never walk again.

Delores sobbed.

"Delores, Delores, he would not want this. You need to be strong for the kids."

She was silent for almost a minute. "You are right. He has been like . . . like a . . . grandfather to them." She gulped. "Jamie's been so quiet. Andrew is devastated."

"Andrew is a strong man, and God will give him strength."

"Is Steffie all right? How long will you be there?"

"I have an appointment in Hong Kong Tuesday, but I plan to spend some vacation time here after that. Stef will be all right."

"Oh, Troy, would you look after her? We should never have let her go."

Wiping her cheeks, Stefanie came to him, pleading with her eyes for the phone. She seemed under control so he handed the phone over.

Edda's eyebrows raised.

"A car struck a close friend. He may die," he said softly.

"I think she will need time with you now, but I am here if you need anything," she said and turned to go to the bedroom.

While Stefanie finished the call, Troy paced back and forth. The daughter of an American scientist is given an unusual opportunity to come to teach on short notice. Her supervisor is a top espionage agent who specializes in stealing technology and now is offering to help gain the release of the American scientist's father. They bug her apartment, watch her, and intercept her mail. Why? Have they connected her to him? As soon as Kong sees photos from Tiananmen Square tonight, they will. It would also bring him into their thinking in connection with Guangmei. Quite probably his cover was about to be blown.

Now, on top of all that, someone tried to kill Zinsser—probably the same man who had killed Guangmei. No question it had to do with his research for Frontiers. Maybe they wanted Stef in hand because of her connection to Zinsser. But if that were the case, they had changed the plan, deciding to kill Zinsser instead.

Troy could think of several possibilities to explain some or all of the facts. Not one of them sounded good, and each cast Stefanie as an expendable bit character in a TV spy drama.

Stefanie cradled the receiver. She walked to the hot plate in the farthest end of the room with her arms wrapped around her and her head bowed.

Troy went to the phone and began dialing.

"What are you doing?" she asked in a voice devoid of emotion.

"*El llamar para dos boletos fuera de aqui.*" No one answered at the airport ticket counter. It must be too late.

Again she followed him into Spanish. "Why two?"

"Because we are leaving on the first plane out."

Stefanie stared at him. "I can't leave. My grandfather."

Troy ruffled his hair in frustration. Still no answer. He slammed the phone down. "How will having both you and your grandfather in the *laogai* affect Nanai's health?"

"I'm an American. They can't—"

Troy pulled her into the bathroom and turned on the water once more.

"You haven't read the latest revision of the Criminal Code, babe. 'Institutions, organizations, and individuals inside and outside the country which subsidize organizations and individuals inside the country' are liable to five years' imprisonment. That's Article 107."

Stefanie propped her hands on her hips. "What makes you think I'm subsidizing anyone?"

He squeezed her shoulder. "You put money in the offering plate, buy anyone a meal, help anyone out?"

She pressed her lips tightly together.

"You're a soft touch, every panhandler's dream."

She brushed his hand from her shoulder. "I'm not leaving without my grandfather."

"And what do you think the Chinese will say about your unflattering articles—especially if they are trying to pressure someone you love to give them whatever it is they want. Think espionage charges. Think death sentence. After what happened to Zinsser, do you think they care what happens to you?"

"So let's assume some of what you say is true. And let's assume that all this has something to do with what happened to Dr. Jim. Where does that leave Grandfather? What would they do to someone like him?" She closed her hands into fists. "Troy, I understand your concern, but I will not leave without Grandfather if there is a chance the door is opening."

She turned away, the fight draining out of her.

Troy put his arms around her and buried his face in her hair. She turned and clung to him. He held her tightly, her tiny frame trembling against him. He thanked God that he was here to hold her as the minutes stretched. He caressed her long, soft hair and pressed his lips against it. He lost track of the minutes of their embrace.

Stefanie stepped back. Wiping the back of a hand across her eyes, she said, "I think you'd better leave now."

"Why, Stef? I only want . . ."

"I know. But please go, Troy." She would not meet his eyes. She turned away.

Troy was frustrated, afraid, and more than a little angry as he strode to the door. *After all I've done . . .* He opened the door, then realized he had left his leather jacket on the sofa.

Stefanie knelt next to a kitchen chair, her head bowed, shoulders shaking, tears streaking her face, lips moving in prayer.

Watching her, wanting to protect her—to fix the situation, he hesitated. Then he tiptoed to pick up his coat and left.

Chapter 33

STEFANIE FINISHED HER floor routine. Her neck muscles had released their tension, her headache had disappeared, and her mind felt clearer.

"I can't leave as Troy wants, but I can be more prepared," she told herself.

Troy. She thought of his strong arms around her the night before, comforting and making no demands, except out of concern for her safety. She remembered the tingle of his aftershave, the tender way he stroked her hair, the safe, protected feeling of his big hands on her back. She had never wanted to cling to anyone as she had wanted to cling to Troy.

So much was fearful and unclear, but one thing had become certain in her evening with Troy. She had to ask him to leave because he was no longer just her friend and adviser. This man loved her so deeply that her welfare was the only focus of his thought. That was something precious, but it could get in the way.

Mentally, she boxed her thoughts of Troy and set them aside to reexamine another day.

Stefanie had gotten lax about wearing the money belt her mother had insisted on. Pulling it from amid her underwear in her dresser drawer, she checked the amount. Her supply had dwindled. Troy was right about her being too generous. She resupplied from the other caches her mother had insisted she keep around the apartment.

Two more months. I have to cut back.

She started to wrap the belt around her waist and hesitated.

What if I do have to leave in a big hurry? It won't hurt to have my papers with me too.

She tugged her suitcases from the apartment's closet. She removed a dilapidated carry-on bag from inside her nested luggage and thrust her hand inside to retrieve the leather folder where she kept the documents. She frowned. It felt too thin, too light.

She opened it. A bead of sweat popped out on her forehead. *Empty.* As she searched the carry-on bag, then the suitcases, her mind replayed the last time she had seen her passport, visa, and birth certificate. She had put them away. *I know I did.*

She peered into every suitcase. She emptied her dirty clothes bag on the floor, searched among the clothes, and shook the bag. She pulled her drawers out, strewing the contents about. She upended her mattress to search the mattress cover and under the bed. She pulled the cushions from the living room furniture and thrust her hands between the back and frame. She removed the backs from her picture frames. She shook each book. She checked every place she had ever considered for hiding anything.

Looking at the havoc she had created, Stefanie sank to the gray carpet between the dumped dirty clothes and the scattered clean ones. She buried her head against her knees. *They have my papers. I'm trapped in China.*

At Tiananmen Square, Troy Hardigan kept an eye on a group of adults practicing *tai chi chuan* while he talked with young people in the English corner. The Chinese, limited in personal space, used their public space enthusiastically. The English corner—many parks had one—attracted people of various ages who wanted to practice speaking English. And as at many parks, thirty adults stretched, bent, and twisted in the ritual movements of the graceful *tai chi chuan* exercises. Beyond them a half dozen couples waltzed to "On the Beautiful Blue Danube" by Strauss. Other people walked, biked, aired pet birds, danced, played with plastic disks, roller skated, painted, even cut hair.

As the *tai chi* group broke up, Hardigan ended his English conversation with two college girls.

He stifled a moan as a stocky Chinese hit a nerve point in his arm with a sledge-hammer sized fist, numbing it to his wrist. "Red, what are you doing here?"

"Waiting for you, Chou. Your wife said that you would be coming by the English corner." Hardigan winced as he opened his hand and tried to wiggle his fingers.

Ulysses Chou had jumped at the chance to take a Marine posting in the United States Embassy security detail. Chou tracked down his family roots in his free time and became knowledgeable about all things Chinese. He had become such a good analyst that he was in danger of losing his guard duties entirely. One reason he was so valuable was an open, friendly manner that made immediate friendships and opened the door to contacts everywhere.

Hardigan spent two hours drinking tea with Chou and a few of his latest Chinese friends. Nothing happened quickly in Chinese society. When finally the two were alone, Chou asked, "What's going down?"

"What do you know of an international agent named Kong Qili?"

The two strolled past the traditional courtyards and stone gods outside the doors along Qudeng Hutong. Chou squeezed his eyes shut. "Kong? The Tiger?"

"Evidently he picked up that name."

"Small silver chin scar? Man-about-town style?"

"That's him."

Chou shut his eyes again as if dredging material from deep within his mind. "Called the Beijing Tiger because he has a reputation for tracking his prey. From Beijing. Spent time in the student movement before the big blow-up. Suspected of being a leading government informant in the Tiananmen Massacre. He definitely gave allegiance to the government afterward and even helped track down several student leaders. Has a degree from Beijing University. I think he also studied in the U.S."

Hardigan sidestepped two young boys running toward him.

"Good memory."

"Better than good. Near photographic."

"Any idea what he's doing now?" Hardigan asked.

"Kong? I haven't heard about anything in particular. He's been working on some sort of high technology acquisition outside the country. I imagine he's into industrial espionage." Chou swigged a drink from the tea flask.

Hardigan nodded. "That's about right, except that now he's working in-country." He assembled his own dealings with Kong Qili and Stefanie's connections.

Chou's frown deepened. "Beijing University? Whatever he's doing there, I bet he's not back for an alumni banquet, and I guarantee he isn't doing what he says he's doing."

"Someone took a photo of Stefanie and me."

"Get out of the country and take her with you, like yesterday."

"She won't go as long as her grandfather is here. Stef has the guts and gumption of a great Marine. A lot like Ramón."

"Sounds great, but if a guy like Kong has her in his sights, she's going to become fish food. Wouldn't she go if you tell her about Kong?"

"Probably not, and how can I tell her about Kong?" Hardigan buried his hands deeper into his pockets. "I haven't even told her about me."

"Women! Believe me, I know how they are."

"Oh yeah, you have, what, four daughters?"

"Six now—that means seven women in the house. Even survival training doesn't help against those odds." Chou stopped suddenly and stared at Hardigan, then guffawed loudly enough to turn stares in their direction. "Oh yeah, I get it now: Hard-hearted Hardigan is head-gone crazy in love."

At least he's speaking English, Hardigan thought thankfully.

"Maybe I am. Is that a crime?" He walked off.

Chou caught up. "Maybe I'm a stuffed rabbit. You've got it bad, Red."

"Look, if you can't help. . . ." Hardigan buried his chin deep into his coat.

"I didn't say that. I'm all for love. It might even make a human being out of you, if it doesn't get you killed." Chou eyed Troy soberly. "You hear that last part, bro? This could get dicey, so keep your wits."

"Yeah, I know."

"I'll see if I can find out what's cooking with Kong. Meanwhile, I remember that he has often been seen with an actress. She's in town performing some minor part. Ren. Ren, what is it?" He snapped his fingers. "Ren Ai-ling, that's it. She's playing at the Experimental Small Theater. Got some money with you?"

Kong Qili signaled for a cab. In the turmoil outside the Beijing airport, someone else reached it first. Another taxi pulled up.

Kong opened the back door, tossed in his suit bag, travel bag, and briefcase. "Qinghe Knitting Mill."

Noting the expertise with which a one-armed driver signaled and flowed into traffic, Kong leaned back. The meetings with Troy Hardigan in Hong Kong were set. His contacts in the United States told him Zinsser was dead, leaving Carla Po free to advance in the satellite research program and open to manipulation. Tzu would convince her to milk its secrets, one way or another. Now if only he could get this Christian thing wrapped up and get back to something important. At least it was coming together. Peng Chongde should be at Beijing Number One Prison now. And Stefanie's value extended beyond the old man's information about the Brother to leverage with her father. That could mine deeper research diamonds.

Kong did like the girl's spirit. Maybe he could avoid having to do anything too nasty to her. If she had won the old man's heart. Just the threat of sending her to the *laogai* might get the information. If not, there was always Ren Shaoqi.

The cab pulled into the parking area for Qinghe Knitting Mill, also known as Beijing Number One Prison. "Go to the gate in the back," Kong ordered.

Kong extended his identification card to the guard at the gate, who waved the car through.

"Wait here," Kong ordered the cabby.

In the office he showed his Public Security badge again before asking the middle-aged secretary, "Have the prisoners transferred from Qinghai Provincial Labor Reform Detachment Number Thirty-Seven arrived?"

"Yes, sir."

"Have Ren Shaoqi brought to a private interrogation room at once." He turned away after acknowledging the woman's response. He smoked in silence as he planned his questions. Meanwhile the woman worked her way through a stack of files, a frown on her face.

"I am sorry, sir," she said at last, turning from a computer screen. "I find no transfer named Ren Shaoqi. We have no prisoner by that name at all."

"He is among the new transfers."

"That is what I am saying, sir. He is not among them."

Kong stared at her. She dropped her gaze to the desk. She picked up a pile of papers, thumbed through them, glanced up, then checked a printout. "He just is not here."

Kong stubbed out his cigarette. *Shaoqi's absence doesn't necessarily mean a problem. I will just have to deal with the old man myself.*

"Then have Peng Chongde taken to the interrogation room."

She flipped through the files again, opened her mouth, closed it, and typed on her keyboard. She glanced at him again.

Kong swore silently. "Would you get me the Qinghai Provincial Labor Reform Detachment Number Thirty-Seven?" Kong said.

The call took forty-seven minutes to go through. Not bothering to hide his exasperation, Kong paced and smoked. When he finally reached the administration offices, a cocky secretary refused to give him the information without authorization from the Public Security Bureau.

Kong stormed from the office. Slamming the cab door behind him, he ordered, "Zhongnanhai."

On the drive he calmed himself. This was only a setback. As long as he had

Stefanie, getting Peng Chongde to come around was only a matter of time, even if he was still in a labor camp halfway across China.

Chen Yuliang hung up the telephone in Kong's apartment office. Assistant Director Chang Rongwen was growing more unpleasant by the day in his demand for the capture of the Brother. Now he ordered her to be at the Religious Affairs Bureau within a half hour.

She checked her watch. She would have to hurry, but Kong was not yet here. He had called from the Public Security Bureau headquarters asking for a list of Peng Chongde's past contacts. He had not called back. *Do I wait for him or go ahead?* After scrolling through the file she had pulled up for Kong, she decided that she could not wait. After all, he had told her to deal with Chang.

The line was busy when she tried to call the Public Security Bureau. She smoked, checked her watch, and tried twice more. When she still could not get through, she typed an on-screen note for Kong and gathered her coat and purse. She checked her watch. There was no way she could take a bus and get there on time. Well, she must do her best. She peeked out the peephole to make sure no one was in the hall, then sprinted out the door toward the buses.

Chapter 34

STEFANIE TRUDGED PAST KONG'S DOOR to reach the elevator. She had spent the last two hours waiting in Troy's hotel lobby, until men had begun making suggestive comments. Though she had filled out forms at the United States Embassy, no one would tell her how long it might take to receive replacement documents.

She paused at the foot of the stairs, dreading to face Edda after the mess she had left in their apartment. Thinking of the apartment brought to mind the microphones in the lights that Troy had found. *I feel like biting someone's head off. Qili is a good candidate and now is a good time.*

She marched back to his door and rapped sharply. It was not latched all the way and eased open. "Qili?"

The computer screen's glow gave the only light in the apartment. "Qili?"

The silence whispered emptiness and reeked of stale cigarette smoke. After peeking both ways in the hallway, she entered, leaving the door ajar. She checked the bathroom and bedroom, but no one was home.

Stefanie decided to leave a message for him. When she jiggled the mouse to bring up the screen. A message was already there in small Chinese characters:

"Immediate meeting with Religious Affairs. Boyfriend now is in Beijing. Peng info below."

Odd that Kong had to go to Religious Affairs. It might be a note someone left for him. *Whose boyfriend? Troy? What Peng?*

She scrolled down and found a detailed report, not about her, but about her grandfather. "What is this?" she muttered.

Footsteps approached the apartment door. Transfixed, Stefanie stared, certain she was about to be discovered. As the steps passed, she released her pent-up breath.

She tiptoed to the door. When she heard nothing, she eased it open, looked up and down the hall and building entrance lobby. Then she closed it, making sure it was fully latched and locked.

She returned to the computer to scroll through the open file but could think of no legitimate reason for Qili to have a complete file on her grandfather. She glanced at the windows with their closed blinds.

After shrinking the file, she opened Qili's directory, hoping for an explanation for so much information. A file named "Frontiers Technology" caught her eye.

Footsteps stopped outside the door. Someone knocked. Stefanie stared at it, willed it to remain closed, prayed. The footsteps left.

She opened the file, scrolled through it. It was too long for her to read, but she saw the names of Dr. Jim and several physicists her father knew. Farther down were Troy's name and Alan Foo's, with addresses, and phone numbers. She saw X's beside the names of the physicist who had been killed in a hit-and-run accident a few months before and by Dr. Jim's name. *It's high time to find out from Troy what Kong's real connection to Frontiers might be.*

She licked her lips to generate saliva. Her heart raced. She peeked behind the blinds for any sight of Kong outside.

Hands shaking, she e-mailed the Frontiers file to Troy. He would know what to do.

Another file in the same folder contained names, addresses, and information about people in the United States. She e-mailed that to Troy too, plus a few other documents that seemed interesting.

I've been here far too long. Her palms were sweating. She checked her watch. *If Qili finds me here, I'm dead—maybe literally.*

Whatever Kong and the room bugs and people following her were about, it could not be good. She deleted his files. Sure, he could probably retrieve the information, but it would take a little time. For good measure, she decided to reformat the entire hard drive. *That might complicate his schemes.*

Reformatting was nearly complete when she heard her neighbor Mrs. Lawrence's voice calling, "Mr. Kong, how nice to see you back."

The two were talking outside the door, Qili's voice irritable, Mrs. Lawrence's cheerily insistent.

Stefanie shut off the computer without waiting for the reformatting to finish. Grabbing her coat, she ran to the window, but students sauntered by in the light of the streetlights. She could not escape without notice.

As she picked up her purse from the desk, she knocked a manila envelope onto the carpet, scattering its contents. She crammed them into the envelope and ran to crouch behind the heavy shower curtain in the bathroom.

Qili excused himself, turned the key in the lock. He growled something to himself about Mrs. Lawrence as he turned on the light to the main room.

What if he notices the computer is off? She licked her lips with a dry tongue.

His coat slapped over a chair. He muttered a curse. The refrigerator door opened. The top popped off a can.

Qili now stepped into the bathroom to the medicine cabinet and opened a medicine bottle. The scent of beer reached her. Praying that he would not decide to take a quick shower, Stefanie hunkered in the shadows of the curtain. She wiped her sweaty hands on her skirt, certain that he could smell her fear.

When he left, she eased her breath out.

The phone rang. His voice seemed so distant in answering that she tiptoed from the tub. She peeked out of the bathroom. *He must be in the bedroom.*

"Yes, Mr. Chang, somehow the prison mixed orders. They released Peng Chongde instead of transferring him. No, but he will not get far. I have people watching. I am just waiting to hear from them," Qili said.

Stefanie eased herself out of the bathroom. She felt nearly frozen with fear, but she had to move quickly. She still held the manila envelope, but she could not cross in front of the open bedroom door to return it to the table. Barely breathing, she tiptoed to the apartment door.

"Once we pick up Peng Chongde, we will have the Brother in a matter of days."

She wanted to stay and hear more about her grandfather, but she had to leave now or never. The nearby roar of a passing bus masked any sound she made in closing the door as she slipped from the room.

She had taken only a few steps when another guest teacher entered the hall from the stairs. She tried to act normal, but he looked at her quizzically.

Not until she had sunk onto the carpet of her own apartment with her door locked could she feel safe. Edda had the lights off, so she must be asleep.

Stefanie dumped the folder's contents in front of her. She brushed a videotape aside to pick up manuscripts. Her manuscripts. Her articles. *How did Qili get them?* The article on the legal churches had a few notes on it. The one on the free unions was heavily marked with notations and legal references.

And there were letters. Her letters to Troy and his to her, letters she had not received. Numerous photographs came next, most of her, photos of her and

Troy at Tiananmen Square. *Those were taken last night, probably the ones we saw Thug taking.* Next, transcripts. Quite a few, annotated with notes and legal references. She lifted these off. At the bottom of the pile lay two floppy disks, and her passport and other legal documents.

Heavy steps paused outside her door. Scarcely breathing, Stefanie listened. When the door across the hall opened, she exhaled. Her hands shook.

"I can't be caught with these," she whispered.

She stuffed her personal documents inside the money belt. She carried the other materials into the bathroom, turning on a light and the noisy bathroom fan. She read each piece of incriminating evidence before tearing it into tiny pieces. She flushed as many of the tiny shreds as she dared but was afraid Edda would investigate if she heard many repeated flushes.

She pushed the window up. The wind had increased, nearly taking her breath away as she leaned out. The occasional sand particle from the Gobi stung her skin and embedded itself in her hair. She flung tiny pieces of paper into the wind.

She took the floppy disk, the film, videotape, and the cassette to the phone. Troy did not answer. She wondered if he was all right.

A piece of paper stuck out from the phone. The note was from Bo Qin. Stefanie glanced around. The apartment had been cleaned, though Qin usually did not come in on Saturday.

The note asked her to meet Qin at the bus stop near Wangfujing Market Street at 8:30 if she wanted to meet her grandfather's brothers and sisters. Stefanie stared at the note. *So that is why Qin seems so different. She's a sister in faith.*

Troy Hardigan followed the stage guard he had bribed to the dressing rooms of the Beijing Experimental Theater.

The guard knocked. "Someone to see you, Miss Ren." The guard rolled his eyes and muttered. "She thinks she will be a great actress."

They waited for her answer. Finally it came. "Come in."

As Hardigan pushed the door open, the guard left.

The actress was probably under thirty, a pretty woman with rounder eyes than Stefanie's. She sat on a stool with her back to him, removing the makeup she had worn during her performance. He studied her studying him in the mirror. She was obviously unimpressed. She winced when she saw his hands, but her eyes lingered on his leather coat, his well-cut suit.

He laid his coat on the plush red armchair and looked around the small room at the small cot, the clothes hanging on the wall, and her face staring at him in the mirror.

"I speak no English," she said in Mandarin.

"I speak some Mandarin, Miss Ren. Will you talk with me? Would you like dinner?"

"I have plans for dinner." She peeked back into the mirror, watching for a reaction.

"Not many were here tonight."

"It is the economy. Few people have a great deal of money, but most of us have nothing."

"That is what I have heard." Hardigan pulled a roll of yuans from his pockets. "How is your mother? Is she still in the hospital?"

She stared in the mirror at him. "Who are you? What do you want?"

He thumbed through the roll casually. The yuans were hundreds.

"She is still in the hospital." She tugged her eyes from the roll of bills, licked her lips, and turned to face him. "What do you want?"

He peeled three hundred yuans from the roll and reached over her shoulder to set them on the dressing table. She shied away, lest his arm brush against her.

"What time have you known Kong Qili?"

She eyed the money nervously, then raised her eyes to his in the mirror. "Why?"

He reached to pick up the money, but she grabbed his hand. "All my life. I grew up with him. My brother and he were best friends. We lived in the same courtyard in Beijing."

He dropped the money into her hand. "How did he get the name Beijing Tiger?" He pulled two hundred yuans from his roll.

She bit her lip while studying his eyes, then shrugged. "It is his own propaganda. He was a government informant. He tracked down leaders of the Tiananmen uprising. Some of them he followed for years. One . . ." She fumbled with her necklace, her turmoil obvious. "One he caught just inside the Tibetan border near India."

"Your brother Shaoqi?"

"Sir, you seem to be paying much for information you already know. My brother Shaoqi was one of the leaders of the Flying Tigers, the motorcyclists who carried messages for the students." She tipped her chin up defiantly.

"Where is your brother now?"

"In the *laogai* for fifteen years."

"This brother was Kong's best friend?"

She nodded.

Hardigan dropped another bill onto the dressing table.

He slowly separated five bills from the roll, making sure Miss Ren saw each. "What does Kong work on now?"

"Who are you? Why do you want to know this?"

Without answering, he held out his empty hand palm up to see what the question was worth to her.

"He does not tell me much until he finishes a job, then he drinks and brags. Now it has something to do with cults." He did not offer the money to her. She tried again.

"He also has been trying to find out who is making some weapon in the West. He infiltrated the scientists but one got greedy and had to be killed."

"Recently?"

She shook her head, her earrings dangling against her neck. Watching the money, she plucked her earrings off. "Months ago. He was frustrated because security was tight, and no one was approachable."

Hardigan dropped two bills. "How long on this? Happy on this recently?"

"Yes, he said he would soon have the information through a woman scientist. He said one of his men would be her lover and get the information soon."

He smiled grimly and laid the rest of the five hundred on the dressing table. "The cults. Why Kong?"

"I know there is an important cultist to capture, but he did not think it worth his time. He is angry about being forced to do this. I also know that there is a girl involved, a girl from *Mei Guo*."

A Christian leader. Must have something to do with the grandfather. Nothing about me, anyway. "Who is the girl?"

"He did not say."

Hardigan folded the roll of money to put it away. She grabbed his hand. "Wait. I can tell you how to find her, what he said about her. That is better than a name in a city like Beijing."

"Tell what you know. I will tell what it is worth. What does the girl have to do with cults? Why Kong?"

Ren's eyes ran over him, paused on his shoulders and hands, and returned to his face. "The undersecretary of the Religious Affairs Bureau wants to torture her in front of her grandfather, who is a cultist, to make him tell where some cult leaders are."

"But she is from *Mei Guo?*"

"He thought it humorous. The laws let him send her to *laogai* as he would any of the rest of us. She is stealing state secrets."

"She knows state secrets?"

"Maybe that is all I should say. It is enough to get me time in the *laogai.*"

Hardigan put down two hundred more and put the rest in his pants pocket, making sure it made a bulge. "If you do not think of anything else. . . ." He picked his coat up from the back of the room's other chair.

Ren bit her lip. He was offering more money than she would earn from her role in the play, money that she needed to care for her mother. Hardigan felt for her, but any remorse fled as he thought of Stefanie and her grandfather.

She grabbed his sleeve. "Maybe if you asked more questions, I would know what to tell you."

He did not drop his coat nor reach for the money. "How would she learn state secrets?"

She shrugged. "It depends on what you think of as a state secret. See, I have given you state secrets tonight." He still did not reach for the wad. "I think that Qili has put someone she trusts near her to give her information, then betray her. Then he took her to see her grandfather and filmed her breaking several regulations."

He dug the wad from his pocket and tossed her two bills.

"What else did he tell you about her?"

She hesitated. "I have known him a long time. I think until the trip to Qinghai to see her grandfather he liked her. He thought her silly but he liked her. When he came back, he was angry. I think he wanted her, and she rejected him."

Slowly, deliberately, Hardigan counted the last of the money, making sure she saw that he had eight hundred yuans. "The last question is for all or nothing."

She nodded.

"What is Kong's weakness? What will make him downfall?"

She shook her head. "He has earned his name 'Beijing Tiger.' I do not know that he has ever failed. He is ruthless and cruel. If you find this girl and leave the country, this may be her only chance. He wants to finish this, so you must act quickly, if it is not already too late."

"Everyone has a weakness, Miss Ren. Kong is human. Think."

"He is terrified of water. You could drown him." He did not loosen his grip on the money.

"My brother used to say that Qili was too confident, that arrogance would be his end. That is the best I can do."

He handed her the eight hundred yuans and picked up his coat. "Thank you, Miss Ren. I hope this helps your mother recover soon."

He donned his coat.

"Wait." She stepped between him and the door and placed a hand on the rich leather lapel of his coat. "You know this girl?"

"Yes, I do."

"Is she very beautiful? More beautiful than I?"

"You are a very beautiful woman, Miss Ren." He pitied her, pitied what Kong had forced her into.

"I do not think you would cheat on this woman," she said slowly.

"Goodnight, Miss Ren."

Chapter 35

AT THE BEIJING DEPARTMENT STORE, Stefanie browsed, watching the time and the crowd around her. By 8:20 she had spotted Thug. The big man was following her today, but a small, beaver-faced man she didn't recognize also lingered nearby.

She followed a line of women into the restroom. In a stall she donned a pair of gray pants that she had brought in a large purse. She twisted her hair into a French knot. She reversed her red coat so that the plaid was on the outside, covered her hair with the pink rain hat that had fooled the soldiers, and tied a dust mask over her mouth to shield her from the storm. She hunched her shoulders as she left the restroom among several other women.

Neither tail had appeared by the time she saw Qin at the bus stop. Qin did not approach her. Stefanie switched buses when Qin did but noticed no one following. They stayed apart until they reached the artists' colony, Yuan Ming Yuan, on the outskirts of Beijing.

Qin waited for Stefanie at the bus stop. To prevent the yellow sand in the wind from scratching their faces, they held their scarves in front of their faces. Qin led Stefanie through a warren of courtyards. She stopped at a door, tapped three times, paused, and knocked twice more.

A graying middle-aged man opened the door.

About forty people of all ages filled two tiny rooms that smelled of coal dust, bread, and paint cleaner. The oldest people sat in the few chairs, the youngest in the least comfortable positions, but no one complained. Children eyed Stefanie curiously. The others smiled their welcome.

Qin introduced her.

An elderly woman grabbed Stefanie's hand and squinted at her. "What Peng? Who is your grandfather?"

The older people babbled in surprise and pleasure, telling her of when they had met or worshiped with her grandfather. The husband of one had been in the *laogai* with Peng Chongde during the Cultural Revolution.

"It is time to begin," the graying man said. "You sisters must sit near our emergency exit." As a foreigner, Stefanie's presence endangered the others.

In the second room, children and young people squatted near the room's only window. A young man with heavily muscled arms, whom Stefanie had seen painting at Tiananmen Square, sat near the window in a wheelchair. An easel with a painting of the Monument to the People's Heroes stood in a corner near him.

The young man in the wheelchair said, "In case of a raid, we will let you out the window. Once you get out, keep low to the corner. Then run."

"Let us begin with prayer. Brother Ningkun," the graying man said. He stood in the doorway between the two rooms.

Stefanie wedged herself into a corner with Qin. They sat shoulder to shoulder, their knees pulled up in order not to kick those in front of them.

A man about Troy's age with a slash of white hair above his right eyebrow rose. "We must remember: 'Little prayer, little power; no prayer, no power.'"

As Brother Ningkun prayed for a spirit of watchfulness and prayerfulness, it seemed that a divine presence filled the room. He prayed for boldness, for those imprisoned for their testimony, for other needs of the church.

Stefanie wondered whether she would have the dedication of these people to sit week after week on a floor, to look over her shoulder constantly, to fear the next knock on the door, to dread the sight of a policeman. Would she risk her future, her career, her family for Jesus as these people did? For the first time in days her thoughts turned from her own situation to her relationship with God. She had become so busy. Had she left the Lord out of her busyness?

Hardigan dropped the phone in disgust. He paced his hotel room swinging one fist against his other palm. *Where is she?*

He tried calling again. This time Edda answered. "No, Stefanie is gone for hours. To church, I think."

Church—he glanced at the clock. He had missed church. He rubbed his red beard stubble. After getting in around two, he had forgotten it was Sunday. "Fraulein Ansgar, have her call me. She left a message for me yesterday, but I did not get back in time to call her."

He was about to hang up, but she said, "You must know. Yesterday, Stefanie spread her things around the room."

"That's not like Stefanie. You're sure it was her?"

"She left a note. She must go to the embassy. If you call, she said she would reach you as soon as she could." Edda's voice lowered, "I am afraid for her."

He was too, but what could he do until he heard from her? He called for breakfast to be delivered. While waiting, he booted up his computer to check his e-mail. At the number of messages logged, he frowned. He scrolled past three business notes.

Two notes from Stefanie! He had discovered that her computer now worked properly with the telephone line. He suspected that Kong had arranged for her inability to e-mail to further isolate her and make her more vulnerable. He had warned her not to send out anything through the university phone lines that she would not want the government to read. Troy quickly opened the first file.

> Troy, I'm sorry I upset you last night. I can't tell you how thankful I am you are here. I became afraid that I was enjoying your comfort too much. Whatever the Lord may have for us, we have to do it His way.

I love you, babe, and you love me too. You're just afraid to admit it.

He opened her second message. Her passport and papers were missing. She was going to the embassy for replacement documents and would call as soon as she could.

Kong doesn't want her to be able to leave the country.

The next message caught his eye. The subject line read "Peng." He didn't recognize the sender's address. He clicked on the message. Blank, but there was an attachment. He clicked on the attachment and struggled through the Chinese characters.

It starts with a note. Somebody's boyfriend is in Beijing.

Below that was an extensive report about Peng Chongde, Stefanie's grandfather. It made no sense at first, and he was not very good at written Chinese characters, but he had a bad feeling that they all meant danger.

Stef must have sent it. Where did she get it? Sent from another computer. No explanation. She must have been in a hurry. *Oh, Stef, don't play spy on me.*

He opened the next file, with the subject line "Frontiers." No message, but an attachment.

His hands were trembling as he clicked on the icon.

Kong Qili enjoyed coffee first thing in the morning, a habit he had picked up in the West. This morning he sipped without tasting, his mind absorbed. Vice-minister Chang had gotten him out of bed to demand to know whether he had found the Brother. The man acted half frantic. Police in Shanghai had no knowledge of Peng Chongde and Ren Shaoqi, although their papers required them to report. Obviously they knew he was after them. It was awkward, but he would pick up Peng Chongde at least in Beijing. He would come for the girl. He had never properly read Chen's work on Chongde. He seated himself at the computer, but before he could turn it on, the phone rang.

"*Ni hao.* Kong."

"*Ni hao,* Mr. Kong. This is Tzu. We finally have Du Guangmei's cell phone calls, including one she made on board the airplane. I thought you would find this interesting. She made a call to Chicago to a cell phone licensed to Troy Hardigan."

"Hardigan?"

"There is something else. We cross-checked that name in our databases. Hardigan was in Beijing representing Frontiers Technology at about the time our stolen *East-is-Red* solid-fuel missile plans reached the West."

Hardigan? No one had suspected an American. Two generals, an industrialist, and Kong's mentor in Public Security had been tried for treason, and now he learned that the government had brought Hardigan in as a Frontiers representative to consult about some of the software. They had told Frontiers only that the communications software had been compromised. They had been subtle, because Frontiers could not know that their technology had been adapted for a military application.

So now it seems the Americans were the subtle ones. Perhaps China had invited in the very agent who could most easily smuggle the material out of the country. And a few months later, Frontiers and other companies around the world were publicly embarrassing the Chinese by exposing their technology deceptions.

And the mole may still be out there, still betraying China. If so, Hardigan may know who it is.

"Find out which military personnel had contact with Hardigan. But, Tzu, have our people be careful."

After hanging up, Kong drummed his fingers on his desk. *Hardigan!* He glanced at the file cabinet in the corner. *So, Stefanie, your boyfriend is CIA. What is he saying to you? Or are you both agents and this is an elaborate ruse?*

He unlocked and searched the file cabinets for the envelope with Stefanie's documents and articles. It wasn't there.

Chen must have taken it with her.

He returned to the computer to review Peng Chongde's file. The sooner he finished with this cult business, the sooner he could deal with Hardigan and the rest of the tangle—and he would do so as an assistant minister.

The computer would not boot. No operating system recognized. He turned it off and tried again. He checked to see that the connections were tight. Still the machine would not boot.

He reached for the phone. When Chen Yuliang answered, he demanded, "What did you do to my computer?"

"Mr. Kong?" Her voice sleepy, she paused before speaking.

"Yes, this is Kong."

"It was fine last night. I left the file you wanted open on the desktop. Did you see my message?"

A chill ran through him. "You left the computer on and the file open?" He tried to calm himself. "Chen, never leave information unsecured. Get over here immediately."

"But—"

"*Never.* The computer was off when I came in, and the hard drive has been reformatted. We do not know who has that information now, and we don't have it."

"So you did not get my message?"

"What message?"

"Stefanie's boyfriend is in Beijing."

"Hardigan is here?" He paused, thinking. "Get over here. We must pull the whole investigation together today." He hung up.

Stefanie first. He would need no help with Stefanie. He would take her himself.

Kong went to his bedroom. Pulling his nine-millimeter Makarov from under his pillow, he checked its loads and dropped an extra magazine in his jacket pocket. Though he thought it superfluous, it would not hurt to be prepared in case Hardigan was with the little hypocrite. He donned his shoulder holster, holstered the Makarov, covered it with a sports jacket, and left the apartment. He jogged the two flights of stairs and strode to her door.

He could hear no movement, but the blare of the Lawrences' TV next door covered any quieter sounds.

He knocked twice before unlocking Stefanie's door with a master key. A pair of pink, footed pajamas with a cartoon rabbit on the front lay on the edge of the bed. Only one side of the bed was mussed, so Hardigan had not spent the night with her.

"Ha! What do you do in my room?"

Kong pulled the gun as he whirled.

Edda Ansgar stood in the bedroom doorway, clutching a quilted blue robe to her throat. The off-white electric curlers in her short hair made her white skin look ghostly, but her pale blue eyes snapped.

"Where is she?"

Her chin tipped up. "Who?"

Kong ground his teeth. "The girl. Who else would I look for here?"

"I thought in church with you on Sunday mornings."

Kong turned back. He opened the closet and pawed through the clothes, Edda's dark and businesslike, Stefanie's bright and varied. If she had taken anything, it wasn't much.

He strode to the dresser and opened the top drawer. Edda was becoming angry, switching from German to Mandarin and back freely to do justice to her feelings.

"What you do? My *Privatleben*." She snatched a pair of white panties from Kong's grasp. "You have no right to search my things."

He holstered his gun and opened the second and third drawers while Ansgar gabbled at him meaninglessly. The third and fourth drawers were Stefanie's, the colorful panties, lacy brassieres, and neatly folded sweaters told him. The drawers, like the closet, indicated that Stefanie had not left permanently.

As he straightened, Ansgar slammed the drawers closed. Unable to express herself adequately, she lapsed into outraged silence as she followed him to the main room.

Stefanie's laptop computer sat behind the table where she kept it when not in use. She would be back.

He stalked to the door. In the doorway he turned. "If you wish to remain a guest of China, you will say nothing to her of this. Call me at once when she arrives."

He closed the door on the woman's icy glare. Kong crossed the hall to knock on the door across from Stefanie's. Qian let him in.

Four men sat around the small apartment watching TV. A fifth worked in headphones at a table. "Where is the girl?" Kong demanded.

The four exchanged guilty glances. Qian licked his lips before admitting, "We lost her at the Beijing Department Store."

A smaller man with buck teeth said, "She went into the restroom, but neither of us saw her come out. After twenty-five minutes we sent a plainclotheswoman in with her description, but she was gone."

Imbeciles! They had lost her at the worst possible moment. Kong glared from one to the next. Gradually the muscles in his jaw relaxed. They were not without means of finding her. He instructed the smaller man to prepare descriptions of Stefanie, Peng Chongde, and Troy Hardigan. "Cover the United States Embassy quickly. Do not allow them inside the embassy. Chen should be at my apartment in a few minutes. Get pictures of the girl and old man from her."

The slender young man with the headphones snapped his pencil in half and threw it onto the table. Kong demanded, "What is wrong?"

"She had a guest Friday night—this Hardigan. They talked a long time, but I cannot understand what they said."

Kong took the headphones. He listened to the recording. He frowned and replayed the few sentences. He passed the earphones back. "Get someone in here who speaks Spanish. The girl's mother speaks Spanish. She must know it too."

The agent with the buck teeth set down the phone. "We will not get anyone for a few hours."

"Why?"

"All extra men are raiding a half dozen suspected house churches this morning."

Kong swore. He turned to the three men sitting by the television, "Do something for a change. Get down to the United States Embassy. And look for someone who has changed appearance. Do not let her or the red-haired ape pass you."

Stefanie listened to the whispered words of a hymn about being faithful to Christ, even to the point of death. Through the open doorway, she watched the rapt faces of the elderly people. Tears slid down one woman's face. Bo Qin's eyes were closed, her hands folded as if in prayer, pressed to her chest. Several children smiled toward heaven as they sang.

Except for singing "Faith of our Fathers" a couple times a year, Stefanie had thought little of martyrdom. She had always thought she loved the Lord, but how often had He been at the center of her goals?

Yet, in spite of facing arrest, loss of jobs, perhaps torture and imprison-ment, these people met faithfully to worship and pray. She wondered if she could keep up that type of commitment. *Do I really love the Lord that much?*

Looking at the people here, some of them in shabby clothes, made her doubt herself in an uncomfortable way.

The graying man who had opened the door read from a slip of paper Mat-thew 6:33 and 34, in which Jesus admonishes his disciples to seek the kingdom of heaven and righteousness first. The preacher's simple message forced Ste-fanie to reevaluate herself and her goals as nothing had ever done. Suddenly a cell phone rang. The painter in the wheelchair answered immediately.

Stefanie stared at him in surprise.

He turned his wheelchair and tugged at the window. A teenaged boy jumped up to help. The preacher opened the stove and tossed the verse of scripture onto the coals. A middle-aged woman set a canvas on the easel near the wheel-chair. She squeezed paint onto the palette and daubed the paintbrush into it.

Then Stefanie heard cars screeching up to the building. In seconds, some-one was pounding on a door farther down the courtyard. By now, the children had scampered out the window and disappeared, followed by parents. The teenagers squeezed through next.

Qin grabbed Stefanie's hand.

"What about them?" Stefanie asked, nodding toward the older people who would be unable to run.

"Pray for them. Go." The wheelchair-bound artist whispered.

Qin squeezed through.

Someone pounded on the door of the apartment.

Stefanie and three others crawled through the window. The elderly woman who had asked about her grandfather sat posing for a portrait as the young artist added to what was already done.

Glancing back, she saw two middle-aged women close the window and draw the faded curtain.

Qin pulled Stefanie after her. The five women darted across in a low, crouch-ing run that seemed amazingly agile and would not show anything to some-one looking out the back windows. Another courtyard opened from the alley. One of the women peeked through a crack in the doorway before entering. The others in the courtyard ignored them. The one who had opened the door led them through the courtyard, into another tiny apartment, past a trio eat-ing their lunch in the front room without speaking, to the back room.

After giving them quick instructions, she whispered, "God bless you."

Qin shoved the single window open. The four women climbed through. They found a gate in a fence and passed through another courtyard.

"Police," Bo Qin whispered.

Two policemen were questioning hungry-looking artisans who shifted around to avoid the assault of the wind-driven sand and sleet. Other police had fanned out and were pounding on neighborhood doors.

Without a word, the other women separated from Qin and Stefanie.

Stefanie tried to calm her pounding heart. "We should go to the bus stop. If we act normally, just talk, they will think they have already talked to us."

One of the Christian women rode a red Flying Pigeon bicycle past them. Another woman joined the crowd around two policemen. Beyond them police herded other residents from the courtyards and buildings into the frigid wind.

Stefanie turtled her head into her coat, wishing she could make herself invisible.

A bus pulled in at the stop ahead. Only four people waited.

"Walk faster." She hoped speeding up would not attract attention. She glanced over her shoulder. That was her mistake. A policeman looked up and noticed the fearful glance.

The last man at the bus stop stepped onto the bottom step of the bus.

The policeman yelled, "You women, stop!" He reached for his gun.

Stefanie grabbed Qin's arm. "Run!"

At a glance over her shoulder, Stefanie saw the policemen shoving through the crowd. One had a gun in his outstretched hand. The gun cracked—somehow she expected it to be louder. She heard the bullet ping off of a rock.

Ahead the bus pulled out. Stefanie threw herself forward.

The police were running now instead of shooting.

Stefanie grabbed a wad of bills from her purse and waved them by the bus door.

The driver, a cigarette hanging limp in his mouth, cracked the door. "Why should I stop if you cannot be on time?"

Stefanie waved the bills through the door. As the door opened, she shoved Qin in. She jumped on the bottom step.

The driver reached for the bills.

"Go!" Stefanie said.

He glanced out at the police, put the bus in gear, and reached for the money.

She shoved it into his hand. She started back into the bus. The driver growled, "You did not pay your fares." He pointed at the fare box.

Returning, Stefanie paid the fares.

She found a seat near the back of the bus beside a middle-aged man who ignored her. Once she was seated, she started to tremble.

Chapter 36

STEFANIE HID HERSELF among a crowd of people entering an elevator at the Friendship Hotel. Crushed between a heavy blond woman doused in costly perfume and an expensively dressed Japanese businessman, she welcomed the invisibility they afforded her.

She and Qin had separated on the bus. Stefanie had switched buses several times. Getting off near Tiananmen Square, she had entered a restaurant's restroom, unpinned her hair, changed back into her skirt, and reversed her coat. After freshening her appearance, she had taken a cab to Troy's hotel.

She exited the elevator on the ninth floor and walked the last two flights of stairs to Troy's floor. At every sound on the stairs, she stopped, afraid that the police or government agents had followed her. But it was only a sweat-dampened man coming back from a workout, and then two giggling maids who smelled of furniture polish. Three Japanese men near the door to the stairs gave Stefanie a start, but they seemed only to be waiting for one of their party to join them.

She hesitated in front of room 1127. Her proper Chinese upbringing was kicking in. What would Nanai say about going to a man's hotel room? A large shape filled the corner of her field of vision and she almost bounced off a big, blocky Chinese man carrying a laptop. Her face growing hot, she apologized in Chinese.

"You must be Red's girl," he responded in New Jersey-accented English. "Didn't he hear you knock?"

He reached over her shoulder and pounded on the door. After a few seconds it opened and the doorway filled with Troy's broad shoulders, smells of soap, shampoo, and shaving cream mingling in his vicinity. After all the fears and dangers of recent days, she wanted to run into the arms of this vision of homey comfort in jeans and athletic undershirt.

"Stef, do you know how worried I've been?"

The big Chinese man with the New Jersey accent guided her into the room with a shovel-sized hand on her back. "Something's up, Red. Police are stopping anyone going into the embassy. We have to get those files sent ASAP."

Troy closed the door, locked it, and turned to study her. "Go ahead and set up, Chou. You're as pale as paper, babe."

The softness of his voice made her throat ache with unshed tears. She wobbled and steadied herself on the back of a chair. At the sound of a siren, she whirled. She ran between the twin beds and pulled the curtain out to peek through the window. A police car screamed past. She leaned against the window frame, her legs unsteady. Troy looked out over her shoulder while the man he called Chou opened the laptop and began assembling what looked like a small satellite dish.

"They're gone," she whispered.

"Cops after you?" asked Chou.

She didn't answer but eyed the Chinese man.

"It's all right. Chou's the head of embassy security. You might remember Ramón talking to me about Ulysses Chou."

"The 'Big Chew'?" Stefanie asked without thinking.

"I've been called that by folks without a proper upbringing," he said with an exaggerated nod toward Troy. "I prefer the name *Ulysses*. It's classier. Say, Red, if I'd known you were robbing cradles, I'd've never taken you home around my girls."

Troy ignored the jab. "What happened with the police?"

"They shot at us, but I switched buses and . . ."

"Whoa, whoa—slow down until we get this all sorted out." Troy pulled her around to face him. He gently squeezed her upper arms, leaned forward, and stared into her eyes. "Who shot at you?"

"The police—at Qin and me."

"And they were shooting at Qin and you because . . . ?" he said slowly, his face reddening, his blue-gray eyes glinting.

"We were running away to catch the bus."

"It's legal to catch a bus in China."

"I mean we got around behind them, and we thought if we reached the bus, we'd be safe."

Troy's fiery eyebrows drew together. "Hold it. It looks like we'll have to fill in the details later. Let's get to basics. Are they after you at this moment? Do they know who they were chasing and did they follow you here?"

"No, you see—"

He touched a broad index finger to her lips.

"Next question: When did you eat last?"

As she tried to remember, her eyes focused on his undershirt. Coarse red hair curled above the neckline, which swelled over his muscular chest. Here and there a red hair stuck through the shirt's weave. She was having trouble concentrating on the question, so she redirected her gaze to the laptop that was set up on the desk. *He must have been working on his computer.*

"Let's simplify the question: Did you eat breakfast?"

She shook her head.

"Anything to eat last night?"

"It doesn't matter, Troy. You have to leave China. Qili has information about you."

"We'll get to that. Let's get you something to eat before you shatter into little pieces."

"Is she talking about the Tiger, Red?" Chou straightened from plugging his modem into the transmitter.

"Yeah." Troy put a hand on Stefanie's back. "You did e-mail those files?"

She nodded, then shook her head. "They're Qili's. I didn't understand them, but they scared me."

"She e-mailed them from Kong's own computer?" Chou whistled. "Not bad, except that will give him a trace."

"I didn't think about that, but there wasn't time to do anything else. I did reformat the hard drive."

"Hey, lady, I'm not criticizing. Sounds like you done good, all things considered." Chou opened a window and began positioning the transmitter toward the Embassy.

Troy was staring at her. "Stef, I know I'm going to be sorry I asked, but how did you get those files from Kong's computer?" His jaw tightened as she described her visit to Kong's apartment and her escape while he was on the phone.

Riffling his hair, Troy stalked across the room and back toward her. "Do you know how close you were to death?"

"Don't be angry." She pleaded, placing a hand on his shirt. "I wanted to confront him about the bugs."

"Bugs?" Chou said, still fiddling with the transmitter. "Unless we are talking about a roach infestation, you'd better give me a full debriefing, Red."

"And I'd better get back to my apartment," Stefanie said. "I don't want to leave my computer alone."

"We'll talk about that after you've eaten." Troy picked up the phone to place an order for room service.

"You don't have those files on your computer?" Chou asked her.

"No, I sent them to Troy."

"Good girl."

"But I do have something." She took off her coat, tore open the lining at the hem, and passed to Troy the floppy disks and film that she had taken from the manila envelope. He tossed them to Chou. She fumbled through the big purse for the videotape. She dug several safety pins from a pocket in her purse to repair her coat until she could sew it. Chou inserted the videotape into the television's tape player.

The picture on the screen looked familiar, but it wasn't until her grandfather entered the scene that she recognized the prison waiting room. "That's my grandfather. Why would Qili tape my meeting with him?"

The two men exchanged glances. "Stef." Troy cracked his knuckles. "This has been a set-up by Kong from the first contact. He doesn't work in education. He's with the Public Security Bureau."

"Police?"

"An agent, a spy for the Chinese government."

Stefanie tore her eyes from her grandfather's image. "I don't understand. Why does he care about *me?*"

"That's a good question, and I'm not sure of all of the answer yet. As best I can figure, you and your grandfather are both means to at least one end— or maybe two. For one thing, your grandfather may know the identity of a Christian leader that the government seems to be obsessed with catching. Kong seems to want to make you a hostage to extort information from Chongde."

She rubbed her forehead. "Would they go to all this trouble just to catch Christians?"

"It is a puzzlement," Chou admitted. "This guy must've really ticked them off. Kong is a specialist at tracking down people who are trying to stay out of sight. But mainly he's been involved in stealing Western research, industrial espionage. He seems on track to be a big player in international espionage. He usually works outside the country. He's set up as a Chinese businessman to buy foreign technology."

"That's why he was at Frontiers that day."

"I hear you got popped in the head that day," Chou said, looking up from his work on the computer. "My money would be that Kong was at least in the room and may have been the one who hit you."

"At least he wears the same aftershave as the man who hit me. . . . So he connected me with Frontiers from the start, then?"

"I'm not sure whether he knows you were the girl who interrupted their safe-cracking gig, but he definitely knows you're the kid of laser researcher Andrew Peng. If Kong is involved, this goes way past hunting miscreant Christians," Chou opined.

"I've been acquainted with Kong the businessman for a few years," Troy explained. "We also knew that someone was trying to infiltrate and access Frontiers' satellite technology. He was my best guess, but we didn't begin to put it all together until you told me the name of your teaching supervisor. I don't think anyone here figured you could connect teacher Kong with technology-buyer Kong."

Stefanie stared thoughtfully at Troy before speaking.

"Sometime you are going to have to tell me how a salesman gets to know so much about international espionage. For now I will assume that goes with the nature of what you sell. But I suspect that you, Mr. Chou, have a portfolio that extends beyond embassy security. I don't even want to add that information to the soup just now. I do want to make sure I understand that from the moment I arrived, Qili intended to arrest me so he could pressure Grandfather.

"That's our best guess. He probably also intended to use you to put the arm on your father and maybe Dr. Zinsser, assuming he knew how close the two of you were."

"Just what did he intend to do to me?"

Troy didn't answer. Chou did: "I suspect he wanted to give your grandpa a front row seat while he gave you a few caresses from an electric baton. That would make the old man spill his guts."

She turned to Troy with her eyebrows raised. "Qili would torture me?"

"Without giving it a thought," Chou responded. "You gotta understand that people like him usually don't get their jollies from it, though I suppose some might. The good ones divorce themselves from any emotion. Torture is an efficient way to fulfill an assignment. Civilizin' virtues ain't particularly high among qualifications for his job."

"He's been out of Beijing." Her face paled. "Do you think he's the one who attacked Dr. Jim?"

Troy squatted beside her chair and took her hand from her lap.

"No, babe, he wasn't stateside. We saw him in Hong Kong."

At a knock on the door, all three jumped and stared. Chou darted across to grab the transmitter. Troy checked the peek hole. "Room service. Get her into the escape hatch. If they see her in here, they could use it as an excuse for a prostitution raid."

Troy pulled her to her feet, grabbed her coat and purse, and unlocked the door linking his room to the next. He shoved her in and closed the door. She stared at the door.

The room was the reverse of Troy's. A single brown suitcase lay on one of the beds. Stefanie looked around, wondering how she would describe her presence to the room's owner. Trying to settle her whirling thoughts, she settled into a chair to wait. In less than a minute, Troy opened the door connecting the rooms. His blue-gray eyes sobered. He closed the door, leaned against it. He was not meeting her eyes again. "Before we go back in, did you check your e-mail this morning?"

She shook her head. Her breath caught. "Nanai?" She rose, holding her hand out to him.

"She's fine. Her blood pressure is coming back up."

"Dr. Jim."

He nodded, his eyes closed. "During the night. Your father was with him. I'm sorry, honey."

There's some mistake. Not Dr. Jim and his big buoyant voice, his contagious laughter. The tears seemed stuck in her throat. Troy encircled her shoulders with his arm; his familiar aftershave smell and touch was comforting.

"When I was a little girl, we went to see Dr. Jim in Boston. I was frightened by the tunnels. The car would burst into the open air, but before you could enjoy it, you were in another tunnel."

A tear slid down her cheek as she sat down again. "When we were out, the sky seemed bright and wonderful. Dr. Jim said we would know true happiness only when we burst through the last of the tunnels into heaven to see the Son shining bright before us. Happiness now is the sunshine between the tunnels, little reflections of that final happiness."

The sobs shook her with her memories of the huge, gentle bear of a man. Troy held her until she could control herself. He patted her cheeks with his handkerchief and placed it in her hands. She blew her nose.

His eyes wet with compassion, Troy brushed a strand of her hair back from her damp cheek. His massive hands were incredibly gentle. She gazed into his eyes to read his heart. Troy bent toward her. "Stef, I. . . ."

The door swung open. "You two going to eat or let the food freeze here?" Chou demanded.

Stefanie jerked back, her face burning at Ulysses Chou's grin.

"Just give us a minute," Troy said.

Chou did not eat anything, but he shot questions at Stefanie and Troy while they ate. Tempted by the wafting aroma, Stefanie dug into the sweet and sour pork, *moo goo gai pan*, and egg's nest soup. Hardigan had never known anyone else who could just forget about eating, as Stefanie evidently had over the last day.

While they ate, he filled Chou in on the satellite password thefts, and they considered possible reasons for the systematic attempts to control communications satellites. Then he turned to Stefanie, who was slumped back in the armchair, her eyes closed, occasionally chewing on a bite of the roll in her hand.

"How are you doing?"

She opened her eyes, blinked, and squinted at him. "I guess it's all catching up."

He reached across the table and squeezed her hand.

"Do you feel like telling me what happened this morning? Why were the police shooting at you?" He pressed a finger to her wrist. Her pulse dragged.

"Qin took me to a house church. I lost my tail at the department store by changing clothes in the restroom and leaving with a bunch of women to meet Qin."

Chou grinned. "This girl is good. We should recruit her."

Stefanie didn't catch Chou's comment. Her head drooped forward. She lifted it as if she carried a load of bricks on her neck.

"What happened after you met Qin?" Troy asked.

"Took buses. Went 'ouse chur'. . . ." Her eyes closed again.

Hardigan went around the table to kneel on the carpet by her chair. He gently shook her shoulders. "Stef, what happened at the house church?"

Her eyes snapped open. "So tired. Sorry. We went out the window when they raided us, got behind them. Uhhh, bus coming. They saw us. We ran." Her eyes were closing again.

"Is that when they shot at you?"

No answer. Stefanie had slumped against him.

"Poor kid's really beat."

A band of anger strapped Troy's chest. If Stefanie weren't passed out in his arms, he would have grabbed Chou by the throat. "What did you put in her food?"

"Just a little lights-out juice to keep her out of the way until we figure how to get her out of the country."

"I ought to knock you out the window."

"Yeah, you could do that, or you could act like a professional instead of a love-sick schoolboy."

"The knock-out drops weren't necessary."

"You been listening to this girl? Everything she does is unpredictable. She must be driving Kong past crazy. That's fine, but she will have us hanging from a couple of meat hooks if we can't control her."

Troy glared at Chou as he stood up and scooped Stefanie into his arms. Hoisting her feather-light frame, he carried her into the other room and set her down gently on the far bed. He pulled her boots off before tucking her under the covers. Against the white sheets, her blue-black hair floated and her face was a deathly pale. He brushed her hair back and kissed her forehead lightly. "It's going to be okay, babe."

Chou was already back at his computer when Troy returned to the room. "I think we are ready to transmit this stuff."

"Fine," Troy snapped.

"Red," Chou said, "don't let your feelings get in the way. Stefanie needs you to keep your head, and so do I."

Chapter 37

Ren Shaoqi climbed stiffly from the train, then stopped in mid-turn instead of helping Peng Chongde down.

Two green military trucks with their beds covered by tarps sat by the train. A half dozen police spread out from them toward the train passengers.

"What is it, Shaoqi?" Chongde asked.

Shaoqi completed his turn to steady the old man. "I think maybe someone has noticed that you are not going to Shanghai. This way, Uncle."

The old man seemed weaker after three long days of train travel. A thin beard was starting low on his chin. He massaged his twisted fingers absent-mindedly. As Shaoqi shouldered him away from the soldiers, who disappeared from view in the crowd, he walked stiffly, leaning on the younger man. Both men smelled of travel in their single set of clothes.

"This is the wrong way. They will look for someone who is running away. Let us sit here and eat what we bought last night." Chongde pointed at a con-crete bench.

Shaoqi tugged his arm. "You do not understand. Kong never meant for us to be free." The old man's silver eyebrows raised, and a smile tugged at the corners of his mouth. *I said too much.* Chongde seated himself on the bench and opened the cloth sack holding his few belongings.

Shaoqi looked around for a path of escape. The government was adept at this kind of search. Those in the crowd who wanted to avoid the police behind them ran into the arms of other police they had not seen.

Shaoqi sat down. The cold from the stone seeped through his pants. "If we are going to be taken in, we might as well have full stomachs."

Chongde thanked God for the food, then handed three hard buns to Shaoqi. The old man tore off a small chunk of his roll. With only a few teeth left, his eating looked as painful as it was slow. He drank from his flask of warm water, then placed a piece of roll in his mouth, allowing it to soak up enough water to become soft enough to chew.

Shaoqi turned away. Watching Chongde made his teeth hurt. He finished his three coarse rolls without tasting them before Chongde had eaten his one. When the old man handed him a bag of peanuts from the knapsack, he cracked the peanuts one by one and watched the police.

The officers were carrying a paper. They would look at someone, then study the picture.

"Let me see your papers," one snapped to a man about Ren Shaoqi's age.

The man stared down at the platform as he handed them over. His eyes darted one direction, then another.

The one policeman called another over. Together they studied the paper and whispered back and forth. Finally they let the man go, and in his backbone Shaoqi felt the young man's relief.

As Shaoqi stood, Chongde said, "Relax, my friend. If they want us, let them look for us."

The old man ground peanuts with a rock on his tin plate. Fearing that the rattle of the peanuts and rock against the tin would draw attention, Shaoqi gritted his teeth.

Sweating with fear, Shaoqi leaned closer. "Just because you have survived forty years in the *laogai* does not mean I want to."

The old man looked up. "My little granddaughter needs me. Please do not destroy my opportunity to reach her by drawing attention to yourself." The old man clawed the pieces of peanut from his plate into his right hand.

Shaoqi sat down and squared his shoulders.

Chongde licked the remaining peanut crumbs from his hand.

"Let me tell you a story about Elisha, the prophet of God. He warned the king of Israel several times that the king of Syria was planning to ambush his soldiers. God told him their plans. The Syrians tried to find out who was betraying them, and their spies heard about Elisha. So this king sent a force of soldiers into Israel to the city where Elisha lived."

A policeman passed, his pants brushing Shaoqi's knee. The young policeman stopped an elderly man with a young man. Chongde was grinding peanuts again. "One morning, Elisha and his servant awoke to see many soldiers waiting outside the city. The servant was afraid, but Elisha prayed that God would show the servant what was really happening."

Peng Chongde scraped the peanut crumbs into his hands.

Two policemen walked by with a wanted poster. Though Shaoqi recognized his own picture and Chongde's, neither policeman glanced in their direction.

"What happened?"

"The servant suddenly saw that the city was also surrounded by God's chariots, pulled by horses of fire. Elisha prayed that the Syrian army would be struck blind." The old man stopped in the middle of the story as if he had forgotten he was telling it. Three policemen next to the train compared their pictures and talked softly. Shaoqi looked at the bag of peanuts in his hand so that they would not see him staring.

"I do not see any flaming chariots, but it is a good story."

Peng Chongde interrupted his peanut mashing to smile his two-toothed smile. "It is a good story because it really happened."

When Shaoqi glanced up, the police were scattering. *They must be flanking us.* But as he watched, one entered the train, another stopped an elderly man and woman, and the third sauntered to the other side of the tracks.

"What happened to the soldiers?"

"They became blind. Elisha led them to their enemy, the king of Israel. Then they regained their sight, only to see that they were helpless, surrounded by soldiers who were eager to kill them."

Two policemen trotted from the train. One waved at the conductor. The train whistle drowned out Peng Chongde's mashing of peanuts. With the black smoke belching from the smoke stack and the couplings clanging, the cars inched forward.

Ahead of the straining locomotive, a police truck disappeared across the tracks. Moments later, gray exhaust swirled out of the other truck.

With the train gone, Shaoqi bent his head against the grit-filled wind that swept at them. The houses on the other side of the tracks were too low and far away to block the storm. "So the king killed the Syrian soldiers?"

"He wanted to, but Elisha commanded him to feed them and send them home."

"That was stupid! I could not have let my enemy go."

"If you hate him so, why do you work for him?"

Shaoqi stared at him. He meant to deny the accusation, but the sharp, old eyes knew. He dropped his gaze.

He could not deny it. He stared at his scarred, callused hands, their knuckles big from hard work. Then he noticed the twisted fingers of Peng Chongde fumbling his plate into his bag. From the time Qili had approached him, Shaoqi had been battling this decision. He sighed.

"Do you remember when Jun was shot, there were rumors that someone else was supposed to supply the kidneys for the general?"

Old Peng nodded.

"I was the one. Kong offered me life, but I turned him down. They took me out to shoot with the others."

He told of the terror of the execution, of being knocked out, of awaking in the darkness unsure of whether he was dead or alive. The sand had scoured his skin, and he'd been unsure whether it was blood or tears that moistened his face.

"Qili gave me another chance. It was the only way I could live long enough to kill him. I did not know Jun."

The old man did not answer. Shaoqi wanted him to understand why he had to kill Qili, how Qili had destroyed him, why he deserved to die. "We had been best friends. We grew up together, but we always competed. The night before the exams for college, my father, who was a policeman, was beaten. My mother, sister, and I spent two days at his side before he died without regaining consciousness.

"Because I missed the exams, I could not go to college. I found a job to help my family. I bought a motorbike, and during the student protests, I became one of the leaders of the Flying Tigers. Qili recognized me and turned my name in. I fled, but he followed. I was a few *li* from the Indian border when he caught me. To show his contempt, he laid his gun aside. We fought. He beat me, but I marked him with that scar on his chin.

"He bragged that he had hired the gang who beat my father with an iron pipe to keep me from taking the exams. He told me that he'd found me by becoming my sister's lover. He has used her all these years. Now tell me . . . TELL ME . . . why I should let my enemy go."

"Because God knows what Kong is, and He will judge. Kong will suffer for his sin. I do not know him, but I would help him avoid what he faces if I could. But I cannot help him." The old man held his twisted fingers out between them. The old eyes carried an ageless wisdom. "So I will try to help you. Kong is not hurt by your hatred. You are locked behind its thick walls. While it rules your spirit, you will never be free."

The train platform was now deserted. Chongde rose slowly to his feet. Turning his back to the wind, he levered his spine straight with an arthritic hand.

He picked up his satchel. "If they are meeting in the place I knew long ago, we have a long walk." He tucked his head to follow the wind and sand eastward.

Shaoqi caught up with him. "You need to know Kong's scheme."

"Kong wants to use little Dehong to force me to betray the Lord and the church."

"How did you know?"

The old man shrugged. "What else could it be? What other influence do I have? Mr. Kong does not understand that he wastes his time. He does not see that I have been in prison too long to have any influence or know anything that would help him."

Shaoqi turned his back to the driving wind. He walked sideways to shelter his face and his companion. "He thinks you can give him the identity of one called the Brother, his headquarters, and a means to betray him."

Peng paused mid-stride. "He was foolish. I am sure he knows far more about the man than I do. Although I would tell him if he but asked that there is no 'headquarters' to find." He stooped to pick up a staff-sized limb that he could use as a walking stick. He said nothing more.

They walked a long time in the scouring wind. Sometimes houses broke its driving force or bounced the sand at them from another direction. Farther into town, walled courtyards sheltered them.

Shaoqi paused. The wind almost sounded to his ears like a song. He couldn't help stopping to listen, then he plodded after Chongde, who had not slackened his pace. Grasping his companion's arm at last, he stopped the older man. "I have to know, Uncle. Why did the police not see us?"

"I do not know."

"Did your God blind their eyes?"

Peng Chongde stared toward the singing. "What do you think?" he asked. When Shaoqi did not answer, he started off again.

Shaoqi ran after him. He walked backward in front of Chongde. "Just tell me? Why do I have to dig everything out of you?"

Chongde surprised him by stopping. He spoke gently, as to a child. "I think you know already many of the things you dig for."

Shaoqi stopped to consider that, and Chongde stepped around him.

The old man suddenly turned into the gate of an old warehouse. As a police van drove by, Shaoqi hung back, then followed. He was amazed to see that many people crowded into the building. He grasped Chongde's arm. "Uncle, if you want to see little Dehong, we cannot go in here. The police are watching."

"It is all right. The police have watched for years, but some of the policemen and the village cadre have many family members who are believers." The old man smiled. "Arresting most of the village would look very bad on the cadre's record."

They went to the rear of the large group, and a girl who wore a scarf offered Chongde the wooden bucket on which she had been sitting. A man in a clear baritone voice was at the front, talking of things for which they should ask God's help. Shaoqi could hardly believe that the man spoke openly of needs for prayer: the need for Bibles, some who were sick, their witness to their neighbors, brothers and sisters in prison, God's supply for the needy, the protection of Brother Peng Chongde's granddaughter, the country's leaders. . . .

Shaoqi lost the rest of the list. He stared at Chongde, who sat motionless, his eyes fastened on the speaker, nodding, his lips moving in thanks. *How do they know old Chongde's need?*

The prayers went on for some time. Some knelt, while others stood or sat. Some prayed silently; others murmured softly. Their arms intertwined in sorrow, an elderly woman and a young one wept. A blanket of peace nestled over everyone but him. He was different than they. Even in their sorrow, they had peace. Since Chu Zhurun's death, Shaoqi had been unable to sleep without nightmares. He longed for their peace.

They sang another song and then a man stood up and spoke with a deep, authoritative voice about God's love. "Not only did God tell us what love does, He showed us. God loved us so much that He gave His only Son to die for us. For you who are parents, think what price you would put on your only son."

Qili had stolen Shaoqi's hope for a family, but every Chinese man harbored a burning desire for a son. If the Christian God loved His Son as the Chinese did, how could He let Him die? Surely He would have blinded the eyes of those who were trying to kill Jesus as He had blinded the men sent for His prophet.

One mother seated on a bucket pulled a small boy onto her lap. Shaoqi could understand her. He could not understand her God.

"Then the Son, our Lord and Savior Jesus Christ, carried our sins, our shame, our guilt to the cross and paid for it so we could be forgiven. Many of us learned about Lei Feng when we were growing up. We were told that this young soldier loved Mao Zedong and his brother soldiers so much that he constantly served them by washing their socks and cooking for them. Then he died for his friends. But the Bible says that Jesus died for us while we were His enemies. We were not His friends."

Shaoqi immediately thought of Qili, his enemy. How could he be an enemy of God as Qili was to him? He squirmed at the thought that he had agreed to betray Chongde, his granddaughter, and the one called the Brother. God might consider that enemy work. He thought of the retarded boy, Jun, who had died in his place.

"How do we love God? He is in heaven; we are on earth. We cannot tuck Him into bed as we do our children. He does not sleep. We cannot buy Him something pretty as we might our wife. He owns all things. We cannot sit with Him when He is sick. He is the Great Physician.

"How do we show God our love? He tells us. If we love Him, we will keep His commandments. He does not give us choices of how to show our love. He tells us, 'Keep my commandments.'"

One of the commandments that Chongde had taught him was love for others, and doing good even to those who had harmed you. Shaoqi shook his head. *Others maybe, but not Qili.* He would not—*could* not—do anything good for Qili. To give up killing Qili was unthinkable. His hatred had kept him alive too long. Then he pictured Chu Zhurun fall over the train railing once more.

Chongde jerked up suddenly. "What was he saying?" the old man asked, turning from one to another. "What was he saying? It cannot be."

Shaoqi turned from his own thoughts to hear what the speaker had said that so riveted Chongde: ". . . manipulation of the Cultural Revolution." Shaoqi had heard people talk about the Cultural Revolution times. Once the excesses were blamed on Mao's wife and henchmen, people began to speak openly of their suffering. What this man was saying about the Cultural Revolution was unlike anything Shaoqi had ever heard. Always people spoke of the awful things done to them. This man described the awful things he had personally inflicted upon others. Now he was particularly describing how he was part of a mob who had arrested a young preacher.

". . . He could have escaped, but he tried to protect the old couple. When he saw our brutality toward the old ones, he told us he was a preacher, and, as he hoped, our fury turned from them to him."

Shaoqi became caught up in the story of one who had admitted being a torturer. His eyes filled with tears. He shuddered with the beating, felt the despair of being locked, thirsty and hungry, in a tiny closet for days, ached with the preacher as he stood in the airplane position for hours while the Red Guards attacked him. Despite their best efforts, the preacher refused to credit Mao with supplying all good things. He would not deny Jesus.

The man telling the story wept. "After several months, another guard and I decided to overcome him. In a self-accusation meeting, we demanded that he recognize Mao as our provider. When he refused, we broke his little finger."

Snap. The speaker broke a twig. Shaoqi and many others in the room jerked.

"When he refused, we broke his next finger." *Snap.* "He passed out. We doused him with water to bring him to. In the end, we broke every finger." Shaoqi heard nothing but the speaker's sobs. "He did not deny Jesus. He did not accuse other Christians."

The speaker blew his nose. "I have often told this story, and only recently God used a young Christian woman to protect me and give me a meal. It was a granddaughter of the same preacher whose fingers I broke. I could not tell her all that I had done. I could not tell how this brave giant of faith humbled me that day. Forty years I have waited to say to this man how sorry I am, how the crack of his fingers haunts me still. In the end, it was his love for Jesus and the old couple that brought me to Jesus."

The hypocrite! What right does he have to ask forgiveness? What has that preacher's pain cost him?

Peng Chongde, unnaturally white, pulled himself to his feet, clinging to the window sill with twisted fingers. "I forgive you, brother." He was trembling. His voice quavered, but he repeated loudly enough for all to hear: "I forgive you."

Shaoqi stared at the old, arthritic hands. Others shifted, turned, stared.

The small, middle-aged man who had been the speaker pushed through the crowd to reach the back of the room. He simply stood before Chongde, then collapsed on the floor, prostrate in weeping. The old man sat on the bucket once more and reached down to caress the head of the younger man. But as he felt the touch of those twisted fingers, the man wailed more inconsolably and laid his face downward on the old man's knees.

"I am so sorry, Peng Chongde. I am so sorry."

Chongde's tears fell on the man's head, which he cradled in his lap. He bent over once more and kissed him gently. "Let us speak no more of it—only the grace that made my sacrifice sufficient."

Shaoqi stood and bolted from the door of the meeting. With head bowed, he walked out the factory gate and down the street, passing the car of a policeman who was watching the factory. He did not give the policeman a sideward glance.

Chongde's words burned a hole inside him.

Chapter 38

"A LARGE MAN IS WITH HIM. Do you want us to take them both?"

Kong hesitated, glancing around his apartment at the men watching TV while they awaited his orders. As much as he wanted Hardigan, he knew that going for him too soon could endanger his plans. Again, the girl was the key.

"Not yet. I want the girl. Find out who is with him if you can. If the girl tries to get to them, pick her up quietly, before she can get there."

At the table, Chen Yuliang combed through transcripts for evidence of where Stefanie might be. After putting the phone down, Kong bent over Yuliang. "Anything yet?"

Yuliang dropped the papers on the table. Removing her glasses, she sighed and rubbed her face. Her eyes were red after the verbal drubbing Kong had given her because of her mistakes. She was trying to put that behind her and concentrate on the task at hand. "I can find nothing here. I do not know where she might have gone. Do the men who have been following her have any ideas?"

"No," Kong said. "She has returned to none of her usual places."

"If only she did not have her documents."

"We do not know that she does. We only assume that she found them in my room and removed them. Chen, you have much to learn about our business." He eased into a smile to cover his frustration. "First lesson: Always have a backup plan. Second lesson: Never leave information unsecured. Third lesson: Never let feelings blind you to a subject's character and motivations."

She folded her arms and leaned away from him. "All right, Mr. Kong, so where is she?"

"Everything is in her apartment. She is a scared little rabbit without resources. If she goes to her lover, we will have her. If she returns to her nest, we will have her."

The phone rang. He answered, "Kong."

"This is Guo. We think we found her."

"Where?"

"Leaving the Friendship Hotel. Fu spotted her getting on a bus that goes by the university. He has a cell phone. Should he pick her up?"

"Have Fu follow her. If she comes back here, I will take her."

He put down the phone and grinned at the frowning Yuliang.

Stefanie drifted in and out of sleep. A yelp from the other room frightened her upright. Pressing her hand above her racing heart, she stared around, trying to place where she was. The room was dark except for a desk light, the computer screen on the desk, and a sliver of light from the door cracked open between the two rooms. *The hotel. Troy's hotel.*

"Do you think your girl knows about this?" She had heard the voice from the other room before, but she could not recall where.

"No, I'm *sure*," Troy said, "but she can't go back to the university, and, with her grandfather at risk, she won't leave."

The university. Beijing. Kong. The e-mail. Things began to make sense. Stefanie propped her arms on her knees and leaned against them, trying to clear her mind. She licked her lips to generate some saliva.

"We can keep her drugged until we've smuggled her out of the country."

What if a specialist cracked my computer? What would happen to the people I've interviewed? What about Grandfather?

Stefanie stuck her feet out of the bed. She had to get out of here, to find her grandfather, to delete her files.

Troy was slow to answer. "Maybe we could plant someone to intercept Peng Chongde and take him out through Shanghai. The files have been sent. Let me do a clean erase on them in case we get raided."

Stefanie eased her boots on. She stood up. Dizziness swept over her, and she grabbed the edge of the bed. She clung to it, hoping neither man would hear her. Gradually, her head cleared.

Her coat, scarf, and purse lay over a chair near the computer desk. She paused as her graduation picture flashed onto the screen saver. A picture of her with Nanai overlaid the first picture. A new photograph she hadn't seen of her with Patty, Troy's younger sister, popped up in the left corner, to be replaced with her family at a Christmas party from the year before. A photo-graph of her holding the bouquet of red roses and white carnations Troy had sent for her last birthday grew on the screen.

Her fogged brain barely registered the pictures, except to think that it was an odd screen saver. Her tongue felt thick, and she was thirsty. She began to stagger toward the bathroom, then remembered that she had to leave now. She felt sick as she eased open the door to the hallway.

By the time she climbed aboard the bus for Beijing University, the weather had worsened, making visibility difficult. Trying to think still nauseated her. She leaned back in the seat and closed her eyes.

The storm had become intense, and she would have ridden past her stop outside the formal gates of Beijing University if the bus driver had not called its name. She squeezed past those standing in the aisle as yellow sand streaked across the headlights' glow.

The wind cleared her mind a little. She met few students as she trudged through the driving gloom with her head tucked forward. *First, I will get my computer and a few clothes. Then I will. . . .*

She paused at the door of her apartment building. She shook her head. *Then I will decide where to go.*

No one met her in the entry. She heard muffled voices as she passed Qili's apartment. *Qili, a spy. Lord, please protect Grandfather from him.*

She glanced at her watch; it was after eight, so the elevator was shut down for the night. She plodded up the stairs to her apartment.

"Stefanie!" Edda, dressed in her heavy green coat, stood above her on the stairs. "Are you all right?" She grasped Stefanie's arm.

"I am a little thick-headed at the moment, but I will be all right."

Edda surprised her by hugging her. "I have been so worried. Your friend Troy called this morning. He was worried."

"I have talked to him."

"Then that Mr. Kong charged into our apartment while I was bathing. He let himself in and waved a gun around. He tore through your things."

He suspects me.

"He demanded where you were and he threatened me."

Fear sharpened her thinking. Stefanie leaned against the railing.

Edda grasped her wrist. "Come to practice with me. I will find you a place to stay until this passes. Perhaps he is just jealous of your friend." But the fear in her eyes belied her words.

Stefanie patted her arm. She couldn't endanger Edda too. "Everything will be all right. I have to get some things from the apartment. Perhaps I will stay away a few days. Maybe you could ask the Lawrences to fill in for me in my classes."

"I will do that. Be careful." Then Edda surprised her again with a hug before leaving.

Stefanie trudged upward. The warmth had a soporific effect. By the time she reached her apartment, she wanted nothing more than to fall into bed and sleep for a week, but she had no time for that. She drank a full glass of water and threw some clothes into a carry-all without caring if anything matched. She tossed in her Bible and Troy's book of poetry. Grabbing her carry-all, leather coat, purse, and computer, she closed the door behind her.

Kong opened the door of his apartment. Fu Qian, the big man who had tailed Stefanie from the hotel, said, "She is here."

"Get back to the hotel. Take reinforcements, but do not go near Hardigan until I call—unless he tries to leave. I want every exit guarded."

He turned to Chen Yuliang who was putting the phone down. She shook her head. "There is no sign of the old man or Ren in either Shanghai or Beijing."

"Do the guards have pictures?"

"Yes, they cannot get on campus without being recognized."

The phone rang and Kong picked it up. Things were coming together.

The agent who monitored the bugs in Stefanie's room called from the room opposite hers. "Someone has entered the apartment. The old woman left a few minutes ago."

"I will be right up." Slipping his jacket on to cover his holstered Makarov, Kong nodded at four plainclothes policemen, who shut the TV off.

As Stefanie placed her key in the lock, she glanced down the hall. Kong and two big men topped the stairs. She glanced in the other direction. The man who reminded her of a beaver stepped from the other stairwell.

"Stefanie!" Kong called, his voice hard.

She threw the door open and hurried through, slamming it behind her. She locked it and shoved an armchair against it.

Kong pounded on the door. "Stefanie, open this door!" No pretense of sweetness or charm here. "Go back into your apartments. This is police business."

Stefanie dragged and pushed the sofa against the door. Kong's key turned in her lock. As big as those guys were, the furniture would not hold them long. She cleared Edda's computer from her desk and toppled the desk onto the sofa.

She peered around the apartment. She had no way to escape. If she could keep them out for a few minutes, she could delete her files to protect her contacts.

The door shuddered under a blow. The furniture inched outward. Stefanie tossed the two kitchen chairs on top of the armchair, then pushed the table across the room. Again the door moved a bit. She shoved back, but the combined furniture did not budge.

She carried her computer and purse into the bathroom and slammed the door, which snickered its peculiar acknowledgment of sticking. Relieved, she locked it and opened her laptop.

"Just a few more inches and I can get my arm through," Kong said.

She did not have time to delete the files. After turning the computer on, she shoved open the window over the bathtub. Cold sand drifted in. Troy had said that dropping a computer while it was booting up would destroy the hard drive. She hoped he was right.

"Get that furniture out of the way," Kong ordered.

One of the kitchen chairs crashed to the floor amid human grunts.

Stefanie leaned through the window. She threw the computer toward the tree. She heard it hit, but the clatter of the furniture being shoved aside drowned the smash of the computer against the asphalt.

The men, apparently more than three, stomped into the apartment. They grew quiet outside the bathroom door.

"Stefanie, open the bathroom door. I promise you will not be hurt," Kong said.

Stefanie glanced around the bathroom. Her blow-dryer and the screwdriver were her only potential weapons. She dug through her purse for her extra floppy disks that contained notes for her articles and the articles themselves. She pulled back the metal guard on a disk and stabbed through the exposed window to damage the flimsy film of the disk itself. She repeated the attack on the other disks.

"Stefanie," Kong's voice came out as a firm but kindly teacher's. "You have no way out. The game is over. Do not be childish."

She climbed into the tub again to view the tree outside her window. She angled her head to study the nearest tree limb—about six feet below her window and three feet away from the building. Shining through the windows of the building, lights lit the tree from various angles, but gusts of sand obscured it. Stefanie brushed the sand from her face. The limb would be slick.

"Stefanie, do not make this hard on yourself. Be reasonable. Cooperate, and we might make an agreeable deal with your CIA boyfriend," Kong said.

CIA boyfriend? What is he talking about?

She closed her eyes to visualize the safest descent. She could break her neck doing this, but she had to warn Troy.

"We know Hardigan's at the Friendship Hotel."

"If I let you in," she said, trying to separate her thoughts, "will you let Troy go?"

"We might come to a deal; now open the door." His voice betrayed his impatience.

"I need a few minutes to think, Qili. Just give me a few minutes."

Kong hesitated. "Okay, hurry up."

She had bought a little time. The bathroom door was surprisingly sturdy, but she knew it wouldn't keep the men out for long. Fortunately, they had decided to try the easy way first. Silently thanking God that the maintenance staff had not repaired the door, Stefanie dropped her coat and then her purse out the window. She wiped the trim with her towel before stepping onto the window sill. Squatting gingerly on the ledge, she pulled herself upright, and leaped.

"Okay, Stefanie, time's up. Open the door," Kong said.

Silence.

"Don't make me knock down the door, Stefanie. That will only make me angry—not in the mood to strike a deal for your boyfriend."

Still silence.

At Kong's signal, one of the men struck the door near the handle with a well-placed foot. The door shuddered but did not yield. Another man stepped forward, and his kick began to splinter the door. As the assault continued, Kong decided that he would grab that pretty hair and soften the girl up with a few well-placed slaps. She would crumple like a dish towel and tell him everything.

The wood cracked around the latch. The two big men shoved the door open and stepped back. Cold wind swept into the room from the open window. Disks lay on the floor. The curtain fluttered toward Kong with a spattering of sand.

"Come out, Stefanie," he ordered. She did not answer. Expecting something to be thrown at him, he dodged into the room. Only the curtain moved. He shoved the door shut and swore. She was gone.

He climbed into the bathtub, slipping on the grit. He saw no movement below him. Either she had broken her neck or escaped. He scooped the floppy disks from the floor on his way back to the apartment's main room.

"She went out the window," Kong told the waiting men. "Go search for her body." He turned to another cop who had a cell phone. "Order the school's gates closed. Have the guards stop anyone trying to go out and check identification cards. If she survived, do not let her get off the campus. Bring in dogs. Check every building."

The guard left at once. Kong pulled out his cell phone.

"Chen," Yuliang answered.

"Send two policemen up here to search. I want all of her personal property confiscated and checked. Order Fu to take Hardigan alive as soon as he reaches the hotel."

"The little rabbit tricked you and hopped into the bushes?"

Hardigan felt good about what had been beamed out of the hotel room. Stefanie had sent them code names and important details of a network of agents covering the United States, Great Britain, Germany, Canada, and Israel. Much of it was encrypted, but it did not look like a first-rate government job. It was probably a low-level cipher for Kong's own use. There also were unencrypted clues in the project logs of the U.S. network that could help uncover identities. This stuff could be immensely valuable.

"Don't wipe our files yet," Chou said suddenly.

"Why not?"

"I'm not getting a transmission confirmation. The communications links at the embassy have been real temperamental. I don't think what we sent was received."

"I already made a disk backup, so we can wipe it off the computer at least."

Chou yawned and checked his watch. "I didn't give Stefanie much sleep aid, and this has taken longer than I expected. I'm surprised she hasn't come to."

The phone rang. Hardigan grabbed it.

"Red," Chou said from the other room, his voice rising. "We got trouble."

Hardigan was already saying, "*Ni hao.*"

"Troy, get out. They're coming. They think you're CIA."

"Stef?" he asked. He looked past Chou into the other hotel room. "*Stef?*"

The phone went dead.

"She's gone," Chou said.

"That was her." Without thinking, Hardigan let his training take over. He closed the laptop.

Chou unplugged the modem. "They got her?"

"No, but they're onto us."

Leaving the light on and his clothes behind, he carried his briefcase and laptop into the adjoining room. He shut the door, went to the suitcase on the bed, and opened it. While Chou dropped acid on papers in the lavatory of Hardigan's room, Hardigan stuffed cheek pads inside his mouth to round his face. He swiftly spread makeup on his face from a tube labeled "acne medicine." He slipped a black wig over his red hair and added a fake gold cap to his left front tooth. Pulling a pair of suit pants over his jeans, he shrugged into the suit coat and an overcoat with Hong Kong labels, and stepped into a pair of black wing-tip shoes. By then, the dark makeup had firmed to a mask. He added a large strawberry burn mark to his left forehead and light-sensitive adjustable glasses.

"Ready?" Chou locked the passage between the two rooms.

"Just the gloves." With no time to remove the telltale red hair on the back of his hands, he had to cover them.

Chou and Hardigan, carrying their laptops and Hardigan's brown suitcase, strolled from the room discussing development of the Golden Triangle near Hong Kong and Guangdong. They were halfway to the stairs when the elevator and stairs on both ends disgorged police and a harried-looking manager.

Hardigan dropped behind Chou when they met the police to allow the officers to pass. He was sweating. He hated the feeling of the cheek pads. He had escaped like this twice before, once in Indonesia and once in Cairo.

He and Chou separated in the lobby. Hardigan checked out as Chang Fangshen, the guise in which he had rented the second room. Should he be stopped, the papers in his breast pocket would identify him as Chang, originally of Shanghai, recently a mid-level manager of a textile firm based in Hong Kong.

He caught a taxi to a small, Chinese-only hotel. Once the cab disappeared, Hardigan slipped into an alley out of the storm. He peeled the burn from his forehead, removed his glasses, and popped a pair of brown contacts into place. He had no problem renting a room for cash for one night.

Once in his room, he dropped his coat over a chair. On a cell phone registered to his alias, he called his contact. Then he threw himself onto the lumpy mattress to pray for Stefanie and await Chou's call.

"He could not have escaped, Mr. Kong. We had every exit guarded. It is a large building, but we will find him," Fu said.

Kong breathed deeply. This was not acceptable. He never had such trouble, and these were nobodies. Hardigan might be CIA, but he obviously wasn't very bright, and he was so large and so Western that he would stand out anywhere. No, Hardigan could not get out of that hotel, and Stefanie could not get off campus.

"Who was Hardigan with?"

"We believe it was the head security agent for the American embassy."

"And the girl? She must have been at the hotel if our men saw her leave."

"We are dusting for prints."

Kong threw the phone at the sofa. He was beginning to admit to himself that he had erred in dismissing Yuliang's warning about Stefanie. He had assumed that because she was not an operative, she was a naïve, emotional little girl, who would collapse with fright if someone threatened her. No, that assessment had proven incorrect at every turn. It was his own fault, not Yuliang's, that matters were falling apart. Yuliang set the phone on the table. She inserted the disks from Stefanie's apartment into a computer.

"Something is wrong with them," she said.

Kong whirled on the big policeman who came in wiping his sleeve across his face. "Did you find her?"

"No, sir. She went over the fence."

"What? She is only 155 centimeters tall."

"Yes, sir, but the dogs led us to a tree near the fence, then lost the scent. It had a limb about two meters up. The dogs found her scent again on the other side of the fence and followed it to a street several blocks away where they lost it."

Chen smiled. "If you studied my report, you will remember that Stefanie is a gymnast. She relaxes by working out on the uneven parallel bars."

The phone rang. Chen answered and listened.

"Wait a minute." Holding her hand over the phone, she said. "Three Japanese businessmen across from Hardigan's room identified Stefanie as being there at about noon today with a big Chinese man. They did not see anyone leave. The elevator operator saw her come about noon and leave around seven."

Kong tried to put everything together. Stefanie had gone into Hardigan's room, but she was not there when the waiters delivered meals for two. The security man was there then.

Kong took the phone. "Did the waiter notice the bathroom door being closed?"

"No, I asked. It was open. The light was on, and the shower curtain pushed back," Fu said.

"Then where was the girl hiding between noon and seven?" He paused to think. "Does this room have a connecting door?"

"Yes, but that was rented by a Hong Kong businessman. He checked out before we had a chance to interview him."

"Has that room been cleaned? Dust it! Also, go to the desk and get a description of this businessman in the next room."

Fu called back in five minutes.

"The man from Hong Kong is ethnic Chinese, 165 to 185 centimeters tall."

That would be about right for Hardigan.

"Black hair."

A wig.

"He wears dark glasses."

To hide his eyes.

"And he has a horrible burn mark on his left forehead."

To distract from attention to his face.

His estimation of his opponent was rising.

"What was his name?"

"Chang Fangshen."

"Chen, call the hotels around for a Chang Fangshen. Fu, leave one man to dust that room and complete the search. Bring the rest here for new assignments."

He hung up the phone and thought out loud.

"We will put men at each place she has done stories about. I want the Chinese she has dealt with questioned, especially the more dissident students and her interviewees."

"Include the cleaning woman. They have become quite chummy," Yuliang added.

Chapter 39

THE CAB DROVE PAST the gates of the United States Embassy on Xiu Shiu Bei Jie. In the streaked glow of the streetlights, miserable policemen in green uniforms hunched their shoulders in the driving storm as they blocked the closed gates.

The plump middle-aged cabby lit another cigarette. "The police must be searching for the dangerous CIA agents trying to get into the embassy."

To avoid the tobacco stench, Stefanie shoved herself back in the seat, her mind racing. She had wanted to check whether the embassy was still guarded, but she had directed the driver to take her to another street beyond the embassy to prevent his suspicion.

The driver glanced in the rearview mirror. "My wife said the television has been showing pictures of three dangerous CIA agents, an American man and a Chinese man and woman. You cannot trust Americans, always trying to cause trouble. Why would our own people ever work for them?"

"What did the announcement say?" she asked.

"My wife did not say. Once I see their pictures, I will keep watch for them."

"Yes, I will too." She wished she could see Troy now. *Oh, Lord, please keep him safe. He wouldn't be in this trouble if it weren't for me.*

When the driver stopped, she paid him, but she kept her back to the light.

Praying, she hobbled away from the lighted area into the duskiness of the wind-blown sand. The ankle she had twisted climbing down the tree slowed her. She turned at the first intersection to face the wind. The storm scoured her skin; her ankle shrieked with pain at each step. The sand pinged off the pink rain bonnet.

In spite of the storm, cars and pedestrians had not completely deserted the familiar street.

Pete Weston had stopped at his apartment on this street to get some batteries for his flash on one of their excursions. She hated to get him into trouble, but maybe he could give her some advice. Gritting her teeth, she limped into the grit-filled wind until she found the apartment building. After trudging to the fourth floor, she searched the numbers until she found his.

He opened the door on the second knock.

"Stefanie, luv. This is a surprise. Come in, and I'll get you a cuppa."

"Hi, Pete. I apologize for disturbing you." She felt so weary she could hardly speak. "I wondered if you could give me some advice."

"And I thought my charm and manly good looks were what you couldn't resist. Never figured you'd want me for my mind. Come into my parlor, luv."

The apartment was larger than hers. A thick flowered armchair beckoned. Pictures of a beautiful petite Chinese girl covered the walls and shelves. From the end table Stefanie picked up a photograph of the girl with her long black hair blowing in the breeze, her eyes smiling at the camera.

"She's lovely."

"Looks a bit like you, actually. That's my Shanshan." He took the photograph from her and peered at it before setting it down and reaching for Stefanie's coat.

"I can't stay. The police are after me. My supervisor, Kong, the one who asked you to leave that first day, brought me here to force my grandfather to betray the underground church. I don't want to get you in trouble too."

"You're balmy." His gaze slid over her. "No, of course, you're not. You'd better sit down before you fall over."

"Pete, they've sealed off the embassy. I don't know what to do."

He pulled her coat off, tossed it over the back of a chair, and guided her to the stuffed chair. "They won't think of coming here. What happened?"

Her whole body ached as she settled into the armchair. Her ankle throbbed. She told him as much as she could without involving Troy or Ulysses Chou. When she finished her account, she rubbed her swollen left ankle. "Would you have some aspirin or ibuprofen? I twisted my ankle."

Pete poured whiskey into his tea and offered her some too. She shook her head but gratefully accepted the aspirin and tea. Soon the warmth of the drink and the apartment began to make her drowsy. They sipped their tea silently while Pete pondered her problem. "I may be able to get you into the Australian Embassy."

He went into the apartment's bedroom. Through the closed door, his voice was muffled. "Hello, this is Weston. I have an American friend here who is having trouble getting into the American embassy. What's that? She didn't mention any bloke."

The warmth tucked her in, but she didn't dare to surrender to it until she knew the outcome of the call.

"Now what about the other thing? Two? No, six, or I'll have her out of here in the blink of an eye." Pete paused. "All right, two o'clock in the back."

On that promise, she let herself fall into the black hole of sleep.

The vibrations of the truck changed with the braking. The Brother automatically raised his arm to ward off the rolling cabbages. He had been unable to sleep during the long ride in the back of the panel truck. It wasn't the reek of cabbage and diesel fuel, the lumpiness of the bed of cabbages, or even the rolling heads of cabbage that assaulted him on every curve or with every braking that kept him awake.

Instead, each time he closed his eyes, he pictured Chang Rongwen, the man who would be the next director of the Religious Affairs Bureau, the man who wanted him dead. His chest ached with each new mental picture of Rongwen and himself as boys, fishing, roughhousing, playing sports at school, always together. *Oh, Rongwen.*

The truck accelerated, leaving some of the diesel fumes behind.

Peng Chongde moaned in his sleep. Beyond him, a cabbage made a thud against something, and the young unbeliever, Ren Shaoqi, cursed softly. The Brother twisted his blanket between his fingers and wondered why the old man was traveling with this unbeliever. Yet Shaoqi seemed intensely devoted to the old man.

The truck slowed and pulled to the side of the street. With the stop the load shifted, launching a cascade of cabbages upon the passengers. The Brother nudged himself between Chongde and the onslaught of vegetables.

The truck's cab door slammed. The driver's steps swished through the driving sand. The stick he carried plunked against the tires as he checked their air pressure. A moment later the metal clasp on the truck's back door clanged. The panel door slid up.

"Lao," the driver whispered.

The Brother crawled over the pile of cabbages.

"I have to let you out here. Police are searching trucks closer to the city, looking for spies."

"Spies?"

"An American man and a Chinese man and woman."

"I will get the others."

The driver grasped his arm. "Wait. The police also are looking for Peng Chongde and Ren Shaoqi. If they catch you with them, what will they do to you?"

The Brother refused to think about it. "I will take care of them."

"But your ministry, the gospel, what about those?"

The Brother pulled a handkerchief from his pocket to clean the sleet from his glasses. "I serve God and his people. That is my ministry, my friend."

The driver looked worried.

The Brother patted his shoulder. "Do not worry. Pray for us. We are in God's hand." He wished the fear gnawing at his intestines would heed his advice.

He crawled over the cabbages. "We have to get out here. There is trouble in Beijing." The Brother folded his blanket and shoved it into his travel bag.

"I will fold that for you, Uncle," Shaoqi offered, snatching Chongde's blanket before the Brother could take it. The younger man turned his back on the Brother, who wondered at his animosity.

The old man extended his hands, opened and closed them to work out the stiffness as he had several times since the Brother had joined him. Once more, guilt gnawed at the Brother. He would not attend to his business with Chang Rongwen until he had seen Chongde to his granddaughter. He owed the old man far more than that.

After throwing his own bag over his shoulder, the Brother helped Chongde over the cabbages and out the back of the truck. Sand from the storm made the floor slick, so the Brother carefully helped the old man down.

"I am sorry, Uncle. I have been listening to the radio. The police are stopping trucks coming into the city to look for you and your friend. Beijing is in a turmoil over some CIA spies," the driver said.

Shaoqi, carrying Chongde's bag and his own, scrambled over the cabbages. The driver did not look at them. His eyes shifted from the Brother too.

"There is a bus stop a few blocks from here. They probably will not stop buses from that stop. It is too close to the city." He glanced at Chongde. "I hope it is not too far for you, Uncle."

"I am stronger than I look. Thank you," Chongde said.

As Shaoqi climbed out of the truck, an avalanche of cabbages tumbled with him.

"Just go back and turn left when you come to the main road," the driver said. He pointed behind them. "I am sorry I cannot do better for you."

All three men stooped to gather the cabbages.

"I can do this. You two start," the Brother said. He watched in the first graying of early dawn until they were out of hearing. "What is it? What else is wrong?"

The driver licked his lips and piled the cabbages that the Brother rolled to him. "I wish you were going to Shanghai or somewhere else. One of the spies the police are looking for is a girl named Peng."

The Brother scowled, finding it hard to think of the sweet-faced girl on the train as a spy. "Well, where there is a will to condemn, there is evidence." He knew that only too well.

"I can't tell you how much I appreciate this," Stefanie said, looking across the Yugo at Pete.

He kept his eyes on the street, although the traffic had thinned. The sandstorm had ceased, leaving the sky with fiery smudges above the factories.

"You are a nice girl. You remind me of Shanshan in more than how you look."

"You've never said much about her."

"No, I guess not." They lapsed into silence.

"I hope you won't get in trouble for helping me."

"They assured me that the wrong people shouldn't find out." He kept his eyes on the road. Despite the assurance, Stefanie knew that Pete must be having second thoughts. He had said little since he had awakened her for the trip to the Australian Embassy. He was uncharacteristically silent.

She closed her eyes and let her head bob to the rhythm of the car's movements. "If I can do anything to repay you, Pete, I will."

He said nothing. Thinking he had not heard her, she raised her head. His knuckles looked white beneath the streetlights as they passed.

"I am sorry to put you through all this," she said.

"We're here. They want us to go in the back. Don't say anything. They're expecting us."

He stopped outside a chain link fence surrounding a large concrete block building. She had expected the Australian Embassy to look more impressive, but this was the back.

Stefanie stiffened as a Chinese policeman stepped to the driver's door. He glanced at the identity card Pete showed him, then opened the gate for them without question.

"Seeing a policeman shook me up a little," she admitted.

"Yeah." He parked the car, got her door, and, tucking her arm though his, led her across the sand-drifted pavement. He opened an unlocked back door. The door closed to leave them in darkness, but Pete pulled her farther into the room. The light came on.

Stefanie lifted her hand to shield her eyes from the light. She blinked. Pete released her arm. The lock clicked behind her in a room that reeked of stale cigarette smoke.

She turned to thank her protectors and stared into the black, glittering eyes of Kong Qili. His hand lashed out, catching her right cheek. The blow knocked her backward. Stunned, she slid down the wall. Her head hurt from banging against the concrete blocks. She brushed her tingling cheek. She touched the tip of her tongue to the corner of her split lip and tasted the saltiness of her own blood.

How did they find us?

"There was no need for that," Pete said. They didn't touch Pete.

"You have done your part. Now it is my turn," Kong said. Reaching her in two strides, he grabbed her hair and dragged her to her feet. She wondered if he would pull her hair out.

She bit her lip to keep from crying. He held her against the wall with his big hand wrapped around her throat. "You have given me much trouble, little lady."

Staring into his eyes scared her. Instead of rage, she saw cold calculation.

"When can I see Shanshan?" Pete demanded.

Stefanie stared past Kong at Pete.

Yuliang stepped into view. Her face was pale and her hands trembled as she handed Pete a key. There was no sympathy in her friend's eyes.

With Kong's hand tight against her throat, she could not swallow. A bead of blood from her split lip tickled her chin, huddled, and dropped.

Pete headed for the door without looking her way. "You said this would take six months off her sentence."

"She will be out in five months," Kong said. "Where will you be if I need you?"

Pete paused as the People's Liberation Army guard unlocked the door, but he did not look back toward Stefanie. "After I see Shanshan, I plan to get roaring drunk."

With the click of the lock behind Pete, Kong's hand tightened on Stefanie's throat. He wrapped her hair around his other hand.

"Where is Hardigan?"

"I do not know," she gasped. *Thank you, Lord. I can't betray him.*

Kong's hand tightened further on her throat. Her breath fought to wheeze out. "Where is Hardigan?"

She tried to form the words "I do not know."

He cut off her breathing entirely with a squeeze. As her head grew light, she tugged futilely at his hand.

"Where is Hardigan?" He loosened his grasp on her throat.

She hauled in air. "I do not know."

Kong released her throat. He slapped her cheek, knocking her head to the right. Then he backhanded her. Silently, she pleaded to God for Troy and her grandfather.

Kong grasped her chin and leaned his weight against her chest. His breath reeking of stale cigarette smoke tickled her cheek. "This is just the beginning. Make it easy on yourself."

She closed her eyes to gain control. She was not about to start crying at this moment.

Kong dragged her by the hair to a chair and shoved her into it.

He dropped a pen and paper on the table in front of her. "Sign that."

She picked it up and tried to read through the blur of tears. The paper trembled. Kong tore it from her hands. "I said to sign it."

She shook her head. "I am not a spy. I am not signing anything before I read it. And as an American citizen, I demand the right to notify the United States embassy."

Kong smiled nastily. "Oh, we will notify the embassy—when it is time."

Sorry, Madre. I will not leave China alive.

Chapter 40

"You have to go in before rush hour," said the skinny man with the ropes in his hand. Soong wore a red jumpsuit with the emblem of his electrical repair unit on the pocket. "If you escape into a traffic jam, the police will catch you on foot."

"This is suicide," Han growled. The large man looked around the scarred green table at Ulysses Chou, Hu Youmei, Hardigan in his Chinese disguise, and Soong the electrician. They were huddled in the cluttered back room of the small electricians' shop where Soong worked, a place notable for its mixed aromas of cigarette smoke, electrical parts, and cleaners. Han studied the resolve in the faces illuminated by the harsh glare of overhead fluorescent tubes.

Hardigan disagreed. The audacity of rescuing Stefanie and the human rights activist that his companions wanted to free would shock the Chinese. It might even work.

Han crossed his muscular arms. "Getting Chang out will be nearly impossible, but I will risk that. Adding the girl will ruin everything."

The cabby, Hu Youmei, shook his head. "We have to get Chang Sitong out before they break him, or all the human rights cells will shatter. Everything we have worked for since the June Fourth Massacre will be destroyed."

"I understand that," Han responded impatiently, "but why the girl?"

Troy responded slowly, uncomfortable with his Mandarin at such a moment when communication meant everything. "She is one of ours. We need to retrieve her. You cannot succeed alone. I take out cell phones. We not help unless girl we get. Ends meet."

"Listen to him," Han spat out with a look of disgust. "A three-year-old speaks better than this man. How will he fool anyone into thinking he is Chinese?"

Hu leaned his elbows on the table and covered his prosthetic arm with his right hand. "He will not speak beyond a word or two. Come, my friends, the time to argue is past. He wants the girl. We want Chang Sitong. He needs us to get him into the prison and to the phones, but we need him to carry our equipment in the box and take out the cell phones. We have to decide right now."

"Our contact will hit the electricity at the prison in under five minutes," Soong added, nodding.

Han nervously crossed his thick arms once more and bit his lower lip. The others waited. No one wanted to push him into something that could cost his life. After a long moment he spoke. "They say the girl is CIA. I will not help the CIA destabilize China."

"She is not CIA," Hu said. "I know her. She is a journalist who has helped us tell the world about Chang Sitong. She wrote a strong story. I have read it, and it already is in the hands of Western media. Now she is in trouble because she spoke out for us."

Han dropped his arms. "We will all die if Sitong breaks."

Hu and Soong nodded.

"What happens next?" Han asked.

"As soon as the power goes down, the guards will turn on the generator and call here immediately. That is what they always do, but we will go in Soong's place," Hu said.

"After leaving me tied, gagged, and beaten." Soong lifted the ropes that would bind him.

"Our contact leaves us the cell locations in the electrical box." Hu waved at Hardigan. "We go after Sitong and the girl while you attach dynamite to the phone lines."

"This will endanger your inside contact," Hardigan said.

Hu nodded. "He will risk it. Chang knows every union and human rights activist in the city, including several people in our contact's family."

The phone rang. Hardigan, Hu, and Han studied one another's faces. Han nodded to Soong, who picked up the phone.

Kong forced Stefanie to trot to keep up. He smirked at her limp. She would not be jumping out of any more third-story windows for a while. Her cheeks and throat were discolored with bruises. Her split lip still bled. She was more stubborn than he had expected—even now her brown eyes sparked with anger instead of terror. He would soon break her and find Hardigan when pain and shock took over her mind.

Two soldiers stood in front of a solid steel door. One of the guards opened the door for them and stepped back.

Bo Qin, the middle-aged cleaning lady, sat at a table with her head lowered. She glanced up and Stefanie gasped, "Qin." Her eyes widened. The woman lowered her head and kneaded her hands.

Good. Chen was right about her attachment to the cleaning woman.

Across from the cleaning woman sat an emaciated, middle-aged man, Chief Interrogator Po. "She refuses to cooperate. Shall I proceed?"

"Yes," Kong said.

"It is not enough for you to pick on the guests you invite to China. You have to pick on my cleaning lady too?" Stefanie said.

Po did not respond.

"I demand to speak to the U.S. embassy."

At a nod from Po, the two guards shoved Bo Qin upright and handcuffed her to the wall opposite Kong and Stefanie with her hands above her head, her face pressed against the rough concrete wall.

"What are you doing to her?" Stefanie demanded. Her arm trembled beneath Kong's hand. She followed the bizarre preparations with wide, frightened eyes.

One of the guards slit Bo Qin's blouse down the back while the other pulled a hemp rope, dripping, from a bucket of water.

With his clipboard held in front of him, Interrogator Po smiled back at Kong and Stefanie. "We are ready."

"You can stop this, Stefanie," Kong said. "Where's Hardigan?"

Stefanie shook her head, her lips parted in shock. "I do not know," she whispered.

"Mr. Po, proceed."

Po's smile broadened. "Mrs. Bo, who arranges the meetings with the traveling cult leaders?"

She did not answer.

The interrogator nodded to the guard who whipped the wet rope across Bo Qin's back. Qin grunted. The interrogator asked another question about the house church meeting. After a few moments of silence, he nodded to the other guard, who touched Qin with an electric baton. She shrieked and slammed against the wall.

Stefanie's face was ashen. She swiped at tears with her free hand. "Stop it, Qili. Make them stop."

"Where is Hardigan?"

"I do not know."

Kong did not enjoy torture as Interrogator Po did, but he would have the information about Hardigan at whatever cost Stefanie deemed that her friend should pay. She was too upset to recognize that Po was asking the woman questions for his own purposes.

The rope *thwacked* across the cleaning woman's back. She moaned. As the guard pulled the lash back, a drop of blood hit Stefanie's cheek. She wiped it off and stared at the woman's blood.

"You call yourself a man?" she snapped at Kong.

"If you want it to end, tell me. I can order the interrogation stopped."

"Then stop it."

"Where is Hardigan?"

With the next jolt of electricity from the electric baton, the cleaning woman collapsed, her body suspended by the cuffs. She pushed her feet into place underneath her, then sagged. The guard swung the heavy rope against Qin's inert body. With the rope's recoil, Stefanie ripped herself free from Kong's grasp and dashed toward the cleaning woman.

In one leap, Kong grabbed her arm.

She rounded on him. She swung her hand to rake him with her nails. Kong caught her free hand, jerked her around to face the beating, and straitjacketed her body against him with her arms.

Stefanie twisted to knee him.

He yanked both of her arms, ripping a scream from her.

She butted him with her head, bringing blood to his mouth.

He cursed and twisted her wrists, popping them outward. She screamed. "Now watch," he demanded.

The guard emptied a bucket of water on the unconscious cleaning woman. Sweat darkened the underarms of the guards' shirts. Beating someone with enough energy to satisfy the interrogator took work. Po blew a column of smoke from his nose before taking another puff on his cigarette.

Kong longed for a good smoke, but forcing the girl to watch occupied both his hands.

The cleaning woman shuddered. Her head twitched.

"More water," Po said.

The guards threw another bucket on the cleaning woman. She lifted her head weakly but did not push herself upright. Blood dripped down her back, puddling with the water on the floor, too thick to coagulate and turn brown.

The interrogator checked his list of questions. "Mrs. Bo, how are these cult meetings scheduled?"

The beatings began again. Kong's nose wrinkled at the odors of burning flesh, blood, urine, sweat, and tobacco smoke. Then Stefanie vomited on him.

Chapter 41

STEFANIE CLAMPED HER HANDS more tightly to her sides. The retching had subsided. Her trembling eased, replaced by shivers in the dank, noisome cell. After rising from the side of the fetid hole that served as a squat toilet, she rubbed her knees where the gravel in the concrete had embedded itself while she vomited.

Beside the open toilet hole, two boards sat across concrete blocks. A blanket lay wrinkled on the top. The solid steel door to the cell stood about six feet away with a bucket of water between the cot and the door. A heavy rusted steel grate leaned against a wall. A single dusty light bulb hanging from the ceiling illuminated the small cell and a black void in the ceiling where Stefanie assumed the grate belonged.

Sinking onto the bunk, she buried her head in her arms. With the board next to the wall thicker than the other, she felt as if she would be pitched onto the floor at any moment.

How did Grandfather survive this so long?

Pictures of Qin's beating filled her mind. *How can one human being treat another like that?*

At the first bite, she jumped up and twirled around. A half dozen black bugs were crawling on her. She slapped at them, knocking some off, and squashing others. One stung her waist on her back. Stefanie pawed at her back until she flicked the bedbug off.

She shook her hair, ran her fingers through it, stamped her feet. Still, her skin prickled with the sensation of hundreds of buggy feet. As quickly as she patted a tickle on her right eyebrow, her left shoulder blade itched, then her right knee-cap. She scratched, slapped, and clawed, but found only one more bug.

By now dozens of ugly black bugs milled about on the cot. *Home. I can't think about home, about Nanai. So I'll think about Qili.*

She picked up the heavy grate and slammed it against the bugs on the boards, mashing as many as she could. Some scurried for cracks in the wall. Men's voices murmured, muttered, shouted, and complained from surrounding cells. When her arms tired of swinging the grate, she let it clatter to the floor beside the bunk. At least she was no longer shivering.

Wrapping her arms around herself, she backed away from the makeshift bunk. *I have to be strong. Oh, Lord, please help me to be strong. I'm so afraid.*

The beating and electric shocks had left Qin unconscious. Kong promised that Stefanie would receive the same treatment if she did not tell him where to find Troy.

"Thank you, Lord, that I don't know where Troy is. Please keep him and Grandfather safe," she whispered.

She squatted beside the metal bucket of water. She could not force herself to put her mouth on the thing. First, she dumped water on her hands, which started her shivering again. She wiped her hands on her skirt. Then she flicked a bug from the water before lapping it. Its heavy iron taste disgusted her. She forced her tongue back into it. Breathing through her mouth helped her to bear the reek of the rank sewage hole that permeated the cell.

The light bulb went out and the darkness bore down on her. She stood, thinking that she heard the buggy feet coming for her again. Or maybe this time it was rats. Sweating and shivering in the dank cold and absolute darkness, she was disoriented, unable to remember where the door was or where the pit of human waste lay.

She dashed her sleeve against her cheeks to absorb the tears. Her heart pounded. She wrapped her arms around her waist to hold down her fear. The rumble of men's protests filtered around the door to her.

When the light bulb came on again, she felt as if she had stood frozen in the same spot for hours, but it might have been only a few minutes.

Though the light from the bulb seemed duller, Stefanie walked around the cell, grateful that she could at least see her surroundings. She estimated the size of the cell at roughly three or four yards long and much less wide. The hole in the ceiling looked to be an open vent. She stopped beneath it and felt a breath of cool air. The grate must have come from there. After another circuit of the cell, she stopped with her gaze transfixed on the vent.

What do I have to lose?

She lifted the boards of the bunk one at a time from the concrete blocks. The first board fell with a clatter that roused the complaints of sleepy prisoners.

She picked up the second, which was heavier than it looked, and staggered beneath its weight. Stumbling over the first board, she pitched the second into the open toilet hole.

She dragged a concrete block across the floor. Its scraping prompted a guard to yell for silence. Standing on the block, she still could not reach the vent hole. She hoisted the second block and waddled to the vent opening, balanced it atop the first one, and climbed on. Though she could reach the vent, she could not get a handhold.

She searched the cell for other ideas or supplies, but she could not imagine any way to use the blanket or boards. Then her eyes settled on the water bucket and she scrambled down to retrieve it. When she emptied the water into the squat toilet, solid waste floated to the surface. She closed her eyes to soothe her quivering stomach.

The wire bail made the bucket tip when it was set upside down on the blocks, so Stefanie set the top block beside the second, laid the bail between the two, and drove the corner of the grate onto the thin bail, splitting it.

"Just add it to my list of crimes against the state, Qili," she muttered.

She restacked the concrete blocks, set the bucket upside down on top, and climbed onto her wobbly scaffold. Balancing on top of the bucket, she poked her head inside the vent. She could see nothing and coal dust tickled her nose. Occasionally coal-tainted air wheezed in her direction.

The metal pipe was gritty with soot, but with a lighter heart than she had felt in hours, she pulled herself up into the vent.

Chapter 42

"YOU MADE GOOD TIME," the guard at the back gate of Beijing Number One Prison said.

Hu Youmei, driving the electrical van, exchanged pleasantries with the guard until the gate opened to permit them through. His neat little artificial mustache, the silver-laced black wig, and his artificial arm disguised him. In a couple of hours he'd be back in his cab, minus all of them, if all went well.

In spite of his doubts, Troy Hardigan, on the far side of the truck cab, was glad to be here. He had to get Stefanie out. She had to know that he had not left her in this bleak, barren place. As he looked around, his old cynicism overcame his Celtic warrior romantic imaginations. Solid concrete block walls rose above him, topped by barbed wire fences and SKS-toting guards.

Next to him, Han muttered, "We are crazy."

Hu Youmei pulled up to a loading dock behind the prison. Hardigan climbed out with the other two. All three wore the electrical company's red coveralls. While Hu talked with the warden, Hardigan and Han lifted a large metal toolbox from the back of the van to roll along the sidewalk. The three men followed the warden past the guards. At a lift of Hu's right eyebrow, one of the guards scratched his nose twice. Everything was in place.

The warden ordered a fresh-faced young guard to lead them to the prison's electrical plant. Hardigan memorized the route in case he had to get out fast and alone.

He and Han unloaded the tools in the prison's electrical plant. To accustom the guards to seeing them, they made several trips out to the van for meters, extension cords, and tools they wouldn't need. After a few trips they would become invisible to the weary guards, who were nearing the end of their shift.

The young guard chatted with Hu, who glanced at his watch. The boy had always thought he would like to be an electrician. He was a pleasant kid, home-sick for Wuhan, serving his country. Hu nodded and grunted his responses, but the boy didn't take the hint.

Hardigan checked his watch. They had to get out of here with Stefanie and Chang Sitong before the electrician, Soong, was discovered beaten and tied at the electrical company's office. They also needed to escape the morning's rush hour traffic.

Han must have been thinking the same thing for he pointed at his watch.

Hardigan nodded. He waved Han to the door. When Han was in position, Hardigan tapped the boy's shoulder. When he turned, Hardigan's fist snapped his head back. The boy's eyes glazed, and he folded.

Hardigan dragged the young guard behind the generators, tied him with orange electrical cords, and gagged him with his own handkerchief.

Hardigan and Hu stripped their jumpsuits, revealing prison guard uniforms beneath. Hardigan's was tight. Hu opened a folded map, which he found be-neath a lantern on a shelf. "They're only a few cells apart. Do you have the forged papers?"

Hu nodded.

Han capped two sticks of dynamite. He glanced up. "You have twenty min-utes before the phones go out. Are you sure you can take out the cell phones?"

"No problem," Hardigan said. "Get the kid out of here before the dynamite blows."

Hu led the way from the electrical room. Hardigan adjusted his green uni-form jacket before following. Either Hu had been here before or he was very good with maps.

The drowsy guards ignored them as they passed.

None of the checkpoint sentries troubled them after glancing over the forged papers. At the final checkpoint, Hu handed over his forged papers to the guard, a weary middle-aged veteran who looked as if he knew what he was doing. "I need the prisoners Chang and Peng."

When the guard turned away, Hardigan glanced at his watch. *Fifteen min-utes left to get out of here.*

The guard stopped in front of a cell to check his keys. "The girl Peng was just brought in from interrogation a couple of hours ago. I am surprised that they want her again so soon."

"They want to keep the pressure on," Hu said.

The guard thought it over before opening Chang's cell. "Hurry up, you."

The middle-aged union leader and human rights activist staggered from a makeshift bunk in the tiny, reeking cell. He carried his left arm against his body, held in place with his right. His face was bruised, and he had lost two teeth. His eyes widened at the sight of the cab driver, Hu, but the guard was already turning away. While Hu handcuffed the prisoner, Chang glanced at Hardigan, who nodded.

"The way the girl has been puking since they brought her back, she will tell them what they want to know with the first kiss of the baton," the guard said.

Hardigan clenched his fists, then forced them to relax. He gritted his teeth against the temptation to throttle the man.

The guard swung the door open. "Come out here, Peng."

When she did not, the guard stepped into the cell and swore. Hardigan looked over his shoulder in time to see Stefanie's foot vanish into the vent in the ceiling. The guard ran across the room and scrambled up her makeshift scaffold. He ran his arm into the vent. "I have you. Come out, Peng."

Hardigan relaxed. They couldn't lose her now, not this close.

The guard yanked, knocking over the bucket. He caught himself on the top concrete block, dragging Steff's leg with him. She kicked him in the face with her free foot. Coal dust covered her skirt and bare legs. The guard lunged for the leg she was kicking. She bloodied his nose with her next blow. The guard wrenched her leg around. Stefanie screamed.

"I will help," Hardigan said. He grabbed the kicking foot. Between the guard and him, they hauled her from the vent. She hung from the vent by her bleeding fingers. Hardigan held her around the knees while the guard pried her fingers loose, muttering threats of dire punishment for attempting to escape.

When she dropped into Hardigan's arms, she slapped his face. She clawed at him, but her bleeding nails did nothing but leave streaks of her blood on his face.

The guard grabbed her arms and wrenched them backward.

She screamed.

"Get your cuffs on her," the guard snapped.

She moaned and would have fallen when Hardigan released her if the guard hadn't pinioned her arms. She pivoted and kicked, but when her foot made contact with Hardigan's shin, she cried out in pain. Her clothes were torn and snagged and black with coal dust, her hair was a sooty, tangled mess, and her hands were bleeding, but her eyes sparkled with black fire.

Hardigan did not dare speak.

"We are late," Hu snapped. "Hurry."

Hardigan wished he did not have to push Stefanie to keep up with the cabby and Chang Sitong. She winced with each step. She limped along with her head down, her face pale behind the soot. After going through the final checkpoint, he whispered, "Not much farther, babe." The lights brightened—Han's signal that they had three minutes left.

Stefanie stopped and stared at Hardigan. "What?"

Ahead of them, Hu turned. "It is clear. This way is faster." He took a side corridor leading to a freight elevator. In the elevator, Stefanie turned to face Troy.

"Listen," Hu said, unlocking Chang Sitong's handcuffs. "We have less than three minutes to get out of here. When we get to the electrical room, you need to put on electrical coveralls, Sitong. Then we are all going to carry out equipment. You will walk out with us. Carry the extension cords up near your face to block the bruises. Once you are inside the truck, stay out of sight."

"Troy?" Stefanie asked. She still stared at him, confused.

"Yeah, babe." Hardigan brushed a wisp of hair from her face while Hu unlocked her handcuffs.

"What do I do?" Stefanie asked.

"We carry you out in the toolbox," Hu said. "Our partner should have a false front in place when we get there."

Hu led them from the elevator to the electrical room. Hardigan tore his police uniform off and tossed it behind the generators with the unconscious guard and the lower drawers from the toolbox. Han lifted Stefanie into the rolling box and shut the lid. The false front looked perfect.

Han helped the other men into their red jumpsuits.

Chang whispered, "If you cannot get me out, do not hesitate. Kill me. They know who I am now."

"I was able to reset the timer," Han said. "We still have three minutes."

Hardigan unbound a small satchel from his waist. "Go ahead. I will be along."

Han and the cabby rolled the toolbox out the door. Each carried all the tools he could manage. Chang carried a bulky roll of extension cord around his good shoulder. He hunched his shoulders to disguise his bruised face. His injured arm hung limp.

Hardigan checked the dynamite and the timer that would set it off. The installation looked good. He carried the unconscious young guard to a nearby furnace room. Squatting out of sight of the door, he attached the wires in a small box that looked like a TV remote. He had seen one of these cell phone scramblers tested before but had never used one in the field.

He snapped the scrambler shut. The green activation light remained dark.

He opened it again, adjusted the wires and closed it again. Still dark.

The young guard beside him stirred.

The squeaking of the toolbox was receding down the corridor.

Hardigan brushed a drop of sweat from his forehead and hoped it didn't smear his makeup.

Forcing himself to be patient, he opened the scrambler again, tightened the battery connections, and checked the wiring. This time, when he closed it, the light blinked green. He set the timer for three minutes. He stuck it in his pocket, grabbed a couple of boxes of tools, and strode down the corridor. The closer he could get it to the office the better.

The rolling tool box sat at the bottom of a flight of stairs. They had planned to take the tools out with Chang. Then, while Chang hid in the van, Hu and Han would come back. Han and Hardigan would carry the toolbox with Stefanie out.

Hardigan was sweating again. What if they left Stefanie and him here? He glanced around and stroked the Glock pistol in his pocket. *Oh, Lord, please don't let them leave us.*

Han and Hu Youmei came through the door at the top of the flight of stairs.

"Less than a minute and a half," Han said. He grabbed one handle of the toolbox, while Hardigan grabbed the other. The cabby carried the tools that Hardigan had brought. Hardigan and Han trotted up the stairs. Stefanie was lighter than the tools they had carried down. While Hu opened the door, Hardigan deposited the scrambler behind the door. At the top of the flight of stairs, they set the toolbox down to roll it. The wheels shrieked their guilt, but the guards barely glanced their way.

Hu signed them out at each of the checkpoints.

In front of the office, they stopped again. The cabby went into the office to sign out. *Forty-six seconds and counting.*

A young, stylishly dressed woman stepped from the office. The bright lights glinted off her thick glasses.

"I checked again," she was saying over her shoulder. "The guard said she has already been taken to interrogation."

Kong stepped into the hallway. "Why would they have taken her before we ordered the interrogation?"

Hardigan tried to look nonchalant. *What's keeping Hu?*

"Perhaps Po called for her," Kong said. In avoiding a group of guards, Kong ran into Hardigan, shoving him against the wall. Hardigan expected the agent to grab him. Instead, Kong pushed away and followed the girl down the corridor.

"Start the van," Hardigan said when Hu emerged from the office. *So close. How many seconds before it blows?*

The two men rolled the toolbox out onto the loading dock. Together, they lifted the toolbox. Han was sweating, staring back at the building. A wheel caught on the edge of the van floor. Hardigan gritted his teeth and slid his body beneath the teetering chest. The toolbox rolled forward into the van.

"I will organize the tools," Hardigan offered as a guard strolled past. He jumped into the back.

Han slammed the door and climbed in the front.

Hu waved at the guard as they pulled out. Han checked his watch. "It should have blown by now."

The guard at the gate did not stop them. Instead, he was noticing that an alarm light had suddenly gone on. He took a step toward the prison, then, yelling at some others, ran toward the building.

"We are going to hit the traffic jams," Hu said glumly.

Hardigan opened the toolbox and helped Stefanie out. He passed her a rag. "Get as much of that dirt off as you can and put those white coveralls and cap on."

He helped Chang Sitong out of the red coveralls and into a coat.

"Did they arrest you because of the article?" Chang asked Stefanie.

"No, Pete Weston set me up, perhaps both of us," she said.

"Weston?" Chang said.

"The photographer?" Han shook his head. "He has been helping us."

Hardigan steadied Stefanie as she tried to put her foot into a pant leg. "He took me to Kong last night in exchange for a shorter prison sentence for his girlfriend."

"That would explain a lot," Han added.

"We did not suspect him," Sitong said.

"How far to our stop?" Hardigan asked.

Hu glanced at the rearview mirror and groaned. "Police behind us."

Chapter 43

"ONE OF THEM HAD WIDE SHOULDERS and a big neck, and his arms were unusually long." The guard was sweating profusely now as he described those who had just escorted the female prisoner from her cell and out of the unit.

"The big one did not say much," the guard added, grasping for any description that might help to soothe the seething Kong. But he had barely got the words out when a muffled explosion filtered through the labyrinthine passages. Dust and smoke poured from the vents. The lights went out.

"What was that?" the guard asked.

Hardigan was here. Kong shoved past the guard and felt his way along the cold concrete and stone wall toward the stairs. Chen Yuliang rounded another corner with a small flashlight she had fished out of her bag. She was out of breath. "An explosion. In the electrical generators."

Kong ran past her and up the steps. "It took out the phones and electricity," she called after him.

Kong felt his way upstairs. He had run into one of the electricians outside the office—the thick one, solid build, wearing gloves. *Hardigan?*

A door above him opened. Several men with flashlights entered.

"You!" Kong grabbed the first one. "Arrest the men in that electrical van. Do not let them out of this yard." He shoved the man back through the group.

From below, Kong smelled smoke. Someone yelled, "Fire! Fire!"

Prisoners screamed. They lunged against the cell doors in terror.

Guards with fire hoses and flashlights blocked the way to the office. Kong fought his way through and found Chen's cell phone on the counter. He punched in a number but nothing happened. He stared out at the closed gate and the scrambling confusion of guards. The electrical van was gone.

"The police have passed us," Han said, his relief evident in his voice.

"Get ready for the next stoplight," Hu said.

Stefanie twisted her hair to fit into the cap. Troy pushed some stray spears of hair in around the edges. He passed her a coat hanging from the hook. It felt big and bulky, but at least it fastened around the throat. *That should hide my bruises.*

"Get ready," Han called.

Stefanie steadied herself and held on to Troy at the back door.

"Once you get out, grab that plastic tool box. Then follow me."

The van stopped. "Now!" Hu yelled.

Troy opened the door and hopped down. Stefanie steeled herself against the pain she knew she would feel when her feet hit the ground. A gasp escaped as the wave of pain spread through her body. *No time to think. Grab the tool box and go.* Hardigan slammed the door. They dodged the traffic to reach the sidewalk, then joined the surging crowds. After a block, the pain was unbearable. Troy was glancing at her with concern. She was trying not to limp, but failing miserably. Sweat popped out on her forehead. She bit her lip and blinked to hold back the tears. Troy slowed a little to help her keep up.

"Two blocks to go," he said.

Two blocks to go. Stefanie kept her head down and plodded on. She felt conspicuous but no one took any notice of them. They were as anonymous on the bustling streets of Beijing as they would have been in Chicago.

The sky erupted in sirens from all directions. Pedestrians stopped and stared. Troy stopped too, blending in with Beijing's citizens. Stefanie trudged on. A half dozen bicyclists, heads turned to look for the source of the commotion, collided. Emergency vehicles' lights flashed on, shrieking demands for the street to clear ahead of them.

Some pedestrians ran to help the piled-up bicyclists. Others continued on their way with nervous glances skyward. Stefanie limped on. Now Hardigan guided her into an alley, across another street, down another block and into a busy parking lot to a parked van.

Hardigan tapped on the side door.

Ulysses Chou laid down his paper and unlocked the passenger door. "If I ever need help with my wiring, I know not to call you. Seems Beijing Number One is on fire after your last service call."

Hardigan moved aside, took the toolbox from Stefanie, and helped her into the back of the van. "How bad?"

"Bad enough that the authorities aren't able to hush it up."

Thinking of the prisoners locked into the fetid cells. Stefanie felt the blood draining from her face. She hoped she wouldn't get sick.

"Can you fit in the well for that third seat?" Chou asked Stefanie.

"I'll try."

Hardigan helped her to the back. Chou had already lined the well with a blanket. "It's the best I could do on short notice."

The hiding place wasn't much. Stefanie lowered herself into the well. Seeing her wince, Troy asked, "What is it?"

"Just a sprain."

She lay down in the well and curled into a fetal position. He squeezed her shoulder. "You okay, babe?"

She pressed her eyes shut, bit her lip, and nodded.

"Save the love scenes for later, Red." Chou started the van.

"Where are we going?"

Chou grinned. "Somewhere the other team will never think of looking."

Stefanie wiggled to make room for the small toolbox beside her, then felt the close darkness as the car's floor mat covered her hiding place. Troy spread some children's toys over the mat, just for good measure.

Chou tuned the radio to a station that played Hong Kong pop while Troy's seatbelt clicked. The mat muffled the sounds. "How's she doing?"

Stefanie wrapped her arms tightly around herself and clenched her teeth, afraid she would burst into tears. *I don't even want to think about that question.*

"The Tiger is not having a good day," said the Dragon with a note of satisfaction in her voice. "One soldier dead. Three in the hospital with smoke inhalation. Eight prisoners suffering smoke inhalation. Furnaces, phones, and electricity out. Two prisoners escaped, probably with the help of a CIA agent. And no closer to finding the man you were assigned to capture. The easy life in America seems to have taken some of your bite."

Kong silently swore to pursue Hardigan to the ends of the earth if he were fired over this.

"We have to add to that Beijing's panic over those television announcements last night," the Minister of Public Security said. "People began rushing to bomb shelters when the sirens went off this morning. They thought the United States was bombing us with nuclear weapons." He shoved back in his chair and peered at Kong. Beneath his bushy eyebrows, his small black eyes were fiery coals.

"I had nothing to do with those announcements, sir, and would not have used them," Kong said.

"I realize that the assistant minister of the Religious Affairs Bureau authorized those television announcements, but the point is that this simple project has been badly bungled. Foreign journalists are smelling a story over the announcements last night and the fire at Beijing Number One. The American Embassy demands to know whether we have any American citizens in custody. The U.S. government is officially and publicly ridiculing the charge that Miss Peng and Mr. Hardigan are CIA agents—especially Miss Peng."

"We would do the same."

Kong forced himself not to squirm. He reeked of smoke from the fire. A hurried washing had not removed the black smudges on his hands and face. He would have to throw out his clothes.

The minister rocked his chair and steepled his fingers. He leaned forward again. "Leave us, Miss Wen."

The Dragon's eyebrows rose, but she obeyed.

Kong wanted a glass of water or a smoke. He could not decide which. His throat burned, but the nicotine would soothe his nerves.

The minister did not speak until the door clicked shut behind the Dragon. He shoved back into his chair again, turned away from Kong, lit a cigarette, and tossed the pack to Kong. Kong relaxed. The minister seemed less threatening surrounded by the familiar haze of smoke.

"Earlier today I counted more than two dozen projects that you have completed efficiently and with creativity." The minister puffed and stared at the smoke-formed clouds. "I also know that you felt this case was beneath you."

"Yes, sir, but I have conscientiously tried. . . ."

"Why?"

"Illiterate cultists in the countryside are less dangerous than America's technological advances. If the province of Taiwan gets that technology, we may never reunite. And I still believe I can take out the cultists *and* prosecute our U.S. plans. They are related to one another. It was a good plan. But obviously we have had some . . . difficulties."

"Start at the beginning. Tell me about this case."

Kong reviewed the events, the meetings with Hardigan in Chicago, the setting up of Stefanie Peng, the visit of Stefanie with her grandfather, the discovery that Hardigan was a CIA spy and in Beijing, the capture of the girl, and her escape from the prison.

The minister stubbed his cigarette out in the ashtray. "What are your next steps?"

"All people entering the English-speaking and Spanish-speaking embassies are being stopped and identified to prevent the fugitives' escape. We are searching all vehicles entering the embassies. A contact in the American embassy assures us they are not there.

"We are monitoring phone calls from the security chief of the American Embassy, who was with Hardigan at the hotel. We have brought in the known religious leaders to find Peng Chongde. Railroads, buses, and airports have increased security and are checking for Hardigan and the girl.

"I would like permission to close off the consulates in other cities, sir, at least the consulate in Shanghai. The Pengs have family in Shanghai."

"What about ports?" The minister asked.

"Of course, sir." *Ports. Why didn't I think of that?* "We will get them, sir. Then we will have the Brother and the identity of Hardigan's contact within our government."

The minister studied him. "I doubt they will attempt to escape through Tibet or Uygur, but we should alert our border patrols. If nothing else, the practice will do them good. Also, beef up security in the parks in case the girl tries to make contact with some Christians or English speakers there."

The spacious and pleasantly appointed apartment of a mid-level bureaucrat was nicer than any other Chinese home Stefanie had seen. She tried to soak away the horrors of the day with a bath, leisurely washing the dirt, sweat, and blood from her hair. The feel and smell of fresh clothing next to her skin was so refreshing, even if the clothes were borrowed from Chou's twelve-year-old daughter.

Feeling more relaxed, though still in constant pain from her ankle and bruises, Stefanie limped into the living room, where Troy was hunched over a simple metal table, working on his laptop. Coming up behind him, she was about to put her hands on his strong shoulders when her eyes were drawn to the Chinese characters on the screen as he scanned and scrolled. Military unit deployments; locations for mobile missile launchers, with missile designations. Now he was making a secure file to send over the telephone line. Her mouth went slack as she considered what Kong had said about Troy and the confirmation that now seemed clear. She drew a heavy breath as she reached the unavoidable conclusion.

The sound of her breath behind him sent Troy jumping almost to his feet as he interposed his body to cover the screen. "What are you doing sneaking up on me like that?" he said angrily.

She drew back. Her hand brushing her bruised right cheek. A man in the same business as Troy had given her that bruise. Troy immediately softened his reaction. "I'm sorry, babe. You startled me. I didn't know you were there."

Too glib, too smooth, like something Kong might say.

"What you were reading . . . it was about nuclear missiles." She stepped back, wincing in pain as her weight shifted to the injured ankle. She looked with new understanding at the man she had known and trusted as "Uncle Troy." She didn't like this new information about him.

"That's something you shouldn't see, something that could get us and several other people killed."

"It's true about you . . . about what you do, isn't it? It was the only thing that explained your part in all of this, but I kept telling myself it couldn't be true. I kept coming up with other explanations."

"I am the same man you've always known, Stef." He moved toward her and reached out to touch her, but she stepped quickly away, feeling new pain as her leg struck an elegant mahogany end table. She sank wearily onto the cushions of the sofa. Troy neither moved nor spoke for a long moment. Stefanie did not lift her eyes from the floor.

"I thought that . . . I thought I knew you. Every man I trust betrays me—Roger, Qili, Pete."

"I have not betrayed you. Your grandfather, your father, Ramón, me—when have we ever betrayed you? Honey, if I weren't what I am, I couldn't have gotten you out of that prison today. I put it all on the line for you."

That was beside the point, wasn't it? No, but did it make up for the lies?

"Yes, you did," she said at last, trying to measure each word she spoke. "You took an unbelievable risk for me. I must seem so ungrateful. It's just that . . . I have entered a very ugly world in which nothing is what it seems, and everyone is playing games. A friend I trusted sold me to the police. A friend I once trusted made me watch awful things being done to a woman I had come to care about—a woman who did not deserve to be tortured. Now suddenly all of that has just gone away. I'm free . . . and the reason is that you are not what you seem to be either. You are all part of the same game. This is your world too. I can't understand how. . . ."

No, Stefanie, do not lose control. She tugged negligently at the skirt she had borrowed from Chou's twelve-year-old daughter, struggling against the feelings that threatened to drown her.

"It's all been a shock," Troy said.

A shock? How condescending could he be? Sure it was a shock, but Troy was missing the real issue here. She rose from the sofa and limped to the other side of the room, leaning against the jamb of the kitchen door, keeping her back toward Troy.

"I have to know something, and I need to be able to depend on the truth of the answer."

"I will tell you the exact truth, whatever it is."

"Has our . . . friendship . . . was it just part of the job? A way to be close to my father and Dr. Jim?" Again she tugged the short, straight skirt.

"You were never part of any work—not ever," Troy said. "I didn't need to insert myself into your life to have a working relationship with your father or Jim. I've been part of your family because I wanted and needed you all. I admit that I took my relationship with you for granted—the whole 'little sister' thing. But it was all real. I got here as soon as I knew you were in trouble. You have no idea how frightened I was for you, honey, especially when I found out about your connection with Kong. All of that is truth."

This time when he approached her, she turned toward him and didn't back away. "It is also pure truth that at that Valentine's Day party, I realized I—"

Stefanie pressed a finger to his lips.

"That's enough for now. I believe you. Please don't say the rest of it yet. I'm not ready."

"I know, babe." He traced her cheek with his finger, careful to avoid the bruise.

"Thank you for coming, for not leaving me in that awful place." Stefanie's eyes filled with tears. "They beat Qin. She was bleeding. Her blood spattered all over the room. And Qili held me and made me watch."

"Don't think about it, honey." He kissed her forehead.

Stefanie looked into Troy's eyes, her lips curving into a sad smile.

"You just broke your promise—about the forehead." Stefanie reached her arms around Troy's neck and pulled his face down to her, closing her eyes as she felt the gentle caress of his lips on hers.

"Seems I am always interrupting these tender love scenes," Chou said from the doorway. Troy and Stefanie jumped and Troy instinctively turned to shield Stefanie from impending danger.

"At ease, Red," Chou said with a grin as he entered the apartment. He shut the door and locked it, then went into the kitchen to fill a watering can. When he reemerged, he proceeded to water the plants in the living room.

"Is this your apartment?" Stefanie asked.

"Mine? The police have already been to mine." Chou grinned again. "No, this belongs to a friend of mine, the chief of police."

Troy rolled his eyes.

Chou thrust his arms wide. "Why would they expect one of their own to be housing the enemies? Besides, he and his wife are in Indonesia to celebrate their thirtieth wedding anniversary."

"Isn't this dangerous?" Stefanie asked. "How did you get in here?"

"I water their plants for them. The police chief's wife and Anne are good friends. They're in our *tai chi* group." He grinned. "What smells so good, little girl?"

He was being diplomatic. The odor from the kitchen was of oil that had become too hot. "Oh, no, I forgot the stir-fry." Stefanie hobbled into the kitchen.

As soon as she was gone, Chou's face darkened. "Our covers are pretty thoroughly blown. Just to be on the safe side, Anne and the kids went to the embassy yesterday. That option's closed now. We've got to find another consulate or a way out of the country."

Hardigan nodded as he walked over to his computer. "We may have another problem. I encoded and sent the document to the company, but I'm getting no response at all." He started the shut-down sequence and closed the lid.

Supper did not go well. Chou ate heartily, despite the fact that the sweet and sour chicken was considerably overdone. Stefanie managed only a few bites, her thoughts consumed with renewed worry about her grandfather. *How can I fight for his release now?*

When she had apologized for the meal, she had felt Troy's hand grasp hers under the table with a sympathetic squeeze. The little gesture made her want to cling to him again.

Chou set his napkin on the table and pushed the plate back. "You leave for Shanghai tomorrow night. The consulate's still unwatched there."

"It may not be safe by the time we reach it," Troy said.

"Then they'll establish a drop point so we can extract by boat."

"Sub?" Troy asked.

Chou nodded. He glanced at Stefanie. "You haven't said much, little girl."

"You won't like to hear what I have to say." She took a deep breath. "I can't leave Beijing without my grandfather."

"Stef. . . ."

Chou raised his hand for silence. "I've got some news on that score, some parts good and some not so good. Peng Chongde has been released."

Stefanie's heart stopped beating. "What?"

"My source says that Kong was bringing him to a prison in Beijing—so his bait would be nice and close. But evidently somebody screwed up the works. They made out a release instead of a transfer. It happens."

"So he's free? He's out? How are we ever going to find him?" Stefanie's heart surged with a mixture of exhilaration and fear.

"Now we get to the not-so-good news. My contact said that Kong has been screaming death and destruction unless they get him back. They are looking for him and another fellow almost as intensely as they are for you two. But he has probably reached the underground church by now. The earth has swallowed him up."

"He will be coming to Beijing. He knows I am here to take him home. I have to find him."

"I think you are forgetting the shape of your situation. There are twelve million people in Beijing. Three of them are wanted rather badly by the police. You two are going to find the third?" Chou asked. "Your grandfather will be a lot safer if he doesn't hook up with us."

"You know he's right, babe."

Stefanie was hardly paying attention. "At the house church I attended Sunday"—she wasn't sure how long ago that had been—"I met an artist who paints at Tiananmen Square. I've seen him there before. He might know."

"Assuming it's not raining, or he hasn't been arrested, or they don't see you before you get to them," Chou said.

Troy shook his head. "Out of the question. The square's full of policemen, and you can bet they all have our pictures."

"What's your idea, little girl?"

"To be what you just called me, Mr. Chou. They are looking for a woman who is a dangerous foreign spy—not a schoolgirl."

Chapter 44

THE BROTHER STROLLED past the front gate of Beijing University. Security guards were checking everyone who entered. If Miss Peng were at the university, how would he reach her without drawing attention to himself? The People's Armed Police had been questioning Christian leaders around Beijing about his whereabouts and identity.

After hearing about the televised announcements the night before, poor Peng Chongde felt certain that his granddaughter had been arrested. Then the radio had broadcast a high-ranking security official who thanked Miss Peng and others for helping them with their emergency "test."

"Our people reacted strongly to what they thought was a threat by the American CIA. The Chinese people are united. They are strong because of their unity." The official had continued praising the people for two minutes.

Reading between the lines, the Brother decided that the test, if indeed that was what it was, had failed.

Rumors tied the fire at Beijing Number One Prison with the announcements last night. A believer whose cousin's husband worked at the prison said a woman who demanded to contact the United States Embassy had escaped.

Stopping at a store, he asked to use the phone. He dialed Miss Peng's number from a note she had given her grandfather.

"*Ni hao*," a woman answered. Her voice was higher than he remembered and she lacked the slight Shanghai accent he expected.

"Would Miss Peng be in?" he asked.

"Speaking."

Now what should I say? She doesn't sound right.

"We met on the train in Xian when you were with Mr. Kong."

"Oh, yes."

"We discussed photographs. Since I was in Beijing, I wondered if you would like to have dinner with me."

"A date? You are asking me for a date?"

"We could continue our conversation about taking pictures." Her voice did not warm nor did she recognize his hints.

"Well, I am quite busy, but if you will leave a phone number, Mr.—"

"I apologize for bothering you." This was not Stefanie Peng, so why was she pretending to be?

"What did you say your name was?" she asked.

He hung up without answering.

As he left the store, he wondered if he had been too vague. No, the voice lacked the warmth he remembered. The tones were wrong. The voice on the phone was pure Beijing.

Now what? He lingered outside the campus until he saw a student with an English book. She was plump with a pleasant face. He noticed several others with English books, but this one stood out, and he took the feeling for God's guidance. He followed her onto the bus and found a seat near her. When she got off, he did too.

"Excuse me," he said, catching up with her. "Is that an English book?"

She smiled. "Yes, I am studying English at Beijing University."

"I have always been curious about English. Is it very hard?"

The girl spoke with him for several minutes about her struggles with the language. When he asked about her teacher, she frowned. She glanced around and lowered her voice. People streamed past without showing any interest in them. "I have a new teacher who does not teach as well as the one I had. Did you see the emergency ads the other night on TV?"

"No, but I heard about them."

"The government has said it was just a test, but my American teacher, Miss Peng, was the woman they were looking for, and she has not returned."

"I see."

"The police are still stopping people outside some of the embassies, and everyone going on campus. A friend of mine is a campus guard. He told me that Miss Peng is one of the people they are looking for."

"And they are still searching for her?"

The young woman glanced at the pedestrians around them. "That is what he said."

He changed the subject back to English, thanked her, and left. He dreaded telling Peng Chongde what he had learned. How would they ever find her now?

Stefanie shoved the white plastic sunglasses with Minnie Mouse on the corners back with one finger. She jiggled her long braid and ran her tongue over the piece of wire that Chou had attached to her teeth to look like braces. The padding disguising her figure beneath the clothes of Chou's twelve-year-old daughter made her feel that she waddled down the aisle of the bus. She tried to remember what twelve felt like, how Amanda had acted at twelve, what the twelve-year-olds at church were like.

"This is crazy," Troy had said again before she left the apartment.

"If Stefanie wants to find her grandfather, this is probably the only way," Chou said. "If you were looking for a woman, would you notice a kid with braces?"

As she had paused at the door of the apartment, Troy had lifted her chin and looked deep in her eyes. "Be careful, babe. I am going to be praying for you every second you are out there."

Roger had never offered to pray for her. Funny how cherished Troy's words made her feel, though she had not let him say that he loved her. She stretched up on tiptoe to kiss his cheek.

With the wrap taken off, her swollen ankle was aching, but she tried to ignore the pain and trotted after a group of kids running across Tiananmen Square, a slightly chubby kid who couldn't keep up, who was carrying a book bag. She stopped to watch Chou practice *tai chi*. He would keep an eye on her in case she was caught. They had agreed they could not risk Troy's capture if she were arrested a second time. There would not be another rescue.

She trudged up the steps to the Monument to the People's Heroes. She took her time walking around it. To anyone who noticed she would have been studying the relief work. The Communist heroes stared at her from their frozen positions in the stone. If they could have, they would have denounced her to the policemen all around, "This woman you seek is deceiving the people again."

She glanced up past the monument to the gray winter sky. The smoke from the factories rose straight up, and Beijing's odor of coal dust, diesel fumes, industrial pollutants, and gas barely touched her.

Were other heroes watching her from beyond the sky, a great cloud of witnesses cheering her on?

Please, Lord, please give me courage and wisdom. Please help me find him.

She had little time. She could not stay in the square when the other children left for school. Troy refused to allow her to remain in China without him, regardless of her grandfather. She could slip away, but where would she go?

Two American Marines from the embassy strolled past, their presence cheering her. She suspected they were part of Chou's protection detail.

There. The artist with his easel and supplies balanced across his lap rolled into the park. *Thank you, Lord.* She shouldn't approach too quickly.

"Are those new braces?"

Stefanie turned to stare into the face of the big man who had tailed her so often. She touched the wire with a finger. She swallowed hard. "Yes, sir. I just got them. I am not used to them yet." Between the cheek pads and the fake braces, she did not sound like herself.

"When they come off, you can smile pretty for our brave soldiers."

Her face heated. He did not recognize her.

"School will start soon. Do not be. . . ." He broke off and stared toward a young woman about her height in a red coat. He walked off in the direction of the woman. He stopped her about a hundred yards away. He must have demanded her papers. Shortly after looking at them, he allowed the woman to walk away. Deciding to play it safe, Stefanie drifted behind a group of college students. Gradually she made her way to the artist who was painting the Monument to the People's Heroes. She stopped beside him.

He glanced up, smiled, and resumed painting.

She waited until no one was near. "You do beautiful work, brother."

He paused, his brush frozen in mid-air. He frowned, shifting his gaze to her. He looked around. "Did you say something?"

"We met Sunday in your apartment. I am Stefanie Peng from *Mei Guo*. I wondered if you know where my grandfather, Peng Chongde, is."

He scowled at her. His hand trembled as he lowered his brush to his palette. "What are you talking about?"

Stefanie twirled on her tiptoes to see if anyone was watching. She tilted the Minnie Mouse sunglasses onto her head, so that she could look the artist in the face.

"The Public Security Bureau set me up to use me against my grandfather. They captured me early Monday morning and made me watch Bo Qin be tortured."

"Why are you telling me this?"

"I have to find my grandfather. I have a way out of the country tonight, but Kong Qili will kill him if he's captured. I don't know anyone else to tell."

"How do I know you are not a government plant, trying to draw me into something that does not concern me?"

"You do not know, unless the Holy Spirit gives you peace that I am telling the truth. The police are looking for me. Look at who they stop today. They may guess that I will try to contact the underground church. I apologize for endangering you, but I did not know where else to go."

"Are you the reason for the raids?"

She stared across the marble paving blocks of the square. Several children, pulling their book bags, scrambled to catch their bus. "Probably. The authorities planned to arrest grandfather and me and torture me to make my grandfather betray someone called the Brother."

When she faced him again, he was staring at her.

Her tail was talking to a man about Troy's size. The tail glanced in her direction.

"If you know of some way to reach my grandfather, we have a way out of Beijing tonight at one o'clock at the abandoned brick yard near the Great Helmsman Toy Factory."

The tail was approaching. Stefanie lowered her sunglasses and flashed a forced smile at the young artist. She raised her voice. "Thank you for letting me watch you paint. I have to go."

She waved at the tail and ran as best she could toward the buses. When she glanced back, the tail was sauntering along the walks, eyeing young women.

"You cannot trust her. It is a trick," Ren Shaoqi said. *Why can't they see it?* He pounded his fist against the kitchen table in the artist's small apartment. The day had left him oblivious to the smells of paint and cleaning chemicals.

Chongde bowed his head and stared at his misshapen fingers.

"It could be," the young artist agreed, "but the police were stopping people who resembled the ones in those TV spots, just as she said."

"She is trying to save her own skin," Shaoqi said. He expected the old man to accuse him of the same thing.

The Brother paused in his pacing. "I have stayed alive and out of prison by being a shrewd judge of character. The woman I met on the train would not betray us. She would not endanger her grandfather unless there was a chance of escape. And the woman I spoke to on the phone was not Sister Peng."

"You are fools," Shaoqi said.

"If my life would save hers, it would be a small trade," Chongde said. He rubbed his twisted fingers, the dry skin sounding like sandpaper.

"There will be no trade if Kong is involved." Shaoqi slipped to his knees in front of the old man. "He is as cruel as a tiger."

The Brother agreed. "He would use you against each other."

The artist looked at the men. "I did not believe her. Then she told me to listen to what the Holy Spirit told me about her. They may be using her, but I believe she is telling the truth as she knows it."

"But we know that the police had her. Then she escaped from Beijing Prison Number One? Such things do not happen," Shaoqi said.

"There was the riot and fire," the Brother said.

"And you think that girl started it or some angel from heaven?" Shaoqi glared at the older man.

"This would not be the first time. A Christian found a broom and swept his way past the guards and out of prison after being tortured," the Brother said. "Yes, I believe she could have escaped from prison."

Shaoqi leaned across the table to glare at the Brother. "Why would you care if Kong finished what you started?"

The Brother blanched.

The artist scrubbed at paint on his fingers.

Chongde looked at his friend. "Shaoqi, you have lived so long with hate. I pray for you all the time that you can understand us, and especially the Brother. When we repent, God buries our sins in the deepest sea and does not hold them against us again. It is as if they never happened. He is our example."

"That is what Kong will do to us when he finds us—bury us in a deep sea, cut in little pieces so the fish will have no trouble digesting us." Shaoqi pointed at the Brother. "It is still because of you!"

"What?"

"If he had you, he would leave Peng Chongde alone."

"Enough!" Chongde ordered.

"Is this true?" the Brother asked.

Held in Chongde's scowling gaze, Shaoqi did not answer.

"The girl said that she would be tortured to make Chongde surrender you," the artist said. He squirmed in his wheelchair. "But your work, Lao. . . ."

The Brother squared on Shaoqi. "How do you know this?"

Shaoqi looked toward Chongde for help, but the old man sat with his eyes closed. The artist and the Brother stared at him.

Shaoqi moistened his lips. "Kong gave me the choice of execution or gaining my freedom by delivering you up through Chongde."

After a long silence, the Brother said, "I see."

"I have not done it."

"I see." The Brother's words cut, though his voice was mild.

"I did not want to be involved in all of this. I just want to live. I am not a Christian. None of you mean anything to me." Shaoqi cracked the knuckles on his other hand.

"Shaoqi, thank you for your help. You have been very good to me," Chongde said.

Shaoqi, still kneeling at Chongde's feet, grasped the gnarled hands. The worn hands felt like wrinkled parchment stretched over dried twigs. "Are you sending me away, uncle?"

"No, but you should risk yourself no longer." The old hands squeezed his. The old man smiled gently his two-tooth smile.

"Then you are going to meet her?"

"I need to pray for the Lord to lead me."

"But you are going?"

"Unless the Lord shows me otherwise, I am going. You have been very good to me, son. You do not need to go."

"If you are going, I am going," Shaoqi said.

"You had better be careful, friend Ren Shaoqi," said the Brother with a smile. "You are very close to love. If you open your heart too wide, more than Peng Chongde may slip in."

The Brother turned to the artist. "Where can I find someone to take us?"

Chapter 45

THE BROTHER STEPPED from one foot to the other in the darkened phone booth as the phone rang. He half hoped that no one would answer.

"*Ni hao*," Jizhong said.

The Brother hesitated. After all these years he hadn't expected her voice to bother him so. Her voice, though still quiet, sounded older, harder.

"Is anyone there?" she asked.

"*Ni hao*, Jizhong. This is Jingyue."

This time she hesitated. "Why are you calling here?"

"I wondered if I could speak to Rongwen."

A brittle chuckle reached him over the phone. "He searches all over China for you, and you call him at home."

"Then he does know it is me. I wondered. Yes, it must seem odd." He didn't know what to say to this woman he had loved.

Jizhong's voice softened. "You haunt him. He has never said that he is looking for you. Never has he described you or used your name. But down deep he knows. No, Jingyue, he is not here, and it would be best if you do not try to talk to him."

"I have been thinking much of him. I have been praying to God for him. We need to talk about some things." He peered around in the subdued light to watch for Peng Chongde and Ren Shaoqi.

"You know that you cannot talk anything out with Rongwen. He hates this God of yours." The silence hung between them.

"We were once so close."

"You cannot doctor a dead horse as if he were alive, Jingyue. *Once* was long ago. Once we were close as well." Her words faded off. He wondered if she meant that she had once been close to him or to her husband. Perhaps both.

He saw Ren Shaoqi and Peng Chongde beneath a streetlight halfway down the block.

"I am sorry to have bothered you, Jizhong. I have to go." He started to put the phone down, but her hurried words captured his attention.

"Jingyue?"

"Yes?"

"It is good to hear from you. Be careful."

Stefanie wiggled her toes inside her borrowed boots to keep them from freezing. Dressed as a child again, she hoped that Ulysses Chou's daughter hadn't had to stand out in the cold in this coat too often.

An edge of the moon peeked from behind a high-flying cloud, illuminating a weed-infested loading yard outside a boarded-up brick factory surrounded by a rusted chain link fence. Only one of the four outside lights glowed.

"What time is it?" she asked.

"Three minutes to one."

Her grandfather had not arrived. Her whole body felt heavy with failure. *Oh, Lord, please, please, don't let me face Nanai without Grandfather. They've gone through so much.*

Troy put his arm around her. "You've done your best, babe, all anyone could do. He is with people who can look out for him."

"The truck's not here yet. He still could come. Maybe he's on the other side of the yard."

"Honey, you're expecting a miracle." Troy pulled her to him. She clung to him, accepting the shelter he provided from the cold eddies of air, wishing he could shelter her from the pain inside. *I am asking a miracle, Lord, but not for me. Only You know how much they've suffered. Please, Lord. Please.*

"I hear the truck."

"Just a few minutes longer, Troy, please."

Staring into the darkness, he paused. "It's not just you or your grandfather. I have information that has to get into the right hands or good people will be killed."

"Just long enough for me to check the other side of the yard?" She pulled her mitten free and brushed a finger down his cheek. She was being unfair. Taking advantage of his love for her shamed her, but the shame didn't stop her. "Please, Troy."

The truck stopped under a darkened streetlight.

He sighed and leaned his forehead against hers. "Promise you won't run off."

"I promise."

"I'll do my best to hold him ten minutes." He released her and walked toward the truck, staying in the shadows. Occasionally she saw his black shadow drift into deeper blackness. The driver switched off his lights when Troy climbed into the passenger side of the truck.

She had told the artist that her grandfather should meet her here, but she had not known how large the loading yard was. In the darkness she glided one foot forward, then the other to avoid stumbling over debris. After fifteen glides, she whispered, "Grandfather."

She wondered how long at this rate in the darkness it would take to get around the yard.

Shaoqi watched the girl from the bushes. She looked like a schoolgirl, but that was how the artist had described her. She crossed the yard between their hiding place in the brickyard and the single working streetlight.

Shaoqi wished he could tell Chongde that this was a policewoman disguised, but what if this was the old one's chance to escape to his family in the West? *I cannot deny him.*

Peng Chongde and the Brother trusted him to decide whether this was a police trap. They were praying for God to give him wisdom. *Why would God, if there is a God, give me wisdom?*

The girl limped toward Shaoqi's hiding place and stopped. "Grandfather?" she called softly.

Her companion, the big man, approached and called. Shaoqi could not recognize what he said. The girl answered him in indistinguishable words. He wished he knew what they were saying. Perhaps it was English.

The girl repeated words several time, her voice pleading, "Please, Troy, please."

If these are police, wouldn't they speak Mandarin?

The big man put his arm around the girl. His tone softened. The tenderness of the man's tone and touch struck Shaoqi as regretful. The man turned the girl toward the truck.

The girl sniffled and sobbed.

The man's voice softened more.

If I only understood.

Taking a deep breath, Shaoqi said, "Peng Dehong?"

The man whirled and thrust himself between Shaoqi and the girl. "Who is there?" he asked in Mandarin.

Shaoqi did not answer.

The girl stepped out beside her friend. "Grandfather?" she asked into the darkness.

"Are you Peng Dehong?" Shaoqi asked. He watched the man.

"I am Peng Stefanie Dehong. Is my grandfather with you?" The girl's voice was hopeful. Chongde said she had a strange American name.

"Stop at the right of the gate. I will get him," Shaoqi said.

"Hurry. We are in trouble. The sooner we are out of Beijing the better," the man said in imperfect Mandarin.

Kong Qili poured himself a cup of coffee and leaned back in his chair. He eased his eyelids closed over gritty, tired eyes. He had not touched his bed since he had rolled out Sunday morning. A police scanner buzzed and chattered in a corner of the room. The sour smell of beer wafted from behind him where two young drunks were being processed for fighting.

The door to the wardroom burst open, barely missing an officer.

Kong stifled his irritation at the sight of the assistant minister of the Religious Affairs Bureau, Chang Rongwen, charging among the scattered staff and desks.

"Mr. Kong, we have him," Chang said.

"Where?"

"He is here in Beijing. We must pick him up at once."

Kong grabbed a pen. "What is the address?" *Ah, Hardigan, I am coming for you.*

"You do not seem surprised that he is here."

"We have had the city encircled for three days. How could he have gotten out? Is the girl with him?"

"What girl?" Chang's jaw slackened, his confusion obvious.

Kong reminded himself that Mr. Chang was an important official whose *guanxi* could deter Kong's climb toward the top. He calmed his voice. "Miss Peng."

"How would Miss Peng have gotten to Lao?"

"Who is talking about Lao?"

The two men stared at each other. Chang drew himself up to his full short stature. "I am talking about Lao, Mr. Kong. He is the reason for all of this."

Kong reigned in his anger. The Brother was an annoyance, an impediment, a fly to be swatted out of the way. He moderated his voice. "Excuse me, Mr. Chang. It is one-thirty in the morning, and I misunderstood. I thought you meant Hardigan or perhaps Peng Chongde."

"But the whole reason for dealing with them was to capture Lao."

"There are other considerations as well."

Chen Yuliang was at a desk nearby, running a pen down a line of telephone transcripts that they had intercepted from Ulysses Chou.

Chang smiled his condescension. "I understand, Mr. Kong. However, now that you are aware that we are talking about the Brother, you will call the police in and have them pick him up."

At least I can rid myself of this annoyance, this illiterate religionist. Kong set his pen to paper. "Very well, Mr. Chang. What is his address?"

"I do not know his address exactly." Chang flushed. "The police must know the illegal house churces in Beijing. Raid them."

"Raid them? All of them? I am not a specialist in this area, but I believe we have far too few officers to approach any raid of this magnitude."

Kong tamped his temper. "How do you know he is in Beijing?"

"Someone contacted me."

"Can we talk to this contact?"

"He is unavailable."

Chang did not meet his eyes. Why was he acting so strangely? Chang opened his wallet, removed a picture cut from a photograph, and passed it to Kong. "This is the man."

Kong held the piece of photograph beneath the light. The grainy black and white picture showed a thin young man in a Mao suit. Though the cap blocked the upper part of the face, he looked familiar. Kong drew a copy of the police artist's description from inside his jacket and squinted at it and then the photo. The lower face in the photo resembled that in the sketch. Kong handed the picture and the drawing to Yuliang.

She looked as bad as he felt when she took the picture from him. After looking at it from bloodshot eyes, she shoved her glasses up and ran a hand over her gray face with its large black circles beneath her eyes. She had not yet complained.

"I do not think that will be any more help than what we have, Mr. Chang," Kong said.

Kong offered Chang a chair, poured him a cup of tea, and studied him. He refilled his cup before returning to his desk.

Chang squirmed. "Mr. Kong, you are staring impolitely."

"You are withholding information."

Chang paled, then blustered. "Mr. Kong, how do you dare. . . ."

Kong skewered Chang with his eyes. "You are the one who wants this man so badly. You expect us to make a seven-course banquet from a morsel when you have other ingredients."

"I assure you, I—"

Yuliang's finger pressed at one item on the transcript. She straightened in her chair. "This is odd."

"What, Chen?" Kong peered across the aisle at her.

"Did you say that the chief of police is not in his office this week?"

"Yes, the family is out of town. Why?"

"Why would the security officer at the American embassy phone the police chief, who is away?"

"What does it matter?" Chang Rongwen demanded.

Kong moved to Chen Yuliang's side. "What did he say?"

"He left a message on the answering machine. 'I will see you soon.'"

It might be nothing. It would be outrageously impudent to hide two criminals in the chief of police's apartment, but no more outrageous than a prison break under the nose of the Beijing Tiger. Kong grabbed his coat and left the Assistant Minister of Religious Affairs spluttering in midsentence.

Chapter 46

IN THE DARKENED HALLWAY, Kong Qili held a hand up to warn the three policemen with drawn guns to be ready. He silently but deftly picked the lock of the apartment of Beijing's chief of police and drew his Makarov.

Prepared to leap in, the policemen nodded.

Kong swung the door open and rushed into the room to one side. The policemen jumped into the darkened apartment, two to the opposite side of the door and one in the middle.

Nothing but darkness greeted them. The officers rushed toward the doors of the other rooms, but Kong knew that the apartment was empty.

Instead of taking chances, he waited until the policemen returned to holster his gun and turn on the lights. Chen Yuliang followed him in.

"No one here, sir," one of the officers reported.

"Look for any sign that someone has been here recently," Kong instructed.

"I was so sure they were here," Chen said. She removed her glasses, rubbed her nose, and turned on the answering machine.

Kong stopped at the wastepaper basket. Empty.

Two policemen returned from the kitchen. One said, "Someone has been here recently, sir. A dishcloth and dish towel are damp."

"The message from Ulysses Chou is not on the answering machine," Chen said.

Kong turned and raised an eyebrow.

"Good instincts, Chen." He returned his attention to the policemen. "Is there any trash in the kitchen? If so, go through it for discarded papers."

Kong lowered himself to the sofa, laid an arm on the back of it, and closed his eyes. *Hardigan and the girl were here, perhaps sitting where I am. If I were Hardigan, what precautions would I take? Does Stefanie know that her grandfather is out of prison? If so, who will she contact to try to reach him?*

337

Kong paced into the kitchen where the three policemen were checking discarded papers.

"Whoever was here ate chicken, sir," one said, opening a day-old newspaper containing chicken bones and skins.

"How many pieces of chicken?" Kong asked.

"Three."

Was old Peng Chongde with them, or was it two pieces for Hardigan?

Kong looked around the kitchen, then strode into the bedroom. The bed was neatly made. They had left nothing in the wastebasket.

In the bathroom he found an empty tube of acne medicine and a broken rubber band in the trash can. Sitting on the edge of the tub, he stared at the two items. He touched the tip of the tube to find what looked like makeup rather than medicine.

Why a rubber band?

While staring at it, he noticed two small shreds of paper on the floor next to the toilet. He picked them up. English script. One piece said "toy tr," the other "rickyard, 1." The handwriting looked like Stefanie's.

She probably had torn up paper and flushed it but dropped a couple of pieces.

Kong returned to the living room where Chen Yuliang sat in an arm chair looking around. "This is what I have always dreamed of, my own apartment with matching furniture."

Kong handed her the two tiny pieces of paper.

Chen's eyes widened. "Stefanie's writing. They were here."

"We must check for shipments that left toy factories and brickyards that are close to one another at 1:00 yesterday or at 1:00 this afternoon. It must be today since the towels are still damp. We are one step behind them."

Stefanie folded the blanket twice as a seat for her grandfather in front of a box of plush stuffed toys that the panel truck was carrying to Shanghai. He seemed more frail even than at the prison, his movements slower, his hands stiffer, thinner even in the warm parka that she had taken for him. She hoped the diesel fumes and the chemicals to keeps bugs out of the toys would not further weaken him.

"You can sit here, Grandfather." She wrapped another doubled blanket around his thin shoulders. "When you are hungry, either of you, help yourselves to what we have here." She pointed out a cardboard box with the glow from a flashlight.

"It is a pleasure to see you again, Peng Dehong," the Brother said.

He looked familiar, but in the flashlight's dim light she couldn't place him.

The little man smiled over his shoulder at her. "If you will shine the light in this direction, I will rearrange some of these crates to give us more room."

The Brother lifted some of the crates atop others. He adjusted the load bars that prevented the piles from toppling.

"Who is the man with you?" Grandfather asked.

How much can I tell them, especially with the Brother here? "Troy—Mr. Hardigan. He is a friend of the family. He and Nanai are very close."

"It is a strange name."

The Brother sat down on a crate on the other side of Grandfather.

"Troy is not Chinese. He is American. I think we are picking up speed." Stefanie caught herself tapping her fingers of her left hand on the floor of the truck. She snapped her hand into a fist. Her abrupt movement jerked the flashlight, sending the light dancing over their improvised cave.

"He sounds younger than he looks. How old is he?"

"He is thirty. Are the diesel fumes bothering you?"

"What is he doing in China?" Chongde asked.

Stefanie wrapped a blanket around her shoulders. "He came to China to help me with my computer. He was in Asia selling computers and technology."

"Is your friend the CIA agent the government is looking for? The one on television the other evening?"

Stefanie hesitated too long again. Both men watched her. "He sells computers and other technology around Asia. His company also works on sensitive equipment. I asked him for help after someone tried to break into my computer."

She pulled her blanket more tightly about her. "When I was arrested, Troy risked his life to rescue me from that horrid prison."

"Innocent people died, Dehong," Chongde said.

"It is not the first time in that place." She couldn't keep the bitterness from her voice as she described Bo Qin's beating and coma.

"Is he a spy?" Chongde asked.

"He is a good man, Grandfather, a man that my father and Nanai both trust and consider a friend. He would not be in danger if it were not for me. He had a way out of China a day ago, but he waited so that I could find you."

"He is a spy. I cannot believe my son would encourage a spy against China as a companion for his daughter."

Stefanie thought this discussion might better be deferred to another time, so she said nothing more.

The truck lurched to the right. Stefanie dropped the flashlight and shoved a box, which tumbled toward her grandfather. The truck surged forward.

"Something is wrong," she said.

Chapter 47

PETE WESTON LURCHED into the white Fiat and laid his head on the steering wheel to quell his nausea. Realizing that he was close to passing out, he forced himself upright and reached for the flask of coffee lying on the passenger's seat. He wrinkled his nose at the smell of the now cold black coffee but gulped it down.

Weary, he leaned his head against the headrest. "This was the one. Stefanie hopped a truck near here." He stared at the sign of the Great Helmsman Toy Factory. The guard had said that a truck left here shortly before 1:00 a.m. transporting a load of toys to Shanghai.

Weston squinted at his watch. *Over an hour ago. Stefanie is getting away.*

He didn't move. His head ached from days of heavy drinking since he had betrayed Stefanie. His stomach boiled. He stank of liquor and vomit and stale coffee.

At first, he drank because he couldn't sleep. When sleep finally came, dreams of his betrayal assaulted him, and each time Stefanie's face became Shanshan's. When he drank to drown out the dreams, they were replaced by nightmares in which the woman he loved accused him of betraying her to Kong. Instead of seeing Kong slapping Stefanie and choking her, Weston saw him beating Shanshan.

Weston shook himself, aware that the maddening dreams hovered nearby. Getting blotto really hadn't helped.

"Once the Tiger's got his claws in you, you live as long as you play with him. After that, he eats you, unless you escape." *Escape.* How he wished he could escape, but there was no escape while Kong held Shanshan. *If I could just get Shanshan away from him.* He pondered the possibilities before he sucked in a deep breath and punched the number on his cell phone.

"Kong," the voice at the other end muttered.

"Did you get more coppers?"

Kong cursed, as angry as Weston had ever heard him in the dozen years that the Tiger had used him. "The Religious Affairs Bureau has pulled strings looking for their cultist. All but a half dozen policemen have been taken from me. Have you found them?"

Weston, sweating, closed his eyes to help him concentrate. "Maybe, but there is a new fish in your pot."

"What are you talking about?"

"I want Shanshan released now and given an exit visa to Australia."

"Do not play games with me, Weston."

Weston ran a sleeve across his sweating forehead. "No, mate, I have stopped playing games with you. Now it is your turn to play my game—if you want the pigeons. I know what truck they are on. I know where they are headed, and when. I know their route. Is it worth Shanshan's release and exit to Australia or not?"

Kong's voice softened ominously. "I could let Shanshan go, but you are still here."

"Is the information worth my price or not?"

"You have my word I will let Shanshan go."

"Not good enough. I will look for the truck. Give Shanshan a cell phone and my number. Take her to my apartment for her passport. When I hear from her after the plane is en route, I will give you everything."

Kong said nothing.

"Well?" Weston demanded.

"Very well, but you had better give me Stefanie and her boyfriend. Australia is not too far away, and you are still here."

Weston folded the cell phone with shaking hands and wondered what he had been thinking to challenge Kong. *Where can we hide from the Tiger?*

He started the car and headed south to the Outer Ring Road, Beijing's bypass. With his stomach roiling, he set out to search for Stefanie. Now, he had no choice; it was Stefanie's life or his own.

"Someone is in a hurry!" the truck driver said.

Hardigan snapped upright, dragging his hand across the red stubble on his cheek. He had drifted to sleep leaning against the passenger door after two nights without rest. "What? What is it?"

"Someone is coming up on us—fast," said Ren Shaoqi, who was sitting between the driver and Hardigan.

The driver's eyes shifted from the road to the mirror and back. Hardigan squinted into the side mirror, expecting to see a police car's cherry light up, praying he would not. The vehicle slowed behind them. Then it pulled around them.

Hardigan's stomach ground its gears when the car did not show up in front of them as expected.

"What is keeping him?" he asked.

All three tried to see out of the driver's window.

"He slowed down beside me, as though he is reading the sign on the truck," the driver said.

"Is he police?" Ren Shaoqi asked.

"I do not think so," the driver said. "He must be drunk."

"What is he doing?" Hardigan asked. He stretched to look into the mirror over Shaoqi's head, but from his corner of the cab he could see nothing.

"I do not like this," the driver said. "He is dropping back."

"Maybe he decided he could not pass us in time to take his exit," Ren said.

Hardigan stared into the mirror on the passenger side of the truck. The lights dropped back but did not turn from the highway. Instead, the car followed at a discreet distance. Studying the vehicle as it passed under a light, Hardigan saw nothing to mark this as an official police car. Likely it was Public Security Bureau.

"How long before we leave Beijing?" he asked.

"I have one more stop," the driver answered. They had made four stops in various parts of Beijing where the driver had picked up crates, barrels, and boxes. The truck box had become so crowded that Shaoqi had joined Hardigan and the driver in the front.

"Can you skip it?"

"This stop?" The driver's eyes widened. "Not this one. I would not dare."

"You said before that you are carrying contraband. What if that is the police and you take them right to your next stop?" Hardigan did not want to know what other illegal items might be on board. They were illegal enough.

The driver scowled and hesitated. "They can take care of the police. It is the next exit and a few blocks. It is safest this way."

Peering at the car lights behind them, Hardigan rubbed his hand over the pocket that held the disk with plans for a military annexation of Taiwan. He felt anything but safe.

The driver drove the panel truck into a small warehouse entrance. Someone raised the door but Hardigan could not see anyone in the dimly lit interior. When the truck stopped, a big man with a face that looked carved from oak climbed onto the running board by the driver's door. "You are late."

"Someone is following us," the driver said. It wasn't the reason he was late, but it served. His prominent Adam's apple bobbed. He glanced at the big man, averted his eyes, and examined the steering wheel.

The warehouse door rumbled closed, but no one turned on more lights. Only lights near the floor glowed feebly in the darkness.

"Who are they?" The big man's eyes fixed on Hardigan and Shaoqi. Hardigan fought the urge to move his hand to his front jacket pocket that held his Glock. The slightest movement was sure to be a mistake. He wondered if the other man held a gun. *What has this driver gotten us into?*

"Passengers to Shanghai and one reason why I am late." He glanced accusingly at his passengers for corroboration.

Why did this man frighten the driver? There was more to it than his bullying attitude. How many were moving about in the dark warehouse beyond the light? Occasionally he saw a shadow cross between the low lights and the truck.

Shaoqi stared out the front window. The driver's eyes followed his hand twitching along the steering wheel. Only Hardigan had continued watching their inquisitor between cautious glances around the warehouse. He recognized his mistake too late with the tightening of the muscles around the man's eyes that were now fastened on him. The big man's mouth elongated into a semblance of a smile. He nodded.

A searchlight burned Hardigan's eyes. He threw his hands up to protect his sight. Shaoqi gasped beside him. Someone opened Hardigan's door and grabbed his arm. He caught a glimpse through stinging eyes of a Chinese face. He swept the arched fingers of his left hand at the other's eyes. He found at least one. The man who had grabbed him screamed and stumbled off the running board.

Hardigan swung around as the black steel barrel of an SKS whisked toward him. He lashed out with his right foot, sending the gun tumbling, then lunged out of the truck cab. He drove his shoulder against the chest of the gun wielder, knocking the man backward.

Someone grabbed his arm. He whirled and sent the heel of his hand into the man's face. Bone cracked.

Men were running and yelling. The driver screamed at him to stop. Two men ran at him from opposite sides. He side-kicked one. The other, a burly worker in coveralls, grabbed him around the neck. Hardigan elbowed him in the groin. The big man doubled over.

Several men surrounded Hardigan. One darted in. Hardigan grabbed him and shoved him in front of another, who lunged toward him.

Stefanie screamed.

Hardigan glanced up, ready to fight his way to her side.

The big goon who had talked to the driver held her with one arm around her throat and pressed a gun to her head.

Hardigan lifted his hands in surrender and stepped back. One of the men clubbed him with a big fist. He stumbled toward two others who grabbed his arms. They forced him upright. The big worker he had kicked in the groin pounded his ribs. He groaned. He doubled as much as the two holding him permitted. He kicked one of assailants in the kneecap.

"Old man, get back here!" the one with Stefanie said.

Chongde appeared before Hardigan, wrapping his arms around him to block the blows.

"No, they will kill you," Hardigan said in Mandarin through clenched teeth.

But his attackers waited for their boss to tell them what to do. The big man thrust Stefanie into another man's arms, shoved Chongde aside, and pointed his gun at Hardigan's head. He cocked the hammer.

Hardigan was sweating. He stared at Stefanie but prayed silently.

"Wait, Dukun, we will give them a chance to win their freedom by telling me a story that pleases me." A small man in an expensive gray striped suit limped toward them.

Shaoqi stepped out of the truck onto the running board. "Taolin?"

The little man swiveled toward Shaoqi, but the two big men kept their guns on Troy. The little man pulled off his sunglasses and squinted.

"Shaoqi?" He ran forward, grabbed Ren Shaoqi's hand, and pumped it. Pulling him off the running board, he hugged him. "Shaoqi, I cannot believe it." He stepped back. "Out of prison. We never thought we would see this day. How did you get out?"

"Remember our friend, the Beijing Tiger? He tried to use me against this uncle in prison. But something did not go as dear Qili wished. We were released by mistake." Shaoqi pointed at the old man who was smiling at them. "But I am trying to help him escape to *Mei Guo* with his granddaughter and her friend," he said, pointing to Stefanie and Troy. "My friend Chongde has been in the *laogai* over forty years altogether."

"Forty!" Taolin stared at Peng Chongde. Taolin shook his head. "How did you do it? Five would have killed me if Shaoqi had not saved my life. He pulled me out of a mine cave-in. I broke my leg, but he got me out." The man shook his head once more. "Forty years." He shook Chongde's hand as enthusiastically as he had Shaoqi's.

The small, thin man, obviously the authority here, wore shoes with one sole thicker than the other to minimize his limp.

"Shaoqi, if I had known it was you, we never would have had this problem. The Tiger hunts you?"

He nodded. "And especially these people."

"Put your guns away," he told his bodyguards. They hesitated. He snapped, "Put them away."

The men released Hardigan but eyed him warily.

"The Tiger and I go back, my friends—almost as far as Shaoqi's relationship with him," Taolin told his fellow smugglers, as well as Troy, Stefanie, and Chongde. "If he does not want these people to reach Shanghai, I, No Taolin, master exporter and entrepreneur, will be honored to sneak the prey past his claws."

"Someone really has followed us," Shaoqi said. "It may be the Tiger or someone working for him."

No grinned maliciously. "Then let us go on a tiger hunt." He waved Dukun toward him.

Weston's cell phone rang as he waited in an alley for the toy truck to emerge from the warehouse where it had disappeared ten minutes before. He had parked on the street and hidden behind a trash pile in the alley.

"Weston." He kept his voice low.

"Pete?"

"Sweetheart, where are you?"

"I am on a plane to Australia."

"That is wonderful, my love."

"It is not true, is it?"

Weston's stomach lurched with fear. A limousine drove past the alley.

"What?"

"Kong said you are earning my freedom by chasing down a Christian girl. It is not true, is it, Pete?" She was crying.

Two vans passed the mouth of the alley.

"Now, Shanshan, you know better than to believe a thing he would say.

He is just trying to hurt us one last time." *I should have known he would do this.*

"He showed me her picture." She was silent momentarily while Weston wracked his brain for a way to lie to her. "Pete, he said you helped them track down Chang Sitong and other human rights activists." Again she waited.

"Don't be balmy. I bribed him. I had a big photo shoot in Bali. The Tiger wanted big money, and I paid him to get you out." He smeared his arm across his forehead to wipe the accumulating sweat away. "Look, sweetheart, go to my folks in Melbourne. Tell them I'm coming for the wedding in a few days and want a big barbie afterward with a few friends over. Just like we planned, Shanshan."

She answered slowly, "All right, Pete, but I will need to look into your eyes and hear you say that the Tiger was lying. I would rather go back to prison than to be part of a plot against good people."

In prison for seventeen more years? You'd never survive. I had to do what I did. I had to. All because she had sent some poverty statistics over the Internet to a human rights organization in Europe.

He didn't speak his thoughts. He'd deal with that later. "Fair dinkum. I'll see you in a few days after I finish this shoot."

"I love you, Pete."

"I love you too." Shanshan was safe. Now to pay off the Tiger and join her. Weston pictured Kong slapping Stefanie in the interrogation room, gentle, little Stefanie. Why did it have to be like this? And what would Kong do to her after she had escaped and embarrassed him?

Weston pounded on the steering wheel. "That's not my problem. I have to think of Shanshan and me."

He reached for his cell phone.

At the police station Kong snatched up his cell phone. "Kong."

"They are in a warehouse off the Fuxing Lu exit. They have not come out yet," Weston said. "They are in a box truck." He gave Kong the truck's license number and a schedule to Shanghai he had bribed a clerk at the first toy factory to read.

Kong grabbed a pen from the desk and jotted the information. "Which warehouse?"

Weston didn't answer.

"Weston, do not play with me. Which warehouse?"

Still no answer. He ended the conversation and dialed again but received a busy signal. Alarmed, he waved the police who were lounging nearby to follow him.

Chapter 48

THE POLICE FOUND WESTON'S CAR in the general vicinity of three warehouses, but they saw no sign of Weston. Kong had tried calling him several times but no one answered. The spymaster ordered three officers each to two of the warehouses, while he and Chen Yuliang took the third.

The sun was coming up, tingeing the buildings with gold interspersed with dark pockets of shadows. Vapor from their mouths and nostrils hung in the air before drifting out of sight.

Kong led Chen toward the warehouse of a man he had tracked down years before. No Taolin was a smuggler by trade—drugs, compact discs, and computer equipment. One had to be cautious with such criminals, for this one was an employee of the Shanghai Triad, a syndicate with the patronage of prominent government officials. It did not matter what the cocky little smuggler did, so long as he stayed out of Kong's way. If the truck driver had come here, No had once again stepped on the Tiger's tail and might now be an *hors d'oeuvre*.

The two moved cautiously forward, staying in the shadows of buildings. Loose stones and debris crunched under their feet. Kong drew his Makarov from under his coat.

At the back of the building, he glided up to peek into a window pockmarked with years worth of grime. Nothing indicated that anyone was here.

He lowered himself beneath the window sill to peek in from the other side. Again no activity. Stacks of crates stood against the wall with rows of pallets loaded with cardboard boxes next to them.

"Mr. Kong," Chen whispered loudly and pointed across the alley to where a cell phone lay on the ground amid piles of trash and pallets.

Kong nodded, peeked in the warehouse to see nothing moving, and slipped past equipment and trash to reach the cell phone. It lay on some old shingles, partially hidden by broken down cardboard boxes hanging from a pile of pallets. Still on, it had not lain there long, for the low battery light was not yet flashing.

Kong punched Weston's number into his own phone. The phone from the alley began beeping.

Kong shut both phones off and pocketed them. He pushed his way past the pallets to where he would have chosen to hide. He found footprints in the dirt and what looked like the print of a fallen body amid overturned barrels and pallets.

Chen asked from the other side of the pile. "Is he there?"

"No."

"What would they have done to him?" she asked. Her voice showed little concern.

"It depends on who has him. Do you suppose our little friend allowed Hardigan to do serious damage to Weston?" He grimaced and added, "I guess I am no longer certain what Stefanie might do."

"I imagine not. But I doubt she would allow harm to come to anyone if she had a choice."

He poked under the cardboard boxes and found a few handwritten pages in English listing names, addresses, and phone numbers. A piece of fabric snared by a splinter on a barrel may have been from Weston's pants.

Beckoning Chen to follow him, he led her to the back door of the warehouse and handed her his gun.

"What do I do with this?"

Annoyed, he glanced at her. "Hold it. Do not point it at me, and do not put your finger on the trigger." He cupped her hands around the gun's grip.

He extracted a lock pick from a case in his coat pocket and unlocked the door to the warehouse. After returning the pick to his pocket, he took the Makarov from the woman, who had grown more pale while she held the weapon.

Inside the silent building, Kong opened the unlocked door to the office. No one was there. He led Chen deeper into the building, past rows of pallets loaded with vegetables and boxes of clothing, around pallet jacks and forklifts. Nothing moved in the shadows. The building smelled of plastics, dust, chemicals, and oil.

He found the central light switches and illuminated the building. Sauntering through, he grabbed a box cutter from the loading dock and arbitrarily cut open several boxes. In one, he found stuffed animals; in another, women's blouses. A third box contained running shoes.

Either No was selling legitimate goods or he wanted the world to believe that he was.

"Mr. Kong," Chen called, "is this blood?"

Chen squatted a few feet from the loading dock, staring at the floor. Kong looked at the reddish brown stains on the floor. He scraped a little of the stain loose from the concrete with the box cutter. "It appears to be."

He studied the surrounding stains. Recent oil stains a few feet farther in suggested that a vehicle had stood here. Had someone from the box truck taken a beating or had Weston been loaded in the truck after being beaten?

Walking around the loading area, he peered at the floor. A red stain a few feet away suggested another vehicle was leaking another fluid. About thirty feet beyond that stain, he squatted to touch another stain—slick, dark, and wet—another oil stain. Perhaps several vehicles had been here.

He wound his way through equipment and merchandise back to the office, with Chen following. "Look through files for anything incriminating."

Kong sat down at the desk. No messages were on the answering machine. He pried open the locked desk drawer with the tip of the box cutter but found nothing interesting.

"Find anything?"

"Not so far." She glanced over from thumbing through the top drawer of the file cabinet.

A door slammed. Someone whistling a popular Hong Kong tune was headed toward the office. Footsteps echoed across the concrete floor. A man called, "Congwen, are you here?"

Kong motioned Chen to stay where she was, but he rose and concealed himself behind the door, his Makarov drawn. Chen stared at the door, her hands frozen on the file folder tabs.

The man stopped in the doorway. "Who are you? What are you doing in here?" He stepped forward. "Get out of Mr. No's files."

Kong slipped from the door to poke the gun into the workman's back. "Who are you? Where's the Australian?"

The workman, middle-aged and wearing a ball cap, raised his hands. "I am Xiao Jiatai. I do not know any Australians."

Kong shoved the heavyset man around to face him. The man's eyes widened. "Do I need to tell you who I am?" Kong said.

Xiao shook his head. "I do not know any Australians, but I will help if I can. Some of the other workers will be here soon. Maybe they know an Australian."

Stepping back, Kong lowered the gun. "What do you do here?"

"I take care of the building and operate a forklift. I load and unload trucks."

"An Australian was outside this morning. We found his car and his cell phone. What happened to him?"

"I just arrived. I did not see anyone except you."

"Who would know?"

"Usually there is a night watchman. I took my son to the doctor yesterday, so I am not certain that one was here last night."

Kong grabbed Xiao's arm and led him to the loading dock. "What vehicles are missing?"

"I think I counted three vans out when I passed the parking area. That is not unusual. And, of course, Mr. No is not here yet, so I did not see the company's car."

Chapter 49

In the back of his limousine, No Taolin regaled his passengers with tales of his "exporting" exploits. Beside Stefanie in the front, Troy listened with taut jaw, occasionally rubbing his tender rib cage.

On Stefanie's other side was the driver, Dukun, who had so recently held a gun to her head. Another bodyguard sat next to No while he entertained Peng Chongde, Ren Shaoqi, and the Brother. At the first stop outside Beijing, Stefanie had discarded the wire that looked like braces, the clothes that were packed around her to make her look chubby, and her braids.

"Who thought of selling our SKSs to American street gangs? Who else could get one of the princelings to support this business activity? Did you ever think of such a thing, Shaoqi?" Taolin asked.

"I would never have thought of it." Stefanie could not tell whether Shaoqi admired his old prison companion or was simply speaking cautiously.

"I said to myself, 'Taolin, what is the richest market in the world?' The answer was obvious. Then I said to myself, 'The Americans want to sell their products in our markets. What products can you get that Americans will want? Think, Taolin.' I did, and we have expanded our operations. What do you think of that, Shaoqi?"

Stefanie's yawn prevented her from hearing Shaoqi's answer. She was weary from the crises of the past day, the long black stretch of highway, No Taolin's high-pitched bragging. From the radio poured the wailing of a Hong Kong pop station. She was caught in a Promethean nightmare, condemned to eternity on the bleak Chinese road, listening to Taolin and countless songs that all blurred into a continual cacophony.

"That is enough of my talking, Shaoqi."

Thank you, Lord. Now could we get rid of the music too?

"Tell me how Kong recruited you," No said.

Stefanie shivered with the former prisoner's account of the firing squad and of waking in the cold, stinking, crawling darkness, uncertain of whether he was alive or dead. *No wonder he agreed to betray Grandfather.*

As if he could read her mind, Troy put an arm around her shoulder and squeezed her arm. She smiled up at him in his foreign disguise, so strange yet reassuringly familiar. He whispered, "Try to rest."

She laid her head against his shoulder.

Shaoqi described life in the prison and how he and Peng Chongde had suddenly been released by mistake. "When we got off the train, police were everywhere, carrying papers with our pictures. But they did not see us. We sat right down next to them and ate, but they did not speak to us. We were invisible to them."

Stefanie shifted her head to listen. Taolin leaned forward. "Why? How did they miss you? Were you disguised?"

"Peng Chongde's God blinded their eyes! He told me of another time many years ago when this happened and his God blinded a whole army's eyes."

"Is this true?" Taolin asked.

"God protected us from them so that I could reach my little granddaughter," Chongde said simply, his aged voice dignified.

The driver also had been caught up in the story. He reached over and shut off the radio.

"This happened to a whole army?" Taolin asked.

The car was now quiet, except for the voice of Chongde carrying them back to ancient Israel. Through his vivid words as a storyteller, they watched as the gathering Syrian army was struck blind at Elisha's request by God's fiery invisible army. Stefanie bowed her head to pray for a receptive spirit in the men listening.

Grandfather finished. No one spoke for several minutes.

"This is an interesting story," Taolin said, "but it is not true."

"Why do you say this?"

"If your God is so powerful, why did you spend forty years in prison? Such a God would have protected you."

"He gave me a hard work to do, but do you think He left me alone? Remember how amazed you were that I survived forty years? To another man He once gave a hard life and even a hard death. Let me tell you His story. Then you tell me whether my God has done good or evil for me."

Chongde told about Jesus, who was God become man, who did the work of God on earth, then died to take the punishment for Chongde and Lao and Stefanie and many others. The Brother picked up the story and told of Jesus' resurrection.

"If Jesus was so good, healing people and all that, why would they kill Him?" Taolin asked.

"He pointed out to others their hypocrisy and sin. Why do the police raid worship services of Christians who do only good for their neighbors?"

"Ahh, they were princelings," Taolin said with new understanding. "This happened long ago." He turned to Shaoqi again. "Tell me how you saw that you were being followed."

Stefanie opened her eyes and almost turned to ask, "How can you just dismiss what Grandfather and Lao have said?" But by now, Shaoqi was telling about the erratic car on the highway, which wouldn't pass. Stefanie sighed and settled back on Troy's arm again.

"It was weaving beside us." Shaoqi waved his hands back and forth like a fish. The driver slowed to let it pass, but instead it dropped behind and stayed there."

No shrugged. "My men looked, but we did not find anyone. Perhaps he gave up and left."

"There is another one, Mr. No," the driver interrupted.

Troy straightened and turned to the driver. "What is it?" he asked in Mandarin.

"We have passed four panel trucks in the past hour that were stopped by the police."

Stefanie watched the dancing lights screaming their authority at the approaching dawn.

"Dukun, call Ching-ching," Taolin said. "You people certainly stop traffic."

"Are they looking for us?" Shaoqi asked.

"You can bank on that," Troy said.

"The bank?" Shaoqi asked.

"He means that you may be certain of it," No Taolin said, "but we will know in a minute." He took the car phone from the bodyguard beside him. "*Ni hao*, Ching-ching, baby. The police are stopping panel trucks. What is going on?"

"Our contact called?" No paused. "No, we will accept his assurances that his people will not bother our product. I will see you soon, baby." No passed the phone to Dukun. "The police are looking for spies, one who escaped from Beijing Number One Prison."

Stefanie peered over her shoulder.

In the pale light, the little man's face grinned a death's head leer at her. "The Tiger is ahead of you, laying a trap. But you need not fear. Not yet."

Morning approached as Kong Qili, Chang Rongwen, and Chen Yuliang wearily entered the Lu Wan District's police station in Shanghai, following a flight arranged by Assistant Minister Chang. The daily noises of the police station and surrounding streets began to grow. Because Kong had worked with him before, the chief of police had offered office space and all the help he could. Kong knew that the chief hoped for part of the glory when the spies were caught. Kong would give it lavishly.

China's unique balance of power between the national and provincial governments allowed more freedom to resist federal directives than seemed wise to Kong, but he had become adept at working the system and he curried favor among the lowest cadres. He freely and loudly spread credit for cooperation. It was the foremost secret to his success: Provincial police were willing to work with him instead of against him.

But now he was tired to death of this hunt for low-threat Christians and their CIA friend. The effort expended had been intense, and he still did not understand how the CIA figured into this whole mess. It was all so untidy and confused. People behaved as expected, then they did not, throwing him off stride.

To give his mind a rest, Kong decided to check on things in the United States through Tzu. He mentally figured the time in Chicago and pressed the phone more tightly to his ear to hear Tzu's report on Dr. Po.

"Our sales target is now a soft contact. She will give us what we want. I have another date with her in two days. We will have the merchandise."

Someone knocked on the door to the police captain's office. Yuliang rose from the sofa where she had been reviewing police reports.

"We think we have your driver," a middle-aged officer with a stiff bearing told Chen.

"A moment please," Kong told Tzu. He placed his hand over the receiver.

"This man is running several hours behind, and he is unusually nervous." The officer stood ramrod straight.

"Do you have the spies?" Chen asked.

"No, but the dogs smelled something."

"Take him to the interrogation room," Kong ordered.

The officer saluted and turned. Before he could close the door, Chen said, "And keep this one guarded. We do not want to have to resuscitate any more with guilty consciences." A few days before, the police had nearly allowed a drug courier to strangle himself with a cord from the blinds in one of the interrogation rooms. He no doubt was anticipating the penalty for adding opium to his cargo of toys.

Kong returned to his phone call. "I am back."

"I will call you as soon as I can get away from Dr. Po with the program."

"Be careful. I want no calls going from the embassy or your residence."

"I am using phone booths in the area."

Kong's mind was already turning to the interrogation. Hardigan was nearly his, and at the moment that was all that mattered.

Kong set the receiver in its cradle, nodded to Chen and Assistant Minister Chang and left for the interrogation room on the second floor. He stopped to watch the driver, a tall, thin man, rub his prominent Adam's apple. The man reached to his shirt pocket, found it empty, and rubbed his throat again. A young policeman stood, straight and motionless, inside the door.

Kong entered the gray room with his prey. He focused his attention on the thin driver. The man's gaze fastened on him. The man's thin hand dropped from his chin to his Adam's apple to his lap, like the hand of a drowning man sinking beneath the waves for the last time.

Straightening to his full height, Kong strode across the room. He picked up the clipboard on the table, glanced through the notes while the driver squirmed, and tossed it back down. He sat on the edge of the table and stared at the driver until a drop of sweat rolled down the driver's face.

"Have you heard of the Beijing Tiger, Ho?"

Ho opened his mouth, moved his lips without making words, and shook his head. Kong leaned toward him. Ho shied back in his seat. He raised his hands to shield his face from Kong's presence. *I will make Hardigan fear like this, make him squirm, make him sweat.* Kong smiled.

"Unless you cooperate fully, you will regret hearing of him. You had a load of opium and contraband compact discs, enough illegal materials to send you to the firing squad. Most seriously, you transported two spies, a man and a woman, enemies of the people, from Beijing to Shanghai."

"No, I did not," Ho whispered. He grabbed Kong's sleeve. "I brought no one to Shanghai."

Kong shook him loose and folded his arms to wait.

"It was not like that. A Chinese man and his little girl paid to ride with me, just to another part of Beijing. They were not spies."

"What did you do to the Australian?"

Ho's face, though sweating, looked blank. "Australian?"

Kong grabbed Ho's shirt collar, pulled him upright and dug his knuckles into his throat. "I ask you once more. Then I call for the electric batons. Then I shoot you unless you tell me what I want to know. Where is the Australian?"

"I know nothing about anyone from Australia." Ho's eyes filled with tears. "I swear it."

He dropped Ho into his chair where the man kneaded his throat. Kong pulled Stefanie's and Hardigan's pictures from his pocket. "You picked these two up in the brickyard near the toy factory. Where are they?"

Ho shook his head. "The man who did the talking was Chinese with gray in his hair. He had big shoulders and arms." He held his hands out to measure them. "He wore glasses, dark glasses. The girl was small and chunky with braids and braces. Her cheeks were much fuller than the girl in this picture. I saw only one of the other men clearly, the young one."

Kong's heart raced. "Describe him."

"He was an average-looking Chinese, but very thin, and his hands were very calloused."

"Were any names mentioned?"

"The old one called him Shaoqi."

So the girl found her grandfather. Now they are all together.

"So there were three men and a girl?"

"No, four, but I did not see the old one and the other one too well. They were in the dark. They and the girl stayed in the box."

Kong nodded. "They were American spies. Where did you take them? Help me and all charges are dropped; protect them, and you will die. I promise."

Ho peeked up at him. "All charges?"

"You have my word."

Ho nodded. "I do not know who contacted me. It may have been the wide-shouldered man. I get messages in a special drop to take some freight or people on my next run. The notes give me directions and part of the payment. That is how I happened to take them. They were at the brickyard where I was told to meet them."

"We will deal with that later. Where are they now?" Kong leaned forward.

"Perhaps they are dead."

"What do you mean, dead?" Kong grabbed the front of his shirt again.

"The wide-shouldered one got in a fight with the warehouse workers at my last stop. I did not ask questions about what they did with them. I need the money."

"And the man in the car that followed you to the warehouse? What happened to him?"

"I do not know. Some of the men went out to look for him while they loaded my truck, but I did not see them again."

Kong sat back to study Ho. He believed him. "Who is this boss?"

"When his men approached me the first time, they told me he was someone that it would be better not to know. I did not ask questions. The money, you know, to get rich is glorious." Ho shrugged.

Deng Xiaopeng's famous dictum had affected the little piranhas like the big sharks.

"I did not know they were spies. They looked Chinese. I will do anything to help you find them."

Kong nodded. "All right. Officer, call for a police artist."

Chapter 50

THE HOT SHOWER FELT SO GOOD that Stefanie hated to leave the luxurious marble-floored bathroom of the Shanghai Hilton, even with the change of clothes from No Taolin. The smuggler had given them false identification papers for Mr. and Mrs. Peter Kong of San Francisco. Using Kong's name had delighted the sly, little man. The three Chinese men received suits and false papers that No's invisible girlfriend, Ching-ching, had provided by the time the car reached the warehouse.

Stefanie emerged from the bathroom to find Troy stretched across the end of one bed with an arm flung across his eyes. Ren Shaoqi gazed from the window at Shanghai's splendid cityscape. Her grandfather and the Brother stared silently from matching easy chairs, one at the carpet, the other at the wall.

"The consulate's locked down," Troy said in English from beneath his arm.

"Locked—" Stefanie sank onto the sofa. "Would anyone else help us?"

"The English-speaking consulates are all guarded. I even checked the Mexican, Indian, and Japanese."

No one said anything for several minutes. Stefanie joined Shaoqi to gaze out the window at the Shanghai skyline. Cars, cabs, buses, bicycles, pedestrians streamed through the streets below, reminding her of Chicago. If Kong Qili were not hunting them like wild animals, she could have walked to the Jingan Temple to see its great bell that was almost a thousand years old or watched Shanghai's famous acrobats perform at the Shanghai Center. She wished she could visit the Bund. Nanai had told her stories about the architecture along the Bund and its famous promenade.

Nanai, you must be worried sick. Father is pacing and Madre's eyes are red from not sleeping.

Shaoqi's curious glance made her wipe away the tears that were building.

359

"Could we take a train to Hong Kong?" she asked without turning.

"Trains, airports, and ships are being watched," Troy said, his voice without emotion. "Hong Kong is always sewn up tight because half of China wants to get in."

"What about some of the American Christian groups working in Shanghai?" she asked. "Would they help us? We're American too."

"You can bet they are watched," Troy said. "We'd endanger them. Their work to bring in a certain number of Bibles each year or to help orphans will end if they don't stay out of politics. And we aren't merely political; we're criminal."

Stefanie turned her back on the skyline. "What are we going to do?"

Troy looked exhausted. His red beard needed shaving again. He ran his hands through his dyed hair. She had set this awful burden upon him, and he had said not a word in reproach.

"Would any of Nanai's family help us?" she asked her grandfather in Chinese.

Peng Chongde shook his head. "I cannot ask. They have suffered from my coming to them before. The authorities will expect me to go to them, especially if they believe you to be with me."

"I wish I could meet Great Aunt Faith," Stefanie said.

"Some meetings are best delayed until heaven. You look so much like my Grace that, if anything harmed you, it would be as if Faith saw it happening to Grace again. I do not think her heart could survive that. She and your grandmother are the last of the family."

At the mention of her grandmother, Stefanie returned to the window to lean against the window casing. *Oh, Nanai, how are you? Hold on. We'll get home somehow.*

"We could see if the brothers have a suggestion," the Brother said.

"I can pay for their help," Troy said, pushing himself up on an elbow.

"I know you mean to be kind, but I think Peng Chongde or I should talk with them." The Brother shoved his glasses higher on his nose. "If they can help, they will, out of love for the Lord and for Chongde. Your offer of wages would offend them."

"But Uncle will be recognized if the police are watching," Shaoqi said. "He needs rest."

Stefanie stared at her grandfather. Why hadn't she noticed how tired he was? His hand trembled as he lowered it to his lap. The fissures had deepened on his face, and his clothes hung on him. He nodded. "I must rest if I can."

"I could go with you," Shaoqi said. He and the Brother stared at one another. Stefanie wondered at the doubt in the Brother's eyes and the defiance in Shaoqi's expression.

"I think that would be good," her grandfather said.

"Are you certain, Uncle?" the Brother asked.

"I have not betrayed anyone," Shaoqi burst out.

"I think you both should go," Chongde said.

Shaoqi and Brother exchanged a long, uncertain look at one another before the older man rose from his chair. Shaoqi trudged unwillingly to the door behind him. Troy closed the door and locked it after they were gone.

"What was that about?" Stefanie asked her grandfather, but he had already turned to Troy.

"If the brothers are being watched, they may not be able to help," Chongde said.

"I have one choice," Troy said in Mandarin, opening his laptop computer. "Two days we have. One day we travel to boat. Instead of through consulate, I can talk straight to them."

"Is that what you are doing now?"

"No, I use Taolin's telephone to send files, in case we do not reach boat. While I do that, you rest, Chongde."

Troy switched to English. "Stefanie, when I am finished, I want you to send a brief note to someone who is not connected directly to your family—someone who would not be watched. Lani would be good. In as few words as possible and without details, tell her to call your mother with the news that we are all right. Remember, no details."

Over the phone line, Troy's computer began to slowly send out the records that Stefanie had copied from Qili's computer.

"Peng Chongde, is there a place you could take everyone if you do not hear from me by eight o'clock?"

Her grandfather bowed his head over his hands as he rubbed them together. He nodded.

"Why eight?" Stefanie asked.

"Because I can hold out that long if I'm caught," he answered in English.

As Chou had instructed, Hardigan called the consulate from the Shanghai Exhibition Centre and asked Linwood Davis to alert the consulate that he was in Shanghai. Through an encoded message, they routed him to a panel of lockers at a bus station.

At the station, Hardigan surveyed the area for anyone who might be an undercover police officer. The uniformed police did not worry him. They paid no more attention to him than to the next Chinese passenger.

Buying a paper gave him more time to reconnoiter. He wondered about two young men leaning on bicycles. His pulse accelerated. He glanced at the front page of the paper, checked his watch, and entered the station. At the sight of another police officer inside, his heart thumped. Had they been able to decipher his telephone conversation with Davis?

Hardigan strode to locker 327 and punched in the code that would open the locker door.

A middle-aged man in a gray trench coat brushed against him while reaching for the next locker.

Hardigan could feel the sweat building under his makeup.

He swung the door open and pulled out a briefcase. It contained a radio programmed to the frequency of a U.S. Navy submarine somewhere in the East China Sea.

The man next to him opened his locker.

Hardigan closed his locker and turned. He tensed, waiting for the other man to grab him, but he did not. While passing the policeman on duty, Hardigan checked his watch to avoid the other's studious observation. Now if he could just get past the two policemen by the bus. . . .

Shaoqi stared at the Oriental Pearl Television Tower gleaming above him. It looked like a flying saucer made of pearl—majestic, luminescent, otherworldly. He started when the Brother clasped his arm. The Brother leaned closer. "You said the police outside Beijing had flyers with your picture and Brother Peng's. They do not know me. If you stay back here with the tourists, they will be less likely to notice you."

The Brother left him scowling in a crowd of smiling, camera-snapping tourists. He watched the small slender man disappear. Then a lump caught in his throat. *What if he is trying to lose me? What if he intends to turn me in to get rid of me or to turn Peng Chongde in?*

He shoved a Japanese tourist aside in his haste to find the little evangelist. He scrambled through a party of smiling Chinese and ran to the corner, looking around wildly. The Brother's brown jacket showed through a hole in the strolling crowd. Shaoqi started after him. As the Brother approached a uniformed policeman, Shaoqi decided he was right, but the older man walked past the policeman to stop an elderly man who was sweeping the street.

The street sweeper waved his hand toward the direction they had come, as if giving directions.

Two policemen glanced over, then resumed their benign alertness, scanning the crowd. Were they looking for him? One of them glanced his way but paid him no attention.

Shaoqi trailed behind a Chinese family that was exclaiming over the Oriental Pearl Tower until he was within a few meters of the Brother and the street sweeper. He attached himself to a group of sightseeing businessmen.

"I am sorry, Lao, but it is not safe," the street sweeper said. Someone had neatly mended the elderly man's worn gray coat. He waved down the street again as though directing the Brother back farther.

"When did the raids start?" the Brother asked.

"Early this morning. Those among the leaders that are not arrested are watched."

"And Sister Faith Chen is watched?"

"Yes." The street sweeper raised his voice. "After you cross the river, turn left on Zhongshan Dong 2-Lu until you reach Renmin Lu. You cannot miss it."

Shaoqi followed the Brother's casual glance to an approaching policeman. His insides felt hollow and cold.

"Can I help you?" the young officer asked the Brother.

"Oh, thank you, officer, but I understand now," the Brother said. "I was mistaken about a place I wanted to visit, but my friend here has straightened me out." The Brother bowed slightly. "Thank you both."

When he walked away, the policeman returned to his vantage point. Shaoqi doubted that he could have identified the Brother five minutes later.

Shaoqi disengaged himself from the group he was standing near to stride after the Brother. He did not join up with the older man until they had rounded a street corner out of sight of the police.

When Shaoqi reached him, the Brother continued walking. "Did you hear that we will not be able to go to our brothers? Those who have not been arrested are watched. It would endanger both them and Chongde."

"Why do you call them brothers?"

"For one thing, we are family as spiritual children of God. Jesus Christ died for us, so we share that special bond of God's forgiveness for the evil we have done. Besides, for over twenty years they have been the only family that I have

had, since the time my family rejected me when they learned I was a Christian."
The Brother removed his thick glasses and cleaned them with a handkerchief.
After returning the handkerchief to his pocket, he strode toward the river.

Shaoqi caught up with him again. "Why do you and Chongde do this? Why
do you believe in this Jesus?"

"He died for my sins and forgave me and has given me peace."

"You could be arrested."

"Yes, but I have done this for twenty years without being arrested." He
breathed deeply, turned away, then back. "The police do not notice people like
me. I am ordinary. They expect nothing from me." He trudged on. "That both-
ered me until I realized that God used my ordinariness to camouflage me."

They walked on without talking for several minutes.

"What will he do now? Chongde, I mean."

"What he has done for years, whatever God wants him to."

Shaoqi halted, staring after Lao. He did not understand what the Brother
meant. Maybe he did not know either, so he covered his ignorance with words
that made no sense.

Chapter 51

Ren Shaoqi thumbed through a magazine in the lobby without noticing either the articles or the pictures. He had needed to leave the hotel room to think. The American spy had left before he and the Brother had returned from talking to the Christian street sweeper. Now Peng Chongde, the Brother, and the girl were praying.

He rubbed his head, wishing he could massage the tangles from his thoughts. *These Christians are a puzzle.* On the one hand, the police had walked past him and Chongde while holding their pictures and had not noticed them. Chongde thought that God was caring for them. Yet the Christians he met barely survived. In prison, they faced daily deprivation, torture, and threats. The Brother was in hiding. The artist in the wheelchair in Beijing lived in the fear that the next raid would take him. Why would a real and powerful God allow His followers to suffer so?

Shaoqi drummed his fingertips on the arm of his chair and stared at a potted plant across the lobby. Though poor, the Christians he had met had been generous and kind, giving him clothes and food. Chongde could not have treated his American son better than he had Shaoqi. Either the Brother, who had broken Chongde's fingers years before, was truly sorry, or he should act in Hong Kong films.

He sighed.

A bright green uniform crossed his line of sight. His pulse quickened. The policeman sidestepped some Caucasian patrons before stopping at the elegant service counter. He removed a poster from his briefcase and showed it to a girl behind the counter who called to several others. They studied it.

Shaoqi's breath caught. He had to see.

Digging in a pocket for some money, he approached the counter. He purchased a newspaper and ventured a glance at the poster. He could not mistake the wide shoulders of the one called Troy disguised as a Chinese. It also held poor quality drawings of Dehong, Chongde, and himself.

"The number to call is on the bottom," the policeman pointed out. The poster offered twenty thousand reminbis for Hardigan's capture.

What could I do with twenty thousand reminbis? He returned to his seat. Kong must want the American badly. He wondered if he could trade Troy for Chongde. No, Qili would expect him to give up all of them. You could not share a dumpling with a tiger without losing the entire dumpling and your hand.

He would have to warn Troy, if only to save Chongde and himself. Spiting Qili should be worth some of that fortune in reward money.

Ren gave up all pretense of reading. He had to warn Troy. He paced back and forth outside, scanning the crowds, hoping that the American would beat the threatening rain. Then a man with a large frame came into view down the block. Shaoqi hurried to meet him. Troy carried a large briefcase that he had not had before. Shaoqi halted before him.

"What is wrong?" Troy's eyes narrowed. Shaoqi cringed as a reflex, for he had trained himself to avoid such formidable people as this in prison. The veins on the big man's hands stood out. *This man could be dangerous, as dangerous as Qili himself.*

Shaoqi nodded away from the pedestrian flow. Hardigan followed warily.

"Where are the others?"

"They are upstairs praying. I . . . I did not want to stay with them, so I came downstairs. A policeman came in with a poster of you with a reward of twenty thousand reminbis. We were on it too, but your picture was the easiest to recognize."

Troy watched him strangely. "That is much money."

Shaoqi looked down. "Kong would have demanded Chongde." It was hard to admit that, hard to hide his wistfulness. He expected to see anger in the big man's eyes or contempt, but Troy only nodded.

"Did they know I was here?"

"I do not think so," Shaoqi said. "The policeman had many posters in his briefcase."

Troy did not answer for several minutes. "We cannot go to another hotel. What about the Christians?"

"They are watched."

Troy stepped into the stream of traffic. Shaoqi followed. "We could go to Taolin."

Troy shook his head. "I do not trust him."

"I saved his life. He is my friend. Where else can we go? It is starting to rain."

Shaoqi wondered if he would have found Taolin's girlfriend, Ching-ching, more interesting if he had not met Peng Dehong first. If Little Dehong, as Peng Chongde called his granddaughter, acted too American, at least she was gracious and caring, a princess to Shaoqi's way of thinking. By contrast, Ching-ching was tall, narrow, and hungry-looking. She sat on the edge of Taolin's desk in a short skirt, swinging her leg and snapping her gum. Her heavily painted eyes squinted and shifted between Taolin at his desk, Shaoqi standing in front of the desk, and Troy standing in the shadows of the warehouse office. She pursed her bright red lips. Her sharp cheekbones stuck out and formed a triangle with her gaunt chin.

"The boat and pilot are all you need, Shaoqi?" Taolin asked. "I can lend you some money, too, interest free, until you get on your feet."

Shaoqi glanced at Hardigan, who stood in the dingy office's shadows. *Twenty thousand reminbis or the old man safe and Qili thwarted?*

Hardigan must have interpreted the glance as a question, for he nodded. Ching-ching glanced over at him, her gaunt cheeks working like a garbage compactor on her gum, her red earrings dangling like bloody hangman's ropes. Her foot thumped a steady rhythm against the desk.

"I think that is all we need, Taolin." Shaoqi knew he was going to regret this. What had kindness ever done for him, other than make survival harder?

Taolin patted Ching-ching's bouncing knee. "Call Mengfu. Tell him I will want his boat later." He rose from the desk and led the two men out of the office into the darkened warehouse. He snapped on a flashlight. "The side door will be open for you."

The shadows of the forklift's prongs reached for them in the light. Wooden crates and cardboard boxes hovered over them on either side, as if ready to pounce. With a fresh gust of wind, rain drummed against a dirty window.

Shaoqi swiveled his head. He thought he caught a movement behind Hardigan, but when he stared into the gloom, he saw nothing.

No led them to the end of a row of pallets piled high with crates, turned right, then left down another aisle. He pulled a key from under an empty coffee cup on a shelf beside a door and unlocked the door.

He pointed with his flashlight down the wharf, but a curtain of rain obscured their sight. "I will have your boat there on the end at the right at two o'clock."

After leading them back to the side door where they had entered, he shook hands with Troy, then with Shaoqi. "Anything I can ever do for you, Shaoqi, is yours for the asking."

Ching-ching's high heels tapped across the concrete floor toward them. Taolin let them out into the alley. They heard the lock click and the bolt slide behind them. They peered into the rain from under the eaves, then huddled behind some barrels.

Hardigan pulled a small tube from his coat. "The makeup is coming off anyway. I might as well take it all off."

His face looked ghastly after he wiped the cream from it. He popped brown contacts from his eyes and threw them into a trash bin. The pale face and blue-gray eyes looked odd against the gray-streaked black hair.

Shaoqi forced himself to stop staring. "Why do they pray?"

"They . . . we believe that God answers prayers."

"Then why does not God help you escape?"

"Who says He is not?" Troy grinned at him. "Because they were praying, you went to the front of the hotel. While they prayed, you saw the poster. Without their prayers, I would now be under arrest."

Shaoqi pondered this bit of logic while Troy opened his briefcase. The big man edged to the end of the eaves, pointed a wok-shaped thing toward the harbor and slipped earphones over his head. Ren watched, but his thoughts revolved around the Christians and their prayers.

Stefanie stilled her restless fingers. Her grandfather and the Brother continued praying, their whispers whistling in the still room. She should be praying, and had been praying, but the vast void within kept drawing her mind back to Troy. He had now been gone for hours. *Where is he? Is he all right? What do I feel for him? Why is everything so confusing? What if he doesn't make it out of China? How can I live with myself if he's taken to some noisome prison when it's my fault?* It occurred to Stefanie that she was experiencing exactly the fears that a young wife and mother had known many years ago while waiting for Peng Chongde at the rendezvous point.

"Please, Lord, keep him safe."

The ring of the telephone shattered the silence. She glanced at the clock. *Not quite five.*

The Brother and her grandfather were staring at her. The phone rang again. She threw herself at the end table and snatched the receiver.

"*Ni hao?*"

"Sweetheart? Is everything all right?" Troy's endearing words had been chosen by No Taolin as a ruse in case anyone had tapped the lines.

She clutched the telephone in both hands. "Yes, I am fine, dear husband. Are you all right?"

"My business is taking longer. I will not be back to change before we go to the theater. Please meet me across from the main door of the Danguangming Theater at 11:45."

"The Danguangming at 11:45, but Grandfather will—"

"Oh, and bring my computer. I may do work at intermission." The call ended with a click. The phone line hung still, empty, and heavy.

"I can give you someone you seek, maybe," a nervous, high-pitched voice whispered into the phone.

Kong covered his other ear to block the sounds of the Shanghai police station. "You have Hardigan?"

"Ha—who? No, no. I can tell you where Ren Shaoqi will be later tonight."

Shaoqi! "Was he with an old man?"

"No, I do not think so. I mean I did not see him well. He stayed in the shadows, but he seemed to be a young man."

Finding Shaoqi would cause some minor inconveniences later, but he didn't want to bother with him now. Shaoqi would abandon the others as soon as he got the opportunity. He started to put the phone down. The girl's next words caught his attention.

"Wide shoulders."

"What?"

"The man with Shaoqi had wide shoulders and really long arms."

"Go on. Tell me everything you can about the man with Ren Shaoqi." It had to be Hardigan. The girl and old man could not be far away. "Where will he be and when?"

The girl paused. He pictured her licking her lips. "How much is it worth to you?"

"Ten thousand reminbis." That would leave him another ten thousand.

She paused again. "Fifteen thousand before you pick him up."

"If you want to cooperate with us, we will pay you twelve thousand reminbis after Ren Shaoqi is picked up. Take it or leave it."

"I will take it."

"All right. How do you know this is Ren Shaoqi?"

She lied, of course. She was covering up for someone, but she told him that Ren Shaoqi and the man with wide shoulders talked with a fisherman on the pier of No Taolin's warehouse. The fisherman agreed to meet them at the pier at two in the morning with his boat.

So my old friend No Taolin did not get enough of prison.

"Where are they now?"

She hesitated. "Will I still get my money?"

"If we capture them, yes."

"I do not know for sure. They were at the Shanghai Hilton. Two of them were registered as Mr. and Mrs. Peter Kong."

Kong! Very funny, this little slap in the face.

"Come in tomorrow morning for your money." He hung up and turned to Chen. "Take two officers and pictures to the Shanghai Hilton."

"The Hilton?" Chen gasped, her shock written on her face.

"They are probably not there now. I will set a trap at No Taolin's warehouse."

"What about the Brother?" Chang Rongwen demanded.

"We are very close to getting the Brother," Kong lied.

Chapter 52

STEFANIE CHECKED THE ROOM for anything they should take with them. They were behind schedule. While her grandfather and the Brother had been talking about the condition of the churches, she had nodded off. As soon as she had awakened, she called for a cab. Now the two men were waiting outside.

When someone knocked on the door, Stefanie tossed her coat over her purse and Troy's computer. They must be coming to tell her the cab was waiting.

She opened the door and was shoved backward and sprawled onto the floor as Yuliang pushed into the room, followed by a middle-aged policeman, who closed the door.

No! We are so close!

"Search the bathroom," Yuliang ordered. The officer pulled a gun.

Yuliang stepped closer to her and peered down at her. "Where are the others?"

Stefanie said nothing. She prayed that her grandfather and the Brother would realize something was wrong and leave. The computer—she should have given . . .

Yuliang reached down and slapped her, rocking her head back. Stefanie bit her lip against the pain.

"I see your master is teaching you well."

Yuliang's eyes were filled with a hatred Stefanie could not understand. She slowly got to her feet.

The policeman returned from the bathroom. He checked under the bed and in the closet. "No one else is here, xiansheng Chen."

"Bring the car around," Yuliang said. "Then come back with your partner."

"Are you sure I should leave you alone with the prisoner?"

"This little gnat? This adorable Christian kitten? Do as you are told. The Tiger is hungry."

The policeman left.

Stefanie rubbed her stinging cheek. "We were friends."

Yuliang's face twisted into fury. "You have always had everything. Then you took Roger away from me."

"Roger said your English was not good enough for him to get the full benefit of your tutorial."

"You think this is about his tutorial?" Yuliang clenched her fists and stalked toward Stefanie. "I did everything he ever asked of me." Her voice rose to a screech.

Stefanie stepped back to put the stuffed chair between Yuliang and her.

"You, with your money and your clothes. You were the cute little hard-to-get dessert. I was not good enough anymore."

"You never told me you were seeing Roger."

"He did not want his father to find out. Then you stepped in."

Stefanie's hip brushed the vase of flowers on the end table, upsetting it. She righted it, but the flowers scratched her hose. As she bent over, she saw the handle of Troy's notebook computer sticking up behind her coat.

"You will be sorry that you betrayed China," Yuliang said, her voice soft and spiteful.

Yuliang pulled her cell phone from her coat pocket and dialed. "Mr. Kong, I have your precious lamb."

Stefanie glanced again at the computer with Troy's secrets. Good people would be killed if it fell into Qili's hands. So many would suffer—her grandparents, Ren Shaoqi, the Brother, and Troy.

"No, the others are gone, but I am sure she can be convinced to tell you where they are." Yuliang sneered at her.

Despite the threat, Stefanie's attention drifted away from Yuliang's conversation with Qili. Somehow . . . somehow, she had to escape, to protect Troy and his innocent people and get her grandfather home safely. She eased back. The silk flowers scratched her legs. She glanced back at the vase as her fingers found the edge of it.

Yuliang set her shoulder bag onto the chair with Stefanie's things and bent to put the phone away.

Stefanie swung the vase with all her strength.

Yuliang saw the movement too late. The vase smashed against the side of her skull. She stumbled backward and dropped. Blood oozed down her face from a gash, and she lay still. Stefanie looked blankly from the piece of the vase still in her hands to Yuliang's head among the shards and peach-colored daisies on the carpet. Yuliang's chest was rising and falling, so she was still alive.

Stefanie dropped the vase fragment. She took a deep breath and picked up her coat, purse, and Troy's computer. She inched around the chair on the far side from Yuliang. She could not take her eyes from the other woman as she backed to the door. With her hand on the knob, she remembered the policeman. She drew in a breath to compose herself. He and his partner would come on the elevator. She could see the lights changing to indicate the elevator's climb, floor by floor.

Expecting any moment to hear the heavy tread and shouts of the police above her, she ran down the stairs at the other end of the corridor.

The hotel parking lot blazed with light, including the rotating strobe of the police car. No police were in sight. The rain had turned to heavy mist. Panting, she pressed through the crowd to the curb. Every minute stretched like ages.

She hailed a taxi and then looked frantically around as one approached. At the sight of her grandfather and the Brother, she called, "Get in. We are late." As her grandfather struggled into the car, she tumbled in the other side and slammed the door.

Not until she had given the cabdriver directions did she allow herself to think what she had done. *I might have killed her.* She could not steady her trembling hands and wanted desperately to see Troy.

Where are they? Hardigan checked his watch again. They were late. Not that it mattered a lot with the police shadowing No Taolin's warehouse.

He crouched amid the trash in the shadows of another building to watch the warehouse. The mist made a halo around the warehouse's outside light.

Gravel crunched behind him and his hand went to the Glock in his pocket.

"Troy?" Ren Shaoqi whispered.

"Here." He kept his hand on the gun. *Never trust a man until he has proved himself, especially when there's a big price on your head.* "Do you have them?"

"They are here," Shaoqi said.

"Did you bring the computer?"

"Yes, Troy," Stefanie whispered. Hardigan relaxed his hand.

"Should we go in and dry off?" the Brother asked.

"Not yet. The local police are having a tea party."

"What?" Stefanie asked.

"No sold us out. The police have staked out the warehouse." This was his fault. He should have been more careful.

"Taolin would not have done that. I saved his life," Shaoqi said. "But he never could pick a woman. I thought I saw Ching-ching follow us into the warehouse."

"What will we do?" Stefanie asked.

Hardigan didn't answer because he didn't know.

"Could you get to the dock without going into the warehouse?" the Brother asked. "If the police are expecting you to go into the warehouse, perhaps they are not watching the dock."

Hardigan checked his watch. He thought of checking both sides of the warehouse himself, but Shaoqi and the Brother insisted on helping. He hated to leave the computer behind as he had at the hotel.

Stefanie read his mind. "I will carry the computer."

"No, honey, stay here with it. If the police get close, destroy it. Lao and Shaoqi, go to the dock on this side; I will go to the far side. Be back before one hour, but be careful."

Stefanie surprised him by sliding her hand into his. She followed him to the edge of the building. He squeezed her hand, but she clung to his. "You be careful, Troy."

He glanced back to where they had left the others, then pulled her gently into his arms. She returned his kiss. "I love you," she whispered.

He swallowed hard, kissed her cheek, and slipped away into the dark.

"We could try swimming," Shaoqi whispered. His back was pressed against the warehouse next to No Taolin's, which overhung the bank. They had no dry route to the dock. The mist hung heavily over the river.

"There. Did you see? The police are hiding there," the Brother said. A spark showed in the gloom, brightened and dimmed.

"Someone lit a cigarette. They are not good at hiding, are they?" Shaoqi commented.

"I am not sure Brother Chongde could swim very far with the water so cold. He needs to be somewhere safe soon. I am worried about him."

Yes, Shaoqi agreed, the old man was growing weaker under the stress of their ordeal. He seemed more frail each day and slept longer when he could. "I thought I was the only one who saw."

"Do not blame the Americans. They have much on their minds, and they do not know him as we do." The words warmed him. He pondered the friendship that he had found with these two older men and found that it filled something he had lost years before. Then the hatred surged back with the thought of Qili.

"How is he going to get out with Qili one step ahead?" he asked.

The Brother sighed deeply. "We need a diversion to draw the police away."

"What kind of diversion is going to draw twenty policeman away from here with the Tiger on their backs? And nothing—nothing short of the Minister of Public Security—is going to separate Qili from his policemen." His anger gleamed like the cigarette of the guard on the wharf.

"You speak too loudly. Do you have any money?"

"A little. Why?"

The Brother removed his hat and took something from it.

"I would like to borrow some money from you for some phone calls. I will leave this with you in case I cannot repay you soon." He caressed a small rectangular package wrapped in a cloth before thrusting it toward Shaoqi. "If I have not repaid you in five days, take it to the street sweeper, tell him that I sent you to him, and ask him to buy it back. If he cannot, he can take you to others who will." The Brother's hand lingered on the package.

"What is it?"

The Brother slowly withdrew his fingers. "This is the book that tells about God. Though they do not have much money, the church will repay you if I cannot."

"You do not need to do that." Shaoqi shoved it toward him. "I trust you for it."

The Brother pushed it back. "Then hold this for me, Shaoqi. I have to go now. Tell the American not to leave. Insist that he not give up and watch for an opening." The Brother backed away.

"What are you going to do?"

"Use a telephone to tie a bleating goat on a chain before your tiger."

The Brother faded into the mist.

Chapter 53

AT THE BUS STATION the Brother stared at the phone number he had written on a scrap of paper. His stomach hurt with the old mocking fear. *If I do this, they may catch me. They will torture and kill me for information about the church, but, if Peng Chongde doesn't escape, they will torture him to betray me. If he does not, he and his granddaughter will die.*

Weary policemen scanned the people passing them. One picked up a foot, shook it a little bit, and switched feet.

Sucking in a quick breath, the Brother straightened and dialed the number before fear could change his mind. The stench of cigarette smoke clung to the phone in the drab waiting room.

The voice answering the telephone was that of Chang Rongwen himself. It was better than he had hoped.

"*Ni hao*, Rongwen."

Silence greeted him, then Rongwen gasped, "Jingyue?"

Now that he was committed, Lao felt at peace in God's will. Rongwen's fear reached through the phone, though. The Brother answered what the other would be thinking. "Jizhong told me where to find you when I called."

It was so strange how he knew what Rongwen was thinking after all these years, just as they had known each other's thoughts at play. How strange that now Rongwen feared him, believing that Jingyue would want revenge, would want to destroy him.

"We spoke only long enough for me to find out how to reach you."

"Where are you?"

"As you suspected, I am in Shanghai. I gathered from the search the police made after I called you in Beijing that you wanted to see me."

"That was Kong, not me. He ordered the search. Do not blame me, Jingyue." The Brother winced at Rongwen's lie.

"I am not calling to accuse."

"We need to settle our differences. We meant too much to one another for us now to threaten each other's well-being."

"I do not threaten you. You are the one with the Tiger and the policemen, not me, Rongwen. I seek nothing but your good."

"Then meet me. I will keep it from Kong and the police. It will be just you and me—like it was years ago, when life was good."

The Brother hesitated as he reviewed a plan fraught with risk. He glanced around the bus station. If policemen were guarding the bus station, they would be at the railroads, embassies, and airports. The Brother hoped that Kong's men would be the ones called in.

"Jingyue? Are you there?" Rongwen pleaded into the phone.

The Brother sighed. "I will be at the Nine Arc Bridge at 1:50. If you come, I want to talk to you about Jesus. You are in a position to do great good."

"I will meet you outside the teahouse at 1:45."

Rongwen, you always had to be richer, stronger, faster, better, earlier. It was just what the Brother had counted on.

He left the bus station and called a taxi. He must reach the Nine Arc Bridge before Rongwen could gather his policemen. As the taxi sped off, he settled back in the seat.

The Nine Arc Bridge joined the Old Town, with its maze of alleys, to Yu Yuan, the Mandarin's Garden. Mentally, he traced the alleys, streets, and river. Rongwen would surround the area with policemen. Trapping him in that maze of streets and alleys would take a lot of policemen, and Kong did not have a lot. The Brother prayed that he would not have enough.

"I could not find a way to the dock." Hardigan asked.

The others were dark shadows in a gray, clinging fog that dampened every sound, turning it into something ominous. A tug's foghorn thrust through the mist. The night songs of the street traffic whispered to them from all directions. A door slammed somewhere. The smells of the river, of boat fumes, and of garbage tinged the air.

"It is well guarded," Ren Shaoqi said.

"We have to be on that dock at two o'clock," Hardigan said. "Maybe a diversion." He had thought about it on his return trip.

Chongde cleared his throat, and Shaoqi shuffled his feet.

"What is it?"

"The Brother has gone to do this," Chongde said.

Shaoqi leaned closer. "He did not say what he would do, but he said not to give up."

"Troy, look." Stefanie pointed at a police car that had stopped in front of the warehouse directly under a streetlight. A policeman in uniform locked the car and went inside by the door that No Taolin had told Ren and Hardigan to enter. "Why would he park there so openly?"

Hardigan did not answer.

Several minutes passed. They watched without speaking. Police came out. Hardigan lost count at twenty with the mass of men in the misty dimness. Several huddled around the police car. Others jogged down the street to cars hidden in alleys.

"I wonder what is going on," Stefanie said.

"You and me both, babe."

"They hear a little white goat bleating," Shaoqi said, fearful of what the sound would mean for the Brother.

"I am sorry, Mr. Kong," the police chief said. "I have orders."

Kong shoved his fists into his pants pockets. He stalked away to calm himself. He said over his shoulder, "This man is merely a cultist. We have the opportunity to break an American spy ring."

The police chief would not meet his eyes when he turned.

"Where is Chen?"

"She is at the hospital. She was attacked by a female prisoner you sent her after."

"How badly hurt?"

"The doctor expects her to be out tomorrow." The chief rocked from foot to foot, unable to hide his eagerness to be gone.

"And the girl—the prisoner?"

The chief cleared his throat. "Chen ordered my man to bring the car around. While he was gone, the prisoner attacked her and escaped."

Kong turned away again.

"Go ahead. Take your men." *It might be better without all these men to warn Hardigan with their stirring.*

"Chang wants you to join us, sir."

"I will come later." He listened to the shuffling steps, the door closing, the last mutters as the officers left. The silence that filled the warehouse stirred his blood. *Yes, this is better. When has the Beijing Tiger ever required help to bring down his prey?*

Chapter 54

WET FROM THE MIST, the Brother squatted in the shadows in an alley a few buildings away from the bridge leading to Yu Yuan. Odors of fish, diesel fuel, and pastries settled around him, held close by the dampness.

Footsteps whispered through the mist that haloed the streetlights. Shadows peeking through the fog coalesced into a short, stocky figure. Mist condensing on his glasses, the Brother waited for the man to draw close enough to be recognized.

Chang Rongwen halted under a light in front of the restaurant. His shoulders hunched inside his dark coat, he peered in one direction, then turned to peer in another. He removed his glasses to wipe them on a handkerchief. He had aged and put on weight, but he was early. That had not changed.

The Brother had prayed for his house church contacts, for Ren Shaoqi, and for the escape of Peng Chongde, his granddaughter, and her friend. The last prayer he saved for himself. "Oh, Lord Jesus, glorify Your name in what comes."

A peace poured down on him as he pulled out his old pocket watch to check the time. Warmth spread through him with a presence so powerful he bowed his head in worship. He lost track of the time while he knelt in the wet alley, tears filling his eyes. Gravel crunched beneath hurried footsteps that approached and receded.

The presence lifted, but the peace remained.

The Brother grasped a garbage can lid to pull himself to his feet. His legs and back protested the time he had squatted in the damp alley.

Rongwen paced with his head jutted forward, a fierce bulldog straining for his prey. After one deep, cleansing breath, the Brother emerged from the alley a few meters behind Rongwen, waited with his arms relaxed at his side. The bridge stretched behind him.

Rongwen muttered something, then wheeled with the feeling that someone was behind him. He threw up his arms and stumbled backward, off balance in his terror.

For a moment they stared at each other. Rongwen had gained more weight and grayed less, but the wrinkles furrowed deeply around his mouth, drawing it into a persistent frown. Rongwen's expensive shoes with their high soles took away the Brother's few centimeters of height advantage. Behind his glasses, Rongwen's eyes sparked with cold hatred.

The Brother looked into the face of his twin brother and saw what he himself might have become without Jesus.

"I did not mean to startle you, Rongwen," the Brother said.

"Jingyue?" Rongwen inched closer.

"You know I am called Lao now. I want to tell you about Jesus, about the peace He has brought to my life, the change . . ."

"Jesus? Your Jewish malefactor god? I know all about him." Rongwen's face twisted into a sneer.

"You know what the state tells you. Do you know that He died to give you new life and forgive your sins?"

Rongwen drew himself taller, jutted his chin forward and advanced. "That is what I thought. You want to convict me of mistakes of the past, because I took Jizhong from you. You want to ruin me."

Lao shook his head. "No, Rongwen, you are wrong."

"You want to destroy everything I have worked for all these years." Rongwen raised his voice.

"No, I want you to repent of your sins so that you can have the peace and happiness that I have found." Rongwen wasn't listening to a word he had to say.

"I did not mean to kill that soldier. If I had not taken the money, someone else would have. You would have. I only did what anyone else would have done."

"That was long ago, in the midst of a gang battle of the Cultural Revolution. I know you thought the soldier was coming to kill you."

Chang Rongwen had struck the soldier over the head with a bottle, killing him, before he realized that the man was a pay clerk, carrying the army unit's payroll. Terrified, he had run with the money. When he found that he was not suspected, he used the money to buy influence and a career.

"You still live in fear after so many years? Rongwen, God forgives any sins and holds them against us no more."

Rongwen laughed, sending a shudder of fear down Lao's back. "No one will hold them against me now, for you are the only one who knows enough to prove my guilt, and no one will believe you." He put a whistle to his mouth.

Before he could blow it, Lao lunged at him. They wrestled for the tiny instrument. Each time Rongwen put it to his lips, his round cheeks puffed like a blowfish.

The Brother shoved his shoulder against his brother's chest and snapped his hand with its grip of the whistle outward. The whistle flew into the stones at the edge of the bridge. Rongwen stumbled backward, hauling Lao with him. They wrestled and rolled on the ground until Rongwen pinned him, hands tightening around his throat. As the heavier combatant, Rongwen was too strong.

Red rimmed Lao's vision. He forced his hands to slide up Rongwen's arms.

He was going to pass out. He jabbed at Rongwen's eyes. One thumb hit the corner of an eye. Rongwen yelled in pain and covered his eye.

The Brother shoved him to the side and scrambled to his knees, his feet. Gasping for breath, he staggered toward the bridge. He ran up the first arc of the bridge. He glanced back to see Rongwen fumbling inside his coat.

"Police! Police!" Rongwen screamed. "Get him! Stop him!"

Officers emerged from alleys and around buildings. On the other end of the bridge a policeman pulled a pistol.

Rongwen straightened, pointed at him with something in his hand. Then an orange flame streaked from the gun in his twin's hand. The bullet's impact knocked the Brother backward against the railing. He staggered and slipped over. The cold waters rushed up to meet him.

The odor of fresh coal, wooden pallets, and plastic-wrapped freight drifted from the open door of the warehouse to mingle with the smell of coal smoke, saltwater, and gasoline fumes outside the building. Beyond the open doorway, a black hole loomed, sucking them into its menace, threatening to capture and hold them forever.

The small group huddled close to Troy Hardigan to hear his final instructions. "If anything happens to me, go, no matter what."

"Troy—" Stefanie objected. Her arm ached with the weight of the computer.

"No arguments. You, your grandfather, and that computer have to get out."

In the blackness, he groped down her arm for the hand that carried the notebook computer. He squeezed her wrist and lifted the computer from her. "Shaoqi, shut the door and latch it."

Shaoqi closed the door. The transmitter he carried was the last thing she saw as the door closed. The darkness swelled to fill the room. It squeezed against her chest, making breathing difficult.

Stefanie could see nothing but a hint of light above the blackness. She thought that must be pallets of merchandise. She followed Troy's soft, sure, steady steps, thankful for the reassurance flowing into her hand from his.

Every rustle of fabric or scrape of shoe against the concrete floor threatened to give them away. The stacks of merchandise on either side loomed over them.

Troy turned the procession left though a gap in the merchant wares. Now that his movements allowed her a glimpse past his wide frame, Stefanie could see a dim light near the floor at an intersection forty feet away. With more light, they moved more quickly.

Troy halted at the end of the aisle before stepping into the light in the cross passage. He passed her the computer. He held a gun in his right hand.

Stefanie quelled her panic. *Trust him.*

The gun swept right and left as Troy scanned the aisle. The two bulbs plugged into lights near the floor created lurking, pouncing shadows. A forklift guarded the door to the dock.

Troy stepped into the lighted area, pressed his back against a pallet rack, and swung the gun in an arc twice. He shifted the gun to his left hand to wave the others forward.

Staying as much in the shadows as they could, they crept toward the forklift in front of the door.

Something is wrong. Be careful, she wanted to cry.

Each step drew them closer to the forklift that sat squarely in front of the door.

The men stared at the forklift.

Stefanie listened to the brooding building. *There. A twist of leather against concrete.* From the corner of her eye a shadow moved.

"TROY!"

He whirled, crouched, and fired as he shoved her away. A flying body knocked him backward against the forklift. The gun flew from his hands. It slammed the top of the forklift and skittered into the blackness beyond.

"Kong!" Shaoqi shouted. He dragged Stefanie away from the fight.

Kong regained his balance first. He whirled and kicked, his long leg streaking toward Troy's head. Troy caught his foot in mid-air and twisted. Kong landed on the floor.

Both men leaped to their feet.

"We have to move now," Shaoqi said. He climbed onto the forklift. "No keys! Help me, Uncle."

Kong shot a knife-edged hand toward Troy's throat. Troy grabbed the hand, dropped to his back, and flipped Kong into a rack of plastic wrap. The rack tumbled backward. Troy rolled to his feet.

Climbing up, Kong grabbed an oar. He swung, catching Troy in the chest. Something cracked.

He swung again.

Troy ducked.

The oar splintered against the forklift where Peng Chongde and Shaoqi were working on connecting some wires. Stefanie could not pull her eyes from the fight.

Kong's swing carried his body too far around and opened him to Troy's blows to the solar plexus and chest. Kong stumbled backward toward Stefanie.

Stefanie scrambled aside to the foot of a stack of boxes. Her eyes darted around, looking for a way to help.

The forklift whirred to life.

Troy followed Kong down to grab him for another blow, but Kong used a kick boxing maneuver upward toward his groin. Troy caught it on the thigh. Pain flashed across his face.

Chongde and Shaoqi could not turn the forklift because of the fighting men. Shaoqi ran it toward them, reversed, lifted the forks halfway, and sped toward the door. At the first blow it cracked. The forklift crashed through on the second blow.

Kong and Troy circled each other.

Shaoqi scrambled from the forklift and ran back for her. He grabbed her arm. "He said to come."

"I will not leave him."

"But the computer—"

Kong's next sidekick caught Troy on the outer thigh, driving him backward. He fell against a cardboard box that burst, scattering stuffed toys.

Stefanie felt the computer's weight for the first time since the fight began. Shaoqi dragged her toward the hole in the door.

"The transmitter?" she asked.

"With your grandfather. Hurry."

Fist or foot smacked against a body behind her. *If Kong wins . . .*

She ran to her grandfather. The mist from the river obscured the dock. They felt their way through the cloud, unable to see the dock beneath their feet.

"Here," someone called ahead of them.

"We are coming. Where are you?" Stefanie called.

In the warehouse something crashed to the floor. How long before the police would come?

"Ahead, to your right."

No Taolin arose out of the mist by the dock. Shaoqi dropped into the boat with the transmitter.

"What are you doing here?" Shaoqi asked. He and Taolin helped Peng Chongde in.

"Do you think the police can invade my warehouse without my learning of it?" No clapped Shaoqi on the shoulder. "You knew I would not let you down."

Stefanie passed the computer down. "Take the boat out a hundred meters and wait five minutes. Do not come back unless I call you."

"Dehong, what are you doing?" Chongde demanded.

"I am going back for Troy."

She had no idea what she could do to help. Perhaps she could find his gun. This was not going to be like Dehong and Chongde. She couldn't leave him now. *Please, Lord, help us.*

Troy's face and knuckles were bleeding. Kong's left eye was swelling and black blood rolled down his cheek. Troy lunged forward with a blow under Kong's raised arm. Kong grunted and spun to kick.

Troy moved to block.

They wheezed like asthmatic engines. Stuffed toys and electrical boxes lay scattered like dead soldiers on a battlefield where boxes had tumbled and burst.

Stefanie edged herself behind a stack of crates. Troy's gun had fallen somewhere near here.

Troy hit Kong, knocking him to the floor a few feet ahead of her. She looked frantically for something to hit him with.

Kong spat. "You are good, Hardigan, but not good enough." He pulled a gun from inside his jacket.

Stefanie stepped away from the stack in hopes of seeing Troy's gun. Rising to his knees, Kong aimed the gun at Troy's chest.

Troy hunched forward panting. He backhanded blood from the corner of his mouth.

Stefanie saw only one weapon, the stack of crates.

"You will have to use that gun," Troy said.

"It is too bad because I would enjoy breaking you."

Stefanie stretched on tiptoe, and shoved. The crates shuddered. She reared back and ran into them. The crates rocked and toppled. Kong turned even as he fired at Troy.

The crates hit him, buried him.

Troy collapsed.

"Troy!" she screamed. She scrambled over crates, boxes, toys, and electrical parts to where he had fallen.

Blood seeped through his fingers where he clutched his shoulder. She pulled him up. "Come on, darling. Lean on me."

His weight nearly dragged her to the floor. Together they struggled until he was upright. She put an arm around his waist. They limped past the unconscious Kong.

"I told you—"

"Later. Hurry." When they reached the dock, she called, "Come get us."

Kong moaned. He shook his head. He shoved crates from his back and legs before he could sit up. He glanced around, recognizing the warehouse. *Hardigan! I shot Hardigan!*

He crawled to his knees, the gun still in his hand. Hanging onto a plastic wrap rack, he climbed to his feet and stood swaying until his head cleared. After the first few stumbling steps, his legs regained their strength.

Hardigan was gone.

He had to stop them. Once they were on the water, they were lost to him. Fear pierced his stomach. *Give up Hardigan or risk the water.*

He had no choice. If Hardigan escaped, he would be relegated to a menial role or lose his job entirely.

Ducking through the hole in the door dizzied him. He leaned against the building to halt the whirling in his head.

Ahead of him something moved, and he could hear the boat's engine.

Stefanie said, "Be careful. He is hurt."

They were getting away. Kong pushed himself from the building.

The mist cleared momentarily showing the mast of a modified junk floating away from the dock. He ran toward it and leaped the last meters to catch the stern. He teetered on the edge, clinging by his fingertips.

The breeze freshened. Beneath him the junk shuddered, then bolted.

As he plunged toward the dark water, Kong screamed.

Epilogue

Tzu Chuin Man straightened his tie, then wondered why he bothered. Dr. Carla Po, Dr. Zinsser's replacement, was delighted to have any male pay attention to her.

He breathed in deeply, composed his face, and rang the bell.

Moments later, Carla opened the door with a big smile. The woman reminded him of an aged Chinese peasant with wrinkles around her eyes and slightly stooped shoulders. Though only in her mid-forties, she looked older. The long skirt and silk blouse looked too young for her.

"Carla, you look lovely." He passed her a box of roses and followed her into the small house. As soon as she closed the door behind him, he enveloped her in a kiss.

"Chuin Man," she gasped, pulling away from him.

"I've missed you. You don't know how long I've waited for this moment."

"No more than I have." Her eyes twinkled up at him.

She cooked much better than he expected. He questioned her vaguely about her work and told her about new deals his company was making. She contributed little to the conversation.

"Chuin Man, I'm sorry. What did you say?" Carla reached across the table to cover his hand with hers. "I've been distracted this evening, but since Dr. Zinsser's death, so much responsibility has fallen on me."

"Yes, darling, I'm sure, but it couldn't be in better hands."

"Did you know Dr. Zinsser?"

Tzu cleared his throat uneasily. "No."

She leaned her elbows on the table and rested her chin on her fists. "He was my dearest friend, my mentor, and someone murdered him."

Tzu carefully placed his silverware across his plate. "That's what I heard."

Carla smiled apologetically. "I'm sorry, but I wanted you to understand that work forces me to cut our evening short."

Tzu tried to cover his relief. The sooner he could leave this woman the better. "Carla, you can't work all the time. You need time to relax, and what about me?"

"I've thought a lot about you. How propitious that we met prior to Dr. Zinsser's death, almost providential that you were there to comfort me."

She looked into his eyes. "I also have been doing a lot of thinking about what you said about world peace and the balance of power. You are right. Both China and the United States need the technology to maintain a balance of power. So I have the program we discussed. It should go a long way in giving you what China needs. I will get the disk for you."

As she left the room, he relaxed. He had feared she would refuse him.

She returned to hand him a disk. "I'm sorry to ask you to leave now, but I have much to do."

He held her. "How soon can I see you again, sweetheart?"

"I'm not sure."

She escorted him to the door.

"I'll call you later, Carla."

As he opened the door, a big black man shoved him inside and a blonde woman in a pin-striped pant suit followed. He whirled, but a balding middle-aged white man stood in the doorway to the room behind him, holding up a badge.

"FBI, Mr. Tzu. You're under arrest for the murder of Dr. J. Derek Zinsser and for illegal possession of classified information." He pulled the disk from Tzu's pocket.

"What about her?" Tzu demanded.

"Is that any way to speak of the woman of your dreams? Only perhaps your dream woman is a little more stupid than I," Dr. Po said, smiling coolly. "Please remove this murderer from my house, Mr. Wingate."

"Hello?" Grace Peng answered the telephone. Her voice sounded so ordinary that Stefanie wanted to cry and laugh.

"Nanai."

"Stefanie?" Nanai gasped. She must have turned from the phone. She was calling, "Hurry. It is Stefanie. Stefanie!"

Stefanie smiled at Troy in his hospital gown, propped up in the bed with his shoulder bandaged. During the submarine trip from the East China Sea to Japan, his wound had festered, but antibiotics were clearing up the infection. It had not stopped serious-looking government officials from visiting him the day before. They had left with Troy's notebook computer.

Troy grinned back, his carrot-red hair tousled, his freckles dark on his pale face. The sight of his grin melted her heart. *I never loved Roger like this.*

Peng Chongde sat in a chair next to the hospital bed. His black eyes sparkled as his gaze fastened on the phone. Stefanie could glimpse the young husband from her grandmother's picture peeking through the age-worn face.

She covered the phone mouthpiece with one hand. "She is calling the family," she said in Mandarin.

"Stefanie? Stefanie, are you still there? Are you all right?" Nanai asked.

"Other than being homesick, I'm fine. Troy wants to know if you have started taking your treatments."

"We have been so worried."

Stefanie shook her head at Troy. "We're all right, except for Troy, who demands that we nurse him back to health."

Nanai shushed her family who babbled questions in the background.

"What is wrong with Troy?" Nanai asked. "We will nurse him when you come home. When come? Where are you?"

"We're at a hospital in Japan."

"Japan! A hospital in Japan!" Her family cheered in the background. "Why are you at hospital?"

"Troy's recovering from a bullet wound in the shoulder." Her own bruises were fading.

Her grandmother gasped. "A bullet wound?" Her family erupted into more questions. "Shhh. I do not hear her. How bad is Troy hurt?"

"Not too badly. He gets out the day after tomorrow. We will be home in—" She glanced at Troy who held up three fingers. "—in three days. We'll get in on an 11:00 p.m. flight."

"In three days at 11:00 p.m.," her grandmother repeated.

Her family squealed. She pictured the hugs, the smiles, the sparkling eyes. She dashed a hand across her eyes.

Peng Chongde reached for the phone.

Stefanie caught his hand. "Nanai, you know I promised to smuggle Grandfather out in my luggage? Well, it didn't quite work out. Someone wants to explain."

She exchanged places with her grandfather.

"Dehong?"

Stefanie slipped her hand into Troy's. He pulled her to the chair beside his hospital bed. Together they watched the tears roll down the old man's face. "This seems like a dream. How many times I have asked God to hear your voice again, and He would bring you to my dreams."

Troy released Stefanie's hand, plucked a tissue from the box on the bed stand, and passed it to her. He grinned at her through watery eyes. While she wiped her eyes, he put his uninjured arm around her to pull her close. She leaned against his good shoulder.

"You know what I've been thinking?" His whispered words tickled her cheek. She shook her head.

"A double honeymoon might be fun."

"Honeymoon?"

"After all these years, don't you think they deserve a honeymoon?"

"That's not what I'm questioning. Who are you taking as the double part of this wonderful honeymoon?"

"The first girl who'll take the size-four ring that's waiting in my safe deposit box, I guess."

She turned to stare up at him. "How long have you had this ring?"

He grinned lopsidedly. "You know that Valentine's party I took you to? Well, when I was in India a couple weeks later, I found this ruby ring. Just your size."

She continued staring at him, unable to speak.

"I'm an eternal optimist. Think you might want to see it?" He squeezed her hand.

She peeked at her grandfather. His eyes were closed, his smile rapturous.

She reached up and kissed Troy's cheek. "Just try giving it to anyone else." Then a cloud seemed to pass over her joy.

Troy caressed her cheek with his index finger. "What's wrong?"

She brushed her hand along his freshly shaven cheek and chin. "I wish Shaoqi, Qin, and Lao could be as happy as I am right now."

No Taolin climbed off the blue Flying Pigeon bicycle. "This seems like a lot of work to return one book."

Ren Shaoqi dismounted a purple version of the same Flying Pigeon. "You did not have to come."

"I want to check with Dukun one more time before we get there." Taolin pulled his cell phone from his coat.

Shaoqi pushed his bike a few feet ahead. He watched the birds flutter from budding branch to ground to bush. They were not far from Shanghai, but the absence of city sounds soothed him. The breeze whispered through the branches.

Taolin pushed his bike beside Shaoqi's. "Still no Ching-ching."

"Has Dukun checked with your police contact again?"

"No bodies." Taolin chuckled. "I always thought drowning was a good way to get rid of kitties, but I did not know it worked for tigers."

Shaoqi frowned. He had expected to rejoice at Qili's death. Instead he mourned their lost childhood friendship. "I will believe we are rid of him when they find his body. What about Lao?"

"Nothing." Taolin stopped pushing the bike. "What have these Christians done to you, Shaoqi? You are not yourself anymore, reading that book, staring into space. What is wrong with you?"

Shaoqi gazed around. He could hear tractors in the nearby fields. The smell of freshly turned earth wafted on the breeze. He shrugged. "It should not be much farther." He flung his leg over the top bar and pushed off.

The street sweeper had directed them to an elderly bird-like woman in a village outside Shanghai. She had caressed the book as if it were her firstborn grandson. Then she reluctantly returned it and sent them to a farmhouse farther west. At the farmhouse, the farmer sent them down a muddy lane.

Taolin was moaning and rubbing the leg he had injured in the long-ago prison mine cave-in. They pushed the bikes down a narrow rocky path. They rounded a curve and almost ran into a man riding his bike the other way.

He hurried past with his face averted. Light was fading from the sky. "That looked like a medical bag," Shaoqi said after he had passed.

"They should have had him wait a little longer. Then they would not have to send for him again when I get there," No grumbled.

Ten minutes later, they reached a machine shed. An elderly man met them outside. He smiled.

"Yiming sent us," Ren said.

"And we are not going any farther," Taolin added.

"No, you are not. Come in." He led the way into the shed, past tractors and implements for the surrounding fields. They wheeled their bikes past pieces of a tractor engine disassembled on a sheet of paper. A large black patch of oil lay under the tractor. The shed smelled of oil, grease, diesel fuel, and soup.

The elderly man opened a door for them. Taolin eyed him suspiciously, as if expecting to be sent off again.

Ren entered a small room with a coal oil lamp burning. The elderly woman from the first house where they had stopped sat on a box beside a cot. She was spooning soup into the mouth of a pale man with a bandaged chest propped against blankets. "Lao!" Ren threw himself on his knees at the man's side. He flushed as he realized he had hugged the older man.

The Brother laughed weakly.

"The police said you were dead!" Taolin said. "They said you were shot and fell in the river."

The Brother smiled up at him. "They were right about everything but the dead part."

"And not far off on that," the elderly woman added.

"But how did you get away? The police scoured the river," Taolin asked.

"The current took me to a tugboat. The mechanic there saw me and pulled me aboard. He was a believer who knew me. He brought me to the brethren. Peng Chongde and the others—did they get away?"

"I saw to that," Taolin said.

Shaoqi wanted to talk, but his relief was too great. His grief since he had lost both Chongde and Lao had surprised him. He had filled his time with reading Lao's precious book and pondering the things the two men had told him about Jesus. Ren removed the book from his pocket. He still had so much to learn.

Taolin looked at the woman. "You could have brought us here with you, aunt."

"We needed to see that you were not bringing the police."

Shaoqi opened the book to the section called Matthew and read the speech by Jesus with the list that Jesus gave about happiness. He said that the poor, the merciful, and the peacemakers could be happy. Could this be so? He shook his head. "I do not understand this," he said. He pointed at the section. "Is this what makes you and Chongde different?"

He lowered the book to show the Brother. The injured man read the words and smiled slowly. "That is just part of it, Shaoqi."

Ren jerked the book back. He looked at the words. "I do not understand it. Why would your Jesus say this? It is always the rich and powerful who are happy, not the poor and meek."

"He is right," Taolin said.

The Brother sighed. "I know a man who is high in the Religious Affairs Bureau, who fears every day that someone will find out the truth about him and that all of his things and his power will disappear."

"True, there is always fear," Taolin answered. "I hold onto everything I have with both hands."

"But then you gave much to save Shaoqi and the rest of us. Did the grasping or the giving make you happier?" Taolin lowered his head thoughtfully.

Shaoqi spoke up. "I have now seen some give all of themselves for others in the name of this Jesus. Chongde is like that. So is Lao." He looked at the Brother. "In spite of everything, you are a happy man."

"I struggle, but where it counts I have happiness—peace."

"I want to learn more. I may never agree about your God, but I want to find out. I think Taolin would also like to know."

The Brother gently pushed the spoon away that the elderly woman offered him. "I could explain it to you. I will be here awhile."

Shaoqi handed the book to him. "I have nowhere to go."

Afterword

"THIS IS JUST FICTION, ISN'T IT? I mean, is this what life is really like for Christians in China?" It is difficult to know how to answer those who have asked these questions after reading the manuscript for *Tiger in the Shadows*. Yes, this is fiction in that Stefanie, Troy, Qili, Chongde, and the other characters we meet do not exist. But, this story also shares the actual challenges faced by Chinese Christians.

Stories of church life and persecutions continually slip out of China through secular and religious sources, so that we can know what a raid is like, what Christians suffer in the *laogai*, and what dangers are posed by the cult on which Budding Rod is based. The following are just a sample of reports:

- The beating of Bo Qin is based closely on the described interrogation of a woman evangelist named Cheng Meiying, who was captured during a church raid. According to the group, Human Rights in China, the beatings left her comatose for several days and permanently brain damaged. (24 November 1998)
- International Christian Concern, an organization that ministers to the persecuted, reported the arrest of thirty-nine Christians in raids in Henan Province. (7 September 1999)
- The Christian Monitor reported raids in Yunan Province resulting in the arrests of twenty evangelists and eight church members. (27 June 2003)
- Photographs of torture, with the names of the policemen and Christians involved were published through Voice of the Martyrs. The photographer is now in hiding in China. (Voice of the Martyrs newsletter, June 2003)

- Much of the chapter on Chinese Christians helping North Korean refugees was gathered from Helping Hands Korea. Helping Hands Korea raises money to deliver food aid to North Korea officially and aids North Korean refugees.
- While the Chinese government allows the printing of a limited number of Bibles, their scarcity remains a serious problem, and Christians do smuggle Bibles and literature into China. The account of the Bible donkeys is based on information from the Voice of the Martyrs and from *The Coming Influence of China* by Carl Lawrence with David Wang (Sisters, Ore.: Multnomah, 1996.) Scarcity of Bibles and of adequate training leaves many vulnerable to false teachings of cults. The one on which Budding Rod is based is one of the most violent.
- Baoti and Sufen's hidden printing press in the cave is based on the work of Kati Li, a young Chinese Christian who lived in such a cave to produce Richard Wurmbrand's book *Tortured for Christ* (Bartlesville, Okla.: Living Sacrifice Book Company, 1998), and other material. (*Voice of the Martyrs* newsletter, July 1998)
- "Work Plan of the Baoding Municipal Public Security Bureau to Prohibit Christian Illegal Activities" is from a translation of this document that was smuggled to the West.
- Descriptions of the *laogai* and the executions come from several sources, including:

  Harry Wu with George Vescey, *Troublemaker: One Man's Crusade Against China's Cruelty* (New York: Times Books, 1996).

  Harry Wu and Carolyn Wakeman, *Bitter Wind: A Memoir of My Years in China's Gulag* (New York: John Wiley & Sons, 1994).

  Harry Wu , *Laogai Handbook: 1997–1998* (Milpitas, Calif.: Laogai Research Foundation).

  Jan Wong, *Red China Blues: My Long March from Mao to Now* (New York: Doubleday, 1996).

  International Christian Concern, newsletter.

- Women are known to ride the buses, holding posters or tracts up for others to read. In the story, the poster lady offered a tantalizing opportunity for Stefanie to see the creativity of evangelism by the church. (Voice of the Martyrs newsletter, May 1999; see also Lawrence and Wang, *The Coming Influence of China*)
- Many preachers, from Watchman Nee to Samuel Lamb (*Bold As a Lamb,*

Ken Anderson, [Grand Rapids: Zondervan, 1991]) and Allen Yuan have spent years in prison. Others like Li Dexian, Gong Shengliang, and Zhong Rongliang have also suffered torture. At the time of this writing, Pastor Gong Shengliang is near death in the *laogai* due to torture and deprivation.

- News reports in the 1990s were rife with accusations of Chinese espionage and interference with electoral processes in the United States and other nations. Numerous publications have carried stories of China's growing influence in Asia.

I also would like to thank Bill Hershey for information on firearms, Sarah Tsai for help with the Chinese language, "Gary" for sharing his experiences in China, Tim Peters for his information on North Koreans, Jon Dee of Persecuted Church Collection for allowing me to use the words of "To Be a Martyr for the Lord," the librarians at the Huntington Township Library for aiding my research, and my critique group for tearing up my work and rebuilding it. My editor, Paul Ingram, really shaped the book and provided immense guidance, expertise, and patience. My husband and sons spent six years of listening, advising, discussing, encouraging, and occasionally arguing. Thank you, each of you. May the Lord bless you.

For additional resources, please consider the following:

Fiction

Randy Alcorn, *Safely Home* (Wheaton, Ill.: Tyndale House Publishers, Inc., 2001).

C. Hope Flinchbaugh, *Daughter of China* (Minneapolis, Minn.: Bethany House Publishers, 2002).

Nonfiction

Brother David, Sara Bruce, and Lela Gilbert, *Walking the Hard Road: The Wang Ming-Tao Story* (New York: HarperCollins, 1989).

Paul Hattaway, *China's Unreached Cities, Vol. 1: A Prayer Guide for 52 of China's Least Evangelized Cities* (Hong Kong: Asian Outreach Ministries, 1999), (available through Voice of the Martyrs, P.O. Box 443, Bartlesville, Okla. 74005).

I Am Looking for My Brothers: China's Christians after Tiananmen Square (available through Voice of the Martyrs, P.O. Box 443, Bartlesville, Okla. 74005).

Nora Lam with Richard H. Schneider, *China Cry: The Nora Lam Story* (Nashville, Tenn.: Thomas Nelson Publishers, 1991).

Carl Lawrence, *The Church in China* (Minneapolis, Minn.: Bethany House Publishers, 1985).

Leslie T. Lyall, *God Reigns in China* (London: Hodder and Stoughton, 1985)

Paul Marshall with Lela Gilbert, *Their Blood Cries Out: The Untold Story of Persecution Against Christians in the Modern World* (Dallas: Word Publications, 1997).

Elwood McQuaid, *Persecuted: Exposing the Growing Intolerance Toward Christianity* (Eugene, Ore.: Harvest House Publishers, 2003).

Nina Shea, *In the Lion's Den: A Shocking Account of Persecution and Martyrdom of Christians Today and How We Should Respond* (Nashville, Tenn.: Broadman and Holman Publishers, 1997).

Organization Web sites

Christian Freedom International: www.christianfreedom.org

Christian Monitor: www.christianmonitor.org

Helping Hands Korea (Family Care Foundation): www.familycare.org/network/p01.htm

Human Rights in China: www.hrichina.org

International Christian Concern: www.persecution.org

Laogai Research Foundation: www.laogai.org

Open Doors with Brother Andrew: www.opendoorsusa.org

Voice of the Martyrs: www.persecution.com

For more links to organizations involved in the persecution and human rights battles of our day and for suggestions on helping the persecuted, please see my Web site: www.onlyinternet.net/boundtogether.